THE END OF LAW

"A powerful and compassionate book looking
into the heart of human dilemma, corruption, and
redemption. This is a gripping story of
depth and insight."

*– **Pen Wilcock**, author of* The Hawk and the Dove *series*

T0326918

By the same author

Only with Blood: A Novel of Ireland

THE END OF LAW

THÉRÈSE DOWN

LION FICTION

Published by
Lion Hudson Limited
Wilkinson House, Jordan Hill Business Park
Banbury Road, Oxford OX2 8DR, England
www.lionhudson.com

ISBN 978 1 78264 357 9
e-ISBN 978 1 78264 191 9

First edition 2016

Acknowledgments

Extract on pp. 314–16 taken from Bishop Clemens August Count von Galen's sermon, Sunday the 3rd August 1941, given in St Lambert's Church. Used with permission from churchinhistory.org.

A catalogue record for this book is available from the British Library

Printed and bound in the UK, **February 2021**, LH57

"Isn't it true that every honest German is ashamed of his government these days? Who among us has any conception of the dimensions of shame that will befall us and our children when one day the veil has fallen from our eyes and the most horrible of crimes – crimes that infinitely outdistance every human measure – reach the light of day?"

First leaflet of the White Rose German Resistance Movement, Alexander Schmorell, circa 1942; executed July 1943, age 26

"How can we expect righteousness to prevail when there is hardly anyone willing to give himself up individually to a righteous cause? Such a fine, sunny day, and I have to go, but what does my death matter, if through us, thousands of people are awakened and stirred to action?"

Sophie Scholl, White Rose activist; executed February 1943, age 21

"It's high time that Christians made up their minds to do something…What are we going to show in the way of resistance – as compared to the Communists, for instance – when all this terror is over? We will be standing empty-handed. We will have no answer when we are asked: What did you do about it?"

Hans Scholl, White Rose activist; executed February 1943, age 25

This is for them and the God they served

CHAPTER ONE

Hedda Schroeder had no reason to doubt she was content and no idea that Berlin in 1933 was becoming a very dangerous place for thinking people. Her father was extremely wealthy. Her mother wafted about their magnificent nineteenth-century house in the salubrious Tiergarten district in a state of agitation, as though she just knew she'd left something somewhere. As she grew up, Hedda watched her mother's inward preoccupation with childish resentment. By the time she was fourteen, the resentment had been replaced by a sullen indifference. At twenty, Hedda no longer regarded with the slightest curiosity her mother's white rabbit fussing. She had learned that nothing ever really happened, nothing changed.

Hedda's father, Ernst, was one of the foremost chemists in Germany, with a seat on the board of the National Conglomerate Trust, IG Farben. His father, Heinrich Schroeder, had been among the earliest to revolutionize German organic chemical manufacture in the latter part of the nineteenth century and made his fortune at twenty-five by joining Bayer as a senior research chemist. Fewer than twenty-five years later, his son had followed suit. In 1933, Bayer was a merged company in the Farben Conglomerate Trust and Ernst was even more influential in the chemical research field than his father had been. He was hardly ever home and when he was, he disposed of Cook's sumptuous meals with rapid, moustachioed jaw movements which signalled his impatience with the distraction from work that was his dinner. Hedda mutated unnoticed at the table from a braided and scrubbed fraulein in pink trying not to wolf her food, to a bobbed and painted beauty whose perfectly pencilled lips were unsullied by dining.

Digested now by the expanding city, the Tiergarten district had begun as a rich hunting ground for Prussian kings. Though the evening air still fell upon the beautiful gardens with the gentility of chiffon, the railway tracks, roads and tramlines of industrial living hemmed, severed and zipped through its delicate finery.

"I shall be out again this evening, Mutti." Hedda announced her plans to the back of her mother's head one evening just before dinner.

"Oh? Anything amusing, dear?" Her mother's reply was standard and the only deference to Hedda's voice was a slight turn of the head. Otherwise, Mathilde Schroeder continued her mince across the parquet towards the dining room, one slender hand given to the other in a pose once contrived to draw attention to her expensive finger jewellery; now, it was as unconscious as anything else she did. "I shall be at the Suzmanns', darling. Daddy will be late – as usual." Then, as an afterthought, stopping and turning to face Hedda across the vast and spotless hallway, Mathilde added, "Do take your keys, dear. It's not fair t..."

"...to wake Cook. Yes, Mutti, I know."

Mathilde smiled and lowered her eyes for a moment. "You didn't say, I think. What will you be doing tonight?"

"I am seeing Walter again – Walter Gunther. You met him already. I believe we're dining at Haus Vaterland. Paul Godwin's orchestra. Do you know it, Mutti?"

"Jazz, dear?" Mathilde recrossed a little of the parquet so as not to appear rude, though she was not eager to continue the conversation. Hedda remained where she was, leaned against the wall and studied her lavishly painted fingernails.

"Yes, though he doesn't just do jazz – quite a variety of styles, really." Hedda's tone was already in neutral; the concessionary modulation in deference to manners, but she was as eager as her mother for the conversation to end. A sudden pique caused her to raise her head and look directly at Mathilde just before a customary number of seconds had passed and her mother could politely extricate herself from the exchange. How elegant and insubstantial Mathilde appeared as she raised an eyebrow in mild alarm at her daughter's sudden interest. "Actually," Hedda began, a note of contrived confidence in her voice, "they say he's... disappeared – you know?"

Mathilde frowned briefly and looked towards the Ming as though its exquisiteness could be restorative following such indelicacy. "Really?" she managed. "Well, perhaps that nice Mr Ginsburg will be on somewhere." Finally releasing herself, raising one hand in departure, Mathilde turned and retraced her steps across the parquet. "Not too late, Hedda."

Later, in the taxi, bumper to bumper along the Bellevuestrasse towards Potsdamer Platz and an eight-fifteen table at Haus Vaterland, Hedda wondered what it was that had made her risk a social faux pas with her mother. No one ever mentioned "das Judische problem" in the Schroeder household. Ernst never discussed current affairs with his wife or his daughter and indeed, such an indelicate discussion would have been most unwelcome. Domestic conversation was never more or less than polite. Mathilde had learned to accept that whatever it was she had lost would not be found, and thought given to its absence or anything which might disturb equanimity was fruitless and emotionally expensive.

Hedda's arrival had served to increase Mathilde's impression of displacement. She hadn't a clue how to deal with her and mainly left her to Cook, whose kindly nature and anxiety to secure her position in times of high unemployment made her only too willing to move into the Schroeders' house and minister to Hedda. The child grew to have, it seemed to Mathilde, a vexingly obdurate manner, as though she had spied the lost thing and was keeping its location secret. Still, there were the parties in the early days as Ernst climbed the executive ladder at Bayer as a senior research chemist and everyone said what a perfect couple they made. If she had been given to reflection, after twenty-five years of marriage to Ernst, Mathilde would perhaps have concluded that it wasn't really that she had lost anything so much as almost found it.

Hedda was not unaware that there was a growing dislike of Jewish people in Berlin. On occasions when someone took her to the cinema, she saw newsreels in which Hitler presented impassioned National Socialist cant, but it seemed to Hedda that all he did was shout. This in itself was anathema to her. No one shouted in the Schroeder family. Even Cook admonished her in whispers when she was naughty for fear of disturbing the strained silence which lay across the house like dust sheets. And though Hedda dated officers of Hitler's new Schutzstaffel, none seemed eager to do more than flatter her and ply her with fine Rhenish in the hope of more than a kiss. Certainly, none was eager to discuss his work. However, it was impossible not to overhear things when out on the crowded streets of the Potsdamer Platz or queuing for a film.

It was surprising how animated and angry people could be. Once, she had even witnessed a fight; an SS officer and a dark-haired young man hurled obscenities at each other while Orchester James Kok played swing in the smoky jazz club, Moka Efti, in the Friedrichstrasse. Tables were overturned and people had leapt from their places to avoid being caught up in the brawl. Hedda was mesmerized. She had turned quickly to her beau, whose arm had slipped protectively around her waist and drawn her to him. When the dark haired man finished the fight by rendering his opponent unconscious with a well-placed upper cut, Hedda had clapped spontaneously. Later, when the tables had been righted, the brawlers removed by police officers, she had blamed the wine for her excitement. The young man she was with, an engineering graduate and son of a doctor, had asked her if she fully understood the nature of the exchange between the two men. Hedda had frowned in irritation and shrugged. "A little – there was lots of shouting about being Jewish – obviously!"

"He will probably be thrown in prison – or worse, you understand?" the student had continued. Karl had been his name.

"Who will? Why?"

"The Jew, of course. He will...disappear, I think." When Hedda did not respond, Karl sought her face in the street-lit taxi. She turned to him and met his gaze, her eyebrows rising to quizzical arches.

"What?" she had prompted, when he didn't speak.

"I thought...for a moment..."

"You thought what?"

"Well, when you clapped like that and then, just now – I thought, perhaps..."

"Goodness me, Karl – please say what you thought! What a puzzle you are making of things!"

How serious he is – and tiresome, Hedda had thought to herself as the strange young man beside her became sullen.

"No, forgive me. It's nothing. Please, don't let me spoil things. It has been a splendid evening."

It has been short of splendid, thought Hedda. Still, there had been a welcome and rare element of excitement, at least. Then, as they entered Tiergarten, Hedda was struck by an interesting thought.

"Do you care if the Jew is put in prison?"

Karl brushed away imaginary dirt from his trousers. "No – no, of course not. Why would I care about that?"

When the taxi stopped, both were hugely relieved that Hedda could get out and leave Karl to his solo journey home. He opened the taxi door for her, saw her to the majestic portal of her family home and then bade her goodnight with a curt bow. She responded in kind and stepped with relief into the light of the immaculate parquet hallway. Karl was aware that the taxi driver eyed him suspiciously in the rear view mirror on many occasions during the drive back to his apartment.

Some three months after her evening with Karl, Hedda alighted from her taxi and drew her expensive tweed scarf closer around her neck, lifted a kid-gloved hand to the tilt of her hat. Recalling how the flecked blue wool of her matching two-piece suit brought out the china blue of her eyes, Hedda smiled and forgot her brief foray into the unpleasantness of politics. And suddenly, here was Walter: tall, impossibly handsome, impeccably shaven. His full, strong mouth creased and eased with smiling. As he carved his way, right hand rigid before him, through the brightly lit crowds in the Platz and then reached her where she waited, she decided he was rather special. Who knew? Perhaps she might even be moved to offer this one more than a lipstick-preserving kiss.

Walter Gunther beamed at her, scanned her from head to toe and whistled his appreciation. Hedda pressed her lips together and looked to one side in mock derision, but her eyes sparkled with excitement.

"Wow! You look even more beautiful than I remember."

"You say that each time you see me, Walter. Soon I shall dazzle you and you won't be able to look at me at all!"

"Well, then I shall simply fall at your feet and worship you."

Hedda laughed, bending forward a little as she did so, reaching to hit his right arm playfully. "You are too silly – but you make me laugh, which is good."

Walter brought his feet together and lifted his right hand to his forehead in an imitation salute, then offered her his arm. "Shall we dine, my lady?" Chatting and laughing, Hedda holding his right arm with both hands, they made their way to the crowded restaurant.

Walter's father had been a Field Marshal in World War One and distinguished himself by service to Germany so that in 1933 the new Führer had made him a General Staff Officer, serving under Chief of Staff Officer Ludwig Beck. His grandfather had been a Prussian general. Walter, twenty-eight years old, wealthy, intelligent, on occasional social terms with Goering, was a newly created SS officer. Berlin was his playground. By the time Hedda caught his eye in a smoky club on the Bellevuestrasse, Walter Gunther was as familiar with the female anatomy and the tactics of seduction as he was with his weapon of choice, the PO8 Parabellum. He handled both with skill, but the gun occupied his thoughts more and held his attention for longer.

Tonight's dinner date at Haus Vaterland was their third meeting. Hedda found herself increasingly attracted to and interested by the handsome officer. She knew instinctively that his charm and foppish humour disguised a sharp intelligence and possibly a temper. She knew this because there was in Walter's eyes a darkness with which Hedda was familiar and which sometimes consumed his expression like un-dammed liquor when he turned from her to put out a cigarette or follow a thought during intervals in their conversation. These unguarded reversions to a more naturally saturnine disposition did not alarm Hedda. Indeed, she saw her father in Walter's underlying intolerance of the frivolity he politely indulged. And, although she was not consciously attracted by the connection, she was given increasingly to thoughts of stability and permanence.

For his part, Walter considered Hedda easy company. She did not lean forward and use the heel of her right palm to thrust her mouth at him in that way women have who want to be adored. She did not seek to establish her intellect by attempting to engage him in ideological discussions about his part in Hitler's rise or his views on "das Judische problem". In fact, Hedda was, he suspected, a little vacuous, but this did nothing to deter him. In fact, he welcomed it. Any woman who might hold his attention for more than a few dates or beyond seduction would necessarily be undemanding of it.

Walter was ambitious and not insensitive to the advantage a good marriage would afford him. Certainly, his social networking could expand to include the bridge and dining engagements of his parents' generation, had he a beautiful and well-connected wife on his arm. Hedda might do nicely. And so, just weeks after their third dinner date, Walter Gunther asked Hedda Schroeder to marry him and she accepted with a gratified shrug and a brilliant smile that enhanced her flawless complexion like a sudden glaze.

The inevitable society wedding followed with well-oiled efficiency, and took place in the spring of 1934. Money was no object and neither were the trimmings essential to the execution of such an occasion. The sun shone, the couple were resplendent. Everyone agreed this was a perfect match. Walter's father and friends attended in full uniform; dazzling dress sabres and immaculately polished boots snared the crisp spring light. A salute of perfectly white gloves complemented the pristine organza froth of the bride's dress when the couple emerged onto the steps of the Kaiser Wilhelm Gedachtniskirch. Walter and Hedda honeymooned briefly in Koblenz. Too much champagne, lights splashing giddily on the sombre Rhein, and a majestic four poster bed. And then back to Berlin.

For Walter, this was a time of consolidation. As well as serving under him, his father was a close and trusted friend of Ludwig Beck, General Chief of Staff, and stationed in Berlin. Beck's distinguished military service during World War One had ensured influence and power as Hitler's Reich took shape. But the Chief of Staff's misgivings regarding Hitler's assumption of absolute military as well as political power, following the 1933 Enabling Act, was well understood in wider military circles. Walter, striving to ensure that his alliance with Hitler and dissent from the conservative Prussian old guard was obvious, saw less and less of his father and confined his socializing to National Socialism circles. He spoke loudly and clearly to whomever might report his views in the right places.

Hedda busied herself with the decoration of her smart town house on the outskirts of the Tiergarten district. She learned to drive and was often seen on sunny days at the wheel of her husband's gleaming Audi DKW. Always gloved and wearing a fashionable matching hat, Hedda was admired and envied by the youthful Berlin set. She was beautiful, glamorous and married to the impossibly handsome and well connected Walter Gunther. What could be more perfect?

Indeed, life for the first months after their marriage was heady and socially exhausting for the newly-weds. Utterly convinced of their beauty, the couple made love to each other for hours each night. Hedda was not interested in Walter's SS duties and Walter was content to fund his wife's caprices. He smiled distractedly at her extravagances and saluted charmingly when he came home late to discover his drawing room full of giddy, flirtatious socialites. He would pour himself a large whisky, loosen his uniform collar and raise his glass to each one before kissing his wife gently on the mouth and withdrawing. The audible "oohs" and other suggestively admiring noises as he left the room never failed to please him. But by the time he sat upon his bed to remove his boots, his mind was once again grappling with the logistics of organizing working groups of ageing Jewish men to clear Berlin's roads of snow or rubbish or horse manure, depending on the season and the district.

Hedda visited her mother on afternoons when neither had anything more pressing in her diary. Dressed in expensive suits and furs, Hedda would sit with her legs crossed, sipping tea from a china cup without removing her carefully pinned hat. Just like a proper visitor. The pregnancy, discovered just six months after Hedda's marriage to Walter, was neither inconvenient nor welcome. It was hardly a surprise, given that neither she nor Walter had made serious efforts to avoid it; so secure was their arrangement that there was no reason to do so.

"Are you happy, Walter?" Hedda turned her head to observe her husband as they lay in bed one Sunday morning listening to the bells rolling across the Sabbath stillness from the north-western tower of the Berliner Dom. He lay on his back, contemplating the ceiling. When she spoke, he turned to her and smiled briefly, extended an arm so that she could move onto it and be pulled towards him. She buried her face in his shoulder as his thoughts resumed.

Herr and Frau Schroeder received the news of their daughter's pregnancy with nods and smiles, but both hoped that becoming grandparents would not interfere with bridge. Only Cook beamed broadly at the news and covered her face with her apron to conceal her tears. It was clear she wanted to clasp Hedda in her arms, but her open gesture was met with an uncertain response and she folded her arms instead and curtsied, repeating her warm congratulations.

For Hedda, the pregnancy brought a new and unsettling lack of certainty which grew as the child began to strain the stitching of her chic clothing. It demanded her attention. The indignity of the vomiting she was forced to endure each morning horrified her. At times, she experienced nothing less than terror when she raised herself from the toilet bowl and contemplated her moist, wild eyes and dishevelled hair in the bathroom mirror. She suffered further indignity upon the examination table at the salubrious offices of Berlin's top gynaecologist, and at every turn, it seemed, was confronted by the rawness, the vulnerability, of her humanity. It did nothing to preserve the precarious harmony of their marriage when Walter came home unexpectedly early to find his wife gorging on apple strudel. Hedda would wipe her mouth guiltily with the back of her hand and start from her plate like a furtive animal.

Hedda was eight months pregnant when Klaus and Agna Gunther turned up unannounced one hot afternoon in August 1935. Hedda was horrified when the housekeeper suddenly showed them into the drawing room. She had kicked off her slippers and removed her stockings, for the heat was stifling. She was dozing in an armchair beside an open window where occasionally, at least, a light breeze disturbed the sullen heaviness of the room.

Agna Gunther was immediately apologetic and genuinely embarrassed at their intrusion.

"Dear Hedda, please – don't get up. We are sorry to land on you like this, but we so wanted to see you and Walter. Well..." Here Agna faltered, lifted her handbag and gripped its handles in front of her as though to defend herself. "Well, he is always too busy to respond to our letters and..." She turned towards her husband as if pleading for help.

"Walter is avoiding us, Hedda," stated Klaus quietly.

"Well," began Agna again, her voice breaking a little as though close to tears, "he is busy, we know... I so wanted to see you, Hedda," Agna smiled broadly, moved towards her daughter-in-law and extended her arms. "How are you?"

By now Hedda had risen from her chair and located her slippers. She moved towards Agna and they hugged lightly.

"I am OK," stated Hedda simply as the women moved apart once more. "Fat!"

Agna laughed. Klaus remained behind them, near the door. He smiled and looked down at his feet, put his hands in his pockets.

"Sit down, Hedda, please," said Agna warmly, stooping to put her handbag on the floor and assuming a seat on a pouffe on which Hedda had earlier rested her feet. There ensued a flurry of exchanges between the women, during which Agna took Hedda's hands in her own and held them, smiling always into her daughter-in-law's beautiful eyes. She wanted to know how Hedda was keeping and if she was eating and sleeping properly. Had she had regular check-ups? Was everything all right? How naughty it was of Walter to give them so little information about this their first grandchild! What was he thinking?

Hedda could not comfort her. She had no idea what Walter was thinking or that he had been ignoring written invitations to his parents' house. He never spoke of them and any attempts she had made to bring them up in conversation were dismissed. Hedda did not yet possess the temerity to challenge her increasingly secretive and serious husband on his behaviour towards his parents – or for that matter on his increasingly frequent and drunken evening forays. But the anger she felt and the resentment at the way in which her life had changed were gathering force as the child within her grew towards unavoidable birth.

Klaus paced the drawing room, concentrating on his feet as though he were not sure if his shoes exactly matched. When Agna stopped talking, Klaus stopped pacing and looked directly at Hedda.

"How is Walter, Hedda? I hear... things about my son, but I know nothing. I don't know who his friends are – how he spends his time. I am not asking you to be disloyal – that would never do. You are his wife. But you can surely share with us a little of what Walter is up to these days? He is so busy. He never writes."

Hedda regarded her father-in-law. After some seconds he began to doubt the girl's hearing – or her wits. At last, she sighed and slumped back in the armchair as though she had given up trying to think of an answer.

"I haven't the faintest idea what Walter is up to," she replied flatly. "He leaves the house at eight each morning and he returns about seven each evening. Sometimes, it is earlier. He dines here or else he bathes and goes straight out again. Sometimes we have people to eat with us here – people Walter works with and their wives. They are all right, but I don't know them well. I don't ask where he goes when he goes out alone and I am generally asleep, or very nearly, when he comes back. Often, he has been drinking and sings in the bathroom. Sometimes he is very serious and quiet and he can't sleep, so he gets up and goes downstairs. He never tells me what he's been doing and he never discusses his work with me. In fact, he barely seems to notice I exist."

Hedda was shocked at how progressively angry her tone had become as she spoke to Klaus. Now she regretted her openness and, in the silence that met her declaration, was ashamed. They would think her shallow and indiscreet. A hot blush heightened further her already high complexion. The heat in the room was overwhelming and she closed her eyes against a slight but rising nausea.

"My dear – I am so sorry." Agna's voice was truly sympathetic and soothing. "I am sorry we have arrived like this and upset you. Would you like some ice water, Hedda? Wait – I shall find your maid – ask her to bring some cold drinks." Agna rose and as she crossed the drawing room to the door signalled to her husband to approach Hedda. Klaus nervously smoothed his moustache and took a seat in a chair adjacent to his daughter-in-law.

"I too am sorry. I fear I was a little abrupt, Hedda. Clearly, Walter is very busy and he does not – quite rightly – want to concern you with his problems, or..." Klaus waved his hand abstractedly in his inability to define what it was about Walter's evening habits that he couldn't impose on his wife. He feared the worst. Much as he hated to contemplate the possibility that Walter might already be returning to his bachelor habits, it seemed a logical consideration. Had he really raised such a shallow and inconsiderate cad? A new and beautiful wife, heavily pregnant, and Walter could not stay with her in the evenings? More than ever, he feared what his son's SS connections and orders might be doing to his conscience. He knew well how ambitious Walter was to make something of himself, to achieve a status that rivalled his father's. He greatly feared that the machine of Hitler's Nazism would propel Walter much further professionally and politically than Klaus had ever travelled. But he could not see how such violent and sudden momentum could do otherwise than cause great destruction, or at best falter to a miserable halt. If he could, Klaus was determined to make Walter see sense before it was too late.

When Walter arrived home from work that evening he was not pleased to discover his parents seated for dinner. Cook was serving finely sliced meats from a large silver salver and placing generous dishes of steaming vegetables upon the table. Walter nodded acknowledgment to each of his parents while saluting in true SS fashion. Klaus and Agna stood up to greet their son, while Hedda remained seated and regarded her husband with the same level and inscrutable gaze with which she had earlier contemplated his father. Although she had truly no idea what or who Walter had become – or really, what he had ever been – she sensed a sort of alliance in his parents' misgivings, and though its nature was indefinable, it was a source of strength. She felt no fear of her husband as he turned his joyless smile upon her and one raised eyebrow questioned her complicity in this unexpected turn of events. It was clear he wished her to rise and greet him.

"Good evening, Walter," Hedda began, her voice clear and steady, though she still made no attempt to stand. "Your parents are here to visit us from Zehlendorf. Isn't this a lovely surprise? I had Cook make something special for dinner: pork in white wine sauce with sauerkraut – your favourite. For dessert we are having plum tart with cream. After all, this is a special occasion! I was not sure if you would be joining us for dinner, or if you might have plans for dining out, but you see of course that I needed to welcome your parents properly – we have not seen them in such a long time."

Walter nodded again. "Of course, Hedda – you have behaved perfectly correctly. I shall join you directly after I have changed for dinner. Please – continue without me for now. Have you asked Cook to bring a nice Riesling to accompany the pork?"

Klaus interjected, "I took the liberty, Walter, of asking your cook to bring wine. We have already started – shall I pour you a glass?"

"Of course – please. I shall be with you soon." And turning stiffly on his heel, Walter left the dining room.

"Oh, dear." Agna's voice was quiet and her words not particularly directed. "I don't think our son is pleased to see us."

Hedda shrugged and looked down at her plate as Cook carefully layered upon it slices of succulent pork. "I wonder if I might have just a little wine? I haven't had a drink of anything more stimulating than fruit juice for such a long time."

Dinner passed awkwardly. Walter made polite conversation with his parents, enquiring after their health and passing occasional remarks on Hedda drinking wine. She regarded him with an apparent imperturbability of which she was master and which served her well when she was feeling anything but calm. Walter studied his wife anew this evening and realized her strength for the first time. It was not a strength he admired particularly, for it was untried and of the infuriatingly passive type he was encountering more often from Jews and Social Democrats who held offices or university degrees and thought they deserved respect, but were too timid – or wise – to demand it.

Finally, Cook cleared away the dessert dishes and brought brandy for the men. Agna and Hedda were discussing baby things and nursery decoration, and Klaus was reduced to sullen silence by the futility of trying to engage his son in conversation. Walter could maintain his composure no longer.

"So, tell me, Father, why is it that you are here – really? If this were only a social visit I think you might have arranged it in advance in the usual way."

Walter's sharpness was startling. Hedda and Agna stopped talking, and all three turned to him at once. The redness that spread from his throat to his cheeks and the burning defiance in Walter's eyes did nothing to reduce their anxiety. Cook withdrew, leaving the brandy bottle on the table. When she had gone, Klaus answered his son. "You do not acknowledge our written invitations or your mother's letters, Walter. I suppose I could try and contact you by telephone at your new place of work – the Air Ministry Building on Wilhelmstrasse, isn't it? I understand you have found favour with Prime Minister Goering. Are you enjoying your new job in Logistics?"

Agna was keen to soften her son and avoid unpleasantness. She knew well that Klaus was increasingly furious at the power and militancy of the SS and Goering's Gestapo, the cavalier contempt with which this new Führer and his "henchmen", as Klaus termed them, treated the army generals. That his own son might be complicit in the smear campaigns conducted against the Prussian army generals, and the recent murders of some, made him sleepless and distraught. Agna was terrified of permanent division between these two men whom she so loved.

"Walter, darling, we have missed you so much. We know you are busy, but – it was my fault. I simply couldn't stay away any longer. I bullied your poor father mercilessly until he agreed to drive me here. I so wanted to see Hedda! You know how we women are when there's a baby on the way. And, darling, this is no ordinary baby. This is our grandson or daughter! I am so happy for you both, Walter. I just wanted so much to see you both. Don't be cross, Wally, please."

Walter heard the love in his mother's voice, and her use of his pet name doused a little the fire of his resentment at what he regarded as an ambush. He did not doubt that his mother was desperate to see him, but he knew for certain that his father would have something to say about his appointment as Chief Logistics Officer to Goering. Walter had, after all, served Goering well in ways of which his father could never approve.

A year earlier, Walter had come to Goering's attention following a particularly zealous demonstration of fealty to the Reich during Operation Hummingbird. The stratagem had been to storm the vice chancellery with a number of other SS and Gestapo officers and shoot certain people who were considered a threat to the Reich. One of the main targets was a close advisor to the vice chancellor himself. When the Gestapo officer holding the pistol at point blank range from the target's head had hesitated, Walter had seized his moment. In an instant he removed his Parabellum from its holster, aimed and pulled the trigger. He had received a letter of commendation from Goering, and there followed an offer of a job in Goering's Reichsluftfahrtministerium. It was the recognition Walter craved.

"Mother, I quite understand your wanting to see us. I just wish you could have waited until I am less busy at work. This new job is very demanding and I have simply no time for anything but work. I would have replied to your letters as soon as I could – when the baby was born, certainly."

"When is the baby due, exactly, Hedda?" Agna was determined to lighten the conversation and, if she had her way, they would leave as soon as Klaus had finished his brandy. She had the most terrible feeling of foreboding.

"Oh... well, in about two weeks' time." Hedda's response was distracted. She had perceived the growing antipathy between Walter and his father, watched the gathering storm of Walter's fury with something like the horrified exhilaration she had experienced when the Jew and the SS officer fought at the Moka Efti club over two years ago. This was only the second time in her life that something had threatened to puncture the veneer of civility on which she had always trodden so carefully.

"And we shall come and visit you at the hospital. Which one will you be in, Hedda?"

"Rudolf Virchow – Augustenberger Platz."

"Augustenberger Platz... let me write that down." Agna retrieved her handbag from where it rested on the floor at her feet and riffled through it until she found a small address book and a pen. She broke the words down aloud into constituent syllables as she recorded the hospital address under "H". "We shall, at any rate, contact the hospital by telephone in a couple of weeks' time. Oh, Walter..." Agna looked to her son with an excited smile. "You are hoping for a boy, I expect, hmm? You men! You always want boys."

Walter, his elbows upon the table, hands joined as if in prayer and fingers pressed to his lips, contemplated his mother's lovely smile for an instant, then slowly folded his hands into each other so that his mouth was free to form words.

"A boy would be pleasing, yes."

"And what would you call him?" Agna was determined to be cheerful. She looked from Walter, to Hedda, to Walter again. Hedda shrugged and contemplated her empty wine glass, ceded the answer to Walter.

"I think... Adolph, perhaps? Or maybe Heinrich or Hermann? It is not decided."

Hedda looked up sharply and could not this time disguise her alarm as she turned towards Walter, though she said nothing. He looked at her steadily and without a trace of warmth. Klaus suddenly snatched his napkin from his knees and rose from the table.

"I think, Walter, it is time you and I talked. Let us leave the ladies and – where can we go? The drawing room? I, for one, would like a cigar." So saying, he picked up the brandy bottle, bowed to Agna and Hedda, and took his leave.

When the men were alone, Klaus remained standing and took an elegant cigar case from an inner jacket pocket and offered a cigar to Walter, who declined with a dismissive gesture from his position in an armchair. Walter never took his eyes from his father as the older man busied himself in cutting off the end of his fine Dutch cigar with a tiny gold guillotine made for the purpose and which he kept in a waistcoat pocket. Then, still without regarding his son, Klaus took his silver gasoline lighter from an inner pocket on the opposite side of his jacket from that in which he kept his cigar case and lit his cigar with great care. Finally, tilting back his head slightly and squinting to avoid smoke, he spoke.

"Walter, you are an SS officer and now Chief Logistics Officer to Hermann Goering, but you are still my son, and though I have not said it in either of our memories... I love you."

Walter could not help the widening of his eyes or the sudden guffaw that escaped him. He said nothing, but continued to watch his father, a look of bemusement on his face.

"I don't blame you for being cynical – I did not much... eh... coddle you when you were a boy. My error perhaps, but I was a soldier and I wanted my son to be a soldier. You understand?"

"Perfectly."

Klaus contemplated his son for a long moment. He was struck by the otherness of him and the distance between them. How angular, how strong and how very much the man Walter seemed now. But what sort of man? That was the question that burned in Klaus's heart. He could not quite believe that he was too afraid to ask it outright.

"I was, in spite of what you suppose, always proud of you, Walter. I know we have disagreed a good deal in the past about how you spent your time – and my money – but I always thought you were a good boy – a good man – at heart. And now... now you are thirty – in your prime and about to become a father yourself."

"Father, what is it you are here to say? I know you will not approve of my closeness to Prime Minister Goering. You do not approve of his... methods. But you will surely know that I cannot discuss my work, and it is better if you and I do not do so." Walter had some difficulty speaking these words, for his father's declaration of love for and pride in him had affected him in ways he could not yet process. The immediate effect was, though, to make him less determined to distance himself from this man whose approbation he had sought openly until it seemed it would never come.

"Walter, you and I come from a distinguished line of military men. Your ancestors were Prussian nobility." Klaus's expression was earnest as he took a chair from beneath a polished occasional table and placed it squarely before Walter's armchair and then sat close, facing his son. Only the repeated movements of Walter's Adam's apple gave away his mounting nervousness. "I love Germany! Goddam it, Walter, your grandfather was a Field Marshal before I was, and gave his life for this country. Your great-grandfather fought Napoleon under Wilhelm and helped to make this nation what it was before the French took their latest revenge upon us with this confounded Treaty. And his father before that lost his life defending Prussia at Saalfeld. For goodness' sake, Walter, I don't think there has been a time when a Gunther was not defending Prussia or Germany with his life on a battlefield. And now here you are..."

"Father, I really..." Walter made to rise from his chair, but Klaus was determined to speak, raised his right hand in a gesture intended to prevent his son's rising.

"No, Walter, let me finish. Von Schleicher was a fine man and an exceptional general. He helped Hitler to gain power, as you know. And now, because he had differences of opinion with the Führer, he is dead. Murdered. Yes, Walter –" Klaus responded to

Walter's raised hand and shaking head by raising his voice – "there is no other word for it. Murdered! Hear me out and then I will go. Von Schleicher was my friend, my true friend. Do you remember how, on summer days, you and your mother and I would visit his house and how he would sit you on his knee and tell you how proud you should be of who you are? He loved you, Walter, and his wife, Elisabeth..." Here Klaus paused and seemed to wrestle with his emotions, unable to look at Walter until he could continue. "She was such a lovely woman – so noble and gentle. She would spoil you, Walter, with sweets and what-not. Do you remember?" For answer, Walter lowered his head and nodded slightly. "Well, they were gunned down like dogs – like dogs – in their own home, and for why, Walter?"

"Father, I am not privy to such things. I..."

"Walter, I hope you never will be privy to decisions to murder honourable men and their wives. This is why I am here – to beg you not to make decisions that will make you more than privy to such things. Be careful, my son, of Goering and of your Führer. They will make a murderer of you if they can." There was a pause during which neither knew what to say, and then Klaus spoke again. "I think they may already have done so." Just as Walter had suspected, it seemed rumours of his actions at the vice chancellery had reached his father's ears.

"That is enough! I must insist you stop this instant, Father, and I would like you to leave." Walter stood up abruptly. Klaus too rose to his feet. It had been a very long time since they had been this physically close.

"You will hear me or you may shoot me, Walter. But I shall finish what I came to say." Klaus's tone was steady and authoritative. "Von Schleicher wanted only to bring back a little Prussian dignity to present political proceedings. He was the voice of reason in the wilderness. If he had succeeded in resurrecting Hohenzollern, what strength, what unifying greatness might we have harnessed once more in Germany! And what sanity might now prevail in this godforsaken Reich! Yes, Walter, and I use the term 'godforsaken' with full intent, for there is no... no... goodness in the dictates of your Führer."

Walter considered whether he should push his father out of the way and fetch his gun. He looked at Klaus as coolly as he could manage and recalled the instant when he had shot the vice chancellor's advisor. Could he shoot the man in front of him?

"Do you know what the motto is of the House of Hohenzollern, Walter?" Walter did not answer. Klaus turned away from his son, contemplated his dead cigar for a moment, then dropped both hands at his sides before facing Walter again and continuing. "It is *Nihil Sine Deo* – Nothing without God. And that, Walter, is precisely what your Nazis are. No matter how powerful, how brutal, how... thuggish they become, they are nothing without God, and Germany will never be made great by such men. My son, you will never be a great man if you walk with such men. There, now I have said what I came to say. I am done."

"You are done? Yes, I should think that is the whole point, Father. You are done – you and all your Prussian friends!" Walter walked away from his father, assumed a central position in the room. "You are finished. You cannot resurrect what is dead, and von Schleicher was a fool to try. He was, as the Führer said, an enemy of the state. He was trying to undermine the new order and take Germany back to a time of... of social division and..." – Walter struggled for fluency against tides of anger and blood pulsing through his head – "...pomposity, which has no place in a Socialist state!"

Visibly shaken by his son's fury and the unambiguousness of his declarations, Klaus had heard Walter's last speech without turning to watch him make it. Now he contemplated the younger man with an expression of enormous sadness. There was a long silence. When Klaus still said nothing, Walter continued, slightly less vehemently, "Move with the times, Father. Embrace the opportunities which are still there for you and do not try and divide the nation you and your ancestors fought so hard to unite. What is honourable about conspiracy? Von Schleicher, Bredow, the others – they are conspirators against this Reich. I... I will not have this treachery in my house."

Klaus looked tired. He reached for the chair on which he had sat earlier, turned it so that it faced Walter, and sat down once more before continuing. When he spoke, his voice was gentle, his tone rather flat.

"Do you know your great and noble Goering is spreading rumours about other generals – disgusting and untrue... filth about their private lives? Is this the mark of a great man, a good man? Every week we hear some new lie about someone. Just yesterday I heard that von Fritsch is supposed to be a... a... homosexual – outrageous! The man is honourable to his bones and would retch at the thought of... well, well... And now – now that Field Marshal von Mackensen has dared to denounce the murders of von Schleicher and his wife in their own home – and poor Bredow, of course – now he has done that, will he be next?"

Walter regarded his father, said nothing. His face was very red and he swallowed often; though in anger or anxiety, Klaus could not discern. He appealed once more to what he hoped was the goodness deep in his son's heart. "You tell me, Walter, is this honourable behaviour? Is this the glorious Germany for which your ancestors fought and died? How did we get from Frederick the Great to Goering, Walter? Can you tell me? Berlin is the birthplace of kings. What will it become under Hitler, do you think? When he has annihilated all possible opposition and forbidden us even to think for ourselves – when he controls the army utterly and when Goering and his murdering Gestapo have succeeded in terrorizing all who dare to express an opinion – tell me, Walter, what sort of Berlin, what sort of Germany, will we have?"

Walter recrossed the room to stand over his father. He feared his intense emotions might affect the pitch and steadiness of his voice and he wanted to be manly and impressive – even now. But never in his wildest imaginings had he thought his father would be so incontinent of thought, so imprudent. As Klaus took out a handkerchief from a trouser pocket and wiped his brow, then relit his cigar with shaking hands, Walter began to collect his thoughts. Father or not, what this man had just said was treacherous. If Goering had heard just a snippet of the spiel that had poured from Chief of Staff Officer Klaus Gunther's mouth he would have had him shot. And this treason was unsluiced in Walter's own drawing room! It spread like poison over the chintz and gleaming brass, the polished furniture and elegant mantle. How unspeakably selfish of this old man to bring this compromising slander to his house – uninvited and unannounced.

Walter knocked the cigar from his father's mouth, then followed it to where it fell and crushed it underfoot. Klaus simply watched.

"I must ask you to leave at once! I did not ask you here. I... I simply cannot believe that you dared to say such things in my own house. Did I ask you here, hmm? Did I?" Walter paced the room, his fury growing with every turn, a note of barely controlled hysteria in his voice. "No! You took it upon yourself to arrive in my house, eat my food and drink my wine. Then you... then you pollute me with all that... all that Prussian old school rubbish! All that..." Inarticulate with wrath, Walter stopped pacing and faced his incredulous father. "Your time is gone. That is what you cannot stand. This is not a time for... for kings and... and Prussian Field Marshals with moustaches who think war must be fought with pistols and sabres. Look around you – Germany is dying on her feet, but we are reviving her – Hitler is reviving her!"

He stood entirely unafraid now before his father, and as he spoke, the contempt he felt was evident. Klaus leaned forward in his chair, rested his arms on his thighs, bent his head and contemplated the ground. Walter struggled to regain composure and stood square before Klaus. "Tell me, Field Marshal, have you even heard of the Junkers 87 dive bomber? No? Let me tell you about it. I am deploying prototypes at this very time – it is part of my job at the Air Ministry. It is a plane which will make the Luftwaffe the finest military airborne force in the world. It can dive at eighty degrees... but the pilot is so comfortable... he is in total control, so... so he can make precision judgments at a practically vertical angle about where to drop his bombs. It will revolutionize warfare. Under Prime Minister Goering, your Prussia will be an almighty power once again. If you cannot see that, old man, then I suggest... I suggest you keep quiet about your blindness."

"Or?" At last, Klaus looked up at Walter. His expression was neutral; his eyes, when they met Walter's, fearless and clear. He stood up slowly.

"Or," Walter stepped back and seemed less sure of himself now that his father had risen and held his gaze, "or else you might find yourself compromised in your work as Chief of Staff Officer for the Führer, Field Marshal Gunther."

"I see." Klaus nodded as though he at last understood something, and then, sighing, he patted his pockets to ensure all the smoking paraphernalia he possessed was in place. He lifted the chair he had used and crossed the room to replace it beneath the table. "You are wrong to presume I have not heard of your Junkers plane – the Stuka, they are calling it? Junkers himself is dead, I think. Yes, yes - February of this year. He was sent..." and here Klaus turned to look at Walter, emphasized the word, "to Bavaria, I think. Did you know this?" Again, Klaus nodded, shrugged his shoulders a little, turned away from Walter and began walking towards the drawing room door. "He owned that firm, you know – of course you know. But he said the wrong things. Just like the others. Just as I have done this evening. I am going, Walter. I shall see myself out." But just as he opened the drawing room door, Klaus shut it gently again and half turned towards Walter, his hand still on the door handle. "In case you are ever... privy to such a discussion, I would rather be shot than sent to Bavaria. I never liked the place. Too much singing." And then he opened wide the door and passed through into the hallway.

Agna knew better than to ask what had happened in the drawing room. Her husband's crestfallen posture and her son's clenched jaw told her all was far from well. With a heart already grieving, she threw herself at Walter and clung to his neck like a stricken lover. He did not raise his arms to return her embrace, but muttered his goodbyes before turning from the open door and marching across the hallway and up the stairs.

Hedda embraced her now sobbing mother-in-law and bade Klaus goodbye. He half smiled at her, but made no attempt to embrace her. Halfway to the car he turned and said only, "I wish you well, Hedda. Look after my grandchild, hmm? There is noble blood in the child's veins. Oh, and Hedda..."

"Yes, Herr Gunther?"

"You might be interested in asking your father what he is working on so hard these days. I hear he is a very brilliant man. Says all the right things."

When Agnette was born fifteen days later, Hedda wrote a short note to Agna and Klaus to inform them that they had a granddaughter and to tell them her name. She promised that she would send a photograph as soon as she had the chance. Walter left the choice of baby's name to Hedda and did not object to its resemblance to that of his mother, although he never mentioned either of his parents again and forbade Hedda to do so. Neither Agna nor Klaus telephoned the Rudolf Virchow hospital to see if they had a grandchild, and Hedda never received a reply from them to her letter announcing Agnette's birth.

CHAPTER TWO

In July 1940, Agnette was almost five years old and her brother, Anselm, was two. Walter was now Oberst Walter Gunther, serving with Flak Regiment General Goering. The same iron nerve and unflinching obeisance under pressure which had first won Walter particular notice in the vice chancellery in 1934 had served him well after war was declared. He had distinguished himself serving in Denmark in April 1940 in Operation Weserubung. The Norwegian air force had had little defence against the might and confidence of the Luftwaffe or its anti-air force battalions. Ecstatic to be serving his country in combat at last, Walter was able to demonstrate his credentials as a warrior of outstanding pedigree. He could not fly his beloved Stukas, but he could jump from one without a second thought and, crystal clear in his objectives, complete any operational task assigned to his battalion.

He was among those who landed at Aalborg in the small hours of the morning on the 9th April 1940 and, largely unopposed, took the airbase, creating a vital refuelling station for the later invasion of Norway. A few days later, Walter's skills with a Flak 38 anti-aircraft gun helped to drive the Allied Forces from central Norway, while the Junkers 87 dive bombers blasted French and British destroyers from the Norwegian Sea. Walter returned to Berlin at the end of April a hero. He fully expected to be deployed in France in a very few months, but for now was basking in his glory and the special regard of Goering himself.

One particular morning in July 1940, Walter was fixing his collar before an elaborate Georgian mirror in the bedroom he occasionally shared with his wife, while shouting to Hedda to get a move on in readying the children. They had a luncheon invitation from Prime Minister Goering himself. They would be travelling by chauffeured car to the splendid Carinhall, a vast Prussian estate in the Schorfheide Forest, north of Berlin, which Goering had acquired in 1935 and where he now lived with his second wife, Emmy, during the summer months.

Walter shouted from his room, giving full vent to his irritation. "Hedda, are you ready now? The car will be here in ten minutes. And can you shut that boy up, please? It is an intolerable racket!"

From Anselm's room a little down the corridor from where Walter was now putting on his jacket, smoothing his oiled hair in preparation for donning his uniform cap, Hedda responded as lightly as she could that she was practically ready. The truth was a little different. Anselm would not remain still enough to have his jacket put on and arched his back against her, screaming his protests and folding his arms rigidly across his chest to prevent her putting them into the sleeves. Hedda tried to soothe the child while keeping her own temper, for she knew that if Anselm were still uncooperative by the time his father wished to leave, there would be punishment – for both of them. Little Agnette sat sullenly on her brother's bed and watched, frowning as her mother lost her balance from her crouching position and tumbled with Anselm onto the floor in an ungainly heap. The child screamed more loudly and Hedda struggled to rise without crushing him, without snagging her stockings or twisting her ankle in an attempt to gain footing in her high heels.

"What is all this? What is all this?" Hedda closed her eyes in frustration that Walter was already in the room. Anselm became quiet, but he lay on his side on the floor with his eyes tight shut and the offending jacket crumpled beneath him.

"Anselm doesn't want to wear his jacket – that is all."

"Anselm!" Walter's voice was loud, and the child opened his eyes but did not move. "Get up at once and put on this jacket, or you will have me to answer to. At once!"

Hedda coaxed the child gently, pulling on the arm uppermost, but he pulled it away from her petulantly and remained on the floor.

Suddenly, Walter crossed the room, took hold of his son's arm and lifted him with one hand, then planted him roughly on his feet. "Do not ignore me, little man, or it will be worse for you. Now, you will get this jacket on – do you hear me? Pick it up and give it to me."

"I will get it, Walter. We don't have time…"

"No! Anselm will pick up the jacket and hand it to me, Hedda. Do not undermine me, please. Anselm, get the jacket – *now*!" The last imperative was shouted and the child visibly jumped and began to cry again, but he did not move towards the garment.

There was a good-humoured klaxon sound from outside the house.

"Walter, the car is here. Please, let me bring the jacket and I will deal with this in the car. He may be too hot in it anyway. Let us see. We can sort it out on the journey."

Agnette covered her ears and closed her eyes at her mother's persistent defiance, for she knew well what could happen in such circumstances. Walter approached his wife and his upper lip curled on one side in a sneer of contempt. He spoke menacingly into her face while she lowered her eyes lest she be accused of further defiance.

"Shut up, Hedda. Now, make the boy pick up the jacket by the time I count to three, or…" He did not finish his sentence, but it was clear from the fierce iciness of his eyes what would follow if he were not obeyed.

"Anselm, darling – Anselm, please, listen to me, sweetness. Daddy and Mummy need to get in a nice big shiny car – would you like to see it? I can show it to you. Would you like to get into a great big shiny car, sweetheart? Would you like that?" Anselm shook with the occasional sob, but he was quiet and nodded solemnly through his tears and snot. A chubby finger went up to his mouth and he hooked it over his lower teeth. "Now then, if you want to get in the car, you must get the jacket from the floor and bring it to Mummy. OK? Will you do that for me?"

Anselm nodded, and still heaving occasionally from the grief of it all, turned from her and walked to the jacket, bent his chubby knees and picked it up.

"There's a good boy! Thank you, Anselm. Shall we put it on now and then go to the big car? Hmm?" The klaxon sounded again, less good naturedly this time.

"Oh, for the love of God, Hedda, put the goddam jacket on the boy and let's get out of here! Herr Goering himself has sent a car for us and we have the discourtesy to be late. Anselm..."

"Please, Walter. Please. Dear Walter, go to the car with Agnette and I shall bring Anselm directly. He is such a good boy, I am sure he will put his jacket on now, hmm?" Hedda looked imploringly into her son's wide blue eyes and smiled. He nodded again and extended an arm. Hedda closed her eyes, this time in relief, and the jacket was applied without further remonstrance.

"About time. Anselm, there will be punishment for this, you can be sure. Come on – Agnette, come. We are late."

Fighting the hatred for her husband that whirled in her breast, Hedda took a handkerchief from the clutch bag she had put in readiness on Anselm's bed and wiped his face, made him blow his nose, before throwing the handkerchief on the bedroom floor and taking her son's hand, heading for the stairs.

The bright July sunshine and the flirtatiously wide smile of the chauffeur who doffed his cap and opened the car door for Hedda were in giddy contrast to the darkness of the previous moments, and Hedda struggled to regain poise. Anselm was not disappointed by the big shiny car and gasped and gabbled his awe, clambering over the ample leather seats and scrambling in an effort to climb the smooth back seat to see out of the rear window. Agnette sat passively as her brother knocked and bumped her in his exuberance, and Hedda curled her body as far as she could away from both of them, staring out of the window in an attempt to shut it all out and snatch a little peace. In the front passenger seat, Walter, in full military uniform, chatted amiably with the chauffeur about the car and the route to Carinhall, smiling and laughing as if, thought Hedda, he were a nice man.

At last, they reached the stately portals that marked the entrance to the estate. Many soldiers stood guard at the gatehouse. Hedda was unprepared for the splendour of Carinhall and, as the Mercedes in which the family was travelling swept up the drive and into a large courtyard, she could not but exclaim aloud at the magnificence of this palatial hunting lodge. Luxurious cars glinted in the sunshine and the chic elegance of those who emerged from them was unsurpassed in Hedda's experience. It was as though they had arrived at a hunt ball or a state occasion. Hedda recognized one or two of the women who stepped daintily from the glossy cars to be saluted by the SS officers holding open the doors. She recognized these women's husbands as colleagues of Walter and former dinner guests at her house, but she could not recall their names. The cars were driven away to be parked by household servants in tailored black butler suits, and a line of neat maids in black and white greeted guests at the door and offered to take their wraps or conduct ladies to cloakrooms.

Walter waited beside the Mercedes and ushered his wife and children before him to the grand doorway of Carinhall. They passed a magnificent statue of a recumbent stag and either side of the doorway were electric mock torches, their heads encased in glass. Antlers protruded from the portal archway and at intervals along the façade of the palace. Above the door was a balcony on which three soldiers presenting rifles stood sentry.

The Gunthers were shown into a magnificent hall. This was the Jagdhalle, 215 feet long and lined from floor to ceiling with timber. The walls displayed yet more antlers, still attached to the skulls of many hapless stags, and before a huge brick canopy fireplace that featured midway along one wall was a bearskin, glossy and ten feet in length, prostrate as if in submission before the shrine of some great hunting god. For the rest, the hall was made merry and festive. Round tables covered in fine linen cloths and glinting silver cutlery were arranged with apparent casualness throughout the room, but each featured carefully prescribed place name cards inscribed in italicized silver ink. Each table was adorned with an arrangement of freshest red roses half in bud among springing gypsophila. Hedda was reminded of a lavish wedding feast.

In a far corner a quartet played Beethoven's *allegro con brio* in F Major, unobtrusive yet distinctively lifting the mood to gaiety. Many guests looked in tingling anticipation at the champagne flutes flooded with light from a picture window. Goering circulated jocularly among his guests, laughing loudly and frequently, urging them to take second glasses of schnapps from the many trays held aloft by bowing menservants. Within half an hour of the Gunthers' arrival at Carinhall, the Jagdhalle was full of chattering and laughing SS and Fallschirmjäger officers of various ranks from Oberstleutnant to Generalfeldmarschall, their wives, children and sweethearts.

Anselm and Agnette were soon running between people, finding other children and crawling beneath tables. Hedda watched her children anxiously, lest they should annoy or bump into anyone, while Walter forgot them and laughed and toasted with his fellow officers. His flirtatious and ostentatious kissing of women's hands Hedda regarded levelly and without the slightest jealousy. She had long suspected that Walter was not faithful to her and the indignation and anger this had first caused had ceded to an icy contempt. She had readjusted easily to sleeping alone most of the time and could not miss a comradeship and intimacy that had never really been there. She noted with interest, however, the admiring looks she drew from many men in the room, and acknowledged their admiration with gracious and increasingly coquettish smiles. The schnapps, the sunlight, the laughter, the exquisite music lightened her mood and reminded her of what it had been like to be twenty and highly desirable. For the first time in her recent memory, Hedda was enjoying herself. She ceased to worry about her children, for maids had appeared from nowhere and were coaxing them into beautiful gardens, where swings and slides and even a mock castle big enough to contain several children at once provided a ready playground. Goering's daughter, Edda, just two years old, was supervised by her nanny and played happily with Anselm and other children near her own age.

The men present at this luncheon were those esteemed by Goering and the Führer himself. Many had distinguished themselves in combat during the Weserubung offensive. Hitler, though, was relaxing at his home in the Bavarian Alps and would not be present.

"So this is the beautiful Frau Gunther! Walter, you are a most fortunate man."

Hedda turned from a light conversation with someone's wife to find herself being solicited by Goering himself to offer him her hand. He took her pale fingers in a firm grasp and bent them to lay flat her upper palm, upon which he bowed to plant an enthusiastic kiss. Hedda's heart jumped giddily, and for a moment she was unsure how to respond, but years of slick Tiergarten etiquette soon came to her aid.

"What an honour to meet you in person, Reichsmarschall Goering. Your estate is completely stunning and you and your wife so hospitable." She smiled warmly into his blue eyes, knowing her own were dazzling him with their crystal beauty.

"As gracious as she is beautiful. Really, Walter, I cannot understand how you ever tear yourself away from her. I think I could almost forgive you for deserting."

Hedda blushed obligingly and curtsied slightly, while Walter, basking in praise and warmed by schnapps, smiled and bowed in acknowledgment.

"I am indeed a lucky man, Reichsmarschall Goering."

"Tell me," Goering continued, withdrawing his gaze reluctantly from Hedda's brilliant smile to face Walter, "have you told your lovely wife just how heroic you are, Walter, or are you too modest?"

Walter coloured a little – more at the assumed intimacy with his wife than the flattery, for he shared little of anything with Hedda. When neither responded, Goering turned back to Hedda, whose expression was now quizzical, one perfectly pencilled eyebrow raised in anticipation of elaboration on her husband's warring credentials.

"He is quite ruthless in his duties, you know, my dear." And, moving closer to Walter, reaching an arm around his shoulders, Goering became serious. "I have seldom seen such... single-mindedness, such lack of hesitation in the execution of orders, such pure courage as your husband exhibited in Denmark, and then again in Norway. He is quite remarkable." And Goering squeezed Walter's shoulders, took his arm away, but slapped Walter's back gently as he did so.

"I can quite imagine that, Reichsmarschall Goering," replied Hedda. "Walter is very determined in all he does."

"Good, good. Well, if you are ready I think we are about to eat – I am famished! Walter, after lunch I should very much like to talk with you. I have a proposition to make, which I think you will find interesting." Goering looked meaningfully and with great seriousness into Walter's eyes so that Walter raised his hand to his forehead and brought his heels together in full Nazi salute.

"It would be a privilege, Sir."

And with a final beaming smile and nod in Hedda's direction, Goering left to give the master of ceremonies the command to bang a burnished bronze gong and announce that lunch was about to be served.

Lunch was a splendid affair, from the cold cucumber and potato soup appetizer, through the succulent selection of grilled meats with potato dumplings and sauerkraut, to the raspberry custard kuchen and richly layered and spiced fruit torten served with cream. Fine Spätburgunder and Riesling wines filled glasses to overflowing throughout the meal, while the quartet rendered appropriately paced excerpts from *Opus 18*. Hedda, seated next to a garrulous, overweight SS general on her right, maintained an apparently effortless charm for the duration of the luncheon, but her head began to ache somewhere near dessert and she grew increasingly irritated by the way in which his moustache caught flecks of food and sauces as he chomped and talked with relentless and equal enthusiasm during and between courses.

To her left, Walter engaged with practised aplomb the attention of Annaliese Hoecker, wife of a senior SS officer said to be a great favourite of the Führer, and so Walter admired her tastes in literature and her preferences for Mozart over Beethoven. Her love of opera placed Mozart firmly at the top of her Liszt – if Walter would excuse the pun. Walter could. Though he knew little of music, he had been exposed, thanks to his mother and father, to enough classical works to be able to hold a superficial conversation about the relative merits of the great Eastern European and German composers. He had been with his family to watch Strauss's *Der Zigeunerbaron* performed by the Berlin State Opera in 1930, and when he was a child his mother would often regale him with the stories behind great operas and operettas, though his father preferred his music without what he called "that infernal soprano warbling". *Der Zigeunerbaron* he had tolerated for his wife's sake, as it was her fiftieth birthday, and for this reason Walter too had consented to sit through what he could see was an accomplished production, though he found it tiresome. Nonetheless, his Prussian background and borrowed critiques impressed Frau Hoecker, who resolved to invite the Gunthers to dinner.

The children had been devouring a sumptuous party lunch in blissful chaos in a room decorated for the occasion. After dessert and before the speeches, Hedda rose from her table, excusing herself from the overweight general's company by expressing her desire to check on her children. One glance into the room decked with balloons and streamers, full of busy maids and frenetic children all wearing plastic aprons covered in cream and jelly, told Hedda all was more than fine with her children. Anselm was sitting on the floor, concentrating hard on manipulating some toy or other. One child was curled up on the floor, evidently asleep.

The children's room opened through patio doors onto the lush lawn and swings, and there Agnette ran from a dark-haired boy who chased her. Her mouth was open, one plait clinging across it, the other flying behind her as she turned to estimate the proximity of her pursuer. Hedda stepped into the summer light and watched her daughter. How tall and lithe and fair she was; how carefree. And Hedda's heart ached suddenly. She could not estimate the damage being done by the indifference and violence that marked their home lives. She did not want to contemplate the dents and fractures in the mould of this child's personality that would shape and set her eventual character; the slaps to her mother's face she had witnessed, the icy terror of her father's temper, the inability of her mother to engage with her emotionally.

Hedda sobered suddenly from the wine and social giddiness of lunch, and the usual numbness dulled her heart. She was still only twenty-seven, but it seemed her life was over. Apart from a brief awakening to possible dreams when she was nineteen, the rest was a sort of detached somnabulance. She was married to a man whom she would soon irrevocably hate; a man who ignored her when she tried to reach him emotionally, or who slapped her if she dared express her frustration at his negligence. She had two children with whom she knew not what to do. She could dress them and read to them and listen to them for short periods, but her cook had a better relationship with Anselm and Agnette than Hedda did.

Now, watching her daughter play and laugh was like watching a cine film. Hedda could no more determine Agnette's eventual happiness than she could step into a love story with a tragic ending and redirect it. The sudden grief that brought tears to her eyes was the most genuine emotion Hedda had felt in a very long time.

She turned from the brief tableau of her daughter's playfulness and made to rejoin her husband in the Jagdhalle. Even from here, she could hear the clang and surprise of clinking glass as the tables were cleared and bottles of vintage champagne and fresh crystal flutes were placed on each one in readiness for toasts.

"Excuse me." The voice was a man's, gentle and enquiring in tone. Hedda instinctively kept her head lowered while her hands flew to her face and she brushed away tears as discreetly as she could, sniffing with minimum inelegance. When she looked up, it was into a familiar face, but she squinted with the effort of placing it in a context that might yield a name. "I don't expect you remember me – I am pretty sure it is you, though – Hedda? Forgive me..." He smiled and extended a hand. "My name is..."

"Karl! Is it Karl? My goodness, yes, I remember you!" Hedda smiled and shook his hand, recalling all the time the dark, strange young man with whom she once shared dinner and then an evening at the Moka Efti jazz club – long ago when things were possible and there were surprises, like a sudden fight between a Jew and a drunk SS officer. "How are you, Karl?"

"It is you! Hedda, yes? I was certain you wouldn't remember me at any rate – it seems a long time ago that we met."

"Yes, it does. I have children now – I have just been looking at my daughter."

"Oh, yes? And which one is she? No – let me guess. She must be the prettiest one. There! The one with the plaits and brilliant smile."

"Yes, that is Agnette, but you saw me looking at her, I think."

"Ah, but it doesn't change the facts – she is the prettiest, and no wonder."

Hedda smiled warmly at him. He had a handsome face and was very tall. But the dark shadow that had always seemed to haunt him, just below his skin, and which made his smiles disappear like sun behind clouds, was still there. This made him less superficially attractive, for his features were somehow strained, and his eyes often narrowed as if against pain. But he was interesting, she decided – his strangeness less irritating to her than when she was impatient and twenty.

"And are you married now? Do you have children?"

"I am married, yes. My wife is not here, though. She's with her parents in Leipzig. We don't have any children."

"Were you in Denmark – or Norway? Somewhere else, perhaps?"

"Norway, yes."

"My husband was there too – and in Denmark – with Flak Regiment Goering. Walter Gunther. Do you know him?"

"I have heard of Oberst Gunther, but I have not met him. I hear he is fearless. Even the SS officers talk about his courage. You must be proud."

Hedda squinted, raised a hand to her brow against the sun and turned again in Agnette's direction before turning back to Karl and speaking. "And you? You must be brave too, or you would not be here."

"Ah, me. Well, they tell me I have a pretty good aim and am handy with an eighty-eight anti-aircraft gun. I brought down a few Norwegian planes. They have promoted me to Oberleutnant."

"Congratulations, Karl."

For answer, Karl nodded but he looked down, and his smile was more a short-lived grimace, which Hedda took for modesty. "I was a medical student before the war. I wanted to make a difference, in a real way, you know? But the war came and my studies had to stop."

"Medicine? Why did I think you were an engineer?"

"Oh, I am – I mean, I already had an engineering degree. Looks like it might be put to good use by the SS, from a conversation I had a little earlier with Herr Goering."

"Oh?" Hedda was amused at the lack of reverence implicit in Karl's use of the simple, civilian title attributed to the Prussian Prime Minister and Reichsmarshall, Goering.

"Yes, it seems there is some sort of job for which I would be ideally suited – with the Waffen. Hygiene Division."

"Hygiene Division? What can that be?"

There was a long pause before Karl answered, during which Hedda watched his bowed head with an expression of quizzical amusement, much like one she would adopt if Anselm said something indecipherable.

"Top secret. I myself need to find out more. I am not sure."

"I see. You always were mysterious, Karl."

"Mysterious?"

"Yes. You know, as if there is something you would like to say but can't, or... I don't know, as if you know something you can't say. I suppose that is, in fact, the case now." She laughed and added, "I am not meaning to be rude or teasing. I am glad you are doing well. I was just remembering that evening on the Friedrichstrasse – we went to see a jazz band."

"Orchester James Kok."

"Yes – that was it! I found you fascinating then – a bit confusing, though." She laughed again.

Karl smiled. "You didn't find me that fascinating. You couldn't get out of the taxi quickly enough, as I recall."

Hedda looked into his eyes. They were deep, rich brown and his lashes were very black. They were very different from Walter's ice blue eyes. Not just in colour but in depth; in the evident capacity for feeling and the sensitivity against which they seemed constantly to squint.

"I was very young then, Karl." The seriousness of her tone and the sudden sadness in her eyes indicated that it was not just the passage of time to which she referred. "Now, everything is different." Then, after a moment: "Will you be a doctor when the war is over?"

"I hope so, yes. Although it is anyone's guess when that might be. I'm not getting any younger either, you know."

"Walter, my husband, seems to think it will all be over in a year."

"Germany may win the war against France – the whole of Europe – in a year. Let us hope she will. But I do not think that it will be the end of the Führer's plans for change in Germany."

"What do you mean?"

Karl was again matter of fact. "I just meant that there will be a lot of rebuilding to do once we have won. I am not sure what role the SS will play. If any."

Hedda nodded. "I think we should go back in now – there are speeches, I understand. And champagne."

As they both began to walk back to the Jagdhalle, Hedda remembered more clearly than ever a similarly unconvincing response to a direct question she had posed to this man on an occasion in 1933, when, in civilian clothes and the back of a taxi, he had feigned disinterest in the probable fate of a young Jew who had been fighting with an SS officer in the Moka Efti jazz club.

When Karl and Hedda re-entered the Jagdhalle, everyone else was already seated and a hush was descending upon the room. At the top of the hall a head table had been placed and it was clear from the organizing of papers in his hand and the intimate, rushed communications Goering was bending to enable with a seated General Chief of Staff, that the Reichsmarshall was preparing to speak. Walter observed his wife's entrance with the handsome, dark Oberleutnant, noted her brilliant smile as she whispered something to him before they parted, and was piqued by a surprisingly virulent jealousy. He had, though, little time to analyse its source or let her know his displeasure, for Goering addressed the assembly and all was quiet.

"Ladies and gentlemen, my dearest comrades and my friends, this afternoon has, I trust, been as much of a pleasure for you as it has been for me and for my dear wife Emmy." There were general murmurs of assent and a few well-wishers lifted their wine glasses to Goering and Emmy in appreciation. "I am aware, of course, that this afternoon is a family occasion. I look around the room and see a most radiant collection of beautiful women…" Goering paused for appreciative noises of concurrence from the men and modest giggles from the women. Several more glasses were raised in enthusiasm. "And it affirms in no small way that Germany is great. That her people are the most beautiful people God saw fit to make and that we have every reason – and every right – to wage war on all that is ugly and deviant and subversive of our great Aryan heritage and culture. We deserve – no, we demand – victory over those who would stand in the way of our rightful supremacy in Europe – indeed, in the world!"

Here there was pause for rapturous applause. The wine that had flowed freely since schnapps was served at midday had, in the intervening four hours, loosened tongues and rendered less Teutonic the general demeanour of the luncheon party. Many banged tables with the combined flats of their fingers, or raised cigars while whooping enthusiastically.

Goering calmed them instantly with a raised hand. "I stand before you now the proudest man on earth. Or perhaps I should defer in that to our beloved Führer!" There was more good-natured laughter. "I am not ashamed to boast that in the last seven years I have stood at the right hand of our most esteemed leader and, with him, have destroyed political subversion in Germany. My Gestapo have routed from our midst dissenters and conspirators; my marvellous Fallschirmjäger –" here, Goering spanned the room with an outstretched arm, following the arc of his arm with his eyes to indicate the assembled Fallschirmjäger men – "...have fought alongside the glorious SS..." Once more there was clapping and table banging and whooping. "... to bring victory in all of our campaigns to date. And now, my Luftwaffe, cream of all known flying fighting forces, is set to make permanent Germany's victory over all of Europe. And all this, my friends, in a few short years!"

Shouts of "Heil Hitler!" and deafening applause and banging followed. Some of the women, smiling broadly, put their hands over their ears. Again, Goering, after a suitable time, raised a hand and all was silent. When he began speaking again it was with a much lowered tone and great gravitas. "As I stand before you now, my brave and honoured comrades, beautiful and loyal ladies, Germany is no longer slave but is master of Europe. In the last few months alone we have conquered Czechoslovakia, Denmark, Norway, Poland, Belgium, Holland and even France! In the next few weeks, England too will kneel before us. Already she is broken and bowed, humiliated on the beaches of France. In a year from now, my brave friends, Germany will be established as the greatest empire the world has ever known!"

At this rousing crescendo, the room erupted. Officers as one leapt to their feet. Shouts of "Sieg heil!" became a chant, and the women, glowing and exchanging glances of feigned alarm or displays of feminine awkwardness, followed suit, while dozens of servants busied themselves with uncorking the champagne and filling the flutes in readiness for the climactic toast. Goering allowed the chanting to continue for twenty seconds or more, then raised both arms in the air to quell it. As soon as it was quiet enough, the general at his side urged a new chant, "Heil Goering!", at which Goering faked demur and lowered his head, but was clearly delighted. Some of the officers exchanged uneasy or quizzical looks, but these were generally shrugged away in the bonhomie and near ecstasy of the moment. All recognized in the chant the commonly acknowledged ambition of the Führer's Second.

At last, Goering silenced them again and bade everyone to raise their glasses before he concluded his speech. "But today, this afternoon, is particularly intended to honour the bravest of the brave – you gathered before me now – who distinguished yourselves in the pursuit of glory in the critical offensive against Denmark and Norway and in the taking of France and Belgium." He raised his glass and proposed the toast, drank. The assembled guests responded.

Goering spoke again. "But we would do well to remember that many of our comrades did not come home, my friends, and it is now to them that I propose a toast and then one minute's silence in respect for their sacrifice and that of their families. Gentlemen and ladies, I give you the absent heroes of the Weserubung offensive, and all those brave men who died throughout Europe this year to make Germany glorious once again."

When this sobering toast was made and all had remained standing, heads lowered, during a minute's silence, Goering again smiled and, raising his glass, said loudly, "And finally, I thank you from the depths of my heart and on behalf of your Führer and your country, and I toast your outstanding daring, honour and achievement on the battlefields of Scandinavia, Belgium, France, Poland. I know that soon many of you will be fighting again, in the skies above Britain, above Holland and on the ground in France, but you will prevail and the fight will be brief, for our victory is assured. Raise a glass now to victory and honour!"

Following the third toast there was more cheering, and Goering's voice boomed above the noise that now there would be music and more wine and dancing. The Beethoven quartet was replaced by a Bavarian band, and Goering disappeared only to re-emerge within fifteen minutes in traditional Bavarian hunting attire. Huge, and glowing with pride and magnanimity, he circulated among his carousing guests with enormous gusto and irresistible bonhomie.

Walter escorted Hedda onto the dance floor, an ample space cleared of tables at the top of the Jagdhalle, and while they smiled and nodded greetings to fellow dancers during a Bavarian waltz, he asked her in as disinterested a tone as he could manage, "Who is the man with whom you came in after lunch?"

Hedda was surprised by her husband's interest, for his disinterest in most things she did had been consistent almost since they married. "You mean Karl? Karl Muller?"

"If that is his name, yes. You seemed very friendly."

Hedda pulled away from her husband enough to look into his face and study his eyes. He did not, however, alter the direction of his glance from somewhere above her head and to the right.

"Walter, are you really jealous? Is that why you want to know?"

"Don't be absurd. I am just curious. Unless you are telling me there is a reason to feel more than curious, that is. That would be interesting."

Hedda grew cold again. For a moment she had thought Walter's concern was based on a measure of feeling he had concealed, and that perhaps he did care for her after all. Now she saw his interest for what it was: concern for appearances, his own ego and a possible dangerous slight on his ability to control and second-guess her behaviour. She was assailed by a sudden anger as she considered the undoubted infidelities indulged by Walter in the last few years and about which she was permitted to say precisely nothing – unless she wanted to invite verbal, and very possibly physical, abuse.

"For a moment there, Walter, I thought you gave a damn about me. Silly of me. Why would you, after all, when you can have any woman in Berlin?"

For answer, Walter said nothing, but Hedda felt his body stiffen and his grip upon her right hand as he led her around the floor became painful.

"Walter, you are hurting my hand," she whispered through a forced smile. "This is ridiculous."

"It is you who are ridiculous, Hedda, and I should have known you would spoil things – disgrace me as I am honoured. First of all you humiliate me by flirting yourself, and then you accuse me of consorting with people like you. I asked a civil question. I still do not have an answer, as far as I recall."

"I will answer you, Walter, if you stop crushing my hand. Otherwise, I shall pretend to faint or something – I promise I shall – to get off this dance floor."

Walter relaxed his grip and a few seconds elapsed while both composed themselves.

"His name is, as I have already said, Karl Muller. I knew him years ago when I was a girl. I had a couple of dates with him – it came to nothing. I do not think we even kissed. He is in the SS, recently promoted. Happy?"

"Delirious. Perhaps you wish to kiss Herr Muller under present circumstances, Hedda? Go on – make my humiliation complete. He is sitting over there, to your left, and seems quite interested in you. Why not ask him to dance?"

The music ceased and all turned towards the band to clap their appreciation. When Hedda turned back, Walter had already left the dance floor and was returning to their table. Hedda glanced briefly in Karl's direction as she followed those wending their way back to seats, and she saw that Karl was indeed watching her progress.

When finally she found her seat, Walter was not there. Looking for him, Hedda eventually spied him at the back of the hall, talking to Goering. At that moment, the children were brought back to their parents, for the maids and nannies had finished their shift, and soon people would start to take their leave. A sleepy Anselm was delivered to Hedda's arms, and Agnette, still smiling and excited, took her father's chair and began to regale Hedda with stories of chases and activities that had engrossed her all afternoon and into the evening. Hedda barely listened, for she was watching Goering and her husband slowly make their way towards her table.

"Get up, Agnette, please."

"Why?" The little girl was peeved at her mother's inattention and concerned by the worried distraction of her tone.

"Because Papa and Herr Goering are coming this way and you have taken Papa's seat. Now get up, there's a good girl."

Agnette huffily obliged, but not without remarking on how very fat Herr Goering was. Hedda had no time to respond to or reprove the rudeness, for the men were upon her.

"Frau Gunther! I hope you have enjoyed yourself today? How do you like Carinhall?"

"Oh, it is beautiful, Reichsmarschall Goering – we have all had a lovely time. Thank you so much."

"Good, good. Someone is tired, I see." Goering tousled Anselm's hair, but the child just turned his face into his mother's shoulder, his thumb in his mouth.

"Yes – he's very sleepy."

"And I should guess my own little poppet is asleep too. She is about this young man's age, I should think." Then he spied Agnette, standing desultorily by her mother's side, playing with her fingers, frowning at them as if she were trying to work out how they moved. "And you, young lady – are you tired also?"

Agnette regarded Goering levelly and shook her head.

"Agnette, don't be rude – speak when you are spoken to."

"Oh, that's all right, Frau Gunther. I know how children are! You know, I think children are the only people who can defeat me completely; one look from my little Edda and I am useless. But tell me, would you mind if I borrowed your husband for a while? There is something I wish to discuss with him."

"No – of course not, Reichsmarschall Goering."

"If you like, I could take that little man off your hands too – I think I have something which will wake him up." Hedda turned her body so that Anselm's face was before Goering's and the latter bent to speak to him directly. "Would you like to see some spectacular model trains, young man, hmm?"

"Oh, Anselm!" Hedda encouraged her son to respond, manoeuvred him so that his hands were on her shoulders and she spoke to his eyes. "Would you like to go with Papa and Reichsmarschall Goering to see some choo-choo trains? Would you?" She smiled and widened her eyes in encouragement and Anselm nodded, started to push away from her in a bid to reach the floor.

"Splendid! Then we boys will adjourn to my model railway in the loft above us here, and if you like, I can show you girls some of my art collection on the way, but we don't expect you to join us in the railway room. Agnette, is it?" The child nodded assent and cocked her head to one side to look up into Goering's puffy, red face. "Do you like pretty pictures?" Agnette seemed to consider the question a moment, then raised her brows, pressed her lips together in a downwards pout and nodded her concession that yes, that could be pleasing. "Splendid! Then I have a treat for you and your lovely mama."

The family followed Goering through the merrymakers, and many eyes watched them enviously. Goering led, holding Anselm's hand. Hedda and Agnette followed, and Walter took up the rear, his uniform cap on once more, his eyes fixed on Goering's movements as he bent and rose in conversation with his son. He could not have been prouder; that much was evident.

In a dimly lit, wide corridor which stretched away apparently infinitely, some way from the Jagdhalle and all the noise, Goering exchanged words with the soldier on guard, who stared straight ahead and saluted. The soldier clicked his heels together, turned rigidly towards a wall, and pressed a number of switches. Immediately, the corridor was illuminated and an Aladdin's cave of glinting gold and sumptuous colour was revealed. The corridor was covered in a deep-pile rubicund carpet, which made silent all footfalls and added to the reverence and mystery of the space around them. On each wall, as far as the eye could see, were affixed paintings of all sizes, expertly hung and spaced. Above many were shaded or muted bars of electric light, which brought depth and texture to the coloured oils of the paintings. Gilt frames shone and smouldered in the silence, and Goering watched the awe on the faces of his guests with unconcealed satisfaction.

He extended an arm in the direction of the corridor. "Shall we?" he said and, without words, the family stepped onto the carpet and began viewing the glorious works of art that presently adorned this particular Carinhall gallery. "These are some of my favourites – and some of my latest acquisitions," Goering informed Walter as they progressed slowly down the corridor.

"Stunning, Herr Reichsmarschall Goering – simply stunning," replied Walter, truly mesmerized by the obvious grandeur of the paintings he beheld. Neither he nor Hedda was an art connoisseur, but there were masterpieces before their eyes that both recognized from magazines or, for Walter, from pre-war visits to galleries in Paris with his parents. Old Dutch and German masters, which they had learned about in school or had come across in encyclopaedias or family Bibles, hung in resplendent surfeit before them, mixed with prints of lesser value or artistic merit. There were hunting scenes and naked ladies from all eras.

"My goodness!" Walter exclaimed. "I recognize this. This was part of an exhibition I went to as a young man, with my parents, in Paris. I thought it the most exquisite thing. It is sixteenth century, isn't it?"

Goering's chest puffed out with pride. "Indeed. This, my dear Walter, I acquired just last month – from Paris, as you rightly say. I am very proud of it. It is of course Gossaert's *Madonna and Child*. Fabulous, isn't it? For me, the Dutch Masters are unsurpassed. Do you agree, Walter?"

"I am afraid, Herr Reichsmarschall, that I do not know enough about art to agree or otherwise, but I bow to your superior judgment. In any case, I love this painting."

"I have many more. You know, I now have well over a thousand paintings here at Carinhall. They come to me from France, from Holland – from many places in Germany. I buy them all, of course."

"You are a man of great taste and culture, Sir," responded Walter. "A thousand, you say?"

"Yes – at least. Matisse, Granach, our own dear Grunwalde – even some van Gogh, although I do not shout about such things." Here, Goering leaned towards Walter and lifted his right hand to his mouth as if he were sharing a secret, and lowered his voice in mock caution. "Our great Führer is not a big fan of modern art, and so…" Goering's plea for complicity was obvious in an exaggerated widening of his eyes as he glared at Walter, and he nodded slightly, "it follows…"

"Of course, Herr Reichsmarschall – I understand completely." Walter smiled briefly and bowed in deference.

"You are a fine man, Walter; a fine man." Goering returned to full volume and smiled. "I have plans, in any case, to trade the van Goghs, I think. Certainly, the Matisses and the Degas will go – if I can just get my hands on the one great prize I yearn for!"

"What is that, Sir? If it is not impertinent to ask."

"Ah, Walter, Walter. Can you imagine? There is a possibility I may be able to get my hands on a Vermeer! There is a Dutchman – van Meegeren – who is believed to have at least one. I may have to pay a very high price, but if I can persuade him to part with just one Vermeer, it would be worth it, my friend. Do you know Vermeer?"

"Alas, I..."

"What a genius! Dutch again, of course. Those Dutchmen – how did they do it? Do you think their country is so boring that they turned to art for distraction?"

"That could be it, Herr Reichsmarschall, sir."

"Ah, and your daughter has impeccable taste, Oberst Gunther. Look at her face; she is enraptured."

While Walter and Goering had been talking, Hedda and her children had walked ahead. Hedda was now entreating Anselm not to grizzle, to be patient, that he would soon see the trains, but the child was very tired and would not be pacified. Hedda had almost decided to take him out of the gallery and wait for her husband and Prime Minister Goering in the hall from which they had entered the gallery corridor, but as she picked up her son he became quiet and then fell fast asleep on her shoulder.

Hedda carried Anselm towards Agnette and studied the painting that had so absorbed her daughter. The painting was very large – as Goering proudly announced, 135 by 173 centimetres – taller than Agnette herself and longer than Goering was tall. The painting dominated the central area of the gallery and was skilfully lit so that its sumptuously decadent colours almost pulsed in richness. The textures of the garments adorning the figures took on a depth and a slickness that made touching them almost impossible to resist, though Agnette could not have reached to do so. The foremost characters were robed in ivory, gold and softly glowing rose salmon. In the bottom right-hand corner as the observers faced the canvas, a basket of pink roses lay discarded in the limp embrace of a carelessly strewn damask and ivory printed scarf, as though dropped in haste. A small dog regarded the abandoned flowers with some interest, apparently oblivious to the imminent tragedy captured in the central tableau.

A devilish figure held aloft a knife and seemed to be about to slay an auburn-haired girl in an ivory dress. None of the assembled figures surrounding them – not even her executioner – could look upon the girl, and had adopted various ways of averting or shielding their eyes. A deer stood before but facing away from the sacrificial altar on which the girl was recumbent, and before the deer, a woman in gold knelt – the owner of the discarded roses? At the kneeling woman's back, a very young boy fled the scene, his right hand raised to his face as if to suppress tears, and in his left hand a bow and broken arrow. A man in sumptuous salmon robes, and wearing a crown that slid from his head, sat beside the dog in a gorgeously upholstered chair and hid his face with his right hand in apparent sorrow or shame. Smoke rose from the altar, and on the top left-hand side of the painting a mysterious ghostly figure seemed to wait, unconcerned, for the knife to do its worst. A crowd of women to the left and of men to the right, dressed variously in garb to denote their station, appeared to argue and remonstrate among themselves.

To Agnette, the entire scene was at once terrifying and wholly absorbing, though anything beyond a simple emotional response and understanding of it was impossible, as she was not quite five years old. Her fascination seemed, nonetheless, as profound as any child's wonder might be upon, for example, beholding the ocean for the first time. She started as if from a reverie at Goering's booming voice.

"You like this one, Agnette? You have excellent taste."

"What are they doing to the lady?"

"Well..." Goering cleared his throat, seemed to search his memory and also for the right words to render simply what he recalled. "That man there is going to kill the lady. Well, in fact he is not, because do you know what?"

Agnette shook her head, never taking her eyes from Goering's face.

"That deer – can you see him? He will be killed instead of the lady and the lady will vanish – pooff!" And Goering widened his arms and eyes suddenly to indicate surprise and nothingness. "Just like magic."

"Why do they want to kill the lady?"

"Hmm. That is a very good question." Goering made a grimace that indicated his inability to explain to a small child the sacrifice of Iphigenia by her father Agamemnon. He looked for help to Walter and Hedda. Hedda shook her head as if to say "Don't ask me!", and Walter bent down, lifted his daughter and sat her upon one arm, supported it with his other.

"You ask too many questions, little Agnette," he said, then kissed her forehead.

"I tell you what," said Goering. "How about I send your mama and papa a copy of this painting and the story that goes with it, eh? Then they can read the story and tell it to you. How does that sound?"

Agnette looked towards the painting and nodded and smiled her enthusiasm, then added quite wistfully as she lay her head against her father's cheek, "I think it is a very sad painting."

Goering laughed briefly, then addressed Walter. "You and I should have that chat now, Walter. It's getting late. I don't want to keep your family here too much longer. Come." And the party turned back towards the entrance of the gallery corridor.

As they walked, Goering explained to Walter and Hedda that he had only just acquired Steen's *Sacrifice of Iphigenia*; that it was a seventeenth-century masterpiece and worth a fortune. He explained that the Jew from whom he had "purchased" it was a phenomenal Dutch art dealer called Goudstikker, from Amsterdam, who had fled the Netherlands as the Nazis marched on Holland. Goudstikker had secured the necessary immigration visas for him and his wife in late 1939, when he had judged – shrewdly – that Germany would invade. On the 13th May, he and his wife had boarded the last cargo boat bound from the Netherlands to England.

"Tragically," Goering recounted, though his smirk and feigned seriousness of mien indicated anything but sympathy, "on the 16th of May, within striking distance of British soil, Goudstikker fell through a trap door on the deck of the boat and broke his neck." Goering snorted in amusement and Walter laughed out loud, then shook his head and tutted in mock remorse. "Luckily," Goering continued, "he didn't have time to organize the export of all his fine art collection. It was fortunate for me that I was able to… *acquire* a great many of Goudstikker's thirteen hundred paintings. The Steen was one of them." Goudstikker had been a nice enough fellow for a Jew, Goering continued, very knowledgable and quite charming. "I did some business with him in early May, in fact," he added. "Goudstikker had handled the sale of an art collection previously owned by a chap who could not pay his bills. The bank foreclosed and possessed the paintings and a friend of mine bought no fewer than nineteen for me. In fact, they were delivered to Carinhall on just the 10th of June – last month."

"You are clearly doing Germany a great service in bringing all these wonderful works of art to Carinhall. What a national treasure is here!" remarked Walter in sincere admiration, though it did occur to him that in May, when Goering was in Amsterdam negotiating prices for paintings, he and Goering's brave Fallschirmjäger soldiers and officers were risking their lives in battle in Denmark, Norway, Belgium and France. On and before the 10th June, thousands more were fighting and dying in France and in the skies over Britain.

"Yes, Walter, my friend, I believe I am. I think of myself as one of the last Renaissance men. In a very practical way, of course," he went on, "we are all Renaissance men these days. We want racial perfection and cultural sophistication – everyone wants to be Greek! In a roundabout way, my art collection is underpinning the entire National Socialist philosophy."

Hedda pressed her cheek against Anselm's soft hair and wondered what part in such a great empire her husband could possibly play and what sort of empire it could be if he had a part to play.

"On a lighter note, come and see my fabulous model railway – I think you will be impressed. Mussolini loved it! Ah," he added more quietly upon beholding Anselm, "is the little boy asleep?"

"Yes, Reichsmarschall, I am afraid he is completely gone." Hedda turned her body so that she could address Goering without speaking over Anselm's head.

"What a pity. Now he will not see the trains. Still, another time, perhaps? Can you ladies find your way back to the Jagdhalle from here? Walter – Daddy – and I need to have a chat, and a very manly game of trains!"

It was not difficult for Hedda to find her way back to the Jagdhalle. The Bavarian band was playing again, though with less gusto. A fairly mournful air was pressed from the accordion, and lightly accompanied by a gentle drumming and flugelhorn – no oompah. People had started to leave and it was easy for Hedda to make her way to her table with Anselm in her arms and Agnette close beside her.

"Hello again. May I join you?" No sooner had Hedda settled than Karl's voice caused her to look up from adjusting Anselm so that both were comfortable. The child was now deeply asleep and his mouth was open, his whole body relaxed and easily cradled.

"Of course. Please..."

Agnette took the opportunity provided by Karl's distraction of her mother to seek more interesting entertainment. "Mutti, may I play outside? I promise to come back lots of times and not go far."

Hedda nodded and smiled at her daughter and then at Karl as he sat down.

"Your children are charming, Hedda. Very sweet."

"Thank you. They are good children." Hedda kissed Anselm's head and held him a little closer to her for a moment. She saw the look of tenderness and longing on Karl's face as he contemplated Anselm's and found herself wishing for a husband who regarded his own children with such open affection. "You don't have any children yourself, you said?"

"No. My wife is very ill. She has been for some time."

Hedda watched the darkness return to Karl's face and his brow furrow. His eyes slid from Anselm, seemed to follow his thoughts downwards.

"I am sorry. Forgive me."

"No, not at all." He looked at her and smiled. "How could you know? Greta is mentally ill. She suffers from severe depression. It didn't begin until after we were married. While I was a medical student I could just about cope with her care, but we were very poor. I would medicate her in the mornings, attend lectures and practicals, then rush home to look after her. At night, when she was asleep, I would study. It was hard, but... we managed. She was not so bad then. When I joined the SS and was posted to Norway, of course I could not take care of Greta any more. She went home to her parents in Leipzig. I don't know if you know anything about depression?"

Hedda shook her head, shrugged her shoulders a little.

"Well, it obliterates the personality – fragments it. You can see the person you know begin to fracture, as if they were trapped in a mirror, and you can't help – there's nothing you can do. It's a slow breakdown. All vitality just ebbs away. The eyes become so lifeless and dull. Drugs slow down the process, but they make the patient sleepy. You lose them either way."

Hedda could think of nothing to say, bowed her face to Anselm's sweet-smelling hair and kissed his head. Karl seemed to need to talk, although Hedda wasn't sure it mattered much to whom he spoke.

"She was a brilliant lawyer – graduated from Leipzig University. That's where I met her. We both come from Leipzig, although we did not get together until 1933 – soon after you and I went out, in fact. We married within a year. She too had moved up to Berlin, as that was where the jobs were. She was – is – beautiful and so sharp. She could make me laugh in spite of myself." Here, Karl stopped and smiled, as if watching Greta waving from far away. He "hmphd" to himself. "That's the irony – she cheered me up all the time."

Hedda watched Karl speak, saw the love on his face, and her heart ached, but it was not for his or Greta's loss.

Then Karl's demeanour changed and he was once more serious and frowning. "Then, of course, the Führer was elected and no women were allowed to practise law – or teach or work at all, really. That's when the depression really kicked in – when she could not work any more. It was as if everything she had worked so hard to achieve, everything bound up with her vision of herself and our future – well, as if it was suddenly..." Karl seemed to search for adequate words. Gave up. "For someone like Greta, having an outlet for her intellect – being independent – well, these things to her were more than privileges she could adapt to being without. They were who she was." Karl's jaw tensed and his deep brown eyes were smouldering with anger. Then he seemed to recall once more where he was. "I am sorry. I didn't mean to go on like that. I don't know what I was thinking."

"Please." She shook her head. "Don't be sorry. I just wish I could think of something helpful to say. It sounds as if you have been through a lot."

"And what about you, Hedda? Are you happy?"

The question startled her and she found herself unable to answer him, because the immediate response was an exclamatory "no", which she could not allow. She stared at him in surprise for a moment, as much at his directness as at the certainty of her response.

"I am sorry – again. People tell me – have always told me – that I am tactless. There is always something I am saying which is too spontaneous or not thought out. Excuse me."

Hedda composed herself once more and began to answer him, to make him feel less embarrassed. "I am not sure what 'happy' means. I am not depressed, like your poor wife – Greta? I have my children." And she smiled again, though her eyes did not, and kissed Anselm's head once more.

Karl looked at her, mildly and levelly, as though about to make an evaluation. This time, though, he did not speak; he only thought how terribly unhappy she suddenly looked. "Do you know much about your husband's work?"

Again, his directness and the apparent unrelatedness of this question to his last one made Hedda frown. She felt a tinge of irritation and was reminded again of their evening in the Friedrichstrasse club, when his intensity and unease so unsettled her.

"No. Of course I know he fought in Norway, like you, and before that he worked for Prime Minister Goering at the Reichsluftfahrtministerium. I don't know what he did – sent planes to places and organized pilot training courses, I think. Then, of course, he trained as a parachutist and joined Flak Regiment Goering. He doesn't talk to me about his work. I just know the obvious details."

Karl studied her eyes. "It is better that way," he said with such seriousness and apparent sorrow that she could think of nothing to say. Then suddenly his eyes ignited with that fervency she found so intriguing. It was the opposite of what happened in Walter's eyes when he grew animated or angry; then it was as if something viscous and cold slipped a sluice gate and swam beneath the ice blue surface. What she saw in Karl's eyes was warm, quickening.

Her own eyes widened in surprised response even before he spoke. "Do you believe in God, Hedda?"

"I don't know! I... I have never really... What a question!" She frowned at him and made a face as if to indicate she thought him strange, though she was at once amused. "You are doing it again, Herr Muller."

"Doing what?"

"You are being mysterious."

"I am sorry." He rose to his feet, and as he did so Hedda was surprised to feel regret that he was about to take his leave. Her conversation with Karl had been at times uncomfortable and even a little vexing, but it was stimulating. His eyes were the most sincere she had contemplated. "I must go," he said. "It has been lovely to see you again, Hedda – and your children. Perhaps we shall meet again?" He and placed his cap upon his head, stood, bowed and smiled briefly into her eyes before turning to leave. She was just thinking how formal and sudden his leave-taking was when Walter reappeared at her side.

"Your friend came back to you, I see." But his tone was surprisingly light.

"He is married, to a lawyer. She is staying with her parents in... can't remember."

"Oh." Walter was now uninterested, full of his own thoughts following his talk with Reichsmarschall Goering. "Shall we go?"

Hedda got carefully to her feet, adjusting Anselm's body as she did so, shifting his weight to her left hip.

"Agnette is outside. Naughty girl – she said she would come in often to let me know she was all right."

"Don't worry. I'll get her." Walter's response was not the irritated rebuke she had expected. "You take Anselm outside, the chauffeur will be waiting."

As Hedda watched him go, she thought a number of things in quick succession: how Karl must have seen Walter coming into the Jagdhalle and how quickly he had taken his leave; how

Walter was in a mercifully good mood and she might not now be punished for her earlier transgressions; and, most keenly, she felt suddenly protective of Karl and determined to keep to herself all he had told her.

CHAPTER THREE

A few weeks after the party at Carinhall, Goering left for France to direct his Luftwaffe offensive in Operation Adler, the long-planned beginning of the bid to neutralize the British RAF and then invade Britain amphibiously. One evening around that time, Walter spoke about Goering's courage and the assured glorious victory of the Luftwaffe offensive. His colour high, his eyes bright but distant, he chewed his dinner mechanically and sawed voraciously at his meat as though the action were an illustration of the rigour and incisiveness of the invasion. He gulped at his Riesling, draining his glass, then refilled it, drained it, refilled it. He spoke at, rather than to, Hedda, his eyes barely meeting hers across the table, and if he appeared to become truly conscious of her presence, he seemed to check his animation and rein in his approbation of Herr Goering's genius, as though remembering her unfitness as an audience. She listened because she had little choice and with the resentful attentiveness of a school pupil who only half understands her teacher's rapid instruction but dare not admit it for fear of reproof.

Hedda did not like Reichsmarschall Goering and she could not help but fear a British reprisal against Berlin. It seemed inevitable and logical. How had her country suddenly become so audacious? A sustained bombing attack on London? Norway, Denmark, Czechoslovakia, Poland and Austria – now France and Britain. She could barely keep track, list the countries assaulted and taken by the Führer in his bid to... to what? Hedda was not at all sure what it was that Hitler intended.

She had gleaned from Goering's comments about Hellenism and cultural superiority that there was a philosophy of sorts behind such aggressive and sudden militarism. She was not sure how it had come about that when she walked to the shops on Bellevuestrasse that she frequently had to negotiate large parties of soldiers supervising the cleaning of the pavement by old Jewish men with toothbrushes; old men who were forced to kneel in the dirt, staring hard at the kerb as if their attentive brushing of small parts of the concrete were restoring a masterpiece. Many of them wept silently, the tears running from beneath their glasses, their hands trembling as they dipped their worn toothbrushes into black soapy water and then lifted them once more to the pavement.

Several times, Hedda had stopped suddenly in shock as a soldier lifted his foot and delivered a vicious kick to an old man's kidneys or even, once, to the side of his face, apparently incensed that he had asked for water. Her startled face and instinctive, wordless shock as she met the soldiers' mocking grimaces engendered patronizing and latently threatening remonstrance – she should hurry on; nothing here to concern such a pretty German lady. One had even taken off his helmet and bowed deeply in an act of mock chivalry. She had walked on, flushing in the wake of their derisory laughter, the chilling wolf whistles.

And here was Walter, more aroused and enthused than ever she had seen him, expressing his hatred of all things un-German, especially Jews. He seemed almost febrile in his compulsion to honour his Führer and the intrepid Reichsmarschall Goering. His eyes shone with hot, furious tears, his face clouded with an expression of barely controlled dejection when he contemplated his inability to be part of the glorious struggle in France.

Hedda dared to ask him why old men were being forced to clean Berlin's streets with toothbrushes. Was it a cost-saving exercise? She knew, of course, it was not, but was genuinely anxious to know why such inhumanity was so openly tolerated in Berlin. Walter contemplated her with barely controlled contempt.

"Cost saving?" he had repeated with affected, tired irony that was supposed to imply her stupidity. Then he paused and smiled, looking with amusement into the empty space to the left of and above his eye-line, his knife and fork separating in a mid-air gesture of mock contemplation. Yes, he supposed it could be seen that way – particularly if they died on the job.

Hedda was unable to suppress her loathing of Walter's viciousness. She flashed back at him that these old men had always contributed to Germany, the country in which they were no doubt born. Should they not now be left to enjoy their retirement?

For answer, Walter banged the table so hard that the silver cruets jumped and rolled in chaotic circles around the table. "Who are you," he bellowed at her, saliva and sauerkraut finding an exit together from the corners of his mouth, "to question the policies of the Führer?" What, he wished to know, would the likes of Hedda know about "das Judische problem"? Should he pass on his wife's dissatisfaction with the treatment of Jews to Herr Goebbels, because he could, she knew; he had occasion to meet the propaganda minister on a weekly basis in the course of his new duties and could certainly question, on Hedda's behalf, the necessity of being unpleasant to filthy Jewish scum.

Hedda eyed her husband with the inscrutable, level gaze behind which she hid when uncertain how to react, and she noted how the vein in his neck throbbed. "What the devil are you staring at? Are you a complete simpleton? Have you lost the power of speech?"

Hedda lowered her eyes and dabbed delicately at the corners of her mouth with her napkin – in disgust at the rivulets of chewed and unswallowed sauerkraut that curved around Walter's jaw, rather than because she had any need herself. She sighed deeply and pushed her plate away from the edge of the table, making to rise.

"Are you deaf now as well? Answer me, damn you! Why should I tolerate this insolence at my own table? Hmm? Can you tell me that at least, Frau Gunther, if it is not too much trouble?"

"I am neither deaf nor dumb," began Hedda as calmly as she could, though her head was a little unsteady and there was a tremor in her hands as they lay her napkin across her plate. "I simply will not respond to being spoken to as if I am an imbecile. I asked a civil question."

"As if you are an imbecile? As *if*? My dear wife, there is no doubt. Your inane questions and your complete lack of understanding of... of anything indicate quite clearly that you are an imbecile of the first order. Do you have any idea at all – at all – what this country is on the brink of achieving? What is possible here?"

"Clearly not." Hedda turned away from his manic glare. She did not want to challenge him further and felt to do so was to invite a beating. He was more incensed than she could remember. He seemed to have abandoned any attempt to allay his fury. Something, she knew, was disturbing him greatly, and there was no guessing what it could be. His work – his life – was a mystery to her. She knew only that whatever it was must be momentous, and if she did not escape, it was likely that she would become an outlet for her husband's terrifying anger. "Excuse me, Walter," she managed with as much gentleness and dignity as she could contrive, "I must attend to the children."

As she reached the door handle, Walter's plate smashed against the door, just inches from her face. She watched transfixed as gravy and shreds of sauerkraut, slugs of cold pork fat, clung briefly to the paintwork, then slid from the gloss surface. The plate splintered, and she was conscious of shards of fine porcelain bouncing off her outstretched hand and forearm and landing at her feet. Gravy splashed across her sleeve and she reflected for a split second that it was silk and would be difficult to clean, but the thought was so rapid it was more an understanding than anything grammatical.

"You're not excused!" Walter hissed menacingly from his chair.

She did not turn to face him, but let her hand fall by her side and waited, her back half turned to him, for whatever would happen next. Her thoughts were as fractured as the plate, and one of them – a briefly glinting slither – was a thin protest at the increasing violence of the language with which he spoke to her. Somehow, this degeneration in itself was indicative of some terrible metamorphosis Walter seemed to be undergoing. Curiously, she recalled Karl's assurance made at the Carinhall occasion; that she was better off not knowing the truth of her husband's work.

The blow, when it came, was numbing of all further thought. Walter had suddenly leapt from his chair and, incandescent with an unnameable rage, had hit Hedda hard across the side of her head with the back of his hand. She stumbled and reached for the polished mahogany sideboard that ran along the wall from the dining room door to the grand bay windows, now heavily draped against the rainy August evening. Still she did not turn to him. Her revulsion was such that upon pain of death she could not have brought herself to look into his face. Fully expecting to be hit again, she closed her eyes and braced for the assault. There was no second blow. Bringing his mouth close to her face Walter hissed into her ear only that she disgusted him and he pushed her out of his way, opened the door and left the room, crunching porcelain beneath his polished boots.

He passed the cook as if she did not exist and the poor woman lifted her apron to her face as Hedda emerged from the dining room. The skin across Hedda's temple had split with the force of the blow, and blood ran down her face and onto the cream silk collar of her dress.

"Madam!" was all the cook could manage when she had let fall her apron and extended a hand uselessly in Hedda's direction.

"I am quite well, Elise," Hedda managed. "Please attend to the children. It is time they were made ready for bed and I really should be letting the maid go home now. Please do that for me, would you?"

"Of course, Frau Gunther." Elise scurried across the highly polished parquet to the foot of the stairs and ran up them as if there were an emergency.

Hedda could think of nothing except finding her favourite chair in the sitting room and pouring herself a large whisky. Walter had gone straight upstairs and he would go out for the evening, she was quite sure. With luck, he would not return before the small hours of the morning. With a great deal of luck, he would find another woman and never return.

The beautifully executed full colour print of Steen's *Sacrifice of Iphigenia* duly arrived, courtesy of Goering and addressed to Fraulein Agnette Gunther. Accompanying the rolled print was a note in Goering's florid handwriting, complimenting Agnette once more on her exquisite artistic taste and hoping her parents would find a fitting frame for the print so that she might hang it on her bedroom wall and contemplate its beauty whenever she wished. Rolled up inside the print was a carefully typed account of the story of the sacrifice of Iphigenia and, with it, a version that a very young child might like and understand, which Goering had had typed by one of his many beautiful secretaries. The letter instructed Agnette's mummy or daddy to read it to her whenever she wished, and stated with mock sternness that Agnette was to brook no refusal at any time. Agnette was delighted with her gift and begged Hedda to send Marguerite, the maid, to buy a fine frame – at once.

"Well," responded Hedda, smiling wearily, "we can't upset you and have you telling tales to Herr Goering now, can we?" And Marguerite was duly dispatched and instructed to order a frame if she could not find one directly, in ornate gold gilt to mimic the Renaissance masters and do justice to the sumptuous golds and softly gleaming lustres of the print. Within two days, the painting was framed and hung and an electrician employed to install a light above it upon the wall facing Agnette's bed, so that she could contemplate its compelling beauty before she slept each night.

Hedda feared that the imminent tragedy evident in the satyr-like executioner's raised hand, the angle of the knife and the evident vulnerability of the intended victim would bring her daughter only nightmares. But Agnette was adamant that Herr Goering was right when he had said the poor deer would become the victim and the girl would be magicked away unharmed. Agnette wanted to know where Hedda thought the girl would go. Hedda contemplated the painting for a long moment before answering, "Well, it says in the story that she went to a place called Taurus, wherever that was."

"Was it like heaven?" Agnette wanted to know.

"Yes. I think it was," replied Hedda, smiling. "Like heaven, or just... a lovely, magical place far away from harm." What she did not say was that in one version of the Iphigenia myth, the fatal blow was not withheld from the girl's throat; that even in versions which delivered Iphigenia from the sacrificial altar and placed her in Taurus, her "sanctuary" was a terrible endurance of lonely enslavement as a priestess to Artemis, condemned to prepare fellow Greeks for sacrifice to the angry goddess who had first demanded Iphigenia's death.

"Tell me again why they were going to kill her, Mutti?" Little Agnette stared at the painting and seemed tireless in her fascination with its heroine.

"Well, Iphigenia's daddy, Agamemnon, had done something very naughty – he boasted that he was better at hunting than the goddess Artemis. She was the best of all the goddesses at using a bow and arrow. Artemis was so angry with Agamemnon that she made the sea go very calm and the wind to stop blowing, so that Agamemnon's army couldn't sail to Troy –" here Hedda anticipated the next question before Agnette could form it – "that's a place far from Greece where Agamemnon's enemies lived. Agamemnon had promised to help his brother rescue a beautiful lady called Helen, because she had left Greece and run away to Troy."

Agnette nodded, looked from the picture to her mother with wide eyes, then back again at the print. "Why?"

"Well, Helen was the most beautiful woman in the world, and when a man from Troy came to visit the Greek people, he fell in love with her straight away and she fell in love with him, and they ran away together to his home in Troy."

"So she wanted to go with him?"

"Yes."

"So why did everyone want her to come back?"

"Well, Helen was married – to the king of Greece – and she shouldn't have run away with someone else."

Agnette considered this. "She was naughty, then! You tell us – me and Anselm – not to go off too far and to let you know where we are, don't you, Mutti?"

"Yes – it was just like that."

"Didn't she like the king any more?"

"No, Agnette."

"Why?"

"I don't know. She just found him..." Hedda was tiring, and irritation was gathering force in her breast and causing her to tense. She made sudden movements to smooth the bedclothes and push back her hair. "She found him... bossy."

Agnette sensed her impatience and was anxious to find out the story before her mother got up and left. "It's all right, Mutti. It's nearly the end, isn't it?"

Hedda looked at her daughter, the pleading in her eyes, the anxiety that made her sit up straight and reach out a tiny hand to her mother in solicitation. Her heart softened. She smiled and hugged her daughter close, breathed in her sweet scent and closed her eyes as she lay her cheek against Agnette's head.

"Nearly, sweetheart. The story ends as we know. Iphigenia is not killed, Artemis feels sorry for her and magics her away to Taurus. And the ships sail from Greece." Hedda drew away from Agnette and, keeping her hands in hers, looked into her face and repeated as simply as she could to the enrapt child the saga of the Trojan offensive: how the Greeks could not begin it until

Agamemnon, King Menelaus's brother, had appeased Artemis following his boasting offence, by offering Iphigenia, his own daughter, as a sacrifice to the goddess. "Artemis was still so angry with Agamemnon," explained Hedda, "that she said she would only make the sea move and the wind blow again if Agamemnon killed Iphigenia."

"Why didn't he just say no? Didn't he love his daughter?"

"Yes, he did love her, but not more than he loved his country." Hedda stopped. "That is enough now, Agnette. Your brother is fast asleep. It is time you were too." Hedda gently pushed her daughter to lie back upon her pillow, and getting up from the bed reached up to turn out the light that illuminated the print, but Agnette cried "No!" in such an earnest tone that she shrugged and left it on.

"Get to sleep, Agnette," she admonished gently, turning to leave the room, heading at last for the sanctuary of the living room.

When the first bombs fell on Berlin in late August 1940, no one was more surprised than Reichsmarschall Goering. Well, it is possible the Führer's astonishment was greater, for he had allowed himself to be so assured by Goering that penetration of Germany's defences was impossible by air that he had simply believed it. In fact, he was not even aware that the Ruhr had already sustained minor damage to industrial buildings from the RAF in May of 1940, for Goering had forbidden the reporting of these raids on Germany's interior, lest Hitler should lose confidence in his leadership of the Luftwaffe. Now central Berlin trembled in the dead of night as RAF bomber aircraft passed over her complacent roofs and blew her a retaliatory shrapnel kiss which, though yet merely flirtatious, was fatal to many lost in trusting sleep.

Hedda leapt from her bed and raced panic-stricken down the hall to the children's rooms, shouting their names while trying to make sense of the whistling noises and the explosions that shook her windows and lit the skies on which they gazed. Walter joined her seconds later, buckling his gun belt around his hips, his SS cap askew upon his head, shirt still unbuttoned beneath his throat.

"Get downstairs," he ordered, striding past their chaos and sleepy softness with automatic determination. "Head for the cellar and stay there."

The cook came flying out of her little room at the end of the hall in a pink nightdress, all plumpness, her grey plait flailing, trying desperately to get her left arm into her dressing gown.

"Quickly, children. We must get to the cellar. Stay close to me," instructed Hedda. More explosions and fiery illuminations increased their terror, but made it easier to negotiate the stairs. Soon Hedda was opening the cellar door with a trembling hand, and, as carefully as she could, guiding the frightened children and the cook down the cold stone steps. She thought she heard the front door slam, but cared little for Walter's whereabouts. She was quite sure he would be safe, wherever he went.

In the cellar, a naked electric bulb trembled and swung as the walls vibrated and the children whimpered into their mother's nightclothes. Elise sat and mumbled prayers to herself.

After some minutes, Agnette lifted her tear-stained face to Hedda's and asked what was happening.

"Our enemies are dropping bombs on us," Hedda replied.

"Who, Mutti? Who are our enemies? Are they the Greeks?"

"Shh!" said Hedda, irritable in her own fear. She preferred to retreat into an inner place when she was afraid, and observe from its quietness whatever was threatening her; she would not be caught easily nor go to meet it. And like such a hiding creature she became one with shadows. She was ready simply to sit on the wooden bench that ran along the cellar wall, contemplating the wine racks, the boxes of fruit and potatoes, and the way the pipes snaked and arched over each other. But Elise suddenly found her voice and stood up, facing Hedda and the children and shaking her fist in front of her while her tears ran fatly down her doughy cheeks.

"Hermann Meier, Hermann Meier..." Elise gasped and lifted her dressing gown to wipe tears from her face, sniffing fulsomely. "Isn't that what Herr Goering said we should call him if Berlin were ever bombed? 'My name shall be Hermann Meier if even one enemy plane should penetrate German airspace.' Isn't that what he said to us, on our streets, in our papers? The great Hermann Goering himself? Well, he's Hermann Meier now, and we..." She could not go on. She sat down heavily on the bench and buried her face in her nightgown and sobbed.

Agnette and Anselm were thoroughly traumatized by so much adult upset and this rude awakening from secure slumber.

"Why is Cook crying, Mutti?" Agnette began to cry anew herself and Anselm's face puckered into a pre-howl grimace. Hedda didn't answer but drew her children to her and contemplated the arrogance of these men in boots and uniforms whose secrets and ambitions had snared their lives. And as she crawled deeper into her own darkness, and the cries of her children and her cook became less troublesome, it was Karl Muller's smile Hedda remembered.

When it seemed that they had been sitting in the cellar for a very long time, and it was as though the coldness of the apples and potatoes, the dankness of the walls, had crept into them and accepted them as inmates, Walter suddenly opened the door and bade them come out.

It was four o'clock in the morning. The house was very still. Occasionally, shouts or sudden cries of women broke the strange numbness of this ravaged morning, but the children were exhausted, and Anselm had already fallen into a troubled sleep in which he frowned and twitched. Hedda's priority was to get them both into bed. Elise begged Herr Gunther to forgive her prying, but she had relatives in the city and would very much like to know if... well, whether... people had been... She could not finish her question, and Walter took a deep, sharp breath and assured her that while he could not be certain how many casualties there were – for certainly there were some, inevitably – there were not many, and building damage seemed to be minimal, given what could have happened. It was certain that the Germania Palast theatre was completely destroyed, as were several other buildings in the city centre – apartment blocks and offices. One could only hope most of the people in the apartments had made for the basements.

Cook was little comforted, and went back to her room wringing her hands and muttering through her tears that it was all too much.

When the children were settled once more, Hedda went downstairs, where she found Walter drinking whisky and staring icily through the large bay windows of the dining room. The sky was a dull red, darkened by heavy smoke, and although the rising sun did its best to lift the night, it found it resistant. Berlin was not ready for August sunshine.

When Hedda entered the dining room, wrapping her night gown closely around herself and hugging her waist with folded arms, Walter turned and observed her for a moment, pausing in his transfer of whisky from glass to lips, then turned away from her again. Hedda considered for a second repeating what Cook had blurted in the cellar, about Goering's inaugural, incautious boast that he had made Germany impervious to air attack. But she thought better of it and said softly to the back of Walter's head, "Do you believe there is a God?"

Walter turned fully around to look at her, an incredulous expression distorting his features and lifting the left side of his upper lip. He contemplated her as if she were mad. "What are you asking now, Hedda?"

Hedda shrugged, looked with affected carelessness at the carpeted floor to her right. "I just wondered if you believe in God. That is all. It occurs to people in such times… " She lifted her eyes and looked at him as neutrally as she could.

Walter hmphed, gulped at his drink and placed the emptied glass on a small table to his left, wiped his mouth. He closed his eyes, lifted his chin and undid his collar buttons before he replied.

CHAPTER THREE

"No. I do not believe in God. Don't be ridiculous." He looked briefly at his wife, then said dismissively, "I am exhausted. I am going to bed."

As he picked up his cap and made to pass her, she ventured one last question, just as her daughter had dared solicit an answer to her burning questions about Greeks and Trojans the night before.

"What do you believe in, Walter?"

Walter stopped, but did not turn to her this time. He seemed to consider the question briefly, then shrugged, made to walk on.

"Do you still believe in Reichsmarschall Goering?" Hedda could hardly believe she had dared go so far. Something she barely understood was inchoate inside her. Something she could not yet name or even see with any definition, but it was coming to birth in the very centre of herself, as a photograph assumes definition beneath chemicals.

Walter hesitated a moment longer in the dining room doorway, but, although there was a definite stiffening of his shoulders, he merely put his cap on his head and strode across the parquet hall to the stairs. Alone, Hedda turned to the window and watched the sun smile helplessly on the wounded city.

Tiergarten Strasse 4 was the place of Walter's new work as a T4 inspector, directly responsible to the chancellery of the Führer. His duties were varied but included inspecting new premises for the expansion of the activities of the T4 project, and he was also charged with "reining in a little", to use Goering's phrasing, the excesses and indulgences of the T4 staff, whose extraordinary responsibilities and attendant stress caused them to seek "outlets" of an often extreme and licentious nature. So much so that Dr Gerhard Bohne, the first designated T4 manager, had resigned in disgust. The orgiastic proclivities of his co-workers caused Walter little thought, but being conscientious he sacked a couple who were found copulating on duty. He also organized an impromptu raid of offices and confiscated many litres of liquor as a signal that his first loyalties were to the chancellery and that he was not a man to be compromised or underestimated. That accomplished, Walter was free to concentrate on the important stuff of his new post and establish a network of centres that would be suitable for the euthanasing of defective people who rendered German society less than Teutonically perfect.

That night in Carinhall, when Goering had asked Walter to accompany him to the room in which he had established his prodigious model railway, had been salutary indeed for Oberst Walter Gunther. Goering had read aloud from a letter written by the Führer himself, in which Hitler had outlined his plans for a policy of cleansing that would be executed under the auspices of the chancellery of the Führer, but which was to be treated with the greatest discretion. Already, Hitler had noted, there had been incidents of irresponsible scaremongering by certain people in the Hygiene Division. It was the wish of the Führer that his most trusted senior officials would identify suitable personnel who would discreetly obey the wishes of their Führer without question in the execution of this most important of political duties.

Goering had recommended Walter, and so the honour was bestowed. Walter had barely been able to conceal his disappointment that he would not be flying to France with the SS. Goering assured him that he was the last person anyone would suspect of cowardice, if it was this that was bothering him. And, he added, the bestowing of the Inspectorate of T4 was the greatest of honours and an ultimate testament to the faith the Reich had in his character. Here, Goering had looked Walter full in the eye and smiled his warmest, most charming smile. Walter had instinctively brought his heels together and raised his chin in salute. Then Goering had turned away and, picking up a clockwork locomotive from his Marklin O gauge track, he appeared to scrutinize it closely before winding it and carefully replacing it, watching as it chugged speedily away then disappeared into a tunnel.

After a minute or so of silence, in which Walter struggled with the impulse to decline the appointment, to phrase his strong desire to continue in active service, Goering finally turned to him and spoke again. "I am sorry about your parents," he had said, looking into Walter's unblinking ice blue eyes. "It must have been painful, no?"

Walter, caught off guard, said nothing, looked down momentarily then back into Goering's eyes. Goering had nodded, patted Walter's right shoulder gently twice, then put his arms behind his back, looking once more to the railway track. "Flossenberg, wasn't it? Where your father died?"

Walter nodded curtly.

"A great pity, Walter. He was, I know, a good man. Sadly misguided, but a good man nonetheless. A fine general in his day. A sorry end indeed."

"Thank you, Reichsmarschall Goering," was all Walter dared in response. He was as much moved by the personal solicitation of Goering as the reference to his father.

"A sorry end for a brave man, Walter," repeated Goering, then he turned to look again into Walter's eyes. "But you were braver – what you did, well..."

Walter coloured at this reference to his denouncement of his father. He felt he must say something in justification, but as he started, Goering waved him silent, shaking his head and pursing his lips in an expression of avuncular indulgence. "I know, my boy; I know. Your loyalty to the Fatherland came before that to your father, eh? Exactly why we are having this conversation." Goering turned away from Walter again and watched the little train slow to a halt on its second lap of the track. "It is no secret that Beck talks of overthrowing the Reich and reinstating the Hohenzollerns; negotiating peace with Britain and France. We owe much of our intelligence to you, my friend. If you had not alerted me to your father's... sympathies with Beck, we would perhaps be at far greater risk of civil strife when we are now most vulnerable – with so many men abroad."

Walter still said nothing. He was remembering the conversation he had had with Goering in his offices at the Air Ministry building on Wilhelmstrasse, when Walter was Logistics Manager in Goering's Reichsluftfahrtministerium. It had not been an easy exchange. Even for one as zealous as Walter in his patriotism and desire to ingratiate himself, the betrayal of a father was no simple matter. Goering had come straight to the point. Klaus Gunther was about to be arrested on suspicion of conspiracy against the Reich, and it seemed there was sufficient evidence to support the idea that in his post at the Chief of Staff office, Klaus was passing vital military information to Beck and other Prussian sympathizers and was even suspected of being party to a plot to assassinate Hitler. In this, he was more extreme even than Beck, for the latter could see no chance of keeping Germany stable if Hitler were removed from office before the time was right.

Walter had listened, fury and excruciating embarrassment causing his face to heat and his eyes to flash. When Goering had finished talking, he nodded, swallowed and said in a barely audible hiss that he was not surprised; that the reason he had no contact with his father was precisely because of his treacherous politics and that he, Walter, was deeply ashamed of his father and hoped sincerely that this turn of events in no way changed Reichsmarschall Goering's view of himself; that he hoped the Reichsmarschall could see that Walter was absolutely committed to the Führer's Reich. Goering had smiled and said he had no doubts pertaining to Walter's loyalty.

When Klaus was arrested, it was at three o'clock in the morning. Loud and relentless banging on the front door got him out of bed, and Agna came anxiously after him, wrapping her dressing gown around herself and tying it with shaking hands. She could only think something had happened to Walter or Hedda or the tiny granddaughter she had never even seen. When her husband opened the door it was to four SS officers, who ordered Klaus to dress in all haste and accompany them at once to Gestapo headquarters. He seemed unsurprised, did not protest. He had paused on his way back to the bedroom to take Agna's hand in his and squeeze it, looking lovingly into her eyes. He would not tell her not to worry. He knew he was unlikely to see her again.

When Agna at last heard that Klaus had been interrogated, accused of conspiracy against the Reich and transported to Flossenberg concentration camp in Bavaria, she had sunk to her knees in abject grief. Walter would not take her telephone calls and she dared not travel to see him. A few days later, Walter was informed at home, by a senior SS officer, that his father was in Flossenberg and his mother had committed suicide by overdose.

He had listened without comment and then saluted and said "Heil Hitler". He poured himself a large whisky, and then another. And no matter how hard he rationalized his father's inevitable demise and his own part in it, he could not prevent the sudden release like butterflies from a box of a thousand blue sky memories of walks by the lakes at Wannsee, his father's dark hair rising from his forehead in the onshore breeze and the way his teeth gripped his pipe as he smiled and talked animatedly of kite flying and fishing. In spite of his best efforts to incapacitate memory with strong liquor, Walter recalled Christmases in the family home; the sweeping staircase, the ten-foot high Christmas tree twinkling in the hallway, how its lights would glint like stars on the marble floor. As a boy, Walter had tried to count the reflections, much to his father's amusement. His father, handsome in his uniform, proud but always gracious. It was strange how clearly Walter saw and felt the affection Klaus always seemed unable to demonstrate; how plain it was now in memories of his father's eyes, as he turned from contemplation of the blue and rolling Wannsee waters to look at Walter, as though he would fill his son with his love of sky and water and the God who made them.

Walter never told Hedda of his parents' fate. He simply had not spoken of either of them since that day before Agnette's birth, when they had turned up unexpectedly and remained for dinner.

Now, Walter tried very hard, through many sleepless nights, to avoid imagining his father labouring all day in Flossenberg, starving, stripped of all dignity. It was almost a relief when he heard, about a year after his arrest, that Klaus had died of pneumonia.

Goering was tired with the constant kvetching by most senior Nazi officials about "das Judische problem" but too politically ambitious to risk voicing his suspicions that eradicating cripples and gypsies might not be as important for Germany as territorial acquisition. Certainly, it had been Goering who had decreed the "Aryanization" of the German economy and had dreamed up the idea of fining the Jews a billion marks for being Jewish. The revenue deriving from this post-pogram tax, following Kristallnacht in 1938, had been most useful – for the acquisition of paintings as well as for financing Hitler's rise to power.

And Goering had lost no sleep when the talks about exterminating Polish Jews began. He had, though, suffered a few restless nights when called to bludgeon the Austrians and Czechs into submission in 1938. Still, victory was glorious, and now he was just a tactic away from German leadership. He needed to indulge the Führer; find men like Walter Gunther who would shoot or gas children without exhibiting distaste, or sell their own fathers to further their careers. Personally, Goering despised such men. If Germany were his, he would stand beneath clear blue skies and smile upon crowds of adoring compatriots, fill halls and theatres with fine music. He would build palaces of art and have the people pay homage to the empire dynasties on whose philosophical excellence he would rebuild the country. Such men as Gunther could have no part in such a nation. He would put them in gloomy offices in grim buildings and inundate them with paperwork. But for now – for now he must deal with them; be seen to do his job as Vice Chancellor to the Führer of Germany, as well as that of Reich Council Chairman of National Defence.

CHAPTER THREE

* * *

Walter's first day as a T4 director overseeing work at Brandenburg-on-Havel hospital prison was hard, even for him. He was to assist SS-Obersturmführer Wirth to dispose of around a hundred mentally impaired and chronically ill *lebensunwertes leben* – those deemed medically to be "unworthy of life" and subjected to what the Führer termed "mercy death". Many children would be among those whom Gunther and Wirth would assist to a "merciful" release from their torment in the gas vans at Brandenburg.

Disposal of bodies was what most preoccupied Walter these days. That, and the images of children arriving in gas vans, twenty at a time, crushed like cattle bound for the abbatoir. But cattle probably didn't make such piteous noises or cry and shake like these "unworthies" did as they waited to die. They stood cold and naked, while the medical staff attached the pipes from the truck engine to the platform beneath the chassis and left the engine running for the prescribed fifteen minutes. It was necessary to monitor the death process through small windows in the vans, to determine how long it took for the children to die. Then measurements had to be done quickly, by scientists, of the CO concentration in the van before the back doors were opened and it was too diluted by oxygen.

Finally, the little bodies were driven to prepared trenches or crematoria and tipped out of lorries in a profuse jumble of limbs and staring eyes. Some had ears missing, bitten off by others in the frenzy caused by a quite remarkable unwillingness to die. Wirth was not plagued by visions. He watched Walter's face during the first few deliveries to Brandenburg and laughed at his colleague's evident distaste.

"You get used to it. You know, in the end, this is just so much... flotsam. Look at them," he had said on one occasion, peering through the gas van at the children and waving at them. Walter had indeed looked at the traumatized children and they stared back at him, some with faces contorted in terror, crying huge tears. He observed how the smallest ones reached out for others, desperate for comfort in this new and ungentle experience. "Would you like to live like that?" Wirth had shouted, slapping Walter on the back. "We're doing them a favour."

Walter envied Wirth. He hoped in a short time to reach such a state of comfortable inurement. He drank more, slept less and grew daily more irritable as his dreams followed him into comfortless sunlight and down cold stone corridors permeated by the odour of gas; corridors whose thick silence was the accumulation of the very moments countless mouths ceased to scream. These days, increasingly, that was almost exactly ten minutes after a precise quantity per head of carbon monoxide had been released into an enclosed space.

And Wirth was right. After weeks of repeated exposure to the most extreme cruelty of which men are capable, Walter attained indifference of a kind. Everyone who worked for the chancellery's T4 programme achieved some state of mind in which they could carry out their duties and still go home to families and tuck children into bed at night. It was that or succumb to mental illness themselves.

The ten thousandth person to be gassed at Sonnenstein was an eight-year-old boy. He had suffered from cerebral palsy and had needed much close nursing care. The staff on the night shift during which Gregor was gassed laid him upon a gurney and covered him in a snow-white sheet. They placed red roses around his head and someone put a teddy bear on his breast, held firm by a carefully placed right arm, as though the child had passed away peacefully in sleep. And then they photographed him. They threw a celebratory "ten thousandth victim" party; the beer flowed and staff gave themselves up to wanton, sexual antics around the gurney. Walter heard of this cabalistic ritual, but shrugged his shoulders. Frankly, as long as the job got done and there were people willing to do it, what did it matter? The boy's mother treasured the photograph of her son in peaceful repose for the rest of her life. She told everyone he had never looked so untroubled – and how caring the staff must have been to put flowers around his head.

By the time Walter was also assigned to the euthanizing administrative team at Eichberg, he was practically insensate to atrocity. He signed the euthanasia requisitions without any thought beyond that needed to move the pen.

On the 23rd August 1940, Hermann Goering made a professionally lethal tactical error. A certain lack of clarity in his orders to a Luftwaffe detail resulted in the accidental bombing of Harrow, just outside London. This destruction of a non-military location triggered a reprisal by eighty-one RAF Bomber Command planes on Berlin on the night of the 25th August. Their targets were industrial and commercial – but it was foggy. On this occasion, there was no time for Hedda and the children to seek protection in the cellar. Elise the cook was killed outright, as her bedroom was at the gable end of the house, which was obliterated in the blast. Hedda's room was ripped apart, but the area of floor where her bed stood was left intact, though precariously close to the ragged and splintered ends of the timber planks that jutted into the open, fiery darkness of the Berlin night. When she had recovered enough presence of mind to process what had happened, Hedda inched her way in a state of barely controlled panic along that part of the wall remaining and onto the landing.

Her head was pounding and her ears felt as though they would burst. She could see Anselm's tiny form, screaming his terror into the open sky, but she could not hear him. She reached for and clung to him. Agnette – where was she? Why hadn't she come from her room? Where was Agnette? Hedda was assailed by a powerful nausea born of shock and agonizing terror. Clasping Anselm's tiny hand, she leaned away from him and was violently sick. Where was Agnette? Anselm's relentless screams were a steady counterpoint to the constant sirens that filled the night, but Hedda could hear only her own blood throbbing through her veins and a rushing, ringing sound like an untuned radio.

The ground beneath her feet was unsteady and flames grew brighter at her back as Hedda made for Agnette's room and found herself screaming "No, no, no!" even before she clambered onto the door, where it lay twisted on the ground, blown from its hinges. Agnette's curtains billowed like tethered birds desperate to be free, and the shattered windows breathed smoke into the room, where it was snatched away instantly by the draughts from the gaping doorway.

Agnette lay several feet from her upturned bed. The blast that had ripped through her room, shattered her windows and blown her door from its hinges had thrown her with great force against a wall, and she had hit her head on the lip of the ornate wrought iron of the mantlepiece. She lay perfectly still, twisted where she had fallen, her left arm beneath her body, her right thrown in front in a most unnatural position. Her eyes were closed and her mouth a little open, so that the thick and steady rivulet of blood that coursed from the wound in her forehead readily poured over her top lip and pooled against the cheek closest to the floor.

Walter and an SS officer, as well as firefighters, appeared at Hedda's side. Hedda dared not move her daughter, dared not check for a pulse, could not countenance leaving her. Traumatized and shell-shocked, she knelt in her nightdress holding the screaming Anselm and stroking Agnette's hair with a violently trembling hand. One of the firefighters put his head to Agnette's breast, felt for a pulse in her right wrist, could determine nothing in the noise and the chaos, and shrugged his shoulders.

As gently as they could, coughing and signalling through the heavy smoke, two firefighters lifted Agnette and laid her on the floor of a wire cage they had hoisted to the first floor level of the house by means of an extending metal arm from a fire engine. Once Agnette was securely within the cage, they beckoned to Hedda and Anselm. Walter watched as all three were lowered to safety. Once Hedda and the children were out of the now steadily burning house, the men made their exit as quickly as they could.

Ladders had been propped against the wall at this and the next window along the corridor, and as they jumped from the ladders to the street, the upstairs floors groaned and collapsed in a mighty rush of flame, timbers and dust.

The night was a cacophony of ambulance and bomb sirens, the clanging of the fire-trucks and the roar of fire and collapsing buildings. Hedda, lost in shock and deafness, clung to Anselm, rocking instinctively to comfort him as they and Walter accompanied Agnette to hospital in an ambulance.

Agnette was not dead. At the hospital, they found a weak pulse, stopped the bleeding from her head and rushed her to X-ray. Walter scribbled "X-ray" on a cigarette box to explain to the frantic Hedda where Agnette was being taken, and then a sympathetic nurse gave him a notepad. Hedda pushed the screaming Anselm to his father and insisted on following the gurney, even though she looked like an escapee from a lunatic asylum in her tattered and bloodstained nightdress, and was in need of urgent medical attention herself. Walter did his best to restrain Anselm as he screamed shrilly and strained against his father's embrace in the direction taken by his mother. The same nurse who had given him the pad of paper relieved him of his child, and he stood still for a moment, then headed for the nearest exit, leaned against a wall and lit a cigarette. More than anything, Walter wished he were in France, pointing a flak gun at the sky and pumping it full of lead. He dropped his cigarette butt on the ground and crushed it beneath his boot. His last thought as he did so was that Goering was no longer very useful to him.

Walter took the pad of paper from his jacket breast pocket and scribbled a note for the waiting casualty nurse and ordered a passing soldier to give it to her. The soldier accepted his errand without question and saluted before running to execute it. Walter smoothed his jacket, straightened the leather belt around his waist, tapped his Parabellum and walked back into the hospital. He asked an orderly to direct him to the nearest office telephone. He dialled the Berlin exchange and ensured that the operator understood he was a high-ranking SS officer, whose calls were a matter of national security and to be given priority. He instructed her to call the home of Marguerite, his and Hedda's maid. Walter himself had taken the precaution of installing a telephone in Marguerite's house in case of just such an emergency.

Marguerite was safe but audibly distraught, and her family and several neighbours had gathered in her small living room to exclaim at the assault on their city. He instructed her to dress hurriedly and he would send a car to collect her and bring her to the hospital, where she was to take care of Anselm. She should also bring toiletries for Hedda. He would return to the hospital in the morning with money, so that Marguerite could buy clothes for Hedda and Anselm. At present, he was going to try and secure accommodation somewhere in Berlin. He made a second call, ordering himself a chauffeured car, a necessity for inspecting and servicing the growing number of elimination centres from Salzburg to Hamburg, Dresden to Stuttgart.

The journey he intended tonight, however, would be a short one. He wanted nothing more than to ascertain that his office at Tiergartenstrasse 4 was intact. He wished only to lie down upon its sumptuous leather sofa and rest. Tomorrow, he would use his connections to find and furnish a new house. Now, he wished only to sleep. He made one final telephone call. He curtly informed Hedda's father that Hedda and the children could be found at the Rudolf Virchow hospital. He informed his parents-in-law that he would be seeking alternative accommodation and noted with an ironic twist of his mouth the hesitation before Ernst Schroeder offered his own many-roomed residence in the Tiergarten as a refuge for as long as Walter and Hedda might need. Walter thanked him, but hoped it would not be necessary to impose.

Finally, before taking his leave of the hospital in the immaculate Mercedes that drew up in the ambulance bay within fifteen minutes of Walter's call, he informed the now terribly anxious nurse who was caring for Anselm that a maid was on her way to relieve her. He found Hedda still awaiting Agnette's X-ray results and demanded to know of the busy staff his daughter's status. He insisted upon seeing a doctor, and ignoring the tired and blood-spattered man's protestations that he had other, seriously wounded, patients to attend to, made him look at Agnette's X-ray and wrung from him a prognosis.

It seemed Agnette had sustained two skull fractures and there was, in all likelihood, a haematoma, which would need surgical attention. The situation was serious. It was possibly fatal. They would not know until they opened her skull. Coma was probable. Walter wrote all of this down on his pad of paper and handed it to Hedda. She wept and wept. Walter noticed she was shivering in her ripped and flimsy nightdress, and made a passing nurse fetch her a blanket. Insisting that his wife and son be given a side-room and made comfortable, he strode away towards the hospital entrance and his waiting car.

Walter watched the pandemonium of bombed Berlin through the Mercedes' windows. There were fewer sirens now. Flames were intermittent, and though there were still places where people milled around in confusion and shock in their nightclothes, most of the city was now quiet. In fact, the bombing had not been extensive, and casualties were "light".

A fine dew spritzed the windscreen as dawn lightened the sky. Walter cursed softly to himself. Sunlight was not what he wanted. He wanted the rest and comfort of darkness. He wanted quietness. In a very few hours, his office telephone would start ringing. He had a very important meeting to attend and he must bathe, and change his uniform. He cursed more loudly. He would need to find alternative accommodation. What had he been thinking? He would get no sleep.

By the time he got to his offices and noted the peach tinge of unripe sun reflecting in the topmost corners of the office windows, he was coldly furious. Damn the British. Damn Goering for an imbecile. Shivering a little in the dawn light, he threw himself onto the sofa, but the leather was cold, the stiffly upholstered arm an unyielding pillow. Unbidden reflections on the irony of his situation presented themselves for his perusal. How many children had he consigned to death – children still smiling, capable of conversation and voluntary mobility? Children capable of love? No telling. And now his own perfect daughter was to undergo brain surgery from which, it was clear, there was little hope she would recover.

Hedda and Anselm left the hospital two days after admission and went to stay with her parents. Each morning, Hedda would leave the Tiergarten district in an SS Opel Kapitan with a designated driver. She would have preferred to drive herself in her mother's car, which, it was made clear, was at Hedda's disposal, but her hearing did not return fully for weeks after the bomb blast and she suffered from terrible headaches, both of which conditions made driving unsafe. Anselm remained sullen and grizzly, and clung to his mother at every opportunity for days after they left the hospital. However, the family cook's gentle encouragement and plentiful sweet treats persuaded him that he was safe in her care during his mother's absence.

Hedda remained long hours of each day by Agnette's bedside, watching her daughter breathe. No other signs of life were detectable in the girl's slight body. As soon as X-rays indicated subsidence of cranial swelling and relative stability of the sizeable haematoma nestled in Agnette's cerebellum, they would operate to remove the clot. What had already been erased of Agnette's memories, higher thought-processing abilities, could only be estimated. Apart from the bruising to part of her face and into her hairline, Agnette seemed as if in a peaceful sleep. Hedda held her hand and wished with an indescribable anguish that she were able to recount to Agnette again, and without the slightest trace of impatience, how Iphigenia was spirited away at the last minute from the sacrificial knife.

CHAPTER THREE

The nurses shaved off Agnette's beautiful hair in readiness for surgery. She seemed smaller and more vulnerable than ever. The extensive bruising to her scalp emphasized the severity of her injuries and made it impossible to avoid contemplation of the likely brain trauma caused by the fracturing of her skull. The vicious criss-cross of surgical stitching following a lengthy operation did nothing to ease Hedda's fears.

Hedda was lost in a deadening silence born of her deafness but, even more, the profound uselessness of words. She would speak to no one and made no attempt to listen to what anyone else had to say. The only way to communicate with Hedda now was to write what was essential for her to know. Anselm was content just to sit upon his mother's knee each evening and fall asleep while she distractedly stroked his hair.

Weeks passed in this way. Walter stayed at his offices, then acquired a smart city apartment on the Bellevuestrasse. He made it clear to Hedda and his in-laws that his work was more important than ever, now that Berlin was in the enemy frontline, and it was better that he remained in the city where he could be called upon at a moment's notice. No one protested. Hedda could barely look at him, and the Schroeders were hugely relieved that they did not have to entertain a high-ranking and tiresomely saturnine SS officer at their dining table each evening – Ernst not least of all because he was encountering Walter increasingly in his professional life. Besides, each man was ever conscious of the abhorrence and incredulity that would be the reactions of their wives should the true nature of their work for the Reich be exposed over dessert.

CHAPTER FOUR

September 1940. Walter Gunther sat in a room with Joachim von Ribbentrop, German Foreign Minister; General Reinhard Heydrich, Reich Security Officer; Joseph Goebbels, Reich Minister of Propaganda and T4 Inspector; and Administrative Director at Brandenburg euthanasia centre, Christian Wirth. Also present was Reichsführer SS, Heinrich Himmler and, considerably less impressively as far as Walter was concerned, were his father-in-law, Ernst Schroeder, and Karl Muller, introduced to the assembly as the Director of Hygiene recently assigned to T4.

Pretty secretaries with glossy hair and crossed legs kept their heads bowed in deference to the sheer majesty of those assembled, though Walter noticed how often the eyes of the great travelled over the slender ankles and lustrous curls of the secretaries. This distraction added to his irritation. Since the bombing of his home and the near fatal wounding of his daughter, he was not in the mood for feminine frippery. In fact, he was aware of a growing contempt for women. Certainly, since his marriage to Hedda he had succumbed frequently to frauleins eager to bed a rich and influential SS officer. But all that had its place. Outside, his beloved Berlin tried valiantly to get to her feet in the early autumn sunshine, her splendour maimed by enemy bombs, and everywhere her pavements soiled by filthy Jews scampering and whining in droves like rats from sewers. Women? Walter had decided they could be confined to two categories – entertainment and weakness. Neither was ennobling and had no place in this illustrious boardroom, where the very future of the Third Reich might be influenced if not decided.

Reichsmarschall Goering was officially a joke since the English had routed the Luftwaffe during the previous two months of humiliating air combat over the English Channel. Goering had assured everyone that victory would be decisive and swift. Just as he had sworn that Berlin would never be bombed. The English were making fools of the German war effort. And instead of being able to pour his fury and shame into an anti-aircraft machine gun and rip the enemy out of the sky, Walter was assigned by Goering to oversee the extermination of cripples and lunatics and now, it seemed, apply his brilliantly strategic mind to the relocation of Jews by train to some godforsaken hole in Poland. He spat on the day he had impressed that idiot Goering.

Himmler had been watching Walter from the opposite side of the boardroom table. This handsome, angst-ridden young man intrigued him. There was in his endlessly working jaw, the narrowing of those icy eyes, something essentially Teutonic. Himmler realized the young SS officer was oblivious to all around him; oblivious even to the fact that the Reichsführer of the SS was scrutinizing his face. Every other young man in the room was shifting uncomfortably and trying too hard to affect the indifference and self-containment Walter displayed effortlessly.

Himmler rose from his seat and walked casually to Walter's side. "Are you all right, Herr Director Gunther?"

At Himmler's address Walter got immediately to his feet and saluted, bringing his heels together and bowing slightly as he did so. "Reichsführer Himmler, sir – a great honour."

"Please." Himmler sighed and motioned to Walter to resume his seat, his cigar leaving smoke trails as he waved his hand impatiently. "We have not met. I have heard much about your work, though. Very thorough. Very efficient."

Walter nodded slightly again, trying not to think about the blush that threatened to rise from his throat and creep across his face. "Thank you, mein Reichsführer. I am, naturally, a great admirer of your work also."

Himmler closed his eyes briefly. This conversation could prove disappointing. "Your part in today's plans will be key. I think you are aware that we are facing... challenges of quite serious proportions?"

Walter nodded and looked up, straight into Himmler's eyes. The blush was forgotten. In spite of Himmler's previous instruction, Walter rose to his feet. "May I speak frankly, mein Reichsführer?"

Himmler looked slightly amused. "I wish you would."

"I wish to do whatever I can to bring Germany to the greatness which is hers by right. We are so close, Reichsführer Himmler – I can feel it! Once we get these filthy Jewish rats out of Berlin we can think straight. We must... forgive me – we must regroup. Our Luftwaffe is the finest military air machine in the world. We have the finest planes on earth. I worked for Reichsmarschall Goering at the Air Ministry and I know what a lethal weapon the Stuka is – we should not have lost!" Walter's pent-up fury and frustration were too evident. He swallowed nervously and began another apology.

"Don't do that! Don't apologize for being honest. I like your spirit, Director Gunther. I can use that."

Walter half smiled, swallowed nervously. Himmler shook his hand, then returned to his seat on the opposite side of the imposing oval table. Walter breathed in deeply, calming himself, and resumed his seat. It was, though, hard to get enough air into his lungs. The sumptuous T4 boardroom was opaque with coils of smoke that intertwined like snakes and, growing heavy, seemed to sleep. The secretaries covered their mouths with scarlet-tipped fingers, trying their best to cough imperceptibly.

On a nod from Himmler, a small man with greased-flat side-parted hair and glasses started from exaggerated stillness, slid his clipboard onto the polished table and crossed the room to open a sash window. The chatter reduced, then died, as people took their places at the table and all eyes turned to the figure standing at the head of the table, Joachim von Ribbentrop, the Foreign Minister.

"Good morning, gentlemen. There are several things of grave concern to us at present. Europe is within our grasp, but there are those who laugh at us – who mock our noble aims and fail entirely to understand our superior intellectual and racial motives. They underestimate us." Here, Ribbentrop paused and looked steely eyed at the assembled company. No one made a sound, several lowered their eyes. Ribbentrop was the most hated member of Hitler's Reich, barely tolerated by Himmler and Goebbels and not tolerated at all by Goering, who openly lampooned him as an idiot to the Führer's face.

But Hitler liked Ribbentrop's barbarity and his inventive, ceaseless sycophancy. Ribbentrop was well known for making notes on even small conversational exchanges with the Führer; for feverishly tracking down people who had been known to have had conversations with Hitler and begging them to recount the smallest details of how the Führer looked, reacted, what he said, that he might write it all down and represent the Führer's ideas as his own thoughts in later conversations. And Ribbentrop's socialist zeal made even Himmler's extremism seem discreet. Hitler had once quipped that where he had to galvanize many to share his visions of non-Aryan extermination, Ribbentrop always out-strategied him, so that he actually had to apply brakes to Ribbentrop's enthusiasm. This, he had stated publicly, was delightful to him. So, the most extreme luminaries of the Nazi party gathered today upon Hitler's orders and listened politely to this man whose favour with the Führer they despised but had to respect.

"You may be aware that I was in Italy in March of this year, on diplomatic business with our illustrious ally, Mussolini. I also had the questionable fortune to be granted an audience with the pope."

Someone sighed, the secretaries scribbled furiously. Everyone wondered what this had to do with the agenda. Ribbentrop, unabashed at his failure to impress his audience, continued, raising his voice as if to compensate for his lack of substance. "Well, he too is laughing at us – from his safe Vatican City in the centre of the capital of our allied Italy. He dared to tell me that we – the greatest race on earth – are barbarians!"

At last, some reaction: Goebbels swore under his breath, a few others mumbled their indignation.

"Yes! As if his position protects him from our censure, gentlemen, Pope Pius dared to list to me a series of our great victories in Belgium, France, Czechoslovakia, Scandinavia, Poland – and call them 'inhumane acts of barbarism'! I tell you, my friends, we must make it a priority to silence this insufferable pontiff, for it is known how he dares to help thousands of Jews to escape us – piling them into Catholic monasteries and convents – even hiding them in his own Vatican City, as though he were untouchable. We should start with the Catholics. Did you hear his Easter homily? He mocked us throughout – to the whole of Europe. He is broadcasting anti-National Socialist propaganda throughout Europe on his Vatican radio station. Have you heard him?"

Ribbentrop was becoming agitated. He took out a handkerchief from his jacket breast pocket and dabbed at his brow. There was a slight tremor in his hand. He seemed to recover himself a little, and when he spoke again the whine of fury had disappeared from his voice.

"Reich Minister Goebbels, I am sure you are fully aware of all the pope is doing to undermine our great war effort. I need hardly remind you of the propagandist pamphlets he enlisted enemy planes to drop on Berlin last year. He has poisoned our Catholic clergy and they betray us beneath our noses. We should start with the Catholics – the Catholics and the Jews in Poland should be exterminated. It is necessary! They are working together to make fools of us!" Ribbentrop looked directly at Goebbels, who regarded him levelly in return with barely controlled loathing.

"You take care of your work, Herr Ribbentrop, and be assured I shall do mine." Several men smirked their satisfaction at the put-down and Ribbentrop's bridling at the snideness of Goebbels' response.

"Very well. Ensure you do – as will I."

"Are we here to discuss the pope, Herr Ribbentrop?" Himmler this time. "Because I understood that it is with Jews we are preoccupied this morning. I should warn you also that my mother is a most devout Catholic and would be scandalized at your heretical denouncement of her beloved pontiff. Are you going to deport my mother, Herr Ribbentrop? I wouldn't like that, I think." Sniggers erupted around the table. "And in any case, surely Mussolini can take care of the pope? Even he should be a match for an old man in a dress."

Even Walter laughed aloud. A couple of secretaries took advantage of the momentary levity to look up from their scribbling and exchange surprised smiles, raise pencilled eyebrows.

"I assure you, Reichsführer Himmler, you will not get rid of Jews while there are convents and monasteries in Europe."

"Let us turn our attention to the big problem, nonetheless, Reichminister Ribbentrop: the countless thousands of Jews who live openly on our soil, who have colonized Europe like rats. Let us excise the vermin we can see, then turn our attention to that which hides when the majority is destroyed. To the main business of the day, Herr Ribbentrop. I am sorry the pope was clearly so disrespectful of your diplomatic status – you are evidently upset." More sniggering, though Himmler held Ribbentrop's gaze while his mouth moved in a tight-lipped smile his eyes did not share. He added, with a sigh, "And anyway, here in Berlin we have our own dear Nuncio Orsenigo to keep a check on El Papa. A true German, Reichminister – I can vouch for him. I have dined with him several times – as indeed have you."

"Yes, yes," Ribbentrop responded irritably.

"As have I," added Goebbels, to general murmurs of interest. "He produced the most exquisite vintage Chianti, as I remember – the old fox wasn't keeping that for the altar boys."

Ribbentrop was now obviously angry. "Well, as you are on intimate terms with our dear cardinal, gentlemen, you are aware no doubt that he has just lodged a formal complaint with the chancellery, citing German brutality against the Polish church!"

CHAPTER FOUR

Goebbels in turn was irritated at Ribbentrop's rebuke and growing tired of the Foreign Minister's petulance. "Unless we receive such a document with a papal seal, we should remain unconcerned. Calm yourself, Ribbentrop." Goebbels' tone was one of affected soothing. "Orsenigo is not a threat to the Reich."

"I don't trust him," retorted Ribbentrop, leafing through papers, the tremor in both hands quite noticeable now.

"And neither, I am willing to wager, does the pope. Now, Foreign Minister, to the point, if you please."

"As you wish. Gentlemen, I refer you to your brief. The Madagascar Plan is abandoned. Given our undeserved – and soon to be avenged – setback at the hands of the British RAF, we of course cannot count on captured British planes to evacuate over four million Jews to Madagascar. The deportation is out of the question. The original plan, to exile them to Poland and use it as a centralized disposal base, is again a priority. As you know, the construction of the Warsaw ghetto is underway once more, and it is envisaged that by October it will accommodate half a million Jews. A further 200,000 can be contained in the Lodz ghetto. There are plans for several more ghettos at strategic Polish locations – indicated in your brief – and then phase two of the evacuation plan, 'Final Goal',will commence within a few months, and a number of specifically constructed camps in Poland, Czechoslovakia and Austria are nearing completion for the accommodation of at least three million more Jews. The Jew as a species is destined for extinction – natural selection at work, gentlemen."

Only Christian Wirth clapped and said "Heil Hitler!" at this impassioned crescendo. Ribbentrop nodded to him, wiped his brow once more.

"If I may, Herr Ribbentrop? I believe I should take the meeting from here."

The voice was one Walter had not heard before and he was intrigued to know more of the speaker. He had heard much about the esteemed General Reinhard Heydrich, Reich Security Officer; of his ruthlessness, efficiency, the esteem in which he was held by the Führer. Ribbentrop seemed reluctant to cede the floor and regarded Heydrich for several moments as if he had forgotten who he was. Heydrich looked amused, then made an expansive gesture with his right arm as if conducting Ribbentrop to a dining table. Suddenly, the latter picked up his papers with great brusqueness and nodded curtly to the audience, moving in the opposite direction to that indicated by Heydrich. Himmler guffawed and Heydrich moved to the head of the table.

"Gentlemen, I need hardly remind you how confidential today's meeting is. Should any details escape the confines of this room and become known to uninvolved parties, the Führer himself will stop at nothing to determine the source of the leak. I am certain such warnings are unnecessary to such a distinguished gathering. Nevertheless, let it not be said that anyone had as mitigation for political indelicacy that he – or indeed she –" and here Heydrich looked over his spectacles at the secretaries, then smiled charmingly – "was not warned of the consequences."

He removed his spectacles and, folding them, placed them in an inner jacket pocket before picking up his briefing bundle and folding previously referenced pages behind those he wanted to address. "Please look at page seven of your brief, if you would, gentlemen. Reichsmarschall Goering has asked me to take over responsibility for 'the Judische problem' from Foreign Secretary Ribbentrop."

Here, there were more indistinguishable amused comments and a couple of faux coughs from Himmler's and Goebbels' side of the table. All knew how much Goering detested Ribbentrop and how much pleasure he took in depriving him of this key duty, and how much pleasure it gave Heydrich to announce it.

"Firstly, to the relocation of Jews from Germany to Poland in the first phase of the revised action following the abandonment of the Madagascar Plan. As the Foreign Minister said, we estimate that around three million Jews and other enemies of the Reich will be resettled in the Warsaw and Lodz ghettoes in the next month to six weeks. My esteemed colleagues, Aktion T4 Senior Directors Wirth and Gunther –" here Heydrich looked directly at both men in turn – "will assist me in the process. Sturmbannführer Wirth has an especial responsibility in readiness for phase two. He will be based at our Brandenburg facility, piloting some special measures by which we may eventually *reduce* –" here he paused and deliberately stressed the word, and contemplated his papers – "the numbers of non-Aryan peoples who are resettled in any one centre. Clearly –" now he looked up again, around the table – "concentrated millions of people will be a huge expense to the Reich at a time when we need to be focusing our economic resources on the war effort. Naturally, most of these resettled people will be put to work. For example, there will be a large camp built – and its construction most generously funded by IG Farben – in the Auschwitz area of Poland. Please see your brief, pages eight and nine, for exact locations and plans. This will eventually be a main camp to many smaller, satellite camps, all of which will provide a new and economical workforce for an IG Farben munitions and chemical factory. It is anticipated that this ingenious and cost-effective plan will be operational within two years."

"And meanwhile, my dear Heydrich," came Goebbels' assured and easy tones, "what will our displaced Jewish and otherwise undesirable friends be doing?"

"Well, esteemed Minister of Propaganda Goebbels, they will be gainfully employed in various ghettoes, and inevitably – often – they will be... dying."

Goebbels nodded and laughed. Wirth laughed out loud, his head thrown back in an unashamed bid for attention. He was already quite an extermination expert and his Brandenburg brief was to find the most efficient ways of dispatching large numbers of people then disposing of their bodies. Wirth enjoyed his work. He looked around the table, chubby cheeked and ruddy with mirth. There was an indubitable glint of stark madness in his black eyes. Walter hated him. Wirth was crass and crude and wholly untrustworthy.

Walter was not alone in thinking Wirth a psychopath. Many senior SS officers with Aktion T4 responsibility thought Wirth certifiable. His penchant for sadism was breathtaking. Recently, he had come up with the idea of disguising execution chambers as showers, and laughed till he cried when unsuspecting "patients" realized they had been assembled to be gassed, not deloused. "Gets me every time – the looks on their stupid faces!" Wirth had babbled to Walter on one occasion as they timed the deaths of the latest batch of "unworthies". Walter had smiled and nodded, secretly bored and utterly disgusted by the whole sordid business. It was unsportsmanlike and degrading. Wirth's credentials for his job were impeccable.

"Today, my esteemed colleagues," went on Heydrich, "we have two men with us who will be instrumental in making the transition smooth from phase one to phase two of the Jewish relocation programme. May I introduce them to those who have not already made their acquaintance: Herr Ernst Schroeder, Chemist and Senior Director from Bayer, now on the IG Farben board, and Obersturmführer Karl Muller, Chief Disinfection Officer, now working for the Aktion T4 programme. Gentlemen, please stand, if you would. Firstly, Professor Schroeder."

Walter watched with close interest how his father-in-law smiled broadly so that his immaculately groomed moustache arched upwards like a mouse stretching. He rose and graciously acknowledged first Heydrich then the rest of the table before sitting down again.

"And Obersturmführer Muller."

Muller was altogether less adroit. He did not smile, merely managed a quick elongation of his lips, and his eyes remained serious, even troubled.

"You will not find either of these gentlemen's presentations in your brief," declared Heydrich. "At this point, I would like all but my own and Reichsführer Himmler's secretaries to leave, if you please. I would also suggest that we have a break for coffee." At this, Heydrich caught the eye of his secretary, and she nodded and smiled, got up, put her pad and pen upon her chair, and left the room with those secretaries asked to vacate it in order to organize refreshments. Goebbels yawned openly.

Ribbentrop did not return to the meeting after coffee – something about an important financial and fiscal meeting with a senior Reich member. No one enquired further.

Agnette was being rushed along tile and concrete corridors on a gurney pushed by an orderly who did his best to control the wayward wheels, but even so, the gurney glanced sharply off the tiled walls and careered across the corridor on a few occasions on the journey from the side room to the operating theatre. An unfit nurse in a starched uniform and cap did her best to keep up, clutching to her chest the clipboard that gripped Agnette's notes. Behind her ran Hedda, tears streaming down her face, her whole visage contorted into a grimace of sheer panic. A surgeon held open the theatre doors, and once the gurney was through, he let them swing shut. When Hedda tried to follow she was restrained by the orderly and thrust firmly back into the corridor. The agonizing waiting must begin all over again. Agnette had started fitting, quite suddenly. The swelling in her brain would not subside. The fluid must be drained, or she would certainly die. More perilous surgery. More risk of infection. More scarring. Less and less of Agnette to hope for.

Hedda yanked her arm from the orderly's grip and addressed him fiercely. "Get my husband!" she screamed. "Get my useless husband – *now*!"

"The problem initially was to do with concentration." Ernst Schroeder was addressing the phase two meeting. "We experimented on small mammals – rats, mice, guinea pigs and suchlike – to begin with. At a CO concentration of 0.3 per cent, we found that the animals were not really showing severe signs of poisoning after an hour's exposure. If we slowly increased the concentration of carbon monoxide – even by fractions of a per cent – then fitting, ataxia and evident narcosis and so on occurred, but not death – even after few hours. At levels above 0.4 per cent, death occurred."

Ernst Schroeder was more animated than Walter had ever seen him. The usually taciturn, laconic little man was in his element. At social engagements, even family dinners, he was withdrawn and preoccupied to the point of rudeness. But give him a pointing stick and a flipchart with sums on it and his beady eyes lit behind his glasses, moustache moving frenetically.

"But Herr Doctor," Himmler feigned fascination, "are these experiments applicable to humans? We are so much bigger."

Dr Schroeder smiled and looked down quickly, as if trying to hide impatience. Walter was reminded of a schoolmaster trying to avoid a sarcastic retort to a class simpleton.

"Yes, yes, all that is easy to calculate: 0.8 – that is 8,000 parts CO per million – will certainly kill a person within thirty minutes after roughly two minutes' exposure. Actually, toxicity is not as respectful of weight as you might suppose. English miners who took canaries into underground mines to detect even slight emissions of CO knew they had not long to get out once a bird began to sway on its perch. Carbon monoxide is a fascinating poison. The molecule binds to haemoglobin many, many times more strongly than oxygen does. We are not entirely sure why. Once metabolized at significant concentrations, CO will cause serious damage to the nervous system almost immediately."

"And so where are we, Dr Schroeder, with our phase two planning?"

"Well, if one wanted to cause death to fifteen hundred people of an average body volume of seventy-five litres in a space of approximately 320 metres cubed, then the most cost-efficient way to ensure death within ten to fifteen minutes would be to adapt a diesel-fuelled vehicle driven by a gas-fuelled generator. With careful ventilation sufficient only to reduce explosive pressure in the room, we can assume a 35 per cent CO concentration in the fuel of such a single combustion chamber vehicle – up to five times more than in a petrol-fuelled engine and more than twenty-five times that of a normal diesel-fuelled vehicle. But there are problems."

Goebbels was falling asleep. The only person paying more than polite interest was Wirth. He was practically on the edge of his chair with frustration, desperately wanting to interrupt the presentation, but still too cowed by the illustriousness of the gathering to do so.

"Problems, Herr Doctor?" Himmler alone encouraged Ernst to elaborate.

"Leaks in pipes, build up of solids in the generator and in feed pipes, which can cause breakdown, inefficient ventilation, so that oxygen levels are kept too high, or indeed, insufficient ventilation so that CO levels become dangerously concentrated and explosion is possible – and of course, engine malfunction is our present greatest obstacle to efficiency. Vehicle diesel engines were not designed to idle at full capacity for prolonged periods. Then we have a shortage of suitably fuelled and driven vehicles. Petroleum is efficient, but scarce and expensive. Most gas fuel generator-run vehicles are needed for our war effort. In short, the direct introduction of CO gas via specially constructed ducts – as recently used and supervised at Brandenburg – is far more efficient, but initially very costly, of course."

Wirth could contain himself no longer. "I get the job done with converted Renault vans. We just build an air-tight chassis and feed a high CO gas/fuel mix into the compartment with a simple pipe. It works very well! I have also used a tractor, adapted to single chamber combustion and with a pipe feeding into a small room. That took longer, but also works. More get killed, though, so it is a question of time or numbers. I do both. It works."

All eyes were now on the agitated and ruddy Wirth. Ernst Schroeder regarded him with an aloof contempt. Goebbels shifted in his chair so that he could get a good view of this hideous little man who was, nonetheless, more entertaining than the good Dr Schroeder.

"Do go on, Director Wirth," encouraged Heydrich. "We could do with some hard statistics. I must report back to the Führer tomorrow on the findings of this meeting. Your presentation was most interesting, Herr Dr Schroeder. Can you have a report to me by tomorrow morning?"

"Foreign Minister Heydrich, sir —" Ernst Schroeder was clearly annoyed by this unseemly and most unscientific interruption from Wirth — "I was under the impression that you were interested in future, longer term, plans for phase two? My brief clearly states that phase two, beginning at the end of next year, will involve the removal of an initial three million persons in the shortest amount of time — and in the least costly manner. Current work under the expert auspices of Herr Wirth is still very experimental, and involves small numbers in comparison. Actually, were it up to me, General, I would suggest Zyklon B. Farben, building on work commenced many years ago at Bayer, have perfected a B Zyklon that will rival CO in both efficacy and cost. I am sure of it."

Wirth was not about to cede the spotlight. He began to stand up, looked to Heydrich then Himmler for permission, received the necessary nods, then took the floor.

"At Hartheim and also at Brandenburg I have set up what I think is a good system. I can dispose of around 250 an hour. This includes time taken for loading, removal, cleaning and so on. Sometimes they are not dead, but that is easily remedied. I know bullets are in short supply, but not many need to be finished off. It is still effective. In any case, garotting is also effective, and with three men on garotting duty, production is maximized. Sometimes the engine does break down, it's true, and then it can set us back a bit, but average weekly production is now about 2,000 — at both institutions. Each van can take seventy-five to eighty at a time, and within ten minutes, boom —" Wirth clapped his hands in a decisive gesture — "they are dead."

The government officials and officers exchanged comments or wrote things down.

"And are the... units... Are they about the same body mass as an average adult?" Heydrich was engaged now. He needed figures and projections for the Führer. So far, the scientist had outlined mainly what was not possible.

"Some are but, you understand, in my work often they are small. Many are just kids."

More murmuring, nodding, note-taking.

"Why do you think, Director Wirth, that production is not much higher, given your stated capacity?"

"Like I said – with respect, Reichsofficers – sometimes we have little to work with. And sometimes, if I may, there are too many... scientists involved."

At this there was open laughter. Ernst Schroeder looked furious.

"Really? And how does this slow things down?" Heydrich's eyes were amused, but otherwise he kept a straight face.

"Well, sometimes there are four doctors and at least two chemists present. They fill in papers and ask questions – play with the gas taps and measure things. I am not allowed to get on with my job unless there are two doctors present at Brandenburg. It slows things."

"Herr Wirth –" Ernst Schroeder could not contain himself – "without scientists, there would be no CO gas and you, my dear fellow, would have no adapted engines delivering the necessary CO concentrations without the efforts of my staff at IG Farben and the excellent engineering skills of colleagues like Officer Muller, here."

At the reference to Muller, Walter turned with the others to look at Muller's face. There was none of the anxiety to ingratiate himself or seek attention evident in the rivalry between Wirth and Schroeder. Muller, by contrast, seemed to shrink under scrutiny. In fact, he looked decidedly unwell.

"Of course, dear Dr Schroeder. We are indebted to your efforts, naturally. I am merely trying to establish possible production figures based on present data and so on. Director Wirth's statistics are most interesting to me." Heydrich continued, "Gentlemen, I think for now we can break for lunch. It has been a most useful meeting so far. Let us reconvene in, say, an hour and a half from now?"

Just then the boardroom doors opened and a junior SS officer entered the room, blushing at the illustriousness of the company, but also at the nature and urgency of his message. He handed Heydrich a note. Once Heydrich had read it, he turned to Walter.

"I think that you will forgive the public announcing of this message, Director Gunther, under the circumstances. I regret that your daughter has taken a turn for the worse at Rudolf Virchow hospital. Your urgent presence is required. Please, leave at once. We shall not expect you after lunch. My secretary will ensure you receive full minutes."

Walter did not move. He considered the message and seemed to contemplate its significance. He was angry. He had spent most of the meeting contriving how best to ingratiate himself with Heydrich and Himmler over lunch. He was also eager to strike up conversation with Muller. Something about that man did not sit right. And also, there was something less than befitting the conduct of a Nazi high-ranking SS officer in the emotional leave-taking from such a meeting to attend to family business.

"Thank you for your concern, General Heydrich, but my daughter has been in a critical condition for many days now. I am sure another few hours will not make much difference. Her mother is with her."

The men had all started to rise from their chairs, gather papers and make for the door. Their minds were on lunch and the fine wines that would no doubt accompany it. Most took little interest in Gunther's news, but Muller sat quite still and contemplated Walter's discomfiture, the growing redness of his complexion. He did not flinch when Walter looked up and caught his eye.

"As you wish, Director Gunther – Walter, I believe? As you wish," conceded Heydrich, "but family is important. When you think about it, Walter, what else are we fighting for here? Take my advice – go to your daughter. Everyone will quite understand. We are all family men."

Walter dared not contradict. He donned his cap, bowed as graciously as he could manage and shot one last challenging look at Muller, who met it with a quizzically arched brow and a slight movement of his head in askance. Muller had still not risen from his seat. Walter rose from his and left the room.

The tempers of both Hedda and Walter were high when their eyes met outside the theatre post-operative recovery room at the Rudolf Virchow hospital. Never kindly disposed to each other under normal circumstances these days, their mutual antipathy was acute at that moment.

"What has happened, Hedda?" Walter asked her this loudly without checking his pace while still a good twenty feet away from where his wife sat alone in the corridor. She rose and, holding his gaze, unperturbed by the annoyance in his countenance, answered equally loudly, "Your daughter is probably dying. That is what is happening."

"Be specific." Walter had reached her and stared into her eyes. His blood was not calmed by the defiance in them.

"Specifically? Her brain swelled again, she began to have fits. Specific enough?" Voicing aloud her comprehension to another for the first time seemed to bring home the seriousness of the words. Hedda was stopped by a sudden, choking sob. She gathered herself, wiped away spontaneous, hot tears and continued less angrily, "They rushed her to the operating theatre again. They said they needed to drain the fluid from her brain. She is in there." Hedda nodded towards the door of the recovery room. "But they won't let me in."

Suddenly she gave in to the pain, the panic, the grief that had been damming against the walls of her heart. "I don't know if she is alive or dead!" The words were half screamed, Hedda's face contorted into an agonized grimace, and she stared challengingly into Walter's eyes. "And where – where were you? I sent for you an hour ago!"

"Calm yourself!" Walter was resisting the urge to slap her full across the face. His eyes returned her hatred. "I came as soon as I got that message. In case you hadn't noticed, there is a war outside. The city has been bombed and traffic is not flowing. It has taken me over forty minutes just to get here – and I was in a high priority meeting..."

She cut him off. The logistics of his journey and the possibility that his arrival was the earliest possible seemed to have no effect upon her temper. "Everything you do is more important than your family. But I'll be damned if you are excused from the death of your daughter! You took no interest in her birth – nor in her life to date – but I will not watch her die alone too. You will have enough respect for our daughter to at least be present when she dies."

Walter regarded Hedda's face. The beauty had ceded to exhaustion and the ravages of anxiety. Her eyes were dulled by tears, and the dark circles below them were more remarkable than their colour. In spite of her rage her complexion was pale, and tears ran in falls across her cheekbones. A man who loved her would have been engulfed by pity. Walter considered her ugly.

"I shall find someone rational to talk to." He pushed her out of his way and walking right up to the recovery room doors he knocked on them loudly in a manner that did not leave anything less than immediate acknowledgment as an option. After five seconds no one had responded. Walter knocked again, even louder. This time, a nurse opened the door. She was frowning in annoyance and her expression barely softened when she beheld Walter in full SS uniform.

"My daughter is in there," he stated. "I want to know how she is."

"She is a fighter. The surgery went well. We are monitoring her post-operative recovery, but it is not easy to say how she is doing, given that your daughter was in a coma to start with."

"Is she going to die?"

"It is too early to say. I –"

"Get me a doctor."

The nurse was about to protest, but Walter's fierce eyes and the menace in his voice made her think again. "Yes. Please wait one moment."

Hedda had moved towards the door, far less interested in Walter now than in what the medical staff had to say. Within a minute, a doctor in a white coat emerged from the recovery room, smiled and extended a hand to Walter. Walter shook his hand peremptorily and waited.

"Officer Gunther, I am Dr Schlieffen. I performed surgery on your daughter earlier today. We successfully inserted a drain to siphon off fluid from the surface of the brain and she is comfortable now. I am still unable to establish reactive signs to stimuli which would indicate consciousness, but there certainly seems to be no deterioration in Agnette's condition, compared with that which was the case before surgery. Now we just wait, I'm afraid. She is, at least, still breathing on her own."

"So. My daughter will not die today?"

The doctor seemed a little taken aback at the directness of the question. "Er, it is possible – though unlikely, I would say – that she will die in the next twelve hours. And if she survives that long, then we are back to where we were before – monitoring her in her coma state, from which she may or may not emerge in due course. We have managed to stabilize her after the surgery. Her chances of survival are better than they were directly before the surgery. I am sorry I cannot be more specific at this point." The doctor assumed a sympathetic demeanour. After all, the terseness of this formidable SS officer could be due to his rank, an assumed military persona. It was possible this was a father in agony trying to be courageous.

"Thank you, Dr Schlieffen. You have been most helpful." Walter saluted the doctor, turned on his heel and walked straight

111

past Hedda and up the corridor in the direction of the way out. If he hurried, he may get back to Tiergartenstrasse 4 without missing too much of the afternoon meeting.

As it happened, the meeting had been ten minutes in session when Walter quietly opened the boardroom door and found his way to a vacant seat at the table. Eyes turned towards him for confirmation that all was well and he answered their concern with a smile and a nod. Attention then turned back to Karl Muller's presentation. He had drawn on a flipchart a precise engineer's layout of an extermination chamber – a model of the one currently in use at Brandenburg. He was explaining in a calm, emollient tone the challenges and specifications of constructing such a chamber.

"The building is an adapted barn. The inner chamber is constructed of brick, and as you can see, a pipe runs along each wall, ten centimetres from the ground. At twenty-centimetre intervals along the pipe are small holes –" and here he paused to point at representations of three of these holes – "which allow the gas to infiltrate the room. The gas canisters are attached to the pipe by a link external to the room. Once they are attached, a simple turn of a tap releases the gas into the pipe. And –" Muller continued – "Dr Schroeder is right. The whole system is constructed on the need for efficiency and accuracy. I am sorry, Director Wirth, but if this system is to work, then it must be run by people who understand its engineering. If it goes wrong, then the result is huge inefficiency and…" here Karl stopped. He took a handkerchief from his uniform breast pocket and wiped his brow. He closed his eyes.

"Are you all right, Officer Muller?" Heydrich's tone was more impatient than concerned. This meeting was going on too long. The wine over a fine lunch had made him sleepy. He wanted to nap for an hour or so before he had to start preparing for his meeting with the Führer, who was, by all accounts, incandescent following Germany's recent defeat by Britain. He would be in no mood to tolerate imprecision or unpreparedness.

"Apologies. I am feeling unwell."

"Not the lunch, I hope?" quipped Goebbels. Muted laughter followed.

"No, no, Minister Goebbels. I have been unwell for a little while now. Forgive me. It will pass."

Walter contemplated Muller's pale complexion, noted again the tremor in his hands, the film of sweat on his brow. He could be ill, or he could be afraid.

"We also want the process to be as humane as possible, one presumes?" Eyebrows raised, Wirth hmphed and Heydrich made a slight, acquiescent gesture. "So engineering is important when operating the gas vans too. I have been present when they have broken down partway through a... process... it was children. They were not unconscious when the diesel engine ceased to function. Herr Wirth's employees were unable to get it to work within one hour of its breakdown. The children screamed and many were vomiting. Some were convulsing. You see, at certain concentrations below lethal the symptoms of CO poisoning include seizures, cardiac arrest, acute breathlessness, severe abdominal pain. They fought each other in blind panic to get out of the van. For an hour. We could clearly see this through the observation window. Many were bleeding. The fits which were induced by the CO caused them to bite their tongues – sometimes they bit them clean off. They slipped around on faeces, blood and urine; they cried aloud for their mothers. Some passed out eventually. A few probably died of cardiac failure."

The room fell completely silent. Heydrich's secretary stopped writing, looked in concern and confusion towards Heydrich and Himmler. Heydrich met her eyes and shook his head. She put down her pen.

"Is this necessary, Officer Muller?" Himmler asked, his tone evidently disapproving.

For response, Muller seemed to rally. He coughed, drew himself up straight and looked directly at Himmler. When he began to speak again his tone had acquired a clarity absent from his previous speech.

"Yes, Reichsführer Himmler. I think so. The details are unpleasant, but do illustrate the necessity to get planning right. An hour to fix an engine and such unpleasantness are counter-productive and bad for staff morale."

"I see. And who were these children – as a matter of scientific record?" asked Himmler.

Wirth interrupted again. "'Unworthies', mentally and physically handicapped from a variety of institutions in the Berlin area. They were certified disposable by Director Gunther – and in the first place, of course, by doctors – lots of doctors!" Levity was returned and the secretaries again bowed their heads, picked up their pens. "Mistakes happen. We learn from them. Even scientists make mistakes," added Wirth petulantly, but his clowning was growing tedious, his increasingly open assumptions of support insolent.

"Your report also, Officer Muller – to my secretary by tomorrow morning," concluded Heydrich. "I am particularly interested in what does work, you understand? There is little point in the relaying of failures to the Führer – particularly at this moment, as I am certain you will appreciate. This meeting, I think, is over. Thank you, gentlemen, for your invaluable work. Heil Hitler!"

The salute was returned, the delegates began to leave. Himmler made a point of shaking Walter's hand and telling him he looked forward to working with him. Walter flashed Himmler his most charming smile. Well worth the irritating crawl back from the hospital through rubble and lines of Jews stumbling pathetically towards the central station and deportation. Then, just as Walter turned to retrieve his briefing papers and leave the room, he was stopped in his tracks by Muller.

"Director Gunther, I do hope your daughter is all right?"

Walter's eyes iced over. "She is out of danger, thank you."

"I was so sorry to hear of her injuries. Please convey my sympathies to your wife."

"Of course."

CHAPTER FIVE

Dinner at the Schroeders' sumptuous residence in the Tiergarten district was promptly at seven, as always. Neither was there the remotest evidence in this household of war rationing. Early October 1940 and venison was in season. Lavish sauces, full-bodied red wines and fresh vegetables of many autumnal varieties adorned the table on this particular occasion. Hedda arrived late, as she often did. Although much had been done to clear rubble and make buildings safe following the August air raids, blackout was mandatory from five o'clock each evening. There were financial penalties imposed on anyone failing to observe it; twenty marks for Aryans, up to 220 marks or a week's imprisonment for Jews careless enough to leave a light in a window after dusk. As the wife of a high-ranking SS officer and agent of the Reich, Hedda often took liberties. Everyone was aware that Hitler's relentless reprisal bombing of London meant that soon Berlin would be bombed again. Hedda hated to leave Agnette alone in the hospital. She sat with her daughter after curfew and blackout for as long as she could, reading to her by lamplight, singing quietly or simply dozing beside her bed before she began the drive home. After a while, soldiers on guard duty recognized her and simply waved her on.

The matron on the acute and trauma ward was a harridan, and patients and nurses alike feared her steely eye and unforgiving tongue. Hedda watched this paragon of Aryan efficiency with an instinctive dislike. For her part, the matron steered clear of Hedda. She was only too well aware of the identity and seniority of Hedda's husband, and the unswerving stare with which Hedda followed her movements about the ward was unnerving, even for such a Valkyrie.

"Any news, darling?" Hedda's mother greeted her daughter in the usual way, expecting the customary dismissive shake of the head. Tonight was no exception. Mathilde was elegant in a verdigris woollen Chanel suit and cream silk blouse. She expertly spooned cauliflower florets from a hand-painted Bavarian porcelain platter onto Ernst's matching plate. "Sit down, Hedda, and eat. You look exhausted. As usual."

Hedda unbuttoned her coat and threw it casually onto a chaise longue, from which Cook discreetly lifted it and took it to be hung up in the hallway. Hedda still did not speak, ignoring her mother's jibe about her appearance. She was well aware of her lack of grooming. Her erstwhile perfectly coiffured hair was dull and had been allowed to grow long, so that it fell in natural waves upon her shoulder. Wiry, stray curls hugged her pale cheeks, and by this time in the evening, what little make-up she had desultorily applied in the morning had worn off. Her eyes were lacklustre and defined by bags. She had lost that vibrant beauty that was hers in full health. Those days seemed like another time to her now, her relative dishevelment more appropriate to the leaden weight of her heart.

Ernst folded down the right-hand corner of *Das Reich* and regarded his daughter over his reading glasses. She was aware of his scrutiny, but Hedda made no attempt to meet his eye, regarding instead her plate as Cook slid thick slices of rare venison onto it and spooned an aromatic wine sauce over the meat. She longed for her father to get up from his seat and come to her, bid her stand, then enfold her in his arms and kiss her head. She longed for him to tell her all would be fine and that he loved her. Ernst hmphed inscrutably, returned to his paper briefly, then folded it in two, placed it to his far right and, removing his glasses, placed them carefully on top of the paper. Same routine each evening. Mathilde put his now laden dinner plate in the space before her husband and eating commenced without further speech.

As Cook was clearing away the plates, Mathilde addressed Hedda once more. "Have you seen Walter today, Hedda?"

"No. I have not seen Walter for three days. And that was for ten minutes when he found the time to come and see Agnette."

"Goodness!" exclaimed Mathilde. "He must be very busy."

Hedda looked at her mother and tried to determine from her features if there was the slightest irony in her remark, for none was discernible from her tone. Mathilde met Hedda's searching and rather hostile glare with a raised eyebrow and a birdlike turn of the head.

"Too busy to bother to find out how I am? Too busy to visit his own daughter properly, or come and see his son?" Hedda was surprised at how angry she had suddenly become in spite of her earlier resolve to avoid such a display. But she was angry at everything: at her disgusting husband, whom she now loathed, at her careless parents, at the defilement of her beautiful child, and always at herself for never having taken the trouble to know and cherish Agnette when she had the chance. The idea that she had lost her daughter without having found her was intolerable to Hedda.

Ernst coughed warningly and Mathilde sighed and brushed imaginary detritus from the tablecloth. "Well, you know, Hedda, Walter is..."

"Walter is an idiot!" Hedda exploded. Cook decided to leave the room with just the dishes she was carrying. "Walter is a wife-beating, unfaithful pig!"

"Hedda!" Mathilde's voice was sharp, though there was a note in her tone that suggested shocked curiosity. "Control yourself."

"Why? Why should I? What is it you are worried about, Mutti? Good manners? My little girl is in a coma. Her head is all... battered and bruised and ripped, with stitches everywhere, and she may never wake up. She's as good as dead, for all I know!" Hedda had risen to her feet and was almost hysterical.

Ernst reached for his glasses and watched his daughter's extraordinary outburst as though witnessing a disappointing turn in an experiment.

"And when was the last time you –" at this, Hedda looked to her father, glared at him, then quickly focused again on her mother – "bothered to visit your granddaughter? When was the last time either of you really took an interest in how I am?"

"Hedda, that is not fair." Mathilde's tone was a little less indignant. "I ask you every day how you are, and…"

"You ask Cook how she is every day! If I were to tell you, do you really want to know? Do you?" Hedda placed both hands on the table and leaned in the direction of her mother. "Shall I tell you how I really am and what I'm going through?" Her challenge was met with silence. "I thought not. Because you don't care. You've never cared."

Ernst spoke at last. "It is perfectly obvious how you are feeling, Hedda. You are mentally and physically exhausted – that much is plain. You are recovering from shock. You are very upset. That much is evident from only casual observation."

Hedda sat down, regarding her father with that same level scrutiny with which she contemplated all those whom she considered a threat.

"There is little to be gained by asking you to go over it all at the end of the day. At the end of the day, people need… peace."

"Hedda…" Mathilde's voice was soothing now. Tears had begun to flow unrestrained down her daughter's face. "It is clear you are suffering, my darling. And we hate to see it. But Hedda, what can we do? You are a grown woman now – married. We… well, obviously you and Anselm are welcome to stay here for as long as you like. We do not see Agnette very often, that is true…" She looked to her husband for support. He looked at the table and shifted uncomfortably in his chair. "But honestly, darling, she does not… Well, Agnette doesn't know we are *there*. If she was… awake, Hedda, then it would be different."

Hedda realized anew the futility of an emotional appeal to these people who above all else feared their emotions. She received the reminder that they were offering her and her son practical assistance, and understood that this was as far as her parents were able to go.

"Excuse me," Hedda said at last, her tone signalling defeat. "I am very tired." And she rose from the table.

"You'll feel better after a good night's sleep, darling," enjoined Mathilde as her daughter left the dining room. When she had gone, Mathilde addressed her husband. "Ernst, do you think he hits her?"

"It wouldn't surprise me in the least."

The expanding Sachsenhausen concentration camp, near Oranienburg, in conjunction with an older, more established partner camp, was roughly thirty-five kilometres north of Berlin and fast becoming the centralized training ground for both the SS and the Gestapo. Both camps were conceived and their construction overseen by Reichsführer Himmler in 1936, and by November 1940 there were more than 10,000 inmates, overwhelmingly male, in Sachsenhausen. Walter's T4 directorate role was expanded to include the administration of Sachsenhausen. Himmler had taken a personal interest in Walter's work and thought him a very likely candidate for promotion to a commandant role in one of the large new Austrian camps under construction at that time.

High-ranking SS officers who were training for promotion, or had been drafted in to train others, were luxuriously accommodated in splendid houses with large gardens in a purpose-built complex in Oranienburg. Brandenburg on Havel prison hospital was located very near to both camps, and as Walter was spending increasing amounts of his time with Wirth, overseeing the running and proceedings at the hospital, it made perfect sense when Walter received the personally signed letter from Himmler, offering him a large four-bedroomed house on the Oranienburg "estate". In any case, Himmler added, he was aware that Walter had lost his house in the August 1940 bombing and, given that RAF air strikes against

Berlin city were becoming increasingly frequent, it seemed only right that a highly valued Aktion T4 director should be rehoused at the Reich's expense.

Hedda received the news of her relocation with indifference. She longed to leave her parents' house, where even breathing evenly at the dinner table was difficult, but she was not eager to be reunited with her husband. Especially as it seemed he was to work in Sachsenhausen prison as well as Tiergartenstrasse, so he would be at home at least half the evenings of the week.

What made the prospect of relocation more palatable, however, was that Walter had made arrangements for Agnette to be moved to a Brandenburg hospital, just eight kilometres from Oranienburg. She would be able to spend more time with Agnette and she would be able to go home more frequently between visits and see more of Anselm. They would ask Marguerite the maid to live in, and they would have a cook. Marguerite would take care of Anselm when Hedda was at the hospital.

And so, on Christmas Eve 1940, Hedda sat in a sumptuously decorated living room before a roaring fire with Anselm on her knee. She contemplated the reflections of the flames in the shiny Christmas tree baubles, while Walter, relaxed in a woollen sweater and slacks, read a paper. All seemed peaceful. The latest light bombing of Berlin, three days previously, had caused some fatalities, and there would be yet more cleaning up and rebuilding to do. But here in tranquil, architecturally stunning Brandenburg, with its woodland lakes, majestic rivers and achingly beautiful landscapes, there was no hint of destruction. The blackout still applied, but curfew was not strictly heeded. Somehow, in this hinterland of snow, ice and water, it was as if the very beauty of the place were a defence against sacrilege.

Roughly 150 kilometres south-east, of Oranienburg, Karl Muller was sipping brandy with his parents, Dr and Frau Muller. His sister, who was five years his junior, and her husband, a non-commissioned officer in the German army, home on a few days' leave, were also present. Karl's nephew was amusing the assembled company by trying on his uncle's SS cap and marching around the living room. Karl smiled, though his eyes flashed darkly over the rim of his brandy glass and his hands shook.

Only two days before, he had installed a gas pipe in a small, bitterly cold room in an institution masquerading as a hospital, and watched as several terrified and naked children were gently coaxed into it by a fraulein with blonde hair. She told them they were going to have a nice hot shower. And then Karl had nodded at Christian Wirth, Director of Operations at Brandenburg on Havel "hospital". Wirth had grinned as he turned on the tap that permitted carbon monoxide gas to travel from its container and into the pipe that Karl had finished installing just a day earlier.

The children, freezing cold, alone, afraid, had huddled together for comfort. Through the glass, Karl had watched a girl sobbing, open mouthed. She stood uncomprehendingly watching the adults at the window. How thin she was, Karl had thought, and how her little chest heaved with the effort of crying. Her eyes had widened in shock as the CO gas reached her. Almost simultaneously, the other children had started to gag. Karl had walked away in as controlled a fashion as he could and sought fresh air, fighting all the while the compulsion to vomit. By the time he had found an outside door and a wall against which to lean, the children were dead.

Dr Schroeder was right. He had calculated beforehand that it would take no more than two minutes of constant high pressure CO piping to poison the air sufficiently to cause the children's deaths in a three by five metre room. Dr Schroeder had been unable, though, to attend the application of his theoretical work, and had left the observation and recording to two medical doctors, Heinze and Gutt, who would be taking responsibility for the Office for the Euthanizing of Children.

"Hey, that's my cap." Karl's sister frowned as her brother suddenly leaned forward and swiped the SS cap from his nephew's head. "Sorry," he muttered. "Long day. Excuse me." Karl left the living room and climbed the stairs to his bedroom; the bedroom where he had prayed each night as a child, before getting into bed, that God would keep his parents and his sister safe from harm. His father was a general practitioner who had cared for the health and well-being of local people since he qualified as a doctor thirty-five years previously. He had been so happy when Karl began his medical studies. How would he feel if he knew his son was occupied daily with ways to kill people efficiently?

On the wall opposite Karl's bed was a picture of the Sacred Heart: Christ with outstretched arms, an expression of infinite compassion on his face. Karl fell to his knees and could not stifle an agonized cry. Frau Muller rose at once from her armchair to go to her son. Her husband stopped her, placing a gentle hand upon her arm.

"He spent most of the day with Greta, remember. It cannot be easy. Leave him."

About a month previously, Karl's wife Greta had become more depressed than she had ever been. She was unable to get out of bed, to dress or even eat unaided. She did not want to eat. She wanted to die. And then she had tried to commit suicide by stabbing her wrists with scissors. The attempt was genuine enough but the scissors too blunt. She wounded herself horribly and made a terrible mess of her parents' bathroom.

Desperate and exhausted, Greta's parents had acceded to pressure from their doctor to admit Greta to a local psychiatric institution. Karl had been unable to get home, for Himmler wanted him to design and oversee the construction of a crematorium at Sachsenhausen. The job needed to be done by Christmas, Himmler had said. In fact, it was completed by mid-December. Plenty of time, then, to convert an old bathroom at Brandenburg hospital into a gas chamber too. Efficiency. Key to the war effort. It was, of course, possible, even likely, that Himmler would have granted him leave for a day or two, had he been aware that Karl's severely depressive wife had been committed to an insane asylum. But Karl didn't want to tell him. He was only too aware of how dangerous it had become to be mentally ill in Germany. It was perfectly reasonable to gas children with polio or genetic disorders, but it was certainly not acceptable to be depressed about it – or anything else, for that matter.

As soon as he was able to get home to Leipzig, on the 23rd December, he had gone directly to the asylum. He had found Greta sitting comfortably enough in a chair on a women's ward. Her wrists were still lightly bandaged beneath her cardigan sleeves. She looked clean, her hair pinned back and her face shiny, but her eyes were so dull. She did not recognize him for a full six minutes, during which time he reverently kissed her hands, stroked her hair and did not try to prevent himself from crying. He repeated her name several times and told her he loved her. Greta had continued to regard him blankly, until suddenly she had spoken.

"Karl?" Her voice was indistinct, as though she had named him in sleep. "Is it you, Karl?"

Overjoyed, he had smiled, nodded his head vigorously, wiped away tears. She had smiled back; a thin, watery smile for which she barely seemed to have the energy.

"Greta, Greta, it is Christmas! I have come home for Christmas, Greta."

Then her smile died, as if she had forgotten him again.

"Do you want to come home?"

She turned her head away. "Sleep," she said. "I just want to sleep." And Greta had closed her eyes. Karl simply sat before her, holding her hand.

The ward was a large, pale green room with a white, high ceiling. The asylum had been built hundreds of years before and constructed on a revolutionary colony model, comprised of several purpose built chalet-type buildings. On the site were also a church, a library and several treatment rooms, a small bakery and a railway station. As far as Karl could tell, Greta had been placed on a ward with female patients whose conditions were non-violent and dysphoric.

Two women, drably dressed and wearing slippers, stood at separate bay windows and contemplated the snow. One rocked gently backwards and forwards; the other stood stock still, arms folded, as though waiting for someone. Three more patients dozed in armchairs, one occasionally opening her eyes to brush imaginary things from her lap and address someone she saw only in dreams of life. Another, the seventh woman on the ward, was little more than a girl. Seventeen? Eighteen? Karl guessed. Certainly she was not older than twenty. She stood in the middle of the ward, one arm gripping her midriff, chewing the fingernails of the other hand. When Karl smiled at her she frowned and began to mutter something. Her dark eyes narrowed and her expression became hostile. She looked foreign, like a gypsy – Romanian perhaps. Karl looked away. God knew she had every reason to fear him; to fear what his uniform signalled to one such as she. Perhaps she had already suffered at SS hands. Perhaps that was why she was in an asylum.

"I want to take my wife home." Karl had been strident in the expression of his wishes to the young nurse in charge.

"I fully understand, Officer Muller, but Greta is very unwell." The nurse looked genuinely sympathetic. "She is... well, she is still on suicide watch and we are trialling some new medication. She really needs to be in the care of her doctor."

"What new medication?" Karl was suspicious of all medical administrative decisions since his assignment to T4. No doctor practising in Hitler's Reich could be trusted. Karl knew all about the processes by which medics were now required to classify people. If a doctor stamped a patient file with a green "minus" sign, the patient was fit to live. A blue "plus" sign was a death sentence. And Karl designed the gas chambers and crematoria that disposed of the countless thousands of "unworthies" who were bussed and brought by rail like freighted cattle, from psychiatric institutions and general hospitals all over Germany, to be gassed at Hartheim, Sonnenstein and Brandenburg.

"I can't discuss her treatment with you, Officer Muller. I am very sorry."

Karl was more incredulous by the second. "Are you saying Greta must stay... in here... for Christmas?"

"I really am very sorry, Officer Muller, sir. There is nothing I can do. If you had come a few hours earlier, perhaps..."

"What?"

"Well, Dr Kaufman left for the holiday this morning. He has finished for Christmas..."

"And there is no doctor on duty over Christmas?"

The nurse looked distraught. Karl realized he had become increasingly irate. He remembered again how intimidating his SS uniform was. He had no desire to bully this woman who was little more than a girl. He just wanted to hold his wife.

"But I shall be able to see her every day over Christmas, yes?"

"Of course." The nurse was visibly relieved. She was close to tears.

"And can I take her out?"

She did not answer, looked towards the bay windows, as though longing to escape.

"It doesn't matter. I shall speak to your superior."

The nurse looked back quickly, her eyes pleading.

"No... no. You misunderstand." He sounded normal now, even soothing. "I will discuss my wife's treatment with a senior staff member or a doctor when I can."

Just before he left the ward, Karl looked again at Greta. She was fast asleep in her chair, head leaning to the left, resting on an upholstered wing. The gypsy girl had crept forward and was staring at him, arms folded, humming something softly. When he met her intense, dark eyes, she nervously lifted a hand, pushed one curtain of thick hair behind an ear, did not break her gaze. He registered her beauty, undisguised by even the drab hospital dress and shapeless cardigan, thick brown tights and worn slippers. His eyes softened. She lowered her eyes from his only to spit on the floor, then lifted them to his again.

The nurse exclaimed loudly, "Nikola!"

"You are the devil! You are the devil!" The gypsy girl's eyes were wide with terror – or hatred, it was hard to tell – and she advanced slowly, then changed her mind and started to walk backwards, pointing all the time at Karl and never taking her eyes off him.

"Nikola!" cried the nurse again. "You stop that! I am so sorry, Officer Muller. Nikola!"

Karl seemed to consider for a moment, then put on his cap, made a dismissive gesture and left the ward.

On Christmas Day morning, around eight o'clock, having left his car on a main road that had been cleared for traffic, Karl trudged through thick snow towards the little house in Riebeck Strasse, Leipzig city, where Greta had grown up and where her parents still lived. Even as he knocked vigorously on the front door, he was aware of the earliness of the hour, the significance of the day. But he was desperate, and he knew they would agree that nothing could be of greater importance than Greta's welfare.

In the midst of Karl's third volley of sharp raps at her door, Clara Erlach appeared and poked her head around it timidly, clutching the front of her woollen dressing gown, a long grey plait snaking lazily over one shoulder and hanging to her waist.

"Karl! Karl, come in! Hans, it is Karl!" she shouted up the stairs to her husband. Clara was clearly delighted to see her son-in-law and ushered him indoors, took his face in her hands and kissed him hard on both cheeks. "Happy Christmas, Karl. How wonderful to see you! Have you seen Greta?"

"Yes, Clara, I have seen Greta. It is why I am here."

"What has happened? Is Greta all right? We only saw her yesterday morning. Has something happened?"

"No... yes. I'll explain. Where is Hans? Is he coming?"

"Hans? Hans, where are you? Karl is here." Clara was impatient now for her husband to come, and fearful for her daughter. While they waited, she put a match to prepared kindling and newspaper in the kitchen stove. "He was never good in the mornings," she confided to Karl as she shut the door on the sleepy flames. She bustled about, automatically reaching for plates from a shelf in a large dresser, locating bread and cheese, placing both on the table. "And now his angina is worse, since Greta... you know."

Finally, Hans appeared, tousled and dressed, still fighting with one of his braces. "Karl, dear boy. It is good to see you. But it is also so early!"

"I'm sorry, Hans. But I wanted to get to you as quickly as possible."

Clara sat down, put her hands between her knees and stared at Karl, an anxious frown on her face. Hans pulled out a chair from beneath the table; sat down also.

"I saw Greta yesterday," began Karl. "You know, it was a bit of a shock." Karl looked directly into Clara's eyes, imploring her to understand there was no accusation in his words. She nodded. Her eyes filled with tears. "I am so sorry I have not been here. I wish with all my heart I..."

All night he had slept only fitfully, waking violently from terrible dreams. Clara saw his exhaustion and distress, and leaning forward took Karl's hands in hers. "No, no, Karl, please... We know you can't get away. We have to read your letters to Greta sometimes... she can't open the envelopes... She always smiles when we read them. We know how things are, Karl. You are a good husband."

Karl, his hands still in Clara's, lowered his head and cried quietly.

"Wait, dear Karl – wait a minute." Clara let go of his hands and went in search of a handkerchief. She kept several large cotton ones pressed and folded in a linen drawer at the bottom of a kitchen cupboard.

Hans sat dejectedly, head also lowered, hands between his thighs and clasped as though in prayer – or embarrassment. When Karl had wiped his eyes and blown his nose, Clara spoke again.

"We know how much you love Greta, Karl. We love her too. She is our little girl. But after that awful day when we found her... in the bathroom... Oh Karl, I thought my baby was dead!" It was

Clara's turn to cry. But she recovered, took several deep breaths. "After that, the doctor said Greta needed proper treatment, in a hospital. He said that we could not possibly provide the care she needed at home. What if she had succeeded? What if my child had taken her own life while we were here – in the garden or making dinner – and she... How could we live with ourselves?"

Karl nodded. "I know, Clara. I know."

"The doctor said Greta's drugs were not working. That they would have to try her on other, stronger, drugs, and that needed close medical observation." Clara's voice was pleading, as if she were convincing herself that she had done the right thing in letting them take her daughter to an asylum. Karl knew what it was to appease one's own conscience, but these people, he was quite certain, had nothing with which to reproach themselves.

"We had no choice." Hans spoke for the first time. His words were a verdict. No one spoke for some time.

Eventually, Karl was able to begin vocalizing the horror that had brought him to their door at eight o'clock on Christmas morning.

"Please listen carefully." He looked first at Hans, then at Clara. "It is very important that you don't ask me too many questions and that you trust me, OK?"

Clara nodded, but Hans was immediately on his guard. All this emotion so early – on Christmas Day. His angina was already playing up. He was very tired. He was worried about Clara. If he became ill, with Greta still so unwell and locked up in that place, what would become of her? Karl was a good man, but he was also an SS officer. Hans had little time for the SS. They frightened him. Two of his good friends, Jews – men he had grown up with and with whom he used to go bowling every week – had been suddenly taken away. Gestapo officers just knocked on their doors in the middle of the night and made them and their families get dressed and put coats on. They had taken them somewhere. That was weeks ago.

"What is this about, Karl? It is Christmas Day, my boy."

"You have to bring her home."

"What?" Hans was suddenly angry. Had this young man listened to anything they had said?

"Please! What do you know about this Dr Kaufman, at the asylum?" Karl's voice was resuming its authoritative tone, though he spoke quietly.

"Well..." Clara spoke again. "He seems charming enough. He treats Greta well, we think. Why, Karl?"

"There are only seven women patients on Greta's ward. Was that the case when you... when she first went in?"

Hans looked confused, then frowned in irritation.

"Please, try and remember."

"What is this about? What is the matter?" Hans demanded.

"Please, Hans," Karl implored, "just answer the question. Please."

Hans shrugged, spoke again. "There were more like... sixteen. Perhaps a few more. Why?"

"And that was a month ago, more or less, right?"

"You are frightening us, Karl," interjected Clara. "What are you saying? People get better... people... die. Sometimes they get moved, to other wards, other hospitals. It is Christmas. People go home."

"Moved? Do you know this or are you just guessing?" Karl was trying hard to hide his great anxiety, but he was aware of how alarmist he sounded, and his heart began to pound as he realized how close he was to showing these people a landscape of debauchery, where the greatest profanity the heart of man could invent had been legitimized; where the grotesque and obscene had been issued with passports to the waking hours of children.

"I heard some nurses talking one time, arranging for some ladies to go to another place, another hospital." Clara's tone was that of someone trying hard to listen again to a long past conversation. Her eyes focused on a point to her left as she conjured the moment when the matron had instructed a young nurse with a clipboard to write down names as she called them out. She had interspersed the roll call with barely audible statements and directions accentuated by gestures, at which the younger member of staff had nodded and made notes. The names of three ladies, Clara recalled, were confirmed out loud by the nurse. The matron had nodded. Then another three. More nodding. Clara had been unable to make out anything distinctly, but she had heard, clearly enough, the word "relocation", and something about a train. She thought she had understood Dresden as a destination, but it was more of an impression than a memory. She looked again into Karl's eyes. "No, I don't know where they went for sure. I think Dresden, but I couldn't say definitely."

"Dresden?" Karl was feeling nauseous. "Can you think why they would move six such women to Dresden?"

Clara shook her head. "Better facilities? Treatment? What? I don't know!"

"Enough! That's enough." Hans was tired and his angina was threatening. SS officer or not, Karl Muller had no right to come into his home on Christmas Day morning and frighten his wife like this. "Say what it is you are trying to say, Karl, for pity's sake. What has all this got to do with Greta?"

"We must get her out of there. Whatever it takes. I will see the doctor straight after Christmas. If you cannot look after Greta here, then she must go to my parents' home."

"Greta is our daughter!" Hans rose to his feet and glowered at his son-in-law.

Karl also rose, and assumed his best SS tone. "She is my wife. I am sorry, Hans, but Greta's safety and well-being are the most important things. I only want to make sure she is... safe. Of course, if you and Clara can look after her, she must come here. If not, she must go to my parents' home in Taucha."

"Why can't she stay in the hospital until she is better? Tell us!" Hans took a few steps towards Karl. Clara had reverted to simply staring wide-eyed at her son-in-law.

"I cannot tell you. I told you not to ask too many questions. She must come home, that is all. If she comes here, I will give you money every month to get extra help – a private nurse. Not one from Leipzig hospital – somewhere else. We'll get her a private physician. Finish with Kaufman. Tell them we want a second opinion. That is our right."

Hans suddenly looked exhausted. "I don't understand anything. So many secrets all of a sudden." He moved behind Clara's chair, leaned on the back of it. She turned to look into her husband's face, putting a hand briefly over one of his. Karl continued.

"I am sorry for... all this. I only want what is best for Greta. You know that." He was not wearing his SS uniform today. In civilian clothes, he was far more like the handsome, well-mannered young man their daughter had brought home from university and later married. But there was a tone to his voice and an intolerance marking his demeanour that were not endearing. Uniformed or not, Obersturmführer Karl Muller, SS, stood before them, and both now wanted him to leave.

"We understand, Karl. We shall look after Greta here. Make whatever arrangements you wish," Hans said calmly.

Karl regarded his wife's parents: Clara, small and frightened in her dressing gown, twisted in her chair to allow her to grip her husband's left hand with both of hers. Hans leaning protectively over her. The tableau they created was one of unity, love, defiance against all that would threaten them. How he envied them.

"I must go." Karl's heart was heavy indeed as he uttered the words. The sense of foreboding he felt, the welling grief at the impression of loss, was another spectre slipping from his nightmares and under his skin. "I shall be in touch, as soon as I know anything definite – about arrangements. Happy Christmas."

Hans looked at him then with an expression clearly intended to convey his incredulity that Karl had just uttered such a wish. The greeting was not returned.

Trudging the streets of an almost deserted city, back to where he had parked his car, Karl looked to the few who passed him, unremarkable: a tall young man in a heavy coat, scarf and gloves, making his way on Christmas morning to an early church service, perhaps, or to some family gathering where he would greet loved ones and assist with the Christmas preparations. Perhaps he was a soldier or officer home on leave, off to see his sweetheart; or a husband and father who had popped out to get something before he ensconced himself in the bosom of his family for Christmas Day. None could guess that Karl was a senior SS officer on the brink of treachery to the Third Reich; desperate beyond the ability of language to convey, to prevent the removal of his wife to Sonnenstein hospital near Dresden, where she would certainly be gassed to death – very possibly in a room he had converted for the purpose.

When Karl arrived once more at his parents' house on that Christmas Day it was about half past ten. His mother was smartly dressed and wearing an apron. She was checking on the progress of the roasting goose when he let himself in.

"You left very early this morning," she said, closing the oven door, standing up to remove her apron and turning to him with a smile. His countenance shocked her. "What is the matter, darling?"

Karl sighed and slumped into the nearest chair. He didn't know what to say. "I have been to see Clara and Hans." There was a long silence as Ellie considered the full implications of this statement. She felt enormous compassion and concern for her son, but she also knew that he would not welcome an open demonstration of maternal solicitation.

"I hardly know what to say, Karl. I am desperately sad for both of you. We go and see her, your father and I, whenever we can. I wish I knew what to do, my darling."

"There is nothing you can do, Mother. I don't know what to do myself."

"How are Clara and Hans? It must be very hard for them. Especially today."

Karl nodded, leaned back in his chair and closed his eyes. His mother crossed the kitchen and stroked his hair for a moment. She contemplated his face, unshaven, pale. She hardly knew him these days. "Why don't you have a rest, Karl? You were up so early. You haven't really... rested since you arrived yesterday. Your father and I are going to Mass." This last statement was said very quickly, and with a degree of awkwardness.

Karl opened his eyes and looked at his mother. "And you don't expect me to come? I have gone with you to Christmas Mass every year – all my life."

Ellie looked uncomfortable, bustling around the kitchen checking things, pointing at bowls and dishes; saucepans containing vegetables and potatoes, sauces and desserts in various stages of preparedness, as if conducting a symphony.

"Where is your father? We shall be late."

"I'm here, I'm here," came a reply from the hallway. "Ready?"

The impression of loneliness that had been dogging Karl increasingly became near panic. Never – not ever – would his father waive the expectation that anyone in his house on Christmas Day should attend Mass. Indeed, until he had left home for university, Karl had been expected to attend Mass every Sunday.

"Don't you want me to come to Mass?"

"I, er... I didn't think you'd want to come, son." His father's voice was sombre.

"Why not?" Karl persisted, though his heart began to beat a warning tattoo in his chest.

His parents exchanged glances. "All right. Well, time is short. We are supposed to be there by..."

"I know what time it starts." Karl shouted his interruption. Growing panic made him vicious. Everything comforting and secure seemed to be spinning away from him.

His father matched his anger in his reply. Such a voice and tone still had the power to instil fear in Karl's heart. "In the last year, Karl, much has changed in this country. You have changed a good deal too, son. This so-called 'government' is not a friend to the Catholic church!"

Erich Muller stood before his son and confronted him

unapologetically. Karl returned his father's glare and braced himself. He could say nothing. The authority of the Reich was a poor rival for the natural, God-given mandate this man had to speak law into his life.

Eventually, Karl responded quietly, "And so I am not a friend of the church?"

Erich closed his eyes, took a deep breath and adopted a more measured tone. "You are and always will be my son. And I love you. But you are also an SS officer of senior rank in Hitler's Reich. I do not love that."

"Erich..." Ellie's voice was fearful, pleading. "Please, Erich. Not now." Both men ignored her.

"I see." Karl could not defend himself. It was like being sixteen again and being punished for some trangression of which his father was suspicious but for which he had no hard evidence. Only this time Karl would not be lying about having stolen a neighbour's motorbike to joyride around Leipzig and finally creep home much too late. How much did his father know about Hitler's Reich and Karl's part in it?

"I am possibly about to be imprudent, Karl, but I'll take the risk. The boy I raised would respect my right to freedom of speech, to a political opinion and to worship my God."

"Of course." Karl watched his father's jaw clench and unclench, heard the slight tremor in his voice when he started speaking again.

"You know, Karl... we know what is happening in Poland. We know and we are ashamed and sick to our stomachs. Polish Catholics – hundreds of priests – are being systematically brutalized and murdered by Germans – by Germans! By men who call themselves Christians! We have heard such stories..."

Ellie was sobbing quietly. She had put on her coat and buttoned it, pulled on her gloves and found her handbag. Now she sat down, put her handbag on her knee and clutched it with both hands, tears running freely down her face.

"The SS, they pull off the fingernails of priests who object to the way their parishioners are treated. They strip them naked and flog them to death in public. They are shooting and burning people. They even crucified a priest last week – strung him up naked on a pole and left him to hang for two days. Did you know all this?"

"No." Karl's answer was truthful. But he was not remotely shocked.

"Well..." Erich was red-faced, his eyes moist. Karl had never seen his father weep. He was not ready to witness such a thing, even now. "Well... well, I am glad of it. I am surprised you don't know, but I am glad."

Karl said nothing, resorting to his teenage ploy of remaining silent under interrogation.

"Our bishop, Bishop Bertram – and the Bishop of Berlin, Cardinal von Preysing – they are outspoken. I am surprised you have not heard what they have been saying against your masters."

Karl visibly darkened at the accusation of allegiance to the Reich. He sat up straight and looked angrily into his father's eyes as if he would refute it, but said nothing.

Erich seemed almost pleased that his son had bridled at the taunt. "Cardinal von Preysing has circulated to all Catholic churches in Berlin and Saxony, with Bertram's help, a copy of a sermon he delivered recently, denouncing the barbarity against Jews and Catholics in Poland – and here, for that matter – right under our noses. We are not stupid! Do you think we suppose the Jews, our friends and neighbours, are all going on holiday? Leaving behind their cars and their furniture? We know what is happening. If *we* know, how can you not know, my son? Can you look me in the eye and say you do not know?"

Silence, except for his mother's crying and the indifferent tick of the kitchen wall clock. Karl closed his eyes and looked down. He had assisted the murders of countless people in the last twelve months. He was as guilty as any of the SS officers indulging brutality against Polish Catholics, Jews, gypsies. As his father's voice finally cracked so that he could no longer speak, Karl felt the blackness finally eclipse him. Further speech was useless.

When Erich collected himself and spoke once more, it was quietly and with considerable bitterness. "I do not for a moment suppose that you should be seen in a church where the Christmas Day homily will centre on all those who today are freezing to death – or worse – in Polish camps. It might not be... politic." Then he added more gently, "I am sorry, my son. Truly very sorry. I know life is not easy for you at the moment." Erich signalled to his wife to join him and he put an arm around her. She rose and leaned on his shoulder and they walked out of the kitchen and down the hall, slowly, as though to a funeral.

It snowed relentlessly. The drive from Leipzig to Berlin took almost seven hours. Karl ran out of petrol once and had to refuel from a can he carried in the boot, his fingers raw and shaking with cold as he tried to direct the flow of fuel into the tank, straining to see through a blizzard of snow. Exhausted and harrowed by the total alienation from his entire family in just one day, Karl finally walked into his Berlin apartment on Potsdamer. He knew it would be foolhardy to maintain contact with his parents now. He endangered them. They endangered him. And his guilt before the humanity and honour of his father was intolerable. If Erich Muller had the slightest inkling of T4 and its domestic euthanasia policy; if he knew that his son worked for Office IV of the Reich Committee and attended secret meetings to present plans for "hygiene" initiatives designed to clear Germany of its imperfect children and mental patients...

But he could not know. The people of Germany did not know that thousands of their handicapped, mentally ill and "genetically impure" children and adults were being systematically poisoned, lethally injected and starved to death every day. Until he had been offered his present post, Karl had not known either.

Berlin, 1940, Christmas Day. Karl did not turn on the light in his apartment nor attempt to heat it. He slumped into the nearest chair and allowed despair to engulf him. Christ, it seemed to him, would not be reborn in Germany this year.

CHAPTER SIX

The top secret meeting at ten-thirty a.m. at 8 Voss Strasse on the 4th January 1941 to discuss the child euthanasia programme and its future was as disturbing and surreal as Karl had known it would be. Present were Drs Brandt, Gutt and Heinze, all key Aktion T4 medical directors with special responsibilities for child euthanasia. Also present were Ernst Schroeder and several logistics and administrative staff members and, of course, the secretaries to take minutes. Nobody's real name would be mentioned in the minutes; everyone had a code name.

The meeting was brief, its purpose to inform the assembled personnel that gassing of small children was to cease and alternative drug-centred methods of dispatch were to be refined and made more effective. It seemed even SS officers and T4 nurses were too much affected by the process of carrying babies and toddlers into gas vans or watching them choke to death in carbon monoxide chambers. There was too high a risk of public exposure from dissenting staff going sick or simply confiding in people they knew.

Starvation was effective in dispatching infants, but it was a drawn-out process, and their crying, as well as the attendant physical ailments which caused them pain and suffering, upset staff unnecessarily. Also, it was hard to starve to death many children at a time while keeping them on wards that could be accessed by non-T4 personnel. Older children were less compliant in taking drugs which made them sick and more difficult to "nurse" on adapted wards. And so the agenda for the Voss Strasse meeting was confined to two main items: what drug or drugs the doctors had decided to use to kill children discreetly and how these drugs would be delivered, stored and administered.

Chief Medical Director of T4 and Hitler's personal physician, Karl Brandt, founder of the code-named Committee for the Scientific Treatment of Severe, Genetically Determined Illness, presided over the meeting. He began by reminding everyone of Hitler's own mandate to them, written in September 1939, that physicians were to be given increasing discretion to determine the fitness for life of their patients, and should be allowed to select those whom they considered suitable candidates for "mercy deaths". He asked if those present were aware that Aristotle himself had said, "Let there be a law that no deformed child shall live," just in case anyone present was the least bit concerned about the civility of this, their solemn duty to ensure the eugenic purity of the German nation. The excising of impurity and disease from society was as much a physician's duty as the excising of diseased or malfunctioning tissue from a body to preserve its life; there was no conflict between the T4 programme's ideals and the physician's Hippocratic Oath, declared Brandt. Incidentally, he had added, medical students would no longer be required to take the Hippocratic Oath. It was simpler that way to ensure compliance by medics with Reich policy.

Having re-established the legitimacy of the process, he asked Drs Gutt and Heinze to present to him their suggestions for the medical expansion of the Reich Committee's work in Berlin particularly, as it was to Brandenburg that most infant designates for mercy killing were being transported at present. He had visited the newly opened and especially equipped Gorden ward at the Brandenburg hospital and congratulated the doctors on their expertise and the efficiency with which the facility was run.

Karl contemplated these three eminent physicians with their expensive suits, their slicked hair and, in two cases, their glasses. They looked and sounded for all the world like normal doctors discussing medical procedures and logistical challenges in a normal hospital. They all had families.

He rather suspected that Dr Kaufman, Greta's psychiatrist, was very much of the opinions shared here, and he quite believed that from now on the esteemed Dr Kaufman would be taking a special interest in Greta's case. For, just the day before, Karl had taken a train to Leipzig and he had, with as much SS authority as he could muster, explained to Dr Kaufman that he was taking Greta home.

"And so, gentlemen, to today's business. Let us be brief, for I am lunching with the Führer in a fine eating establishment today, and I shall not be picking up the bill." Brandt smiled a charming smile. "Dr Gutt, I understand you favour barbiturate use in the elimination of infants. Is that correct?"

"It is, Director. The advantages are significant over other methods, in that increased doses over two to three days induce fatal pulmonary congestion, which is recordable as natural death. Luminal and Veronal are most effective, based on trials, and as they are widely used throughout the country for the treatment of a broad spectrum of disease, suspicion need not be aroused by the ordering and delivery of relatively large amounts of either drug. Discretion, of course, being of the utmost importance." Gutt finished speaking, removed his glasses as he did so and looked frankly at Brandt.

"Quite, quite," Brandt agreed, "and presumably, Herr Schroeder, there is little difficulty in accommodating demand?"

"None whatsoever, Director Brandt." Ernst was animated once more. Karl thought him a most enigmatic little chap. He sat almost mannequin-like for much of the time, straight-backed and serious until addressed, and then it was as if he came to life. "These are drugs isolated and developed in the first instance by German chemists at Bayer. Their production is now a staple business of IG Farben and most cost effective."

"Excellent." Brandt appeared delighted at how smoothly everything was proceeding. He would be full of praise for the positivity and efficiency of the T4 staff when he met the Führer for lunch later. This was, after all, a reflection on Brandt's own organizational skills.

"Are we dismissing the morphine-scopolamine option, then?"

Dr Kaufman had been too well bred and was too wary of assertive SS officers to show openly his disagreement with anything they might say. But he had seemed genuinely affected by Karl's suggestion that Greta should be removed from his care.

"But why, if I may ask, Officer Muller, are you taking her from the security and specialist care we can provide here? How will you ensure she does not relapse or deteriorate? Your wife is still a suicide risk, you know."

Karl had contemplated Greta sleeping open-mouthed in her armchair. He had been unable to rouse her. "I don't think Greta will kill herself, Dr Kaufman."

"How can you be sure? How will you monitor her medication?"

"What medication are you giving her? She seems almost comatose."

"Hardly." Kaufman frowned in irritation, then smiled at Karl just as quickly. "She is sedated. And she doesn't sleep so well at night. It is normal she should be tired."

"When I was here last week, she could talk. She recognized me."

"What are you saying, Officer Muller? That Greta is being progressively drugged?" Kaufman's tone was more assured as Karl seemed less confident.

"I don't know." Karl decided to challenge this psychiatrist who was so unwilling to release his wife into his care. He allowed his eyes to show some of the mounting hostility he was trying to stem, and he held Kaufman's gaze just a little longer than politeness allowed.

"I assure you, Officer Muller, Greta is being well cared for. I am most reluctant to hand over my patient to you without knowing how her medical and care regime will be monitored. You can understand that?"

Karl looked for the gypsy girl who had been so vociferous and fully ambulant on the occasion of his last visit. His eyes scanned the room and found her eventually. She was curled up on her side in a large armchair near a window. Her face was buried in the crook of one arm. Her other arm hung loosely from her shoulder towards the floor; its attitude of limpness was such that she could not be conscious. No one stood or walked.

"I am taking her home," he had pronounced with finality when he turned back to Kaufman. Get me her notes, if you please. And her coat. It is cold outside."

"Obersturmführer Muller, are you quite well?" Brandt was looking directly at Karl, an expression of quizzical concern on his face.

"Forgive me, Director." Karl coughed and straightened himself in his seat. "The excesses of the season – still recovering." There was good-natured laughter.

"Indeed! They must have been most absorbing. I am sorry to tax you with work, but I would value your opinion on the logistical side of all this. We are going to need your expertise to coordinate delivery of the suppositories and also the Luminal. You will need to create new storage facilities and it will be your job to distribute the supplies to the various wards and liaise with T4 staff regarding their administration and further orders. We shall be relying on you to make us effective, Officer Muller. Do you think you will soon be operational again?" More good-natured laughter.

Karl smiled and nodded. "Of course. Forgive me, Director. I already have ideas for storage and distribution. We have an idle warehouse on Lutzow Ufer – number three – and also a couple of spare offices on floor two, following IV Office's transfer to Voss Strasse. Some dedicated admin staff can work from there – receive consignments, etc. PO Box, er – " here Karl consulted his papers – "PO Box 120, Lutzow Ufer will be the correspondence address."

Karl looked briefly at Ernst Schroeder, who nodded peremptorily and wrote it down. "We have two trucks already, in the warehouse, awaiting conversion to gas-mobiles. If you think the drug distribution is a priority, we can recommission these trucks immediately. It is not a problem."

"Excellent. Then I shall leave you, gentlemen. I am quite certain that the remaining details can be addressed without me. Good work and Heil Hitler!" And the handsome Dr Brandt gathered his papers, placed them in his elegant calfskin briefcase, smoothed his tie and rose from his chair before shaking Gutt's and Heinze's hands and leaving.

When he had gone, Heinze seemed to carry on from something he had been saying while Karl had been inattentive. "Neurologically, scopolamine in overdose is highly anticholinergic, depressing the central nervous system – lethal to an adult at 0.6 milligrams and at 0.3 causing extreme drowsiness and tachycardia. The combination with morphine makes the administration most humane and effective. The analgesic properties of morphine reduce pain caused by tachycardia while in overdose, inducing infarction, so speeding up death. It is more costly initially, but death is practically instantaneous – useful for older children and those more resistant to barbiturate poisoning. And of course, there will be a considerable saving in the mid to long term, as maintenance costs are eliminated."

"Quite so. Production problems, Herr Schroeder?" Gutt seemed to have assumed Brandt's role as chair.

Ernst just shook his head slowly and emphatically, closed his eyes and pursed his lips as a way of conveying just how problem-free the manufacture of scopolamine-morphine suppositories in 0.6 milligram doses could be.

"Splendid," concluded Gutt. "Dr Heinze and I shall estimate the required consignments of both drug types and get an order to Officer Muller by the end of tomorrow. Obersturmführer Muller, you then will liaise with Herr Schroeder to get them delivered, stored, distributed. A most useful meeting, gentlemen. Heil Hitler."

CHAPTER SIX

* * *

Karl practically had to carry Greta to the waiting taxi from the Leipzig asylum. Unable to get her coat on, even with a nurse's help, he put it around her shoulders and secured it as best he could. Then he heaved her to her feet and half dragged her to the car. She was not heavy. It was the first time he had held his wife in his arms in months. She smelled of chemicals and cheap soap, and he could feel her ribs quite clearly, even through her coat. Once in the back seat of the taxi, Greta slumped forward, her head lolling heavily, so that Karl had to prop her up against the back of the seat and gently lift her head by placing his hand beneath her chin. Her eyes flickered, and he glimpsed their whites, but she could not open them. *That swine, Kaufman! What has he been giving her?* he thought to himself, fighting tears of rage and love. Out loud he said tenderly, "Soon have you home, my darling. Soon have you home." And he sat close beside her in the back seat, pulling her head onto his shoulder and stroking her hair.

When they arrived at the Erlachs' house, Hans came out in his slippers, trying not to fall over on the icy garden path. Karl asked the taxi driver to wait once more, then lifted his wife out of the back seat and carried her into the warm house. He lay Greta on a sofa, and Clara, talking to her daughter and crying the whole time, removed her coat and covered her with a blanket.

"I do not know why she is so drowsy," Karl announced with difficulty to his anxious parents-in-law, "but you must find another physician as soon as you can. Kaufman will not release her notes to me. He will have to give them to another doctor – another psychiatrist perhaps. You must keep her hydrated – that's very important."

Karl could not go on. He bent and kissed his wife tenderly, took a large amount of money from an inside jacket pocket, and handed it to Hans. Then he wrote a blank cheque and made it payable to his father-in-law; gave him that also. Finally, he said simply, "Look after her. I'll come when I can," and he had left.

Ever since, Karl had been in a state of near reverie; a weird semi-aware state in which he was no longer sure what was real and what was not. With effort, he could rouse himself to full consciousness in order to function, but he was increasingly reluctant to do so. Somewhere deep within him, a small voice was warning him to wake up.

Walter was bored. By the end of January 1941 Germany was again bullish in her fighting confidence. German troops had been mobilized for Italy, to bolster Mussolini's flagging effort, and legions of Spanish soldiers, tokens of Franco's alliance with Hitler's National Socialist ideals, were arriving in Germany for training. They were going to be deployed in the planned offensive against Russia.

How Walter would have loved to be assigned a fighting commission! But it was so difficult to know how to play the political game. If he wrote to Goering asking for such an assignment, his actions could be seen as disobedience to the Reich Office. There was no shortage of military SS and commissioned army officers. Fewer on the ground were senior SS men with the right credentials for advancing the ideological war front of pan-European hegemony. How sick he was of hearing T4 officials and Reich officers expound the virtues and equal value of T4 in the accomplishment of the Führer's grand design for Aryan dominance. While Walter had no argument against such lofty ideological aims, he was positively vicious when he contemplated how ignoble it was for the son of generations of warriors to be reduced to gassing cripples. He wanted to serve under Rommel, be a hero. The desire was an obsession; the frustration of it a cause of savagery.

Walter felt love for no one. He was permanently angry, resentful or disgusted. If he allowed any softer sentiment to colour his thoughts it was self-pity. As for Hedda, he loathed her. Loathed her tired, permanently sad, mooning face; loathed the insolent reproach of her sidelong glances as he passed her in rooms they couldn't bear to share. He no longer dined with her, preferring to eat in his study or at some seedy club in the city. Sex was therapeutic and he easily found it, usually free of charge. There was any number of willing women on Bellevuestrasse or Potsdamer. He never engaged with them on any other level than the carnal; made little attempt at conversation. A few drinks, a few knowing glances and the occasional smile were enough. His teutonic good looks and uniform did the rest. It was all too easy. Too easy and too boring, like everything else.

As for his children, Walter was objective, in the main. He had grieved a little for Agnette when she was injured, but he could not afford to luxuriate in such an emotion if he was to eliminate effectively other people's children. And when she did not recover after some weeks, he consigned her to death and preferred to remember her as she was. The shaven-headed, skinny little thing under a hospital sheet reminded him too much of the dead "unworthies" piling up daily at the Brandenburg institution that Wirth ran with unfailing enthusiasm. Walter stopped visiting Agnette at the hospital. It was futile.

Anselm had never really occupied his thoughts for long. The way the child sat on his mother's knee and sucked his thumb, pushed his head into his mother's breast and watched Walter with those big "Hedda eyes" irritated him. Everything, actually, was pretty irritating. Now, as he prepared to inspect Sachsenhausen camp in his impeccable uniform, SS-issue pure wool greatcoat and shiny leather boots, Walter's lip curled in renewed disgust. The place stank. How he hated the furtive attempts by the inmates to go unnoticed as he passed them. Useless, terrified scum.

The male prisoners at Sachsenhausen were divided into hierarchical categories by coloured triangles sewn on their camp overalls. At the apex of the pyramid were the criminals: rapists and murderers mainly, but some political insurgents. No triangles for them. Secondly came Communists, denoted by their red triangles. Then came the homosexuals, with their pretty pink triangles, and lastly, the lowest of the lowly scum on whom all others legitimately trampled for survival, the Jews, with their yellow triangles.

One of the "services" performed by Sachsenhausen inmates was the testing of the durability of shoes and boots produced by certain East German manufacturers, often for soldiers on the frontline. Today, another consignment of test footwear had arrived and just for fun, the consignment included women's shoes. When Walter arrived at the roll call area he found three camp guards in high spirits, their laughter could be heard well before Walter requested access through the main gates.

The semi-circular yard was crammed with hunched and desperately skinny men in ragged, dark overalls, and in a space in the middle, the guards had assembled some twenty homosexual prisoners and were making them put on women's shoes. It was several degrees below freezing. As Walter surveyed the scene ahead, he clapped his gloved hands together to encourage increased circulation to his fingers, and considered returning to his warm office on Tiergarten Strasse. There would be hot coffee and those little sugar cakes his secretary always brought in. But there was also a mountain of paperwork waiting to be signed, and the coffee and cakes would be there whatever time he walked into the office, so what the hell. He could do with a little entertainment.

When they saw him, the SS camp guards became instantly quiet and saluted him. The prisoners, shaking uncontrollably from cold, many of them too weak to stand up for long, tried desperately to stand to attention also. This was less easy for the two who had been forced to squeeze their feet into women's high-heeled shoes two sizes too small for them. The two men wobbled and stumbled, wavered and tottered, tried to help each other remain upright, and fell over again. One of the camp guards could no longer suppress a snigger and his face was red from the effort. This set off another, whose shoulders began to quiver, and he giggled uncontrollably like a nervous schoolgirl. Walter could not help but grin. He made a dismissive gesture with a gloved hand and the men relaxed and laughed at will.

"What is the matter... *gentlemen*?" The last word was deliberately delayed and stressed to signal their sexuality. Walter directed his words at the two men who now clung to each other in hopeless support. "Don't you like your nice new shoes?" The camp guards were doubled over in helpless laughter. "I should have thought they were right up... your street?" More ribald laughter. Walter came closer to the men. They tried again to separate; one remained upright, wobbling. The other was weaker, and in fear as much as anything else, his legs buckled and he fell to his knees. Tears fell silently down his face.

"Ah, don't cry," continued Walter mock soothingly, lifting the man's face by his chin. "I'm going to teach you how to walk in your nice shoes. You'd like that, wouldn't you?" The camp guards' laughter had subsided to the occasional guffaw. One rubbed a tear from his eye. Walter's tone changed suddenly and he struck the kneeling man hard on the side of his face. "I am talking to you, you pathetic pansy! I said, would you like to learn how to walk in your nice... new... shoes?" With each of the final three monosyllables, Walter kicked or hit the man while walking around him, once in his lower back, once hard against his upturned soles, and finally he slapped him hard around the head. The man sprawled on the freezing ground, sobbing and shaking, tears and snot all over his face. He tried to wipe them away with his sleeve as he pushed himself up to the kneeling position again. His friend, still wobbling and swaying on his heels, also shaking violently with terror and cold, could take no more.

"Please, Herr Commandant," he began in a small, piteous voice. "Please, sir – the shoes are too small. If we could have larger..."

The camp guards glared at him. One made an exaggerated "ooh" shape with his lips and his eyes grew wide in surprised amusement at the prisoner's audacity.

Walter rounded on him. "What did you say?" This was precisely the outlet his pent-up frustration and rage needed. "Did you speak to me?"

Walter punched the man twice very hard in his gut and then delivered a bone-breaking upper cut to his jaw, which sent the prisoner flying across the yard. The man lay still, moaning a little but barely conscious. Walter removed his right glove, unbuttoned his coat and took his Parabellum from its holster in a smooth series of swift movements and shot the man in the forehead. One of the huddled homosexual prisoners cried aloud in horror. The one on the floor hung his head and seemed to wait for his bullet. Instead, Walter paced over to him, pulled him to his feet and pushed him roughly away from him. "Walk!" he commanded. "Walk, you degenerate scum!" The man fell and pushed himself up, and stumbled and fell and cried, then pushed himself up with his hands again, like a toddler learning to walk. At last, Walter was excruciatingly bored with the spectacle.

The camp guards were no longer tempted to laugh. Walter's fury had banished humour and made it dangerous, even for them. The other inmates shivered and bowed their heads, huddled closer together. Walter shot the stumbling man and signalled to the camp guards to remove the bodies. A guard in turn motioned to two prisoners to see to the bodies, and they ran forward, dragged the dead men out of the way by their feet, their ridiculous shoes still on and the blood from their wounds leaving smears in their wake on the frosty ground.

"Now listen to me, you pathetic queers," shouted Walter at the remaining homosexuals. "You are going to wear your new shoes on a nice long walk. And you –" he raised his voice even more, addressed a section in front of him of other prisoners, mainly Jews – "you are going to walk with them. That should warm you up!"

Walking towards one of the camp guards, a huge man whose belly was barely contained by his jacket, Walter said, "Make the queers and Jews walk till they drop – the full twenty-five kilometres.

Kill any who survive. Choose at least sixty more by the end of the day and get rid of them too. We're behind on quota."

The guard saluted, clicked his heels together and began rounding up prisoners, herding them into the perimeter trench, shouting and delivering glancing blows all the while. The other two supervised, steely-eyed and taciturn now. The last thing they had needed was for a bit of fun to turn into an all-day supervised death march. They could have delivered his quota on time and also spent most of the freezing, miserable day indoors, drinking schnapps and eating liverwurst. They hated Walter almost as much as the condemned men who staggered and stumbled across glass, rocks, gravel and an assortment of other surfaces designed to test shoes. They were setting out on the first lap of what would be the most gruelling and the last twenty-five kilometres of their lives. Walter, his inspection over, left the camp and drove home to Oranienburg.

"The crematorium at Sachsenhausen is not working." Walter was speaking to Karl Muller by telephone. It was nine p.m. A jolly fire roared and danced in his office hearth, and his belly was full of pork and saurkraut. As he spoke, he fingered the stem of a crystal glass in which glinted and winked a crisp Rhenish wine. The last thing he had needed was some hesitant, simpering camp guard on the phone telling him the crematorium had packed up. He had been very sorry to disturb the Oberführer, but they had tried everything they could to get it going again. There seemed to be some sort of problem with the fuel feed. What should they do? They still had about fifty bodies to dispose of.

Walter was damned if he was going out again to that godforsaken place. The temperature had dropped to around minus six and he had spent all afternoon in his office at home signing requisitions and writing letters to people working at various T4 institutions, advising them of his imminent inspections. He needed to unwind in peace.

When he had replaced the receiver following the camp guard's call, he took a swig of his wine and drummed fingers on his desk. He was aware of noises from upstairs as Hedda bathed Anselm and kept up a constant chatter with him. Then it occurred to him: Muller! Karl Muller had designed and supervised the installation of the crematorium, so he could go and fix it. Brilliant! As a senior T4 officer, Walter had Muller's private number in his directory.

"I don't know why it is not working."

Walter rolled his eyes in impatience, but tried to remain polite. "That is the point, really, Muller. Something to do with the fuel supply or combustion process – or something. An engineering problem, you see. I am sorry to ask you at so late an hour, but I believe the situation is quite critical, Hygiene Director." Walter used Karl's T4 title as a means of firmly placing responsibility for this digression from efficiency at Karl's feet. Walter could not resist a smile to himself when after a few seconds' hesitation, Karl assured him that of course he would see to it. "Excellent! Please report back when it's all sorted out, will you?" Walter sat back in his chair and raised his glass to himself. He thought he would listen to a little Wagner on the phonograph – drown out the racket from upstairs.

The thirty-five kilometre journey by car from Berlin to Sachsenhausen on a freezing, dark night took almost two hours. The roads were so slippery with black ice that the tyres could not grip the surface, and the car frequently turned and glided across the road like a drunken ballerina. Karl could only steer into the skids and pray that there would not be an oncoming vehicle around the next corner, or that the side of the road was flanked by a level grass verge and not a ditch. He cursed the darkness, his tiredness and the inhumanity of the situation that required him to drive this perilous route in order to facilitate the motion of a huge and insatiable killing machine. But why should this not be the case? He was one of its designers. It had a right to expect his attention.

CHAPTER SIX

Karl slammed the car into first gear, gently let his foot off the clutch for the umpteenth time, coaxed and willed the car from a horizontal position across a narrow road to a head first one in the right direction. Well then, he supposed to himself, clenching his teeth and then cursing through them, he was a sort of gimp – a serviceable, fawning thing who dwelt in fear of displeasing its overlords. "Well, not for much longer!" he shouted aloud in abject frustration as the car once more slid away from his control and turned another slow pirouette in the wrong direction.

But no definite plan for his or anyone else's liberation had formed in his mind. He could not even imagine where he would start to subvert or elude the regime to which his country was so wholly in thrall. For the first time since he was little more than a child, Karl prayed. He addressed a God whose existence, he saw with sudden, revelatory clarity, was not negated by the evidence of evil all around him, but was a logical corollary of it. How could there be darkness if not light? How could anyone be appalled at evil if there were not an innate notion of what was good? And as he prayed the Lord's Prayer repeatedly and out loud with a fervour born of desperation, it seemed to Karl that something perceptibly shifted; the eclipse of his soul was not quite so total.

Sachsenhausen at midnight, in 1941, was hellish. But not as hellish as it would become, or even, at midnight, as diabolical as it was by day. Presently, at least, it was quiet. The few hours between late night and dawn were the safest for the inmates; even Nazi guards got tired. During the day, the guards had nothing to do but invent relatively amusing ways of torturing and killing quotas of inmates. But those on the night shift mainly drank and slept. Even the soldiers who manned the gun turrets relaxed after two a.m. and took it in turns to sleep, for they knew their charges were too sick and traumatized to cause trouble.

Usually, the impression that one was passing through the gates of Hades on arriving at Sachsenhausen by night was enhanced by the eerie red halo around the crematorium chimney, the belch of greasy smoke inching its way like a phantasmic snake over the twelve-foot-high walls to the camouflage of darkness beyond. But that night, there was no crematorium glow as Karl's car finally crawled quietly through the gates and into the roll call yard. A soldier bearing his rifle loosely against his shoulder saluted Karl and waited while his superior officer got out of the car, put on his cap and indicated that he was ready to be escorted to the crematorium.

Still ten feet away from the crematorium, Karl could detect the muffled sounds of voices, and these assumed knife-edge clarity when the soldier opened the door and light burst into the yard, as though it too would flee from the scene below. There was a sudden up-draught on which came a stench, the like of which Karl had never experienced. Instinctively, he put a hand over his mouth and nose. Men were shouting and swearing good-naturedly at each other. Women's voices, softer and laced with laughter, were an unexpected counterpoint to the gruff male tones. And then, having gone down two flights of narrow, concrete steps to the floor of the crematorium itself, Karl was indeed under the impression he had entered a circle of hell.

By ten-thirty, the night shift guards had given up expectation of an engineer to fix the crematorium oven. So they had resorted to drinking, and after a few drinks the idea had occurred that it might be pleasant to invite a few Aufseherin to join them. And if their female counterparts were too shy to indulge in a little drunken debauchery, perhaps some of their charges would be more obliging. There were about 2,000 women prisoners at Sachsenhausen, occupying a few barracks at the far end of the prison complex.

Under the amused and less than sober auspices of their female comrades, a couple of camp guards had turned on the lights in one of the female prisoner barracks and forced the women to stand to attention so that they could be inspected. No Jews – that was punishable by court martial or worse. But gypsy girls, Communists, Catholic dissenters and Aryan hiders of Jews – these were all fair game. They singled out a few young ones, pretty girls whose emaciation and exhaustion had not destroyed their looks entirely. They chose a couple of older women too: a political anti-Nazi activist in her early thirties and a Catholic schoolteacher who had hidden a Jewish family in her loft. She had been troublesome, that one, protesting in fine language at the inhumanity and degradation of her treatment, so she was pistol whipped. A few of her teeth flew from her mouth and hit the filthy floor in a stain of her blood and spit. She wasn't so desirable after that, or even very conscious. So they left her huddled on the floor, head forward, and bleeding in dark gobbets from her open mouth.

The rest they took, whimpering and freezing, across icy expanses of concrete, to the main roll calling yard and then on to the crematorium, where they were pushed and bundled down the steps, and the door shut behind them. Even SS camp guards could be shy in front of ladies, so, to warm up proceedings, the men drank plentifully and quickly with their female colleagues before they turned their attention to the cowering, shivering women on the crematorium floor.

At the moment Karl appeared, the fun was just getting started. An overweight camp guard had grabbed a gypsy girl and was whirling her around the floor to a discordant, giddy polka in his head. Her feet left the floor and her eyes stared fixedly in terror. She was limp and paralysed in his embrace while he leered from her face to the spectators, who lifted bottles in salute and cheered him on as he dipped and lifted her at will. But it was not the grotesqueness of this tableau alone that particularly arrested Karl's ability to think or remain convinced he was conscious and not in some fiendish nightmare. It was also that all around the walls of the crematorium building, at regular intervals of about four feet, corpses of male prisoners hung like gruesome marionettes, their heads pushed to one side as a function of the hooks penetrating the other side of their heads, just beneath the ear. Their eyes stared ahead glassily in the naked electric light, and their hands and arms hung limply by their sides. Blood dripped along the lengths of their fingers, congealed on the floor in flamboyant chrysanthemums.

And then, just distinguishable in the poor light of a far right-hand corner, was an amorphous heap of naked corpses, thrown higgledy-piggledy one on top of the other: Jew, Communist and homosexual in a last, levelling embrace.

The music in the drunken dancer's head seemed to stop abruptly and he dropped the girl when he saw Karl. She simply fell; remained quite still at his feet. He saluted uncertainly. The Aufseherin jumped from the knees of SS guards and bottle-crate seats to add their homage to a superior officer, smoothing and adjusting their uniforms as they did so. Karl still could not speak. He looked at them with an expression they could not discern, but which could not safely be construed as merely mock horror. They were used to the dramatic posturing and ironic verbal parrying of senior officers who liked to toy with them then suddenly attack. It was the pecking order, the privilege of rank. They got their turn with the prisoners.

After some moments, one, more daring than the rest, began to offer an explanation. He was not too drunk to interpret the insignia on Karl's shoulder, so began respectfully, "Mein Obersturmführer, sir, we waited a long time for an engineer. The furnace, it will not work. We did not think anyone would come –"

Karl cut him short, raising a hand. With as much dignity as he could summon, he turned and, pushing the accompanying soldier out of his way, he took the steps two at a time and still only just made it to the yard before vomiting copiously.

The soldier was soon behind him. "Are you all right, sir?"

Karl sniffed, took a couple of deep breaths. "Yes, yes. It's the stench." Then more assertively: "Are they animals? Are they pigs down there?" Karl drew himself upright, searched inside his coat for a pocket from which he drew a handkerchief. He wiped his mouth. "Right," he declared, "let's sort out this disgusting mess."

In the crematorium once more, in the stench of blood and

faeces, sweat, body odour and other things less definable, Karl faced a rapidly sobering and worried row of male and female camp guards. One of them started again to explain. "We didn't think anyone was going to come, sir. We —"

"Clearly." Karl cut him off. The gypsy girl was still in a heap on the floor, head down, not daring to move, her long dark hair falling over her face. She looked like a flower picked and discarded, wilting where it fell. Karl stepped forward and, putting a hand under her left arm, lifted her to her feet. When he was sure she could stand, he walked her back to the other prisoners. Karl then turned, addressed himself to the women guards. "Get out." They darted like startled gazelles across the crematorium to their prisoners and ushered them back up the steps into the freezing night and the relative security of their barracks.

His shock and horror were now giving way to cold fury. When he shouted, even he was startled. "Why have you put these men on hooks?"

The guards exchanged quizzical looks. One answered him, his tone full of confusion at such a question. "We always do this. It is a way of keeping the floor clear... while we're getting the furnace hot enough."

"It is what we were told to do," offered another, also emboldened by the absurdity of the question and the evident eccentricity of this SS officer who showed kindness to gypsy scum and got upset by queers on hooks. Karl lowered his face into a hand for a moment and tried to clear his thoughts. He was bone-achingly tired. He seemed never to sleep these days. His reality was no respite from his dreams, and his dreams were only marginally more frightening. Either way there was no rest. Ever.

"Well," he said at last, much more quietly, "I am Obersturmführer Muller. I am in charge right now and I am telling you to get these men down from the hooks. Do it now."

They moved at once, lifting and manoeuvring the corpses from the hooks. Rigor mortis made it impossible to unhook one or two, and Karl watched one of the guards cross the room and pick up a huge club, intending to break the men's limbs to make them more pliable. The club was bloodstained and clearly used regularly for this purpose, among others.

"No!" cried Karl. "Leave them." Then, adding with affected nonchalance, "We have work to do." So saying, he turned from them, closed his eyes, and for the second time that day muttered an earnest prayer for strength – and forgiveness.

He removed his coat and placed it on a crate, saying, "Now, try turning on the furnace, if you please." It was soon obvious to Karl that the pressure pump in the fuel tank of the double four-muffle furnace was broken. Without pressure, the diesel fuel would not rise through the main valve and combust when it met the heated coil, so no gas and no ignition.

"It needs a new pump," he pronounced. "Get me something to clean my hands, please." One of the guards found him a rag. "I shall have a new pump sent with one of my junior engineers tomorrow." He saluted them, they saluted back. He was on the steps when he half turned and addressed the men again. "Tell me," he demanded, keeping his tone as even as he could, "out of interest. Were those men dead when you hung them on hooks?"

There was a brief silence, then the dancer, sober now and feeling rather cheated by this killjoy officer with mad eyes, answered him, "Not all of them, sir. No."

Karl proceeded up the stairs without further speech and was greatly relieved at the prospect of a long, arduous drive home in the icy night. His thoughts needed the discipline of the concentration that would be necessary to get home safely. He had a very important letter to write.

CHAPTER SEVEN

February 1941. The snow fell intermittently, but there were many days of rain, when the people trudged through streets scummed with waves of blackened sludge. The pavements were often icy and it was hard to travel anywhere with haste. Feet and tyres alike proceeded cautiously. What struck Karl as he made his way on one such day to a small coffee shop on Bellevuestrasse, was that nothing was what it seemed. The realization was vertiginous. The men and women who smiled quickly and nodded at him as he passed them in the streets were good Germans of pedigree Aryan stock, for no one else was allowed to be on the streets outside certain hours. Jews, for instance, could shop in a very few locations, and only for certain low-grade goods that were still in reasonable supply, between the hours of four and five p.m. – when there was hardly anything left to buy. As Karl approached the coffee shop it was almost twelve-thirty in the afternoon.

The people who smiled at him did so because he wore an SS uniform and made them feel safe. Many had either consigned their Jewish neighbours to death or were busy pretending their deaths did not concern them. Yet even these accessories to mass murder would have been scandalized if they knew of the thousands of helpless Aryan children and adults dying horribly in the local hospitals to which they had entrusted them – or to which they had been forced to relinquish their defective relatives.

Karl became dizzy, fought a rising nausea that had become an almost daily feature of his existence, as he reflected yet again that this was just Berlin. Zoom out quickly and look down on Dresden,

Frankfurt, Leipzig, Hanover, Hamburg, Nuremberg, Munich, Stuttgart, and it was plain: the grotesque shadow of evil beneath the skin, conducted from hell into the fabric of Germany's waking life. "We've got it all wrong. This is all wrong!" was the simple mantra of Karl Muller's life these days. The good, harmless and sane were being gassed and starved and shot and overdosed and choked to death by exhaust fumes, and the bad people were calling it civilization. Was this not obvious? Who else realized? Whom could he trust with his thoughts? He feared for his sanity. Certainly, he was not well. So hard to eat or sleep or think straight. And his hands shook much of the time, so that he was afraid to take off his gloves in a meeting, or hold a pen. He wasn't sure how long he had before they guessed he was an imposter.

"Karl?" Hedda's voice was timid and quiet, but it made him jump. He looked at her without comprehension for a few moments.

"Hedda! Forgive me – preoccupied, with work... and things. You know?"

Hedda nodded. She knew well enough how preoccupied men could be. "How are you?" Hedda was glad to see Karl. She had often thought of him since the previous July when she had spoken to him at Carinhall. He looked gaunt and undernourished, she thought. His dark eyes had acquired a nervous quickness, as though unable to light on anything for long. "Haunted" was the word that came to mind when she contemplated his badly shaven face, pallor and sunken eyes.

"I am quite well." Karl forced his eyes to smile, but was eager to get away from the wife of Walter Gunther. He counted Gunther among those to be most feared and mistrusted.

"Are you having coffee here?" Hedda smiled at Karl's apparent confusion at the question. He seemed to survey his own hand upon the coffee house door with some surprise.

"Er, yes, I was going to... yes, I think." Hedda was amused in spite of manners and a genuine concern for this SS officer in full uniform, who seemed to have caught himself sleepwalking.

"Karl, are you sure you're all right?"

"Yes, yes! Just... er, surprised to see you and thinking of all sorts of things... to do with work. Yes... you are going for coffee too?" He stood aside and held open the door to let Hedda past him and into the welcoming embrace of the warm and aromatic café. Coffee was in short supply. Patrons of this establishment were strictly Aryans and then only the wealthy. Poor people could not afford the luxury of pure coffee, let alone cups of it made for them and served with fresh milk or cream. A huge sign on the door warned "STRICTLY NO JEWS".

Hedda and Karl sat together at a table, and Hedda removed her coat. Karl thought she was more attractive than ever. Her hair was not bobbed and precisely curled, smoothed and sprayed into place, nor were her eyes heavily made up or her mouth expertly glossed and pencilled, as they had been on the previous occasions of their meeting. True, she looked tired, but her loose, long hair, gripped back on one side to prevent the annoyance of stray curls, was thick and healthy; her blue eyes were remarkable, in spite of shadows beneath them. And although her face was thinner, her full mouth and high cheekbones ensured an unarguable natural beauty that Karl much preferred to that enhanced by artifice. But his appraisal of Hedda Gunther's beauty was merely observational. Of far more concern was her identity. A waitress duly arrived and took their orders.

"I have not seen you here before." Karl's tone was almost accusatory. He was fighting the paranoid thought that she was spying on him. He couldn't think why, though. Unless Cardinal von Preysing of Berlin was a traitor and not at all the man Karl's father believed him to be. If that were the case, then, yes, he might have alerted the Reich Committee to the fact that SS Obersturmführer Muller had written to him recently, asking for his help in bringing to the world's attention what was happening in Sachsenhausen, in Sonnenstein, in Brandenburg, in Lodz, in Warsaw... Karl could feel panic rising in his chest. He put a shaking hand to his forehead.

"Karl –" Hedda's tone was insistent now, and quite familiar – "you are not well. Please – do you want me to get you a taxi? You should go home, perhaps?"

Karl fought the rising fear, drew himself up straight in his seat and placed both hands flat upon the table before looking at her directly. "It's nothing," he began as levelly as he could. He thought her concern very genuine. Such a concern would be hard for a traitor to fake convincingly. It was so hard to tell! Change the subject. "Are you still in Berlin? I have not seen you here before. I, er, I come to this place quite a lot. I live in Berlin – on Potsdamer. This is quite local for me. The coffee is good."

Hedda decided not to pursue the topic of his apparent illness. "No, I don't live in Berlin now. Walter was given a house in Oranienburg. Our house in Berlin was bombed last August. We lost it."

Of course! It all came back to Karl as she spoke: the little girl in hospital – she must be visiting her at... where was it? Rudolf Virchow. "I am so sorry," he began. "Forgive me. How is your daughter? Are you visiting her?" Then it occurred to him that the meeting Gunther had left to see his daughter was months ago. Was the child dead? Karl felt himself colouring. How could he have been so gauche, so utterly caught up in his own preoccupations?

Hedda was confused. "How did you know about Agnette?"

"Your husband – I work with him. He left one day to go and see her. It is a tragedy. I am very sorry." He could not ask how the child was.

"You work with Walter?" It was Hedda's turn to be incredulous. She composed her features, assumed a more characteristic, detached demeanour. Sat back.

The coffee arrived. Neither spoke as the waitress placed the steaming cups before them, asked if they required anything else, was dismissed by a head shake and raised hand from Karl.

Hedda's surprise and evident displeasure at Karl's declared professional association with her husband brought him instant relief. She could not be spying on him, then. He would make sure. And he would also make it as plain as he could without being obvious that he had nothing in common with her husband, the administrative director of Sachsenhausen and senior director of T4 operations, SS Oberführer Gunther.

"Yes. I am sometimes in meetings with him. He is senior to me, of course. He makes decisions. I do as I am told, mostly." He did not smile, did not look at her, lifted his coffee cup to his lips as best he could without removing his gloves. His head shook a little with the effort of not seeming unnerved. Damn it! He could not master this way others had of seeming calm. Were they calm? The doctors, the senior SS officers – the Reich officers? Did they look so in control because they were? He replaced the coffee cup too quickly. Coffee splashed over the rim and into the saucer.

Hedda saw the tremor in his hands. Nothing he said could convince her more entirely than this did of his difference with Walter. The thought struck her: *He is afraid of something.*

"Walter has never mentioned that he sees you at work," she said softly. She took a cigarette case from her handbag, removed a cigarette and, placing it in her mouth, searched her handbag for a lighter. She lit her cigarette and contemplated Karl. "I had no idea." Her voice sounded flat. She picked up the packet and lifted it towards Karl.

He declined, shaking his head. He spoke again. "And your daughter?" Karl could still remember the pretty little girl with flailing plaits who ran around in the July sunshine at Goering's party.

Hedda sank in her chair and sighed heavily. She rubbed her forehead hard with the heel of the hand in which she held her cigarette, as though she would rub away the images in her head. She was not anxious to talk about Agnette. She long ago understood that no one really cared about her daughter except herself – and Anselm, in his way. Karl Muller was hardly going to be making more than polite conversation. What was the point? She shrugged. Inhaled, exhaled decisively. "Agnette is... well, she's not really conscious yet – a light coma, they call it. She was in a deep coma for weeks. Lots of surgery. The doctors say that there is some evidence of reactive behaviour now, but she just lies there. Doesn't talk. I think sometimes she recognizes me. I don't know." Hedda finished by shrugging again. She drank her coffee absently.

Karl considered her words. His thoughts flashed to the little girl he had watched die from gas poisoning in Brandenburg. He often saw her, in dreams, in unguarded waking moments. When he again expressed his sympathy, his tone was sincere and Hedda was moved. It was a long time since anyone had spoken to her kindly.

"And are you visiting her today? Is that why you are in Berlin?"

"No, no..." Hedda balanced her cigarette on the lip of an ashtray, found a handkerchief in her bag and blew her nose as genteelly as she could. "Agnette is at a hospital in Brandenburg now – very close to where we live. I am going to see my mother. She has flu." Hedda smiled briefly. "My mother is hopeless when she's ill – positively a martyr. She sent me a card telling me she was terribly unwell but 'not to worry'. I'm not worried, actually." Hedda could not suppress an ironic laugh, less at the juxtaposed triviality of her mother's illness with Agnette's than at her mother's own great concern for herself. Mathilde had not even sent a card to Hedda for the duration of Agnette's hospitalization.

But her expression changed from amusement to concern again when she saw the sudden horror on Karl's face. "What on earth is the matter now, Karl?" she said, irritated anew at this man's unstable temperament.

"She is in Brandenburg? Which hospital?"

"The big one in the town. Why?"

"The new one? The one that used to be a prison?"

"No! I think that is a... what are they, places for... insane people?" She remembered Karl's wife was mentally ill, and relied on years of good breeding to recover without showing she was aware of a faux pas. "Something like that? No, Agnette is at the general hospital – on a children's ward. Why? What is the matter?"

"Please. Don't be alarmed. It's only that I have... worked at the big one, the one outside the town. It's not very nice. No place for a child. They haven't sorted it out yet – still too much like a prison."

"Why would they send a child there?" Hedda was curious and annoyed. Why was this man always so full of mysteries and half-spoken ideas? "Agnette is not well. Her brain was damaged, yes, but... that's a physical thing."

"Of course. But there is a war. Casualties mean that some hospitals will be given military priority. They will send patients to wherever there are beds. That's the only point, really. I don't think there will be the resources soon to make distinctions between the insane and the injured or just sick."

"Oh." Hedda seemed satisfied. She took a final drag on her cigarette; stubbed it out. "Anyway, I am just stalling in here before I see my mother." She smiled again. ""And I have to admit it's rather nice to be sitting in a coffee shop in Berlin again, without children or... anyone else to worry about. I don't get much time to myself these days. I left my son with the maid. After all, you can't take a three-year-old to a flu-ridden grandmother." Hedda suddenly became animated, her eyes widening in mock drama. "And if I don't visit my mother she will sulk and tell all her friends I don't care about her so they will be sympathetic. I won't give her the satisfaction."

This time they both laughed. Karl was aware as he did so that it was a very long time since he had had anything to laugh about. But the anxiety was creeping back even before he stopped.

Why did he have to bump into Hedda Gunther now and learn of her child's removal to Brandenburg? Another huge weight on his shoulders! How could he tell her that no children's ward in a Brandenburg hospital was a safe place; that the new Gorden paediatric wing that had been opened at Brandenburg general hospital was a euthanasia centre? It had been constructed simply because the staff at the converted Brandenburg prison hospital were not happy to gas infants and children under eight years old, so more "humane" methods of despatch by specialized personnel had been devised for the purpose in a general hospital paediatric unit. How could he tell her that he was personally responsible for the imminent delivery of a drug consignment from IG Farben, via T4 offices, made up of three kilogrammes of Luminal barbiturate and two of morphine-scopolamine suppositories, to the Gorden paediatric wing, Brandenburg hospital?

Hedda noted the change in his eyes again and wondered anew what made this man so odd. "And what about you?" she questioned him. "How is your wife? I'm sorry – I can't remember her name – in Leipzig, I think?"

Karl frowned and nodded, as if mention of Greta was a natural progression to the conversation. "She – Greta – is still quite unwell. But she will be fine," he said, tipping his now empty coffee cup on the saucer and rolling it from side to side on its base. He looked up and into Hedda's eyes, found them soft and concerned. What he wouldn't do to be able to scream his torment, spill the filth from himself in confession to her right now. If it were just his own life he would endanger by doing so, he would do it in an instant. He had contemplated suicide many times. The very possibility was a comfort, as was the thought that there was still at least one aspect of his life over which he had control: his continued existence. But who would protect Greta? "I saw her at Christmas," he found himself saying. "She is still with her parents in Leipzig."

"That must be hard for you. Do you get home often?"

"No. There is much to do and Leipzig is far away. There's a war on, after all. Men at the front don't get home. I am lucky. At least I can go every few months or so. And you? You are lucky, I think; you can see your husband every day."

Hedda could not disguise the expression these words prompted and which denoted how very much less than fortunate that made her feel. "Walter works here, in Berlin, and also in Sachsenhausen prison," she replied. "He is at home about two nights a week. When he needs to work in Berlin, he prefers to stay in the city. It makes sense."

Karl recalled his own traumatic journey to and from Sachsenhausen just a couple of weeks before. "Absolutely," he agreed.

"Anyhow, Walter and I..." She stopped. He looked at her quickly, but she was careful not to meet his eye. "Well, we don't mind being apart. Put it that way."

Karl nodded. He was not surprised she did not love Walter. So why had she married him? Karl studied anew Hedda's languid blue eyes, remembered the stunning young girl he had escorted on a night out in Berlin long ago, in another life.

"What does he do all day, anyhow?" Hedda was probing, genuinely curious about Walter's work, not least of all because Karl worked with him. How could such totally different men do the same thing? Karl closed his eyes and put his hands to his face. Hedda took the gesture for embarrassment at her probing and an inability to discuss with her such things. "I'm sorry," she said in a sing-song voice. "I know I'm not supposed to ask such questions. Top secret, right?"

Karl, tired and suddenly wishing more than ever that he could just go to sleep, just lose consciousness completely for at least a while, pursed his lips and nodded. Said nothing.

"Well, I hope whatever it is that you end this stupid war quickly. I don't think I like Germany very much any more."

"Me neither." He couldn't resist saying it, but added quickly, "I'm working on it – promise."

They paid their bill, left the coffee shop, emerged once more onto the street. Then they embraced amicably, smiled at each other and wished each other well. An officer from the Tiergarten 4 office passed them, tipped his cap and met Hedda's eyes. "Frau Gunther," he said in greeting before walking on without slowing his pace.

"I know his face, but I can't remember his name," remarked Hedda. "He came to dinner once – must be more than a year ago."

Karl had not taken notice of the man. He shrugged. "Well, I must be getting back to work," he said.

"And I to my dear mother. Can't put it off any longer." And they parted.

It seemed to Karl, as he walked away from Hedda in the direction of Voss Strasse and his office on that slushy February afternoon, that everything had become a lot worse since he had started praying again.

A few days later and Walter was working from his T4 office in Berlin. It was ten a.m. and he was sifting through the post. Requisitions for supplies, responses to his letters announcing his intention to inspect various premises. He put these to one side for his secretary; she would need to compile a schedule. Bills for supplies – mainly from IG Farben; an invitation to drinks and dinner at a function being organized by Ribbentrop at the embassy for senior T4 personnel – a little morale booster and opportunity for the tedious ambassador to hog a microphone and announce T4 programme statistics as if he were personally responsible for them. Tedious, but given the likely prestigiousness of the guests, he would go. Who knew: perhaps even the Führer might be there this time? Walter still had not spoken with Hitler, and that prospect was one of the very few things he was living for.

The final envelope he opened was one addressed to The Reich Committee, Post Box 101, Berlin W9. This was the code address for requisitions from the child euthanasia team. It contained duplicates of several closely typed sheets of children's names and accompanying justifications in medical terms for their imminent euthanasia. Walter had to sign off the requisition in duplicate, then have his secretary send back one to the originating doctor at whichever institution. The copy was kept on file. He had to put his signature next to each child's name to show he had read the medical record, just in case anyone should try and query the death later and things became legal. So, sighing, he sat back, pen poised to flick and tick his way through the list of thirty or so names of children deemed unworthy of life at Brandenburg hospital.

CHAPTER SEVEN

When he saw Agnette's name he instinctively sat up and frowned. His heart skipped a little at the significance before his thoughts caught up. He could not at once understand fully the name as his daughter's. This was partly incredulity and partly that he couldn't place her in his working context. She belonged to a box in the attic of his mind marked "unsuccessful", in which resided his family and his marriage. At last he was able to focus on the words before him.

Gunther, Agnette Marie: Severe head trauma following injuries received in bombing raid August 1940. Comatose four weeks following surgery to remove subdural haematoma; follow-up surgery to relieve intracranial pressure. Prolonged coma. Aphasia. Seizures. Prognosis poor.

Walter sat back once more and stared into space. He saw Agnette smiling, mixing cake ingredients in a large bowl while the cook looked on in benign encouragement; Agnette, sullen because she could not have some toy or sweet; Agnette, younger, an unsteady toddler, fluffy blonde hair and face serious in concentration as she sought to preserve her balance; Agnette, at five years old already beautiful, the chiselled beauty of her mother detectable beneath the chubbiness of childhood. But Agnette did not have Hedda's moon blue eyes; she had her father's eyes, ice-blue and Aryan. She had been a Teutonic ice maiden of rare beauty in the making. She had been perfect. Walter put his head in his hands. Now, she was hideous. The last time he had seen her, her eyes were dull. Her hair had begun to grow back in tufts. The tufts seemed darker than before, as though trauma had turned off some inner light. The scars from her operations were livid and criss-crossed cruelly over her skull. They would be hidden by her hair when it eventually grew back, a nurse had said, but at that moment, Agnette looked like something Dr Frankenstein might concoct.

As far as he was concerned his little ice maiden was long dead. There was, though, which was curious to Walter as he sat, head in hands, trying to think it through logically, a difference between his "objective" definition of his daughter as dead and actually decreeing the termination of her cardiovascular and respiratory system by lethal drug overdose. He had watched hundreds of children die in gas vans and had remotely decreed the deaths of thousands more. It seemed that Walter's hestitation in authorizing the termination of this "unworthy" was that the child was his own. Not logical. He decided to wait until after lunch. As long as the requisition was signed and sent back by the end of the day, the child euthanasia programme for Brandenburg would be on schedule. He just needed time to adjust.

Following his chance meeting with Hedda, Karl was much disturbed. The knowledge that he would have to tell Hedda that her daughter was in mortal danger was yawning awake and soon would dominate his consciousness. He decided to take a long lunch break away from the offices. He crossed the city by tram to an area of Berlin characterized by large expanses of open land. The Lichtenberg district was relatively quiet and beautiful. He would be able to think there. The snow had thawed a good deal in recent days, so it would be possible to see the grass and contemplate the sleeping trees.

He saw the assembled crowd on Weitlingstrasse before he alighted from the tram. An assortment of people had gathered and were looking with great interest at some spectacle in their midst that Karl could not discern. Curious, he walked towards the excited group and was increasingly aware of the high level of activity and energy that defined the gathering. Soldiers with rifles and wearing army-issue helmets milled among the people, apparently unsure of how to behave. Should they disperse them? One seemed to think so and put a whistle to his lips in readiness to silence the people and give the order to move on, but he saw Karl approaching at the last moment and let the whistle drop from his mouth. He disappeared into the throng of people, no doubt to alert his comrades that an SS officer was coming.

As Karl got closer, he became aware of raised voices. One man's voice in particular rose above the others in assuredness and clarity. It was angry and came to Karl's ears in punctuated, irregular ejaculations. He could not make out the words. Occasionally, soldiers issued orders to the crowd, though in tones less convincing than that used by the speaker who seemed to be central to the hubbub. As Karl reached the fringe of the crowd, a thoroughfare opened up as people noticed and made way for him. And then it was clear what was causing such excitement. Karl had to stop and process the spectacle for himself before he could formulate any coherent response.

The soldiers led a street-cleaning detachment whose job it was to ensure the main streets in this area of Berlin were kept free from snow, and when there was no snow, dirt and litter. The people who were forced to clear or clean the streets were Jews – young and old of both sexes. This was now common practice throughout the city and in other cities of Germany. Those who had not yet been deported to ghettoes in Poland were put to work in this fashion. Even if the streets were already clean, they must be cleaned again. And again. For the object was not hygiene and urban aesthetics. The primary object was the systematic humiliation, abuse and murder of as many Jews as possible. The more Jews who dropped dead of heart attacks, hypothermia, pneumonia, exhaustion, the better. After all, the only reason they had not yet been deported was administrative or logistical; a matter of delayed paperwork, congested trains or temporary overcrowding of the Lodz and Warsaw ghettoes.

This particular "hygiene" detail, consisting of men and women ranging in age from fifteen to forty, had been consigned to clean Weitlingstrasse with toothbrushes. One look at the Jewish people kneeling on the ground was enough to inform any onlooker of how they had been abused. None of them was dressed well enough for the cold weather. The soldiers had deemed coats too restricting of the necessary vigorous movements for street cleaning and had ordered their removal. The people shivered violently. A young girl was in particular trouble. She seemed to be very unwell, flu perhaps, and slumped where she knelt. On the couple of occasions Karl saw her lift her head, her face was flushed with fever and she struggled to keep her eyes from closing. Women in headscarves took advantage of the distraction to edge closer to the adolescents in surreptitious bids to comfort them. It was not unusual for whole families to be assigned to street-cleaning duties. All were shivering violently, all had bare hands that were red raw and chilblained, and all were exhausted. Some were silently crying with eyes closed as if praying.

The man who was the cause of the disturbance was dressed in an expensive, tailored suit. He had removed his pure wool brown coat, his fine fedora hat and leather gloves and his suit jacket, and had folded them neatly on the pavement. He worked in his waistcoat and rolled-up shirtsleeves, kneeling on the road, punctuating his rhetoric by occasionally scrubbing the tarmac vigorously with a toothbrush he had taken from an old man beside him. As Karl contemplated him, the man looked up from his scrubbing to shout abuse at the soldiers, and rebuke the crowd of onlookers.

"Have you no shame?" he yelled as people gasped and pointed at him. "Madam –" he looked directly at one well-dressed Aryan lady, who took a step backwards in a vain bid to shrink from his attention – "would you like to get down on your knees in the filth on this road and scrub it with a toothbrush? No? What a surprise! Yet you are happy to walk past this woman." And here, he leaned backwards, put his arm around a middle-aged Jewish lady who buried her face in her hands and began to sob loudly. "You will stand by," he continued, "and allow her to do what you would never consent to. Shame on you!" He took his arm away from the Jewish lady, but she did not lift her head or uncover her face. "Shame on you all! Call yourselves Germans? The Germany I love would never have consented to such an abomination. Are you really going to stand behind the tyranny of Hitler's Reich and support this?"

He fell to scrubbing again, stopped once more, aimed his invective at Karl this time, whose appearance some moments earlier seemed to have made no impression on him whatsoever. "And you – you are proud to stand there in your SS uniform and represent a nation which treats its citizens like this?" Then the man stood up, threw down his toothbrush and approached Karl, looking him fiercely and directly in the eye. "Are you mad?" More gasps.

The soldiers were paralysed in their confusion. Should they shoot him? Should they arrest him and take him to Gestapo headquarters? Two things prevented either course of action: one was now the presence of an SS Obersturmführer and the other was that the man had earlier produced evidence that he was the brother of Reichsmarschall Hermann Goering.

Karl met Albert Goering's angry glare with bemused calmness and genuine admiration, which made Goering falter in his confrontation and frown. For a few seconds, their eyes were locked and then Goering stepped back.

"So, Herr SS Officer," he challenged, "what are you going to do with me? Shoot me?" He made an expansive, provocative gesture with his arms. "Tell me off?" He grinned, but his eyes did not lose their ferocity. "Arrest me?" He held both his arms out straight in front of him as if asking to be handcuffed. "Well, what are the SS going to do to stop the bad man from embarrassing the Reich?"

Karl seemed to consider for a moment, smiled, raised his eyebrows before turning to the nearest soldier. "Get rid of the people."

The soldier blew his whistle and signalled to his fellows to move the people along.

"Oh! So you are going to shoot me; is that it?" Goering roared this at the top of his voice, turned a 360 degree exaggerated circle, swinging his arms dramatically. "I am to be murdered in cold blood for speaking my mind. This is Germany, folks!"

"Who is this man, Private?" asked Karl of one of the soldiers.

"Well, mein Obersturmführer, he says he is Reichsmarschall

Goering's brother. These are his papers… it seems." The private passed the identification papers to Karl. Karl could not prevent his guffaw of complete incredulity following the soldier's statement. Goering meanwhile had gone back to scrubbing the road, shouting all the while that he and the Jewish citizens of Germany had inalienable human rights and were being unjustly and outrageously persecuted, and he demanded justice.

"He said what?" Even as Karl perused the papers and considered the likeness of the photograph to the face he had just contemplated at close quarters, he could not believe his ears. "Is he drunk?"

The soldier shrugged. "I do not think so, sir. I am not sure."

Soon, all the people were gone. Two soldiers stood guard to ensure more did not convene, and Karl continued to quiz the private. "How long has he been doing this?"

"Just about fifteen minutes, sir. What shall we do?"

Karl was trying not to laugh out loud at the sheer absurdity of the situation. "I'm really not sure, Private! Let me see." And he handed the papers back to the soldier and stepped forward. "Herr Goering, a word, if you please, sir."

At the mention of the Reichsmarschall's name, the Jews in the road were startled anew. They looked in terror at the well-built, obviously wealthy man on his knees and suspected some kind of perverted trick.

"Fear not, my friends," said Albert Goering loudly. "I am not Hitler's dogsbody. I am the dogsbody's brother. Nothing to fear from me, I assure you. Now, good people, get off your knees, get your coats back from these fiendish soldiers and go home. Better still, get the hell out of this godforsaken country in any way you can. Go!" And Albert Goering threw bank notes to the confused people. They looked at each other. "Pick them up – please!" urged Goering, and the frozen, frightened people stooped and gathered up the notes, bowing and nodding thanks.

The soldiers looked frantically from one to the other, then to Karl, expecting him to countermand Goering's instruction, but it didn't come. Goering meanwhile was helping the people to their feet. He lifted the chin of the sick girl and looked with compassion into her face. He said something to her; she responded. He spoke again and she nodded. He helped her to her feet, then supported her while one of the women brought her coat, put it around her shoulders, then led her away slowly down the street.

"Hey, SS Officer, that girl's name is Rachael Eisenberg. She is not to be asked to do any more stupid things for these soldiers, do you hear me? She is very sick. Give me your word – if you are a man." Goering stood, feet apart, shivering in the cold now that his angry euphoria was spent. He simply stared soberly and completely without fear at Karl, and waited for the assurance that the girl would be safe. The dumfounded soldiers gawped at the confrontation.

"You have my word," said Karl. Then he addressed the soldiers: "See to it." The private to whom he had just spoken nodded. The others merely regarded him, inscrutable expressions on their faces. "Bring me a truck," Karl commanded the private again, and the soldier began to run to where he had parked his army vehicle earlier that day, a mile or so south of their present location. Karl approached Goering. "I must ask you to accompany me to Gestapo headquarters, Herr Goering," he said loudly and assertively, all the while conveying his admiration with his eyes and allowing himself to smile warmly into Goering's.

Goering again frowned, tried once more to determine the mien of this dark eyed, unusual SS officer. He decided not to trust him. "Of course you must," he responded. And he again held out his arms for handcuffs.

"That won't be necessary," said Karl. "I am sure this will just be a formality."

Goering picked up his discarded jacket and put it on, then his coat, gloves and hat. He took a cigar and lighter from an inside pocket and, still shivering with cold, put the cigar in his mouth, then lit it, inhaled deeply and walked towards Karl. He offered him a cigar.

"No, thank you," Karl declined graciously, then added, "That was quite a performance."

"A performance? No. The performance is making decent people get down on their knees to clean the road with toothbrushes. It is a sick, perverted... it's..." He seemed unable to find adequate words to describe how he felt, drew again on his cigar, narrowed his eyes and scowled in disgust, then found some more words, shouted them, all the time glaring at Karl: "A fiasco! A judicial travesty... profane barbarity!" He tapped his head with gloved index finger and took a step closer to Karl, searched his eyes. "Have you SS blokes lost your minds? Have you relinquished all reason? Can you not see how... abominable this is? They are people. Flesh and blood, with hearts and minds like you and me. Well," he added wryly, "like me, anyhow."

Karl was very mindful of the soldiers who were listening to every word but could not see his face. Holding Albert Goering's gaze, he allowed his expression to register the harrowing profundity of the horror he daily carried in his heart but had not dared to show to anyone. How he ached to cry out in gratitude to God for this extraordinary affirmation of the conviction he kept alive in some inner sanctum of his soul, that he could not be alone in realizing the insanity that had gripped his entire country. And while his eyes threatened to fill with tears, he replied in a voice remarkably calm and assured, "Unfortunately, Herr Goering, not everyone agrees with your point of view."

The soldiers took his words and demeanour for practised SS irony and a tactic to placate the clearly insane Albert Goering, and they exchanged knowing grins. "Perhaps you can persuade your brother of the sanity of your view and the utter perversion of his?" Then he turned from Goering and announced in his best SS senior officer tone, "Ah. Here is the truck."

When the truck drew up alongside them, Karl stood back and ushered Goering into the front seat, beside the driver. He climbed in the front after him. The two soldiers clambered into the back and they set off for Prinz Albrechtstrasse, near Potsdamer Platz, and the headquarters of the Gestapo. Albert Goering was very quiet all the way there, stealing frequent glances at Karl, who stared ahead with apparent stoicism.

The last scene of that extraordinary afternoon for Karl was of Albert Goering laughing and shaking his head at what he considered out loud to be the asininity of the Gestapo officers who began to question him and pass his papers between themselves. One immediately telephoned the Reich Main Security office, also on Prinz Albrechtstrasse, and asked to speak directly to Reichsfürer SS, and Chief of German Police, Himmler.

The function of the Main Security office was to deal with all "enemies of the Reich", among whom Albert Goering was becoming prominent. Albert listened to the phone call and the account of his misdemeanours with mock seriousness, nodding his head and frowning, then he gestured towards the Gestapo officer who was trying to turn his back on Goering and speak at a volume he could not overhear. "Don't forget to tell Himmler how I said you are all mad," he shouted. Then he laughed again, lit another cigar. Karl saluted in Goering's direction from the doorway of the office, watched him tip his forehead in a return salute. Then Goering's face was lost in wreaths of cigar smoke, and Karl backed out and closed the door. He had no wish to encounter Himmler. The soldiers had seen more than enough to furnish a formal report.

On his way out of the building, Karl met the two soldiers who had kept guard on Weitlingstrasse while the third had gone for the truck. They were smoking and laughing together, no doubt recounting highlights of what they had witnessed that day.

"Well done," he shouted to them, and smiled. "What an unusual person Herr Albert Goering is, eh?" And he made a face as if to imply what he really meant was "mad". They laughed, one of them throwing his butt on the ground and stamping it out, the other drawing long on what remained of his cigarette and nodding vigorously in agreement. "Still," continued Karl in a more sober tone and drawing closer to them, acquiring a conspiratorial demeanour, "we can't be too careful. Strange or not, he is the brother of the Reichsmarschall and head of the Luftwaffe – the vice chancellor of the Reich. Take my advice: humour him about the sick Jew – you never know what trouble he could cause for you lads. Heil Hitler!" And they snapped to attention, returning his salute wearing suitably appreciative expressions. Smiling to himself, Karl put on his cap and made his way to his office, from where it was his intention to order lunch, then ponder the enormity of the thing that had just happened.

CHAPTER EIGHT

When Cardinal von Preysing received Obersturmführer Karl Muller's letter he was shocked, to say the least. He was impressed by the fluency of the prose, the evident intelligence of the writer and, most of all, by the apparently heartfelt outpourings of grief at what Muller claimed he had witnessed. Karl pleaded earnestly that von Preysing would alert the Vatican, and anyone else he could reach outside Germany, to the unspeakable atrocities of which he wrote and which were, he assured the cardinal and Bishop of Berlin, just a sample of what was happening all over Germany – and what was to come.

Not only did Karl describe in harrowing detail what was happening to children in Brandenburg, to prisoners in Sachsenhausen and to mental patients in Brandenburg on Havel and Sonnenstein, he also warned von Preysing of what was intended for the Jews being sent to Lodz and Warsaw; what "phase two" would involve. He made it plain that if nothing were done to stop the roll forward of the killing machine as it gathered momentum, it would be unstoppable. He revealed secret plans and strategies of T4. Karl ended by begging the cardinal to open his eyes to what was happening in the hospitals and asylums of his city and surrounding districts, then he signed and printed his name and rank.

Von Preysing faced a dilemma. Just a month before, he had written to Pope Pius XII asking for the Holy See's intervention in the terrible persecution by National Socialist Germany of Europe's Jews. He had also preached against cruelty and persecution of the Jews, and his sermons had been circulated throughout Germany.

He knew Hitler was furious with him. This latest letter could be a trap; it might be designed to inflame him and move him to some indiscretion that would incriminate him and the church. He had to be careful. His duty was first of all to protect his church and obey his pontiff. He could not openly counter the intentions of the Reichskonkordat between the Catholic church and Hitler's Reich, which allowed the church to determine its own liturgical direction in Germany in return for an oath of loyalty to the government. As a bishop, he had a particular duty to maintain the treaty. If the Catholic church were caught in flagrant breach of the agreement, who knew what Hitler would do – to the church, to the clergy, to the Vatican? If he, as bishop of the capital city of the Reich, were too outspoken in defence of the church and against Hitler, he might single-handedly endanger the Catholic safe houses that were springing up everywhere in Germany to protect Jews from persecution. Monasteries, convents, Catholic households throughout the country were now numerous in their protection of Jews – many funded by the church and, indirectly, by the pope himself. Two of the priests in von Preysing's own diocese had already been imprisoned in concentration camps for being too outspoken in defence of Jews.

The bishop had little doubt that what was described in this letter was at least based on truth, although he had not heard of T4. He certainly could not afford to answer this letter. And he could not see this Karl Muller, in case he was walking into a trap. Furthermore, von Preysing needed to warn Cardinal Orsenigo, the papal nuncio seated in Berlin, that he had received this letter, lest the possible entrapment extended to the nuncio himself and was designed to oust a papal representative from Berlin. Then, God help them! In truth, von Preysing was very worried about the frequency with which Orsenigo dined with high-ranking Reich officials and how he was most reluctant to discuss with his bishops details of these meetings. Nonetheless, von Preysing was aware that a less "sympathetic" nuncio might well alienate church from state once and for all.

CHAPTER EIGHT

Without delay, Cardinal von Preysing had a copy made of the letter and had it delivered to Cardinal Orsenigo with a note warning him to be on his guard. If the letter proved to be genuine, then the church was obliged to take action of some sort. Then he prayed for wisdom and guidance from God on what he should do next, while making up his mind immediately to forward a copy of the letter to his good friend and trusted confidant, Cardinal von Galen, Bishop of Munster. Von Galen was well connected, born of a long line of Prussian aristocrats and was a personal friend of the pope, having worked with him when Pius was Nuncio Eugenio Pacilli in Berlin in the early thirties. Von Galen would know how to ascertain the truth of these claims and this T4 information. He was powerful and outspoken, with a direct line to the hearts of countless Catholics throughout Munster. Even Hitler would think twice about upsetting so fearless and influential a prelate.

Two days after his encounter with Albert Goering, Karl was sitting in his office on Voss Strasse completing paperwork when Walter Gunther knocked on the door and walked in. Karl was startled by this unexpected visit from so senior an officer, and Gunther in particular; he wondered if he were aware of Karl's meeting with his wife the previous week. His heart lurched at the possibility of treachery by von Preysing or someone in von Preysing's offices. He quickly collected himself, however, and stood up, returning the "Heil Hitler" greeting.

"Please, as you were, Obersturmführer Muller." Walter smiled briefly, gestured to Karl to sit down. "I have business with Dr Brandt and thought I would drop in on you to thank you personally for your most efficient repair of the furnace at Sachsenhausen."

"Most gracious, Oberführer Gunther. I trust all is now working to order?"

"Oh, yes. Fine," replied Walter, simultaneously looking around the room, noting the untidiness of the desk. Then he added, "I understand from one of the guards that there was some...

unpleasantness when you arrived on the night you diagnosed the problem?"

Karl was immediately wary; assumed as confident a tone as he could muster. "Yes – it seems the men had decided to find some... unorthodox ways of amusing themselves while they waited. It was not behaviour respectful of their stations... their uniforms."

Walter sighed exaggeratedly, looked at the ceiling, eventually looked at Karl, and replied, "So why did you not report this incident?"

"Well, I dealt with it. The fault was diagnosed. I considered the whole thing insufficiently serious for a formal complaint."

Walter contemplated Karl, nodded slowly. "I see. In future, Obersturmführer Muller, I would be grateful if you would bring directly to me any discoveries you make of insubordination or... unfitting behaviour among my staff. As a T4 administrative director, I advise the commandant of Sachsenhausen. You were sent there by me; you should have reported everything to me when you relayed the cause of the crematorium malfunction." Walter smiled suddenly, a wintry smile that did not thaw his eyes. His tone lightened. "I hear you were... unwell at the scene?"

Karl reddened. "It was the stench. It stank down there. What can I say?"

Walter laughed briefly. "You get used to it. You get used to a lot in this job, wouldn't you agree?" Walter reached into a jacket pocket, took out a packet of cigarettes and a lighter. "Do you smoke?" Karl shook his head. Walter lit a cigarette, drew on it and raised his head so as not to lose sight of Karl through the smoke he exhaled. Karl pushed an ashtray to the edge of the desk and Walter leaned forward, took it, then, drawing a chair towards Karl's desk, sat down and crossed his legs, holding the ashtray in the palm of his left hand. "And I heard another rumour involving you, Officer Muller," he began once more. "Your life is becoming quite eventful, I think." Again, Walter smiled coldly.

Karl concentrated on keeping his facial expression as natural as he could in response to the statement Gunther had just made, but his heart was thudding against his ribs and he fought increasing light-headedness. "Oh? What rumour can that be?"

"Oh, come, my dear Muller. I am referring to your encounter with the extraordinary Albert Goering. Berlin is buzzing with it."

"Ah."

"Ah? That is all? The fellow is outrageous! Himmler is furious. If he could have, I believe he would have had him shot. What the hell did he think he was doing?" Walter was animated, his voice raised inversely with the depths of his outrage and incredulity.

"It is not for me to... comment. I..."

Walter guffawed. "Then you are on your own, Muller! The man is an 'enemy of the Reich' – classified. If he were anyone else, he would have been executed months ago. Problem is, Reichsmarschall Goering keeps getting him off the hook; insists he is 'not right in the head'. This time, he even sent a car for him and Goering junior left Gestapo headquarters laughing and inviting them to kiss his ass!" Walter watched Karl's face closely for his reactions. "Did you know, Muller, that Goering has got his brother a job?"

Karl shook his head, assuming an interested expression. "No, I didn't know that. What job?"

"He's put him in the Skoda munitions factory in Pilsen, Czechoslovakia. He's only made him Export Director! What do you think of that?"

"I think..." began Karl, who really hadn't had time to think anything of this information, but who was very uncomfortable and felt increasingly unwell. "I think it's odd?"

"Odd? I'll say it's bloody odd, Muller! Why would anyone make a lunatic the export director of a German munitions factory? How can you excuse openly treacherous behaviour like Albert Goering's on grounds he is 'not right in the head', then give him an executive position in a factory making weapons for the Reich? You tell me that." Walter's eyes were alight with outraged incredulity. He stared at Karl intently, leaned forward and waited for his reaction.

Karl merely shook his head in theatrical disbelief; made a face as if he agreed the whole situation was crazy. What he wanted to say but did not dare was, "Why the hell are you here, telling me all this?"

Walter drew hard on his cigarette, narrowed his eyes and exhaled extravagantly as he stubbed it, leaned forward and replaced the ashtray, then sat back in his chair. "By all accounts, Muller, you handled the situation impeccably the other day." Karl inclined his head in acknowledgment of the compliment. There was a marked silence, during which Walter never took his eyes from Karl's face. "Shame the Jews got the day off, though, eh?" Karl looked quizzical, then remembered how the street-cleaning detail had been dismissed by Albert Goering, and half smiled, nodded. "Still –" Walter crossed his legs, folded his hands on his upper thigh – "I hope they enjoyed it. The Gestapo had them all shot first thing next morning." He watched Karl's face, caught the brief startle as his eyes widened in shock. "That upset you, Muller?"

Karl shrugged, looked at his desk, then directly at Gunther. "Why should it? I expected nothing less. It is what happens."

Walter stared at Karl, smiled again briefly. "You know, you are interesting to me, Obersturmführer Muller." Karl raised an eyebrow once more, looked askance at his superior officer. "You are an enigma, I think."

"With respect, Oberführer Gunther, sir, I am very ordinary. I am just doing my job."

Walter stood up, turning his cap by its rim using both hands before placing it on his head. He made a "Hmph" sound, accompanied by a jerk of his shoulders, the combined effect implying his lack of concordance with Karl's claim to ordinariness. "Talking of your job," Walter added just before he reached the doorway of the office, "we have plans for a new gas chamber in an Austrian camp. It will be operational by the end of this year. It will be key for phase two. You will hear details soon enough, because you are to design it and its crematorium."

"I see." Karl thought it wise to show an interest. "And where will it be, precisely?"

"Mauthausen," responded Walter tersely, turning to look directly at Karl. "It is in Mauthausen. Top secret, Muller, obviously. Heil Hitler!" And he left, closing the door behind him. Karl waited a full five minutes before he allowed himself to breathe easy. Then he put his face in his hands and quietly wept.

Karl increasingly had the impression that it was only a matter of time before his disguise was realized, and his life would have been futile indeed if by that time he had succeeded only in contributing to the insanity of Hitler's Reich. He had received no reply from von Preysing. Very well then, he would seek a face-to-face meeting with the papal nuncio Orsenigo himself. He had listened attentively to Ribbentrop's disparaging comments about the pope. Surely the pope's own nuncio shared his pontiff's sentiments? The nature and extent of the treachery otherwise was unthinkable, and as a Catholic, however lapsed, Karl could not admit its possibility. He remembered also Himmler's and Goebbels' mocking gibes that Orsenigo was more sympathetic to National Socialism than he ought to be, but Karl understood only too well the necessity for counterfeit diplomacy when working for and against the Reich simultaneously.

In the same determined mood, Karl arranged for a car to take him on an official visit to Brandenburg hospital. He needed to inspect the delivery arrangements for the new drug consignments to the Gorden ward and to speak with the T4 staff there about discretion and procedures. But what he needed to do most of all was see Agnette Gunther and, if possible, her mother, to ensure they were all right.

The paediatric ward at Brandenburg-Gorden hospital was a special wing that none but authorized personnel could enter. In this respect, it was immediately different from the children's ward of the main hospital. No one visited the children receiving "specialized care" on Gorden. Karl presented his T4 IV Office ID at the door, and a guard punched a code into a panel on one of the double doors and allowed him to enter.

It was quiet. The main corridor to the ward was short and flanked on each side by a staff office to the left and a locked storeroom to the right. Karl introduced himself to the nursing staff – a matron and two young nurses – and said he would be needing a tour of the ward, access to the storeroom and to speak to the staff about procedures and security. The matron nodded without smiling and indicated that they should proceed at once to the ward where, she said, the children were mainly sleeping at present.

It was late March. Timid spring light was doing its best to cheer up a glowering sky, and largely failing. The only two windows that were not covered by blinds were high, and admitted just enough light through narrrow panes to allow nurses to check on their charges and administer drug doses to each child. Further than this, the light collided with more gloom and was lost.

Karl stood at the opening of the ward and waited for his eyes to adjust. Stretching away from him on both sides in ordered rows was a number of cots. Large canvas cradles on metal legs. Karl and the silent matron walked up to the first cot and looked in. A child of about three years old lay flat on its back covered in a light blanket. It was impossible to tell the sex of the child. The infant's eyes were half open and rolled upwards so that the whites showed, and the mouth was open. The eyes flickered, so it was evident the child was alive, but it was skeletal, hardly making an impression beneath the blanket, and its skull looked like that of a fledgling, covered only in a little downy hair.

"What is this child's name?" asked Karl quietly, without looking at the matron. He was aware she went to the foot of the cot and read the notes.

"Eugenie," she said.

"She is so thin." The matron said nothing. When he tore his eyes from the child and looked at her, she regarded him sternly and not, Karl thought, without a degree of contempt. It was his job to understand that this child was being starved to death. If Eugenie were not dead of starvation by Wednesday – three days' time – then she would be disposed of by a single overdose of Luminal barbiturate. It wouldn't take much to sabotage the respiratory system of this little girl.

Karl straightened up and put his hands behind his back, assumed a less scrutable expression, and moved to the next cot. It contained a baby of no more than eighteen months old. A tiny thing, so light and small he could have scooped it up and held it in one hand. The child opened her eyes and beheld Karl. The baby could make no sound, but Karl started as if the child had screamed. She was too dehydrated to cry, but her tiny face crumpled into a pout and her dry lips parted in a silent wail of incomprehension and misery. The matron, prompted by the SS officer's reaction to the child, bent over the cot and touched the baby's face gently. The child turned her head to look at the nurse, her agony plaintive in tearless eyes.

Time and again in the loneliness of his apartment, Karl would be brought to his knees, sobbing, at the burden he carried from that ward; at his betrayal of that child and of all the children in hundreds of wards throughout Germany in which helpless children starved and thirsted to death. He thought himself incapable of hating anyone with greater passion than he hated the matron as she touched the baby's cheek.

"I have seen enough."

"But Officer Muller, don't you want to see the supply room or speak to the nurses?" she had said quietly as he walked away.

"I have remembered I am late for something. I shall brief you in writing regarding protocol," Karl had responded without turning around. Just as waking brought no relief from his nightmares, the light and comparative airiness of the main corridor outside the darkened Gorden Wing paediatric unit afforded no relief to Karl from its horror.

The children's ward at Brandenburg-Gorden was for boys and girls from infancy to twelve years old. It appeared to be a normal ward, but of course it was not entirely; it was also a filter for admission of children to the euthanasia programme, particularly those whose parents were "difficult", or reluctant to hand over their children to "special care" units that would not admit visitors. Older children and teenagers were admitted to adult wards, and from there to Brandenburg on Havel to be gassed, then cremated.

Little by little, "assigned" children at Brandenburg-Gorden "took a turn for the worse", aided expertly by increasing doses of barbiturate with their regular medication. As they became too ill to be nursed on the regular ward, they were transferred to the Gorden Wing for "expert and specialized care", usually at night, when their parents were not around to object or insist on accompanying them.

When they were dead, parents were informed and often sent photographs of the body. There was a standard letter that was issued to parents in all such cases. It condoled politely, detailed a cause of death, and explained cremations without parental consent on grounds that there was a war; new regulations for the control of infectious diseases dictated that staff had no choice but to comply with orders from the Reich to cremate all dead without delay.

An urn containing the son's or daughter's ashes could be provided at the parents' request, and any complaints should be directed to the Reich Committee, Berlin. "Heil Hitler" was the standard subscription to such letters.

In contrast with the Gorden Wing, where the children had no energy to make much noise of any kind, the children on the main ward included many who were recovering from a range of non-fatal ailments and conditions. Several were sitting up in bed chatting, or walking around in their dressing gowns, visiting other children's beds or playing with toys. There were several visitors, some laughter and generally an air of bustle and energy. There was no sign of Agnette, however.

Karl reasoned that a child in a near catatonic state would hardly be among these noisy, recovering children, so when a nurse asked if she could help him, he explained who he was and that he had come to inspect the ward in light of new childcare protocols. He needed to see all facilities for children's care, including any side rooms. She nodded curtly, asked him to follow her. No doubt she had been told that not all children were to be cared for routinely. No doubt she was aware that the medication she was asked to administer to several children in her charge was highly unlikely to assist their healing. It was likely she dreaded being assigned to shift work on Gorden paediatric wing and faced with the inescapable evidence that her worst fears were facts. No doubt she had been warned that if she wanted to keep her job – or even her life – she would do as she was told without question and keep her mouth shut.

The displeasure evident in her eyes and curt gestures as the nurse led him away from the main ward to the side rooms was gratifying at least, thought Karl. He often wondered what long-term psychological damage was being done to people who worked daily for the Third Reich against their conscience; who dreaded sleep and the garish terror of their nightmares.

Karl entered each side room in turn. A child connected to a drip slept soundly in one, her rosy face and plump arms testament to her predominant health. In another room, anxious parents attended the cotside of a small child. They both looked around quickly when he walked in, desperation evident in their expressions. They looked away when he wasn't the doctor they were expecting. Their child was grizzling and restless. Karl excused himself and closed the door quietly.

Agnette was in the last room he tried. He assumed the small, thin figure in the bed was her, from the uneven tufts of fair hair that covered her scalp and the stillness with which the child stared at the window. He confirmed her identity by unhooking the clipboard from the end of her bed and glancing at her notes.

Agnette didn't react to his presence immediately, but when he drew close to her face and greeted her by name, Karl saw her eyes flicker, and her attention seemed to return to the room from somewhere far away. He introduced himself as if she could hear and understand him, and he told her that he knew her mother and was her friend. He very much hoped, he said, that she was feeling better and he was very sorry that she had been so unwell. Karl then paid careful attention to her notes. And there it was. The tiny blue plus sign stamped apparently innocuously in the top right-hand corner of the second page. It would be ignored or dismissed as insignificant by anyone outside T4.

Though he had been expecting this, Karl was still surprised at the virulence of the emotion he felt. He feared he would vocalize his fury in some way, so he closed his eyes, breathed deeply. He had to keep a clear head if he was going to do something to save this child. He could not save all the children condemned to murder at this hospital but, if he kept his nerve, he might save this one.

Karl put the board back on the end of the bed and approached Agnette once more. He touched her face gently and stroked her soft, short hair. "I am going to look after you, Agnette," he whispered, "and that is a promise." Her clear blue eyes flickered again but did not turn from the window. She seemed to him like a bird that had lost its freedom and its song, but could not die as long as it could glimpse the sky.

The young nurse to whom he had spoken earlier opened the door. She was wearing gloves and carried a bedpan in one hand. She appeared startled to find Karl standing over Agnette. "I am sorry, Officer Muller," she began, though she sounded more resentful of his presence than sorry she had disturbed him. "I must check Agnette – empty her catheter bag."

"Of course – please. I was just leaving." Karl smiled at her, bowed quickly in half salute and left the room.

Walter was at home. He had decided to join Hedda and Anselm at the dinner table. This was a rare occurrence and his usual absence had licensed Hedda to include her son at the table for the evening meal. Hedda hated dining alone and had been teaching Anselm table manners while enjoying his company. Although he was not able to manipulate alone a full-sized knife and fork, Anselm was now very good at sitting up straight for minutes at a time and had almost mastered chewing with his mouth closed.

When Walter walked into the dining room in full SS uniform and took his place at the head of the table, both Hedda and Anselm stopped chattering and laughing, and could not disguise how disappointed they were. Hedda became serious and lowered her voice, urged Anselm to be a good boy and sit up straight as she had showed him. Anselm frowned and stuck out his lower lip, folded his arms petulantly and made a "hmphing" noise. Walter was immediately irritated by the evident displeasure the boy exhibited at having to share the table with his father.

"Do as you are told, Anselm, or leave the table and go to bed. It's quite simple." Walter's voice was measured, but ice cold. The child looked at his mother as if to say "What do you think?" and she widened her eyes, nodding at him to comply.

"Eat, Anselm," she added. "Good boy."

The cook arrived, placed a plate full of chicken, creamed potatoes and cabbage before Walter and then left the room, returning with a bottle of white wine and a glass.

"So," began Walter deliberately, while pushing chicken onto his fork, "how are you, Hedda?" He put the food into his mouth and looked directly at her.

"I am well, thank you." There was a long pause during which Walter continued to eat, chewing rapidly, washing down his dinner with intermittent gulps of wine.

"Although you did not ask, I too am well," he said at last, smiling at her briefly, his eyes brittle.

"No! I will do it, Mutti. Stop it!" Anselm was suddenly cross and pushed away the fork Hedda held to his mouth.

"All right, Anselm. Do it, then." Hedda was becoming irritable in her nervousness. She wanted Anselm to finish his dinner quickly so that they could both escape Walter's company.

Walter watched them, chewing ruminatively, seeming to relish their obvious discomfort. "How is your mother? You went to see her last week. Is she over the flu?" he asked, shovelling mashed potato onto his fork and consuming it with automative enthusiasm.

"She is better now, I think – it was just a mild dose. Of course you'd think it was the Black Death or something…" She checked herself. It no longer felt natural to make conversation with Walter. Her husband nodded, threw rather than placed his knife and fork together on his plate and wiped his mouth with a napkin, pushing away his plate.

Anselm folded his arms, pursed his lips and closed his eyes. "No more." Hedda was happy to push his remaining food to one side of the plate. Immediately, Anselm opened his eyes and beamed at her. "Pudding!"

"Anselm, what have I told you about manners?"

"Pudding, *pleeease.*" The child scrunched closed his eyes again and leaned towards his mother, shouting the last word.

"Anselm, stop being silly!" Walter's tone was sharp.

The boy started visibly, eyes opening wide in shock, then he frowned sullenly at his father, put a finger to his lips and hissed, "Shh!"

"How dare you tell me to be quiet! Get down from the table this instant and get to bed! There will be no pudding for you this evening. Go!"

Anselm began to cry loudly, looking abjectly at Hedda. "I want pudding, Mutti. I want my pudding!"

Hedda shot Walter a resentful glance, then said, "Well, Anselm, I don't want any pudding tonight either, so how about you and I go to bed, huh? Come on, I'll read you a story. Would you like a bath?" The child nodded, turning in his chair so that he could use his hands to push himself off it backwards, to the floor.

"Please, Hedda, call the maid and tell her to put Anselm to bed. I would like to talk with you."

Anselm began to cry again; looked imploringly at Hedda and shook his head vigorously. "No, Mama. I want you to put me to bed – you, Mutti. I want a bath with you, Mutti."

"The child is out of control!" roared Walter, snatching his napkin from his knee and slamming it down on the table. "Get to bed this instant! Do as you are told!"

"For goodness' sake, Walter!" It was Hedda now who raised her voice. "He is three!" Anselm's crying became screaming. Walter rose, approached his son and pulled him from Hedda's embrace, put him under his left arm and walked out of the room. The child became hysterical.

"Walter!" Hedda leapt from her chair and followed him. "Walter, don't you dare hurt him!"

Walter stopped in the middle of the hallway and turned to look at Hedda. "What did you say?" he shouted above Anselm's cries. He began walking towards his wife, apparently forgetful of the small boy kicking and straining against him in the vice of his right arm.

Hedda closed her eyes, took a deep breath, spoke more calmly. "Please, Walter, don't hurt him. He's just a baby. Please." Walter seemed to consider her words. The maid had come into the hall and now stood uncertainly in the shadows beneath the stairs. Hedda called her, not taking her eyes from Walter's face. "Marguerite, would you please take Anselm to bed? No need to bath him. I'll do it in the morning."

Walter seemed chastened by Marguerite's presence and put the boy down. Anselm ran to his mother. Hedda crouched down till she looked into his eyes, took a handkerchief from her sleeve and wiped his nose. "Goodnight, darling. Be a good boy and go with Marguerite. I shall come and kiss you goodnight later, OK?" She smiled, and Anselm, red-faced, nodded, and without looking at his father crossed the hallway to where the maid stood, holding out her hand.

Walter walked back to the dining room. Hedda remained still for a moment, bowed her head as if in defeat, and turned slowly to follow him.

"So," Walter began menacingly through clenched teeth, "you humiliate me yet again, in front of the domestic staff this time."

Hedda rolled her eyes, shook her head.

"Don't roll your eyes at me!" His voice was low and vicious.

Hedda had no idea what was causing him to behave so abominably, but she was certain of the danger she faced. "Shall we just get to the bit where you hit me, and skip the nonsense in between, Walter?" She stared at him levelly.

"You insolent slut!"

Hedda screwed up her face and looked at him with utter contempt. "What are you talking about? You're completely mad! You need help, Walter!" Hedda knew that whatever the root of his fury, when Walter behaved like this he needed an outlet, the release or catharsis of violence, and she was his scapegoat. It was inevitable he would hit her. She would rather precipitate the violence than parry with or cajole him. It saved time and energy.

Walter swept his dinner plate, cutlery, the half-full bottle of wine and the crystal glass to the floor with one sweep of his right arm. Hedda raised an eyebrow and that familiar calm, that distant, eye-of-the-storm feeling, settled in her heart. Good. She would feel nothing until it was over.

"So," he began, his chest heaving with the effort of breathing through the anger and talking without shouting, for he did not want the maid to hear. "So, you went up to Berlin last week just to see your mother, did you?"

Hedda looked totally confused. Her tone when she responded was mock quizzical, as though he already had the answer and she had to guess. "Yes?"

"So you didn't use the opportunity to meet a man?"

"What? What man, Walter? I haven't a clue what you are talking about."

"You are a filthy, foul-mouthed liar and an adulterous whore." The statement was made as if he were announcing that she had the winning ticket in a raffle. "One of the officers who works for me saw you – he saw you kissing a man outside a coffee shop on Bellevuestrasse. He saw you embrace in the middle of the street. He said it was an officer, but he couldn't see his face. I suppose he's lying? Hmm?"

Hedda threw back her head and laughed out loud in derision. "You mean Karl Muller?"

He knew it! "Who?"

"Karl Muller. The man I spoke to at Goering's bash last summer." She was suddenly exhausted, her tone became flat. "I did not plan to meet him." Hedda put her head in her hands for a moment, then pushed back her hair and looked up again at Walter. "I met him by chance at the coffee shop. I have already told you, I knew him once – years ago. I dated him twice – a few times. He was nice, but..." She stopped. She no longer thought Karl boring.

"But what?" Walter was now sneering. He had what he wanted. She was clearly telling the truth; she was not having an affair. But of far more interest was that Walter had had a hunch the man she was with was Muller, and Muller was occupying his thoughts more and more these days. There was something about that man which was not right, and other people had noted it too; the camp guard at Sachsenhausen, for example.

One of the soldiers at the Albert Goering incident was surprised at how lenient Muller had been with the Jews and had mentioned it to Himmler. Himmler had mentioned it to Walter as they chatted over drinks at Ribbentrop's embassy gathering. Himmler confided in Walter that if he had had his way, Albert Goering would be dead. He could not understand why Karl Muller had allowed the Jews on road-cleaning detail to simply walk away on Goering's instructions. How humiliating for the SS! Still, that was remedied by their executions a few hours later.

And why had Muller not said that he had had coffee with Hedda? He could have mentioned it to Walter when he spoke to him in Muller's office days before, but he had kept quiet. Did Muller have designs on Hedda? Well, if he did, it was pretty clear from Hedda that his feelings were not reciprocated. Walter could tell that meddlesome little swine, Schitzel, that Hedda had met an old friend at the coffee shop and nothing more.

"I don't give a damn who you sleep with, quite frankly," Walter sneered into Hedda's face. He grabbed her face and squeezed it hard, twisting her lips. "But if you make a fool of me, I will kill you." He released her.

She flashed at him, chest heaving with loathing and anger. "Always about your ego and your image, isn't it, Walter? I have told you, Karl is married."

"And this is the only reason you don't sleep with him?"

"Make up your mind, Walter. Am I sleeping with him or not? Do you care or don't you give a damn? I'm a little confused."

"Where is this wife? I never hear of her. Perhaps she does not exist? Perhaps the way is clear for you to leap into bed with him after all!"

Hedda rolled her eyes, tears of frustration welling in them. "She is in Leipzig, with her parents. She is not well... apparently."

"Oh? What is wrong with her?"

Hedda tried to think clearly. Her instincts were to protect Karl. "She has some sort of... mental problem or something. Look, I'm not sure. You know what, Walter? It is none of my business. Is that all this was about? This whole... the shouting, the... Why don't you just ask me, Walter? Why don't you just ask me if I am having an affair and I will tell you and that is that?" She shook her head again, dropped it into her hands.

Walter contemplated her distress with interested detachment at first, and then the thing he could not, under any circumstances, say that evening came back into his mind with a startling, stabbing sensation that took him by surprise.

A few days before, after a good lunch of veal and Riesling in a rather nice restaurant off Potsdamer, Walter had gone back to the office and put his signature next to his daughter's name, where it had appeared on an alphabetical requisition list from the child euthanasia team in Berlin. He could not tell Hedda how, at Ribbentrop's embassy "do" the following evening, he had discussed his decision with Himmler, who had put a comforting hand upon his shoulder and commiserated, but commended his great courage. Himmler had been effusive in expressing how impressed he was by this, Walter's ultimate gesture of loyalty to the Reich. The Führer himself would hear of this great sacrifice for the war effort and the glory of Germany, Himmler had assured Walter, and he had added that it was men like Walter who made Germany great. "Have some more champagne, my dear Gunther," he had urged, refilling Walter's glass. "You have done a noble and courageous thing. Heil Hitler!" And Walter had reciprocated the toast and drunk heartily from his champagne glass.

Now, as Oberführer Gunther straightened his jacket, ran a smoothing hand through his thick blond hair and surveyed the shattered crockery, he forgot about Muller. His eyes passed over the smashed wine bottle, the gravy and wine soaking into the dining room rug. Then he stepped over the debris and made for the door. It was as if an irritating puzzle had suddenly been solved. The stabbing sensation in his chest, he understood as he crossed the hall to his study and a bottle of finest malt whisky, was guilt. That, he realized, was what had been bothering him.

CHAPTER NINE

Karl had to think of a way of saving Agnette Gunther. He was more motivated to save her above the other children dying on the Gorden ward because he knew her mother, but, more importantly, he actually could, if he acted quickly enough, save her. He was limited, though, in what he could do. He had already accepted and signed for the consignment of drugs from IG Farben and had supervised their loading into the warehouse on Lutzow Ufer. They were to be distributed to several euthanasia centres – "special paediatric wards" – throughout Germany, by truck, in the next two days. He had until Wednesday before the morphine-scopolamine suppositories and the Luminol barbiturates would arrive at Brandenburg hospital. It was Sunday.

They were to be loaded onto the delivery truck the following morning. In spite of it being the Sabbath, there were still people in the T4 offices. Servicing the Reich machine was a seven day a week job. At the end of the day, Karl stayed late, bade colleagues good evening, complained good-naturedly about the paperwork he had to get through, and waited. He waited till about six-thirty and everyone had gone. Then, estimating that it would take him about thirty minutes' fast walking to get to the warehouse on Lutzow Ufer Strasse in Tiergarten, he left his office. No taxis operated after blackout.

Karl really had no idea what he was going to do to the consignment of drugs. He had thought of setting fire to the warehouse, but that was too obvious. He had thought of opening the crates and stamping all over the boxes of drugs. Again, too

197

obvious. Finally, he had decided on covering the labels marked "Brandenburg-Gorden" with labels marked "Sonnenstein" or "Grafeneck" or "Hartsheim" instead. Of course it had pained him terribly to imagine the other consignments reaching their destinations – the thousands of children in west and southern Germany, in Austria, who would certainly die from Wednesday onwards. But if he dwelt on what he could not do, Karl felt he would be completely paralysed or even lose his sanity. He had to concentrate on what he could do.

It was a dark and rainy evening. More like November than March. A vicious wind whipped his face, and freezing rain joined the assault, stinging and numbing his skin. The blackout and the filthy weather meant there was hardly anyone on the streets of central Berlin. For both, Karl was grateful. He was extremely nervous. If he was caught in the warehouse and subsequently Brandenburg did not receive its delivery, he would be interrogated. If he was caught sabotaging the drug consignment, he would be shot – or worse. The only truly terrifying thing about either prospect was that he would be unable to stop this drug consignment arriving by Wednesday at Brandenburg hospital, in which case Agnette Gunther would certainly be dead by Thursday evening.

As he walked, Karl prayed. He prayed for courage and forgiveness: forgiveness, because he was trying to save just one child, and courage, because he needed it to do even that. He did not try and mitigate his T4 actions with God, considering it futile to construct a legal defence before omniscience. He just prayed for the complicity of God in this one instance; in this one good deed he might actually be able to effect.

The rain began to thunder down, slamming into his cap and driving into his eyes. At one point it was so heavy that he had to turn his back against it, for it was impossible to proceed while facing into it. And so it was that he first saw the enemy planes.

The sirens came a little while afterwards. Visibility on that night was so poor that the RAF pilots had to fly a lot lower over

Berlin than they would have liked. But it also made it very difficult to see them approaching, and the anti-aircraft guns in the towers on the city's periphery were slow off the mark. The drone of the bombers finally became a distinct sound above the roar of the rain, and the sirens wailed mechanically above it all. Karl ran into the road. He was not likely to be a target or even clearly visible to the MK II RAF pilots, but the buildings were. Karl ran as fast as he could beneath the planes' heavy fuselages and turned left, heading for the location of the nearest bunker of which he was aware. Before he reached the bunker and was ushered down by soldiers, he heard the first explosions. He tried to pinpoint the likely impact, given his estimation of the sound, but one explosion was followed swiftly by another. He gave up imagining the damage, waited it out.

Two hours later, the all-clear was sounded. Karl emerged from the bunker into cold and gusty darkness. Fire engines screamed around streets near to and far from where he stood. People shouted, the eerie glow of flames at intermittent locations made visible the driving rain, fire conspiring with water to confuse and sabotage the recovery efforts. Karl still had to get to Lutzow Ufer Strasse and the warehouse. The chaos of Berlin bombed provided the perfect cover. If he were asked, he could say he was checking on trucks, buildings, supplies.

What he really hadn't thought he would see, even in his wildest imaginings, as he turned into Lutzow Ufer Strasse, Tiergarten, were the flames licking hungrily around the rubble of the erstwhile T4 offices, gorging on the crushed consignments of drugs and the crumpled trucks inside the flattened warehouse.

The day following the Sunday 24th March air raid, Berlin picked herself up again and began the dogged recovery. Casualties were light; the buildings hit were mainly on the outskirts of the city. The main Berlin target seemed to have been the Putlitzstrasse Station in Tiergarten, and many buildings and a few houses in that area had been hit. Had he set off fifteen minutes earlier, Karl might well have been a casualty.

At eleven on the Tuesday morning following the air raid, Karl was back at the Brandenburg-Gorden hospital, explaining to paediatric staff, including Dr Heinze, that the IG Farben drug consignment had been bombed and there would now be at least a week's wait until a new delivery and distribution system was established. The inconvenience was regrettable, but that was war. As he walked away from the meeting, he couldn't help but smile. Small victories, small victories.

As he had hoped, Hedda was visiting Agnette. He had made up his mind that had she not been there he would telephone her house and ask her to come to the hospital. He had Walter's private number, as Walter had his, and he had already checked that Walter was working in Berlin.

Hedda was more alarmed than pleased to see Karl Muller come through the door of Agnette's hospital room after Walter's outburst the previous evening.

"Karl! What are you doing here?" she asked, rising from her chair beside Agnette's bed.

"I have to speak with you," he replied, and the urgency in his eyes set her heart racing. Had Walter said something gauche and threatening to him? She coloured at the thought, was about to start apologizing for her husband, when Karl continued: "About Agnette."

"Agnette?"

"Yes – can we talk somewhere? It is not safe here."

"Not safe? Karl, what is going on? What can you have to say about Agnette?"

"Please, Hedda." Karl took her by the shoulders and looked earnestly into her eyes. "Do you love your daughter?"

"What? Of course I do! What a stupid…"

"And do you want her to get better?" Karl searched Hedda's beautiful eyes for the slightest betrayal of anything less than candour. Found none. Hedda had never seen Karl Muller look so unambiguous about anything. His eyes were bright and passionate;

there was a determination in his tone that was uncharacteristic in her experience of the man.

"What is happening, Karl? What is this about?"

"Trust me," came the imperative response. "You can trust me, Hedda. Meet me in about five minutes in the small garden near the casualty area. Do you know where that is?"

She nodded.

"Good. We can talk there."

The emotions Hedda experienced during the course of the ensuing conversation with Karl Muller were varied to say the least. What she learned was that there was such a thing as a Child Euthanasia Programme, started by the Führer himself in 1939 and managed by some of the finest and most qualified doctors in Germany, as well as by senior SS personnel. Her own husband and, he was mortified to admit, Karl Muller himself were part of the scheme to eliminate children diagnosed as unworthy of life. She understood that if Walter – or any other SS officer for that matter – knew he was telling her this, he would be shot, and in all likelihood so would she. It was vital to the running of T4 that no "ordinary" people should get to know of what was going on, or there would be a national outcry.

He was very sorry to have to be the one to tell her, but Brandenburg hospital was a training centre for child euthanasia methods under the auspices of Drs Heinze and Gutt. If she did not believe him, she should show an interest in the new Gorden paediatric wing. She would get the same decoy-spiel response from all medical staff she asked and nothing more would they offer. And she should check out the entrance to the ward; there was a coded lock on the doors and a twenty-four-hour armed guard. Why did she suppose that was necessary for a children's ward? They would tell her it was to minimize infection risk. But she could take it from him: he had visited that ward and none of the children was infectious. Dying, yes, but not from infectious diseases.

Hedda tried to take it all in, but it was hard to believe such a horror story. "It is too far-fetched," she had said. "I cannot believe this and I don't know why you are telling me." And so he had proceeded to the immediate reason for this indiscretion, which could cost him his life: Agnette had been assessed and selected for euthanasia.

At first, Hedda had reacted with furious denial. She accused Karl of taking some sort of sick vengeance against her and Walter. Walter had probably accused him of having an affair with her and now he was getting revenge. Well, it was sick! And what was more, she would tell Walter all about it and Karl would be sorry he had ever concocted so vile and cruel a story.

"I do not know what you are talking about, Hedda," Karl had cried. "Walter has said nothing to me about any affair. I am telling you the truth at the risk of losing my life, because I want to save your daughter. Because it is the one decent, true thing I may be able to do in my miserable, godforsaken life, and if you do not believe me – if you do not believe me, then even that... Hedda, even this one good thing will not happen."

There was such desperation, so profound an agony, in his expression and voice that Hedda was arrested in her protestations, and the angry flush in her cheeks gave way to pallor. She folded her arms across her middle as though suddenly very cold.

"I will tell Walter," she said, "because if he is so senior, he can stop it. He can stop them hurting Agnette."

"No!" Karl had finally shouted, then he looked around nervously lest he had been heard by any passers-by. "You cannot tell Walter because, Hedda, Walter signed the requisition slip. He was the one who gave permission for Agnette to be killed."

Hedda almost collapsed. Karl caught her, held her upright, apologized again and again. "I have seen Agnette's records," he said. "My job means I have access to supply rooms, staff quarters, nurses' offices. I looked at her file – her full doctor's notes, forwarded from Virchow to Brandenburg when they moved her.

There is a copy of the requisition and Walter's signature next to Agnette's name. The doctor has included another note, a standard form on which are written the words 'Eligible for Special Paediatric Care', and he has stamped 'Authorized – Reich Committee' and in brackets – in handwriting – 'parental consent'."

"When?" Hedda had finally asked in a tiny voice, pushing herself away from Karl and staring at him. The March breeze lifted her hair, blew her dress against her legs, and tears sped across her face. She was shivering violently. Karl thought with an aching heart that she looked like a child herself. A desperately hurt, lost child.

"I cannot be certain," he had answered, stemming his own threatening tears by pressing the corners of his eyes with the forefinger and thumb of one hand. "I think you may have a week now. But we cannot take anything for granted. There's a number of ways they can do it. You must keep a watch on her chart – any change in drugs regime, any injections, question them immediately. Assume the worst."

"Oh, dear God in heaven!" Hedda sobbed, fell to her knees on the wet March grass. "Oh, no, no."

"Get up, Hedda. You must get up. If someone sees us... Have you got a cigarette?"

"What?"

"A cigarette? Come on, get up. Light a cigarette. That way you have a reason to be here. Here..." he took off his jacket, put it around her shoulders, lifted her to her feet. She fumbled in her handbag, but her hands were shaking too much. "Let me." Karl found the packet, took two cigarettes out, lit them both, gave her one. It was obvious in seconds that he did not smoke. He coughed and almost retched as he inhaled the smoke. "You cannot leave her alone at night. They may move her to the Gorden Wing and then there is no one to stop them there. You will get a letter telling you she died in the night."

"Stop it!" Hedda hissed at him. "Stop it! I have to think."

"There is no time. Go back to the ward. Look at the second page of her observation notes. In the top right-hand corner, there is a blue plus sign. It means she has been selected. If you get time and you can do it discreetly, look at the other children's notes – children in the side rooms. Some will have a green minus sign and some the blue plus sign. Green is good. Stay beside her. Don't ask too many questions all at once. We have to stop them from being suspicious until..."

"Until when? What, exactly, are we going to do to stop it happening?" Hedda looked at him in desperation.

"I shall think of something. Stay by her side. If you have to go home, get a maid or a nanny or someone to stay with her, and give them strict instructions not to leave her side. Tell the matron you have decided to sleep on the ward."

"Well, that will make them suspicious. I haven't slept there since we moved to Oranienburg. We live eight kilometres from the hospital, for goodness' sake."

"That's up to you, Hedda – think that one through. I have to go now. I have stayed long enough. Too risky. I will find you." Then, more gently, "My life as well as Agnette's is now in your hands, Hedda. Hers is more important. Just give me the time I need to save it. Please, don't speak to Walter. Everything I have told you is true – before God."

"God?" Hedda widened her eyes in exaggerated surprise, almost choked on the word. "You think there's a God, after all you have just said?"

"Hitler and the SS are killing these children, Hedda – not God." And he threw his unsmoked cigarette on the ground, took back his jacket and walked away from her.

Back on the ward, Hedda asked a nurse if she could make a private telephone call.

"Of course, Frau Gunther," came the reply. "Please, use the office."

"Marguerite?" Hedda kept her voice as low as she could, kept checking the door to make sure no one was approaching the office. She asked her maid to listen very carefully. "Marguerite, I need you to do exactly as I say, OK?" Marguerite agreed at once. "I need you to pretend that Anselm is unwell... I don't know, Marguerite – think of something, something infectious – a rash and a temperature – nothing too serious, but... yes, yes... keep it vague. Leave Anselm with the cook and come at once to Brandenburg hospital. Get a taxi. Ask it to wait when you get here; I'll give you the fare. Come to the children's ward and ask for me. Bring with you a bag with some overnight things in it: toiletries, change of clothes – you know. And Marguerite –" Hedda paused, realizing how very strange all this must sound to the poor woman – "Don't tell anyone, please. It's very important that you say nothing. Even to Walter – if he turns up."

Hedda stopped again. What if Walter came back from Berlin? He didn't usually come home during the first half of the week, but he was unpredictable. "If he turns up and asks where I am, just say... just say you think I have gone to stay at my mother's, but you are not sure. He shouldn't come home, Marguerite. Don't worry. I'm sorry this is so mysterious. Just trust me, OK? Yes, yes. That's right. Good. See you very soon."

When she got off the telephone and left the office, Hedda spoke to a nurse, affecting as much charm as she could. "I am so sorry, but I cannot go home tonight. I was worried about my other child, my son Anselm, when I telephoned this morning – I've been staying away on some family business. The cook said he was a bit off colour – grizzly, you know? I have just called the house to see how he is. It seems he has a temperature and a little rash on his tummy. It may be nothing, but I don't want to expose myself to whatever it is. I don't want to be prevented from seeing Agnette."

"But you may already have been exposed to the infection," answered the nurse. "These things are often contagious before the spots or fever appear, Frau Gunther."

"No," said Hedda stridently, "absolutely not. As I said, I have been very busy lately – away from home. The cook has been looking after Anselm." Then, with great indignation, "Do you think I would expose Agnette knowingly? I know how infections work. I am not an imbecile!"

"So, what would you like us to do, Frau Gunther?"

"Well, I'd like to stay here tonight, please – until Anselm is well again, actually, or until we know it's nothing to worry about." The nurse looked perplexed, began to protest. "I will not expose my daughter to an illness!" Hedda was suddenly fierce, fixing the nurse with an uncompromising glare. "I think you of all people can understand that?" The nurse nodded, said she would see what she could do, but would have to speak to Matron.

"Do that," said Hedda. "I think Matron will understand. Either that, or she will have to explain to my husband why I cannot stay with my child."

The nurse coloured. She had never seen Hedda like this. She was only too aware of the identity of Hedda's husband, but Hedda had always been so polite and modest; she had never used her connections to command special treatment before.

Back at his Voss Strasse office, Karl wrote two letters by hand. One was to His Eminence, Cardinal Orsenigo, papal nuncio in Berlin, and the other was addressed to Albert Goering, Export Director, The Skoda Munitions Factory, Pilsen, Bohemia. In the first, Karl asked for a meeting with Orsenigo, to discuss with him matters of the utmost importance to the church. He would hand it to the nuncio himself first thing in the morning. In his letter to Albert Goering, Karl reminded Goering of who he was and how they had met. He expressed his great sorrow that the Jews of the street-cleaning party had been shot to death by the Gestapo. He told Goering of the T4 Child Euthanasia Programme and what he had seen on the Brandenburg- Gorden ward. He told him of the murders of mental patients, the appalling treatment of prisoners in Sachsenhausen. He told him about Agnette Gunther and Hedda, and how Oberführer Walter Gunther, Administrative Director of Sachsenhausen and Agnette's own father, had signed the papers condemning his daughter to death. He explained that the child's mother, Hedda Gunther, had known nothing of her husband's actions.

Karl added in his letter that Agnette was semi-comatose in Brandenburg and would not last much longer now that she had been assigned "unworthy" status. He asked Albert Goering to use his influence to save Agnette in any way he could, to sabotage the work of T4 in any way possible. Karl finished by stating that he cared little for his own life, except that he might use what remained of it to do some small good before he was, inevitably, caught and disposed of.

It was just over 300 kilometres from Berlin to Pilsen, a little further than the distance from Berlin to Leipzig. Karl intended to deliver Goering's letter by hand. Although he could not afford to meet with Albert Goering, because the Pilsen Skoda munitions factory would be crawling with SS and army personnel, he could pull up in a taxi outside the factory, assume his most authoritative SS demeanour, choose a soldier, and insist the letter be put into Goering's hands immediately. He would order that the soldier confide discreetly to Herr Goering that the letter was top secret and to be read only in private. He would demand to know the soldier's name and then threaten that he would be checking that Herr Goering had received the letter. He would say that he could not spare the time to deliver the letter himself as he was busy pursuing top secret Reich business, but as soon as he returned to his office, he would be telephoning Herr Goering to discuss its contents. Then Karl would be driven back to the station to catch the next train to Berlin.

He applied for twenty-four hours' leave to attend to an urgent family matter in Leipzig. He submitted the application to Dr Brandt's IV Office on Vosse Strasse. Brandt and his team of doctors were most impressed with Karl's work; he was a dedicated, quiet man who worked Sundays. If he were requesting leave, it must be urgent. It was granted within two hours.

* * *

Marguerite, Hedda's maid, duly arrived at the children's ward, Brandenburg hospital, with a bag containing a change of clothing and other essentials for an overnight stay, and asked for Hedda. She found her employer in a highly agitated state, pacing Agnette's room, biting her fingers in impatience and anxiety. As soon as Marguerite was shown to the room, Hedda shut the door on the receding nurse, took the bag from her, then took Marguerite's hands in hers and looked straight into her eyes. "Please, Marguerite, listen very carefully. There is something I must do and I have to know I can trust you absolutely. I cannot tell you, or anyone, what it is, but it is..." She struggled for words that would convey the life-and-death importance of her mission without terrifying the maid. She decided to exploit what she knew of Marguerite's loathing of Walter. "Walter has done something... something terrible, and I have to try and put it right." It was not difficult to allow her eyes to fill with tears as she pleaded with Marguerite, and the immediate heartfelt sympathy evident in the maid's eyes encouraged Hedda's own emotional expression. "I have told the staff here that Anselm is unwell, as I explained to you on the telephone. I shall tell them that you have had no contact with Anselm; that he is being looked after by the cook. You tell them the same if they ask, OK?"

Marguerite nodded, but she looked confused, waiting for Hedda to explain how this was necessary to the righting of Walter's terrible wrong.

"I must stay with Agnette tonight. I don't want to come home in case Walter turns up."

Marguerite nodded.

"Then tomorrow morning, no later than seven o'clock, you come straight to the hospital, OK? You come here – seven o'clock?"

The maid nodded again, still waiting for the final pieces.

"You need to stay with Agnette tomorrow until I get back to you. And listen, Marguerite, this is so important! Please don't leave her side. Don't let the staff take her anywhere – scream at them if you have to, but don't let anyone take Agnette anywhere. Do you hear me?" Hedda was crying freely, her eyes wide, desperate.

Marguerite was frightened and thoroughly confused.

"It's OK, Marguerite. It's just that I don't let them do anything with Agnette without my permission. Don't let them take advantage of my not being around. Tell them I am coming back very soon."

The maid looked less alarmed, nodded again.

"When you get home this evening, tell Cook she will be looking after Anselm tomorrow. Tell her I'll explain everything when I see her." Hedda let go of Marguerite's hands, took a handkerchief from her sleeve, wiped her eyes, and sat down in a chair near Agnette's bed and put her face in her hands.

"Don't worry, Frau Gunther, I will do as you say. I understand what to do." Her tone was full of sympathy for Hedda's evident distress. "I brought you some food. It is in the bag. And a flask of coffee – how you like it. Anselm is... well." Marguerite lowered her voice for this last word and Hedda looked up. They both laughed briefly. "And I will see you tomorrow, here, seven. You go and do what you have to do. God bless."

"You, Marguerite, are an angel. Thank you." Hedda smiled warmly at the maid, then added, "I shall pay you – and Cook – double your wages for this, OK?"

Marguerite beamed and nodded delightedly. "It is my mother's birthday soon, so that will be perfect! Thank you, Frau Gunther." And she left, having first procured from Hedda enough money to pay the taxi fare.

About an hour after Marguerite had gone, the matron appeared. She was the same one Karl had encountered on Gorden Ward, for she had authority over all paediatric nurses at Brandenburg.

"Frau Gunther, my nurse tells me that you wish to stay with Agnette tonight. Is this correct?"

"It is." Hedda could not keep all the outrage and loathing out of her eyes when she looked at the matron. She knew this woman had to be complicit in the deliberate harming of children. But she managed a brief smile.

"This is irregular, Frau Gunther. Only in very exceptional cases do we allow a parent to remain with a child. And Nurse Berning also tells me you have a child at home with an infectious disease. Is this also correct?"

"It may be – it may not be infectious. In any case, I have not been exposed to him lately and neither has the maid, who will remain with Agnette tomorrow, while I attend to some important business. I do not like Agnette to be without company during the day and I do not know how long I shall be busy. I like to feed her myself – it takes a long time, as you know. I am sure your nurses are glad I do it. And she likes me to read to her and talk to her. Agnette relies on me, Matron."

"Be that as it may, Frau Gunther, I don't think it is appropriate that you stay overnight. Why must you stay with Agnette overnight?"

"Well, obviously I do not want to go home to Anselm, my son, in case he is infectious. If what he has turns out to be infectious, then I shan't be able to come back to Agnette for days, shall I?"

"Quite, but... Forgive me, Frau Gunther, is it not possible to stay in a hotel or a boarding house?"

"Why would I spend the money, Matron, to do that, if I am perfectly happy to sleep on a spare mattress beside Agnette? There is a war on, you know!" And she smiled at Matron, relaxed her tone. "I can't see what your objection is, Matron. It is hardly a great inconvenience for you to set up a spare bed in here. The room is plenty big enough. What is your objection, beyond 'irregularity'?"

The matron was not used to being gainsaid and looked icily at Hedda for a moment. She could not, though, summon another objection that would not sound impertinent to this woman whose husband was so senior in the SS. And then there was the other matter, of which Matron was of course aware. Agnette had been designated "unworthy" and the father had signed the paperwork.

She could not be sure if this display of sudden maternal agitation were in spite of or because of this fact. For now, diplomacy was the only prudent way forward.

"Very well. I shall inform the doctor of your intention."

Hedda held her gaze, then smiled sweetly. "Please do, Matron, and thank you. It is not for long. Just until I find out what is wrong with my poor little Anselm – get the all-clear. You do understand?" Another winning smile.

Matron nodded and left. Within an hour, a large armchair appeared, carried by two orderlies. "Matron says this is the best she can do; that there's a war on," one of them said, then rolled his eyes complicitly at Hedda.

"Please convey to Matron my enormous gratitude. Tell her it will do very nicely, thank you."

"I am very sorry, Officer Muller, but His Eminence Nuncio Orsenigo cannot see you," a formally suited official of the nunciature had announced to Karl in a quiet, gentle voice. The luxuriously decorated and spotlessly clean ante-room in which Karl had waited for a response to his request for a meeting with the cardinal was expansive, hung with portraits of past popes and Berlin nuncios. Gilt and polished silver glinted serenely in the early morning spring light, which seemed to fuse reverently with the peace in the room.

Until this quietly officious man had entered, Karl had been unable to detect a sound of life in the building during the fifteen minutes he had waited.

"Perhaps it is too early? Shall I come back later?"

The man closed his eyes and shook his head, clasped his hands before him. "No, Obersturmführer Muller, sir. It is simply that he cannot see you."

Karl struggled to understand. "He is busy? I know I should have made an appointment, but my business with him is urgent – absolutely urgent."

The man nodded, seemed to understand that Karl thought his business urgent. He looked at Karl directly, so there would be no misunderstanding, and repeated what he had already said twice.

Karl fought his anger, contemplated the man and considered begging, shouting, demanding. The room was oppressively still. The authority of hundreds of years of Catholic prelature, captured in the slickly oiled portraits, was stifling. He felt again the weight of his father's moral censure; the awe before the mysticism of the priest he had served as an altar boy; the sense all Catholics have that they are serving at the feet of men whose obeisance to the pope endows them with a measure of his authoritative infallibility. Karl's anger subsided before the implacability of the nuncio's secretary. In its stead came resolution. He picked up his cap from the elegantly turned table on which he had placed it. Wordlessly, he took his letter from an inner jacket pocket and gave it to the secretary to be handed at once to the cardinal. Then he put on his cap, walked past the man and out of the room.

Outside, Karl reorientated himself in the sunshine and busyness of early morning Berlin, then walked briskly in the direction of the station, where he boarded the first train for Pilsen.

Hedda spent an uncomfortable, cold and fitful night at Agnette's side. The ward seemed normal enough. She could detect all the sounds one might expect on a children's ward: whimpering, occasional loud crying and remonstrations between children and nurses; long periods of near silence, the occasional banging of doors, nurses' lowered voices as they chatted or exchanged information.

In her side room, however, Hedda could see nothing and so could not see how the children were treated; could not tell if any were rolled away silently in their beds or in wheelchairs to a place from which they would never emerge alive. The thought terrified her. It seemed that every time she began to nod off, she started awake. Twice she jumped, startled by the door to Agnette's room being opened. Each time, a nurse entered, put on the light at the head of Agnette's bed and checked her breathing, her catheter and the sheets for cleanliness, and wrote down her observations on the chart at the foot of the bed.

Hedda watched these procedures intently, reading what had been written as soon as the nurse exited the room. One of the nurses, a young one, smiled kindly at Hedda, offered her tea. It was so tempting to question her, to seek solace or assurance that those who cared for her daughter were not all monsters. But she dared not. She refused the tea, although her flask of coffee was long since emptied. She would trust them in nothing.

Hedda watched her daughter sleeping. On inestimable occasions Hedda wondered what was going on in her daughter's head. For the first five weeks after the bombing, Agnette had fought for her life, slipping in and out of consciousness then falling precipitously into a deep coma. For a month, she lay still with her eyes closed, and Hedda had talked to her, sung to her, read to her, wept over her daily.

And then one day, Hedda had come in to see Agnette at the Rudolf Virchow hospital in Berlin and her eyes were open. The doctors had said there was very little reactivity, the pupils hardly responded at all to direct light and Agnette certainly showed no signs of recognition of her mother, but it was progress, they had said. At that stage, Agnette could not swallow anything on her own. Even water simply pooled in her mouth and dribbled down her chin onto the sheets. So she had been fed through a tube into her stomach. But gradually, over weeks, Hedda's persistent attempts and gentle cajoling seemed to work. Agnette rediscovered her swallow reflex, and though the tranquil, doll-like expression in her eyes did not change, she started to swallow water, then soup, then finely mashed food.

The process of feeding her was painstaking, but Hedda was infinitely patient, finding a reserve of selflessness and love she hardly knew she had. The doctors had agreed this was more progress, but still Agnette remained motionless; made no attempt to move her limbs or speak. On just a very few occasions, though, Hedda had witnessed signs of life from her daughter that she regarded as miraculous indications of healing but the doctors dismissed gently as wishful thinking: neurological "spikes" of brain activity that were simply random.

Once, Agnette's lips had moved and she emitted a small sound, different from the occasional sighs or low moans she sometimes made. It was an obvious attempt to say "Mutti". So convinced had Hedda been of this acknowledgment of her presence that she had cried out, run for the medical staff and made them come and check her daughter for signs of new life.

That was a month ago. Other signs indicated to Hedda that Agnette was coming back. She was sure her daughter had returned the grip of her hand on at least two occasions in the last few weeks and sometimes, Hedda was certain, Agnette registered her mother's entrance to the room with definite flickers of her eyes.

Each night, Agnette's eyes closed in sleep, and every morning they opened to stare and blink upon a new day. Nothing the doctors said – no matter how often they looked into Agnette's eyes and shook their heads as they lifted her hand, then let it drop limply again – nothing would convince Hedda that Agnette was not making progress. She just knew her daughter was looking for a way back, trying doors within her head, exploring avenues, until one day she would turn the handle on the door that led to recovery and freedom. It was Hedda's job to be there when she arrived.

Ernst Schroeder was sipping his morning coffee from a china cup with such precision his moustache remained dry. One hand held the morning paper before his face. Then the maid admitted his daughter. He looked up mid sip and his eyes widened in surprise behind his glasses. "Hedda!" he exclaimed. "What are you doing here so early? We are not expecting you, are we?"

Mathilde came into the dining room, both hands busy with the application of an earring to her left lobe, her hair elegantly swept into a small beehive, figure hugged smugly by a Schiaparelli suit. The effect was finished by immaculate Italian shoes. "Darling!" she exclaimed upon seeing Hedda. "I thought I heard the door, and wondered who could be here so early. Is there something wrong?" She approached Hedda and almost recoiled in horror at her daughter's pallor, unkempt hair, the soupçon of body odour. "Hedda, whatever is the matter? Not another crisis, surely?"

Hedda began to cry. She was aware that her arrival and evident need of attention was hugely inconvenient. It was barely eight-thirty in the morning. When Marguerite had arrived at the hospital at seven a.m. promptly as promised, Hedda had rushed to her car in the hospital car park, applied some face powder and lipstick, and brushed her hair hurriedly in the windscreen mirror. Then she had driven the forty kilometres from Brandenburg to her parents' house in Tiergarten as quickly as she could in the new Audi DKW Walter had bought for her to replace the one destroyed in the August bombing.

"Hedda, sweetheart, whatever can it be?" Mathilde looked at her husband with an expression beginning as concern and ending with a confidential widening of her eyes that denoted exasperation. She could not understand why her daughter's life was so complicated and overemotional. If Walter was beastly, then Hedda should dress up and spend his money. If he was unfaithful, well, that was not necessarily disastrous. Guilty husbands were often indulgent of their wives. Hedda should stay out of Walter's way, hire an excellent nanny, divert herself. The pain and indignation of neglect, Mathilde had discovered after a few years, dulled to indifference. It was simply a matter of finding ways to fill one's time after that.

"Inge!" Mathilde called the maid, who appeared almost at once. "Be a dear and tell Cook to bring Hedda a nice breakfast and some coffee, would you?" Then, to her daughter again: "You look absolutely dreadful, darling – and so thin! Have some food and cheer up. There's a good girl."

Hedda closed her eyes and smiled ironically to herself at her mother's practical encouragement. She accepted a proffered lavender-scented handkerchief and wiped her eyes.

"You are obviously just about to go out, Mutti. Don't let me stop you. It is Father I came to see."

"Really, dear?" Mathilde's voice was tinged with relief. "Well, I was just about to go and breakfast at the Kaiserhof. A number of your father's work acquaintances are in town and staying there – some very senior men in the government. We dined with them last night – it was simply wonderful, Hedda." Mathilde was suddenly in her element, had found a wall mirror in the dining room and was primping her beehive, ensuring her lipstick hadn't smudged. She grimaced to stretch her lips, running a perfectly manicured middle fingernail along the edge of her bottom lip. "I am meeting the wives for breakfast at nine, then we are going shopping – the men are in meetings all day. I am going to suggest they dine with us here before they go home – that would be so lovely!" She was satisfied with her appearance, and eager to leave. "I can't be late, Hedda. If I had known you were coming, well... Will you be here when I get back? Probably not?"

"Probably not. Goodbye, Mutti. Enjoy your day." Hedda watched her mother cross the dining room and pause briefly at the door.

"Do try and cheer up, darling," enjoined Mathilde finally. "Life need not be so grim – war or no war. Goodbye, Hedda." And she was gone.

The cook, anxious to see Hedda, brought the breakfast tray in herself. She beamed, then her face fell as she took in her unkempt appearance. Hedda greeted her as warmly as she could manage, eyed the scrambled eggs dubiously but thanked her anyway. When the cook was gone, Hedda poured herself some coffee and looked at her father. He had sat silently through the flurry and bustle of the last eight minutes or so and wondered what, precisely, his daughter could possibly want with him. Money?

It was likely Gunther didn't give her enough. Did she want to consult with him about getting a divorce, moving back home? That would be too inconvenient. Hedda and Anselm were noisy and he liked his life quiet. Then there was all that to-ing and fro-ing to hospitals, and tears at dinner.

By the time Hedda was ready to speak, Ernst had decided to buy his daughter an apartment, wherever she wanted to live. He didn't blame her for wanting to divorce Walter Gunther. Personally, Ernst couldn't stand the man. But neither did he want to get involved. The last thing he needed was Oberführer Walter Gunther breathing down his neck about divorce settlements and access to his children. He hoped Hedda wasn't going to take too long or get emotional. Ernst needed to be at work by nine-fifteen, latest. He was entirely unprepared for what his daughter said next.

"Father, I know you are just a chemist."

Ernst raised his eyebrows, looked at Hedda indignantly.

"No, I don't mean to be rude – not like that. I mean that I know you are not a military man, or a Gestapo officer or something, so I know you won't have anything to do with what I am about to tell you... and you may be horribly shocked."

Hedda wondered how she could break to him what she had learned from Karl Muller only yesterday. Already, she felt as though she had lived with the knowledge a long time. She was sorry to inflict on her father the malaise such knowledge brought. She did not have much time to hold his attention, however, and he was not a man to indulge fantasy or rumour, so she would have to be direct.

Her father was the single most powerful figure in her life apart from Walter, and the only one she could assume was on her side. He was rich and he had a very senior, influential position in a major German company. He consorted with government officials. He was her only chance of help. There was no knowing if Karl Muller was trustworthy or really in a position to help her daughter.

"Don't ask me how I know what I am about to tell you," Hedda began, "but I can assure you my source is reliable and I am not just being hysterical... or... or... having a breakdown or something."

"Go on." Ernst took off his reading glasses, folded them and put them in a case that he took from an inside jacket pocket. Then he looked in the opposite inside pocket for another glasses case and opened it, took out his distance glasses and applied them in order to clearly see Hedda in her seat halfway down the dining table.

"I know about something – some secret government plan called T4." Ernst was unable to hide his surprise. Hedda saw his discomfiture. "You have heard of it!"

Ernst coloured a little, recovered his composure. "I have... that is, we hear rumours."

"Well, what I am about to tell you is not a rumour, Father. I am sorry to come here and burden you with such a horrible thing, but... I have no one else."

Ernst wanted desperately to go to work. He simply could not afford to discuss with his daughter anything to do with T4. No civilians were supposed to know about T4. This was a potentially very compromising situation.

"Hedda, I cannot be late for work. And what you have just said, well, if it is true, it is highly secret – dangerous to discuss. Who could possibly have said such a thing to you?" But the suspicion that Walter had been indiscreet or that Hedda had discovered some carelessly discarded document in Walter's office at home was occurring to him. This was preferable to her having learned it some other way. He drained his coffee cup, began to stand up, decidedly nervous now.

"No, Father!" Hedda shouted and made Ernst jump. "You may not just leave me this time. You need to listen to me. It is a matter of life and death – Agnette's life or death!"

"How dare you speak to me in this manner, Hedda!" protested Ernst. "Whatever has become of you?" He stood up and walked to where she sat, regarding his daughter directly.

Hedda in turn jumped to her feet, knocking her chair over. She faced him. "I dare speak to you like this, Father," she began again, more quietly, "because I have it on good authority that Walter – my husband and Agnette's father – has consented to have Agnette killed!"

Ernst could not speak; could hardly process the statement at first.

"Something to do with a child euthanasia project: this T4 organization. They round up children they think are too sick, or mentally helpless... I don't know. I know it sounds insane, but you have to believe me, Vati!" She had not used the diminutive to address her father since she was a small child. "Walter has actually agreed to let them kill my little girl with drugs, because they do not think she will ever get better and that she is..." Hedda tried to recall the words Karl had used, the term the government used, to describe children of no use to the Reich – "oh, some horrible term... 'useless' or 'not fit to live' or something. I know how absurd it sounds, but apparently even doctors and nurses are taking children to special places where they actually murder them! I have to stop them from hurting Agnette. Vati, I need your help. You might be able to speak to Walter or... or get Agnette out of the hospital for me. Help me get her away from here. Give us the money to escape – please, I am begging you. Help me to stop them killing my child – your granddaughter!" Exhaustion, grief, desperation all overwhelmed Hedda as she stood before her father. She covered her face and sobbed.

It had been a long time since anyone had touched her gently or held her. She was almost shocked when Ernst placed tentative hands on her shoulders. She suddenly collapsed into his chest, and he put his arms around her and held his daughter as she wept. He could not think what to say. After some moments, Ernst gently pushed Hedda away, looked into her face. So much grief! How very tired and helpless she looked.

She had grown into a beautiful young woman right in front of him, with hardly a sound. Her expression had changed from open smiles and round-eyed happiness to studied, pencilled pouts and detached resignation. Her school grades had been unremarkable; she seemed uninterested in anything that required concentration. Her only reading matter was glossy magazines. But it was true that he had never tried to engage her interest. Ernst had assumed Hedda was unintelligent, and in any case, given her gender and class, intellect was superfluous. Her mother schooled her in all she needed to know about make-up and couture. Ernst and Hedda had had no common ground from which to begin a conversation. Until now.

"Hedda," began Ernst, "I do not know who has been filling your head with all this... dramatic information... " She pulled back violently, began to protest. He silenced her by closing his eyes and raising a hand. "I have not finished. I would very much like to know who has been talking to you." His voice was quiet, concerned.

Hedda was tempted to confide in him, but she recalled Karl's face; how terrified he had been when he had spoken to her; how he had said they would kill him if his treachery were discovered. She shook her head and looked away from her father's searching eyes.

"Then I must surmise such talk is rumour, but –" again he cut off her nascent protestations – "I will look into it. Listen to me, Hedda." Ernst regarded his daughter with renewed focus and his tone was prescriptive. "You must not speak of this, of our conversation here, to anyone. Do you hear me?"

Hedda was startled by his earnestness, but at least he was not dismissing her.

"I mean it, Hedda. Speak to no one of this. I cannot help you if you do. I will speak to you again shortly, when I... know a little more." He kissed her lightly on the forehead, pulled her gently to one side so that he could proceed from the dining room. "I have to go – I will certainly be late for work. Please, drink some coffee, have a little breakfast, Hedda. You look so tired."

"But what can I do right now to save Agnette, Father? How can I stop them from hurting her right now?" She turned to watch his progress from the room.

Ernst halted, turned to look at her once more over his distance glasses, removed them, replaced them in their case and returned them to an inner pocket. "Be calm. Try to be calm, Hedda. Stay with her. Try not to arouse suspicion. Act normally. Say nothing to anyone – least of all Walter. Do you understand me?"

Hedda sighed, nodded. "Thank you, Vati." Then, as he turned from her again she added, "I do love you, you know."

Ernst stopped suddenly, placed a hand on the door frame, bowed his head as if trying to remember something, then left.

Following the series of phase two development meetings with several senior Reich ministers and IG Farben board members that Ernst had scheduled for that day, he telephoned his son-in-law and arranged to meet him at Walter's T4 offices.

"I will come straight to the point, Walter," Ernst began, coughing nervously, removing his glasses and cleaning them with shaking hands. "Someone has told Hedda – or she has found out somehow – about T4, and..."

"What?" Walter was instantly furious. "How is that possible? How can you know this?" he shouted, rising from his chair.

"Please, Walter!" Ernst hastily put on his glasses again and lifted a hand as if to stop Walter advancing. "I am only telling you what I know. Naturally, I had not assumed you knew already..."

"What are you implying?" Walter leaned on his desk and glared at his father-in-law. "Are you suggesting I have told her? Because I certainly have not."

"No, Walter. I said I had not assumed you knew!" Ernst raised his voice in frustration at Walter's refusal to let him speak or to listen. "If you would do me the courtesy of listening to me, please. This is very difficult." Ernst tried to collect himself. All morning, Hedda's distress, the horror that he was now involved in a potential violation of the essential secrecy with which the T4 work was conducted and the inevitability of this encounter with Walter had distracted him terribly. It had loomed like a gathering storm just below the veneer of normality he was obliged to keep intact throughout the day's phase two meetings.

His own board presentation of cost and profit projections regarding a proposed new plant construction near the Auschwitz camp had been nerve-racking enough. He had long been working on the calculations and research necessary to present viable costings for the use of camp inmates as labour to produce the chemicals that would exterminate them. Once the war was won, the factory would become an industrial chemical centre providing work for the local population. But Ernst had not been prepared for how the science and theory of extermination became harder to expostulate with conviction when one's own granddaughter was a designated victim. And he had been most unprepared for how moved he had been by Hedda's grief and her declaration of love for him. It had been decades since anyone had said they loved him.

"Please, Walter –" Ernst spoke again, sadness usurping his anger – "sit down. I do not know how Hedda has discovered this, but she is aware that... Well, she says..."

"What? Spit it out! What did she say?" Walter consented to sit down again, but he was in no mood to be patronized by this old man for whom he had little personal regard. He had no choice but to work with his father-in-law and he understood Ernst was an excellent chemist, but he did not like him.

When first Walter had become infatuated with Hedda, Ernst seemed lukewarm and indifferent. His demeanour hardly changed after they were married. At some level, Walter had been terribly hurt and then angered by Ernst's lack of enthusiasm at his daughter's choice of husband. Part of him had hoped that marriage would bring him a degree of paternal surrogacy, a share in his wife's rights to fatherly affection. But it soon became apparent that where Walter's own father had alienated him by expecting too much of him, a similarly unbreachable gulf had developed between Ernst and Hedda, caused by Ernst's indifference. Walter could not hope to be included by extension in a bond that was not there, and the evidence in Ernst's demeanour that the acquisition of Walter as a son did nothing to inspire paternal interest was doubly galling.

Now, Ernst regarded the angry young man before him and sighed. Everything suddenly seemed so hopeless. "She says you have agreed to let Agnette die. She says she knows this from a reliable source. Is it true?"

Walter's expression changed from glowering anger to shock. His face relaxed into a sort of neutral bewilderment.

"I can see that it is true," remarked Ernst. He took off his glasses again, looked for a chair and sat down.

When Walter spoke once more, his voice was quiet. "Agnette is not going to get well." It was the first time he had voiced aloud any feelings or opinions about his daughter in a very long time. Indeed, he had not even said her name aloud for weeks.

"So it seems," Ernst responded, then looked quickly at Walter to ensure he was not misunderstood. "I mean, apparently this is the prognosis of the doctors at Brandenburg." There was a short silence during which both men contemplated the little girl whose life had been measured and valued so slightly.

"How could she have discovered this?" Walter was still subdued. He even sounded sad.

"Hedda?" Ernst sighed again, made a face he used when estimating chemical reactions. "Perhaps she saw the records? She is in the hospital a long time each day. It is possible she had access to the files, became curious?"

Walter shook his head. "No. Everything is coded. Nothing is stated – we are very careful of that. She could not have understood what the notes meant. Someone must have told her."

Ernst began carefully, only too aware of the volatility of Walter's temper. "Forgive me, Walter, but is it certain she has not found out from you?" Then quickly he added, "You know. Perhaps a mislaid document, a phone call overheard, sleep-talking – I don't know…"

Walter considered each possibility then, dismissed them all definitively. "Absolutely not."

"Then… how?"

"'Who', you mean." Walter narrowed his eyes, put his hands together as if praying, then brought the tips of his fingers to his lips in an attitude of focused thought. His eyes widened suddenly and something like triumph lit his eyes. "I may have an idea who did this."

"Who? One of the nursing staff?"

"Perhaps, but I have another suspect."

Ernst waited expectantly when Walter did not enlighten him, then he grew irritated. "Well who, in God's name, man?"

Walter, however, had recovered control. Distracted from his own culpability in the betrayal of his daughter and wife by the treachery of another to the Reich, he was busy transmuting his guilt to a desire for vengeance. He got briskly to his feet. "I am afraid I am not yet at liberty to say, but I must start investigations. You must excuse me, Ernst."

But Ernst was not to be so easily dismissed. Having been stirred to consider anew the importance to his life of his daughter and granddaughter, he wanted to discuss the advisability of proceeding with the planned disposal of Agnette by whatever means Walter had authorized.

"Just a minute, Walter." He too rose from his chair. "What are you going to do about Agnette now? Surely you cannot… go ahead as planned? Hedda knows! Think, man. Think of the consequences!"

Walter seemed to pause, lowered his head, half nodded. "I'll speak to Brandt," he said. "In any case, he must know that the whole operation is possibly compromised. Now please, I must go. Heil Hitler."

Ernst returned the salute and without further words left Walter's office.

Back at the hospital in Brandenburg, Hedda had ascertained from Marguerite that no one had tried to move Agnette and, apart from changing her catheter bag, changing the sheets and giving Agnette a wash, the nurses had not attended to her. Certainly they had not tried to administer drugs. The painstaking spooning into Agnette's mouth of prescribed amounts of fluids and mashed-up cereal with fruit, they had gladly left to Marguerite. There was a definite flicker of recognition when Agnette heard her mother's voice.

"You see? Did you see that?" Hedda had smiled delightedly, looking at Marguerite. "She knew I was back!"

Marguerite had seen and she smiled back warmly at Hedda, but she felt great compassion for both mother and daughter. She had sat at Agnette's side for four hours, and she was bored and cramped in this silent, isolated room. Used to a big, noisy family and the demands of a busy life, Marguerite was ill equipped for the patient silence that was Hedda's natural sanctuary. The prostrate little girl, scarred and staring at the window with far-away eyes, seemed unearthly to Marguerite. The room was morgue-like and oppressive to her.

"What shall I do now, Frau Gunther?" Marguerite had asked quietly.

"Go back to the house, Marguerite. Help Cook with Anselm, carry on as usual. But remember, if anyone here asks, you are not looking after him – OK? They must think you cannot be infectious. I am hoping Walter did not come home last night. He usually doesn't come home till Wednesday when he works in Berlin. If he does turn up, act normally. Tell him I am staying with Agnette because..." She fought the hatred that rose spontaneously in her chest when she thought of what he had done; remembered she must not divulge it to Marguerite. Then an idea occurred that gave some satisfaction to her burning outrage. "Tell him I am staying here because there are definite signs of improvement in Agnette's condition and I am so excited I wish to stay with her." The idea grew into more than a way of scalding Walter's conscience; she grew excited. "Yes, Marguerite, tell him that I am of the hope – the belief – that Agnette may be going to wake up."

Marguerite looked involuntarily at the girl in the bed and adjusted her doubtful expression before responding to Hedda, "Yes, Frau Gunther. I will tell him." Then, as she collected her coat and the bag she had brought to Hedda that morning, now containing washing and the empty coffee flask, she said, "Shall I bring you more clothes and coffee tonight? Some nice toiletries, perhaps? More magazines?"

Hedda smiled and nodded. "Yes please, and bring some more books. Here –" she crossed to the windowsill and retrieved a number of children's story books, put them in the bag, "some more books for Agnette, please. We are tired of these now." Marguerite smiled again, turned to go. "And Marguerite..."

"Yes, Frau Gunther?"

"Give Anselm a very big kiss from me."

Marguerite smiled broadly, saying, "Of course I will." And she was gone.

CHAPTER TEN

Walter met Dr Brandt for dinner at the Hotel Adlon Kempinski in central Berlin. The early evening light allowed spectacular views of the Brandenburg Gate from the restaurant windows. Brandt ordered goose liver pâté, lamb with sage and lime sauce, champagne. Walter said he would have the same. In truth, his appetite was depressed by the burden of his business. Possibly, he was about to divulge most unwelcome information to Hitler's private physician and overall director of the top secret T4 Child Euthanasia Programme. Even worse, the divulgence would invite close scrutiny of Walter's own loyalty in what might be a most compromising breach of security.

For his part, Brandt would not have chosen to dine with Gunther had Walter not insisted that he had business of great import to discuss. He did not like SS Oberführer Gunther; his taciturn manner and ascetic demeanour were not to Brandt's extrovert tastes. He preferred the company of sophisticated people who were not afraid to laugh out loud and enjoy themselves. Walter Gunther seemed always on the verge of petulance. Still, by all accounts he was efficient, and Himmler thought highly of him.

The splendidly lavish Adlon Kempinski was Brandt's favourite place to stay and dine when he sojourned in Berlin on business, and he had reserved a table before Gunther had tracked him down late in the afternoon and insisted on a meeting at his nearest convenience. It was not convenient to invite Gunther to join him for dinner, but his diary was otherwise full for days, so here was the Oberstumführer, flushed and clearly anxious, at Brandt's table.

Enough to spoil a man's appetite. Brandt was relieved when the champagne arrived. It might help loosen things up a little.

"So, Officer Gunther, what was it you wanted to talk to me about?" Brandt poured Walter a generous glass of champagne. Walter nodded his thanks, took the stem of the glass and lifted it to his mouth, took two successive deep gulps. Brandt raised an eyebrow, refilled his glass. "That serious, eh?"

"Herr Director Brandt," began Walter, "what do you know about Obersturmführer Karl Muller?"

"Muller?" Brandt looked surprised, considered a moment. "He seems a good man – clever, quiet, gets on with things. Why?"

"Because I am not entirely sure yet, but I am almost certain that Muller might have... leaked certain top secret information to... to a civilian."

"Really?" Brandt considered anew, sipped his own champagne. "What makes you think so?"

Walter felt, to his horror, the dreaded creeping redness rising hotly up his throat to his face. His anger at his vulnerability to this tell-tale sign of his emotional instability added to the speed and intensity of his blush. He compensated by sounding increasingly authoritative and officious. "It has come to my attention that Muller has informed a member of the public that... that a child is to be... to be..."

Walter was experiencing a sensation close to panic. He seemed to have no control over the fear that was spreading throughout his body and making his throat close. He was trembling so much that he wanted to grip his chair to steady himself and take deep breaths to slow his heart, but he had to try and carry on talking and acting normally. His wholly unexpected discomfiture was not alleviated by the knowledge that he was before one of the most gifted and illustrious physicians in Germany and a close personal friend of the Führer himself.

Brandt, preoccupied with the champagne and trying to remember anything untoward about the apparently modest and likeable Muller, did not realize Walter's difficulty until he could not finish his sentence. Now he looked at Gunther, saw how flustered he had become, assumed he was embarrassed at this possible betrayal of a fellow SS officer, and paid closer attention.

"He has told a parent that their child is to be killed. Is that it?"

Walter nodded, grateful for the interpretation. He used the pause to recover his composure a little.

"I see." Brandt frowned and looked at the table, raised an eyebrow, took another drink. "Poor devil."

Walter's immediate indignation at Brandt's sympathy for Muller was distraction enough from his own acutely anxious state to allow less self-conscious speech. "I don't understand, sir."

The goose liver pâté arrived and Brandt smiled delightedly at the waiter. "Splendid! Many thanks." The doctor applied his napkin to his lap with an expert flourish and took another sip of champagne. "Well, it all makes perfect sense." Brandt spread some pâté on a geometrically perfect square of finely toasted white bread. Walter waited for the revelation that must follow such a statement. "You see, I remembered, while you were talking, that I received a letter a few weeks ago – perhaps longer, let me see..." Brandt chewed, nodded, looked at Walter and said before he had entirely swallowed the pâté, "This is excellent pâté, my friend. Try it."

Walter by now was sufficiently unimpressed by Brandt's casual reception of his confidence to be almost composed once more. He did not even make the effort to smile at Brandt's prandial encouragement.

Brandt seemed unperturbed, and continued, "Yes, some time after Christmas I got a letter from a chap called... Kauf... stein? Kauf... man? Yes, I think – a Dr Kaufman. I think I had met him before at some meeting. Anyway, this Kaufman is a psychiatrist in Leipzig – the asylum." Brandt spread a little more pâté on toast; chewed thoughtfully.

"What did he say, sir?" Walter was barely able to control his impatience. He had decided Brandt was a fool. He wondered how the Führer could hold him in such high regard. This was no way to do business. Why wasn't he taking seriously this breach of confidentiality?

At last, Brandt stopped chewing, looked straight at Walter and continued. "He said that Muller had removed his wife from the asylum at Leipzig. He phrased it politely, carefully, but he said he thought it irregular that an SS officer, even a senior one, could suddenly turn up and withdraw a patient from his care – even if the patient was that officer's wife. He said he understood family ties were important, etcetera, etcetera, but he still felt SS officers should observe protocols and have respect for professional procedures. He was clearly furious." Brandt allowed himself a chuckle at Kaufman's expense, shook his head, savoured his pâté.

Walter was fascinated – his fears once more allayed by this divulgence of the contents of so confidential and incriminating a letter. He was hugely impatient to know how this situation had been resolved. "I see," Walter said, "and what happened?"

Brandt looked irritated. This man was rude and spoiling his dinner. Gunther hadn't touched his appetizer, and now he was on the verge of accusing Brandt of some sort of professional negligence.

"What do you imagine 'happened', Gunther?" Brandt looked directly at Walter again. "Nothing 'happened'. You cannot blame a man for looking after his wife. Apparently, Muller took her out of the asylum and made alternative arrangements for her care – with her parents, I believe. Wouldn't you do the same?" He lowered his voice, leaned towards Walter, his eyes now deadly serious. "If you knew what might become of your wife in such a place because you had... inside knowledge, wouldn't you use your position and influence to save her from possible harm?"

Walter felt the panic returning; sought to respond before it rose again to his throat. "And how does this excuse his recent breach of confidence, his betrayal of the Reich Office?"

Brandt sat back, took his napkin from his knee, rolled it and placed it carefully on the table to his right. He had decided to speed up this dinner, much as it pained him to leave his pâté unfinished.

He could, however, see how Himmler liked this Oberführer Gunther. They had much in common. Both were more reptilian than human.

"It does not excuse it, Oberführer Gunther, but it does explain it." Brandt sat back once more, cleared some toast from a back tooth with his tongue. "I can turn a blind eye to a colleague exploiting his rank to benefit his family. Within reason, of course. It makes no difference to the Reich if Muller's wife is removed from an asylum in Leipzig." Here he paused, then continued in a tone that was probably close to the one he employed when discussing diagnoses with colleagues. "But Muller is clearly suffering from a guilty conscience and he has taken pity on some poor parent. He has *empathized*, Officer Gunther." Walter said nothing. Brandt sipped his champagne, seemed to reflect a moment, then resumed his train of thought. "And for that reason alone – if what you say is true –" and he looked at Walter coldly – "he must be disciplined. Probably removed from the programme."

Walter's glowering expression dissolved in pleasant surprise. He smiled, took a deep breath, raised his champagne glass to Brandt in a toast.

"Pity," added Brandt reflectively. "I liked him."

"Heil Hitler," Walter smiled charmingly, his voice warm with renewed admiration.

More like it, thought Brandt.

"I understand, Director Brandt," added Walter as an apparent afterthought, "but what shall we do about... about the child?"

The medic frowned once more, responded matter-of-factly. "The child should be left well alone," he pronounced. "Muller should be made to look like a mad man for suggesting such a thing." Then he drained his glass, looked directly at Walter. "What is wrong with the child?"

Walter took a handkerchief from a pocket and pretended he needed to blow his nose. Brandt looked away discreetly.

"Some incurable paralysing disease – I am not sure."

Brandt nodded, lost interest. "Well, see whichever doctor is responsible. Get... him – her? – off the list. Explain there has been a potential security breach. Don't go into details. Get the child home, away from the hospital and access to staff. And, Gunther..."

"Yes, Dr Brandt?"

"Make sure this is the only one. Find out if he has spoken to others."

"Yes, sir," Walter replied.

"Excellent. Good work, Gunther. Now for pity's sake, man, eat your pâté – it's absolutely marvellous."

Back at his office, Walter telephoned Dr Heinze at Brandenburg hospital. He discovered that Hedda had remained overnight at the hospital with Agnette and that she was most insistent on remaining that night also. Yes, he could confirm that Muller had visited the hospital within the last week or so, to talk about drug consignments and to visit the wards, prior to the warehouse bombing. Nothing seemed to have been done since; they were still awaiting a new consignment. They were now behind schedule. There were now many spaces on Gorden Ward and several patients on the children's ward who could occupy those spaces. But should they proceed according to the old regime or wait for the new 'treatments'?

Walter had responded that they should proceed according to previous protocols and he would personally look into the delay with the deliveries. And then, as if he had just remembered, he added that there might possibly have been a breach in security. It was most regrettable, but his daughter was no longer entitled to special paediatric treatment. He was not questioning Drs Heinze and Gutt's judgment, but it might be prudent to take Agnette off the special list for now. He could not elaborate further at present.

"That explains a lot," Heinze had commented wryly, clearly referring to Hedda's unusual behaviour. Of course he would comply immediately. Might he ask about the source of the indiscretion?

"Have you noticed anything unusual about Obersturmführer

Muller's behaviour?" Walter had replied. "For example, has he been speaking to any nursing staff in particular, or to Frau Gunther, by any chance, on his visits to Brandenburg?"

Dr Heinze said he would conduct discreet enquiries.

But Walter was in no mood to wait for enough circumstantial evidence to be amassed on which to arrest Muller as an enemy of the Reich. He had already thought of a plan to precipitate his conviction.

"Emilie!" He shouted for his secretary through his open office door.

"Yes, Officer Gunther, sir?" Emilie was present in seconds, notebook and pen at the ready. A young, plain girl of diminutive stature, she was unfailingly nervous in Walter's presence. This, however, made her quick to obey and super-efficient, for she dreaded his censure.

"Get me the number of a Dr Kaufman in Leipzig. He works at some lunatic asylum down there. There can't be many. As quickly as you can, please." And Emilie was gone. Within ten minutes she reappeared with the number. "Thank you, Emilie. Now, shut the door."

Moments later, Walter was speaking directly to Kaufman. He apologized for the tardiness of the response to the good doctor's letter regarding the sudden removal of a Frau Muller from his care, around Christmas time? The letter had received the close attention of Dr Brandt himself, and Dr Brandt had confided in him about the incident. Now Walter was telephoning, he said, to discuss what he agreed amounted to a most regrettable breach of protocol; procedures should of course be observed at all times. After all, continued Walter, he understood the patient was very ill and needed to remain hospitalized?

Dr Kaufman emphatically confirmed this. The patient was suicidal when he last treated her, he said, and needed heavy sedation to ensure she was not a threat to herself. The prognosis was very poor. Frau Muller was certainly a candidate for ECT, in Kaufman's opinion, and it was not at all appropriate that she should be in a domestic setting.

Walter made sympathetic noises and said how deeply regrettable the whole thing was, but that SS Officer Muller was now fully understanding of the need to respect Reich protocols and was in agreement that his wife should be returned to the asylum. Authorizing paperwork from Dr Brandt's office would follow in the next few days by priority post. From now on, Dr Kaufman's assessments of the patient's welfare, and no one else's, would be paramount, and the Reich Office would watch the development of the case with interest.

Kaufman thanked Walter for his courteous and most professional call, and confided further that he had been most insulted by the manner and behaviour of Officer Muller – very abrupt and rude. And, if he was not too impertinent in suggesting it, in Kaufman's professional opinion, Muller seemed to be suffering from a nervous disorder of some sort himself – he was highly strung and anxious; his professional judgment obviously questionable. Oh, and he had terrified one of the nurses before Christmas; threatened her, Dr Kaufman believed.

"Emilie!"

Again, with the speed and demeanour of a nervous rabbit, Emilie popped her head around the office door. "Yes, Herr Oberführer Gunther, sir?"

"Come in and take a letter. Stamp it officially, send it immediately, high priority post, Reich business. Ready?"

Hedda had spent two nights at the hospital, as well as most of three days, and she was exhausted. It was almost impossible to sleep properly in the armchair she had been given, and she suffered from bad dreams when she did doze off. The end of March weather was grey and rainy, and a chill wind swept in from the east, so that even getting outside for a few moments' fresh air was unpleasant. In any case, she hardly dared leave Agnette.

But the more time passed without incident, the more she began to wonder if she had been insane to listen to Karl. She had noted the blue plus sign on Agnette's notes, but had not had the opportunity to check other children's notes for similar symbols or the green minus signs Karl had mentioned. It was hard to tell from a side room if other children were being moved suspiciously and not just going home. Certainly, she recognized a few children and their regular visitors. They seemed to be getting better and Hedda could detect nothing out of the ordinary in the days she remained with her daughter.

When she doubted Karl's story, she felt hot flushes of embarrassment. What had she been thinking, rushing to her father like that with such a story? He would think her hysterical. And her anxiety was compounded by the silence of Agnette's room and the increasing loneliness Hedda felt, isolated as she was from Anselm, whom she desperately missed.

The two days since she had spoken with Karl in the hospital gardens seemed much longer ago, so slowly the quiet hours passed. Marguerite's brief visits with clothes and coffee and food from home were welcome punctuations in the monotony, but she longed to talk to someone; to share with someone trustworthy the terrible fears and sadness she felt by turn as the slow hours slid by.

And then something astonishing happened. Something that confirmed she was not insane and that Muller was to be trusted and that she had done the right thing in speaking to her father. Upon returning from a short walk to the hospital gardens for a cigarette, Hedda checked Agnette, checked the chart at the end of the bed – as she did compulsively every time she returned from the bathroom or a cigarette break. But on this occasion there was an amendment that she was certain had been made in the ten minutes since she stepped out of the room. Hedda carried the notes to the armchair, sat down heavily. She was trembling violently. The second page with the stamped blue cross in the top right-hand corner had gone.

And then, on the evening of the same day, the last Wednesday in March, Ernst and Mathilde Schroeder arrived to visit their granddaughter. Mathilde was elegant in grey, gloves to match, handbag dangled daintily across one forearm.

"Your father was most insistent we come, Hedda, and he was right: we have been too negligent." She kissed Hedda on each cheek, looked into her eyes, tutted at how exhausted she seemed.

Ernst stood, hands in pockets at the door, his jaw working fiercely as though fighting some strong emotion. His eyes were fixed on the bed where Agnette lay staring at the dark March sky through the small window. Only when Mathilde had stopped fussing and had moved to her granddaughter's bedside, smiling into Agnette's clear eyes, did Ernst look at his daughter. He held her anxious gaze, nodded. Hedda could not dam the tears that spilled down her face.

"Is there any change, Hedda? Darling! You're upset!" Mathilde looked for somewhere to put down her handbag, hesitated a moment, looked apologetically at Agnette, then placed it on the bed. She opened it and took out a handkerchief. Carefully in her tight skirt, she hunkered down before her daughter and dabbed at her eyes with the handkerchief. "Darling, everything will be better from now on, you'll see," crooned Mathilde soothingly. "We know you have had a very difficult time and you have been so brave. Your father has told me a few things..." Hedda looked to Ernst in alarm. He frowned, shook his head quickly. "Oh, don't worry, just outlines, nothing detailed. You know your father. But we do know that life is not... easy for you, Hedda. We want to do more. We have been talking and, well, we want to help, don't we, Ernst?"

Ernst nodded, looked again at Hedda, looked down at the floor.

Hedda could not speak for some time, crying as if her heart would break.

"Oh, darling." Mathilde sounded genuinely moved. "It is not as bad as all that – you'll see. It never is." She fingered her pearls agitatedly, looking to Ernst for help.

"Hedda." At last, Ernst spoke. "I have something to tell you that even your mother doesn't know." Mathilde stood up, an exaggeratedly surprised expression on her face, and stared at her husband. "The doctors say you can take Agnette home. I can arrange for an ambulance to collect her tomorrow morning."

"But... how? When did you hear this, Ernst? Why didn't you tell me?" spluttered Mathilde. "How can you possibly know such a thing before Hedda does?"

"I bumped into Walter, at work. He won't be home this evening, by the way, Hedda, so he asked me to pass on the news." Mathilde looked confused for a few seconds longer, then she shrugged, turned back to Hedda, who was smiling and crying and half laughing, then crying. Suddenly, Hedda leapt to her feet, kissed her mother, then crossed the room in seconds and pressed herself against her father's chest.

"Thank you, Vati," she sobbed into his neck. "Thank you, thank you, thank you."

Ernst held his daughter tightly and could no longer fight the tears that had been pricking at his throat since he had opened the side room door and beheld her – forlorn, alone, dishevelled; guarding her daughter against harm.

Since Hedda had come to him, Ernst had hardly slept. It was as if he had been shaken from some sort of limited consciousness state in which he functioned without any real sensibility. It was not difficult for Ernst to detach himself from feelings, and proceed logically; he had been trained to do it from an early age by a father whose own eminent scientific career had required the same objectivity. In fact, until very recently, it had been devilishly difficult for Ernst to feel anything that was not generated by a series of logical choices or responses. The difficulty, he was discovering, with assuming life was chemical, was that the premise was unable to explain a number of stubborn irreductions. If thoughts were simply neurons firing in the brain, why was his heart breaking? And why was he now unable to redirect his thoughts to paths the corollaries of which were not emotionally debilitating? And how was he now to reconcile, logically or otherwise, the work he had done to reprieve from death his own granddaughter, with the orders he would soon receive to supply replacement drugs for the T4 Office Child Euthanasia Programme?

Karl, increasingly, had taken to praying. He could do nothing more in his own strength. There was not a circumstance in his own life over which he had control. He had done all he could do to save his wife and Agnette Gunther, and he had not instructed Herr Schroeder at IG Farben to supply a new drugs consignment following the bombing last Sunday night. Neither had he any intention of doing so. By now, someone would have mentioned the absence of communication regarding supplies. It was simply a question of time before he was held to account.

He had tried his best to alert the church authorities to the T4 programme. They would not listen. He had taken a huge risk in travelling to Pilsen with his letter for Albert Goering. Now, he could only pray Goering could do something to help. If not – if the letter had been intercepted or Goering suspected a trap of some sort – it was only a matter of time before Karl was arrested.

The only reason he did not simply walk away, go to Leipzig, collect his wife and make a run for it, was because he knew the trap that would ensnare him was already sprung. If he drew attention to Greta now, who knew what they might do to her? He had to find a way of seeing her discreetly one last time. The problem was, he had recently requested emergency leave for family business in order to travel to Pilsen. Another such request would focus attention on him sooner than he would like. He had resolved not to have any more involvement in killing anyone. This would prove difficult, as it was his job. If he refused to do it, he would be incarcerated or worse. That was preferable to killing children, but what about Greta? How could he protect her if he was in prison or dead? And so, paralysed by lack of choice, lonelier and more desperate than he would have known how to explain, Karl turned to prayer as an alternative to suicide.

Raised on Catholic liturgy, Karl began with the prayers he had learned by heart in catechism and then from attending Mass every Sunday with his family and as an altar boy. He derived immense solace from the Lord's Prayer and the idea of a benevolent Father who understood perfectly his heart and his difficulties. In relinquishing to God the impossibility of his situation, and trusting that he had the power to provide solutions where human beings could not imagine them, Karl unburdened his soul and found the strength he needed to wait with a level of equanimity and even peace, the denouement of his life. "Lord, I am not worthy to receive you, but only say the word and I shall be healed," he repeated over and over again. That he was repentant of his sins was beyond doubt. Nonetheless, Karl was determined to make his Confession. He walked to St Michael's Church in Kreuzberg. He would confess to a priest the terrible, abominable details of the T4 programme. He would spew it all from his guts and nightmares in an attempt to purge his soul, but also to solicit aid. He knew Catholics throughout Germany were openly assisting persecuted Jews, but someone needed to prevent the helpless "unworthies" from being sacrificed upon what Karl had decided was a satanic altar.

Where was God? It was a good question. As far as Karl could tell, he had been rejected as surplus to requirements when Hitler had vowed publicly at an SS training event at Vogelsang Castle in 1939 that he would crush Christianity beneath his boot like the "poisonous toad it was". God had been deprived of authority in Germany when he was systematically deleted from the Old Testament because he was a Jew. Jesus, Hitler had asserted openly, was an anti-Semite, driving the "enemies of the human race out of the temple".

It was no secret in SS circles that Hitler's "Reich Church" was to replace Christian churches of all denominations once the war was won. Rosenberg, Hitler's cultural and educational leader and main proponent of Nazi ideology, had stated publicly on several occasions that he spoke for Hitler when he said all Catholic and Protestant churches must eventually disappear, making way for what Goebbels pronounced would be a "National Reich Church", within which Hitler would be the intermediary between the Aryan race and the throne of God. Hitler had a hundred thousand copies of a revised "Bible" created by the "Theological Institute" in Eisenhach, which he founded in 1939, expressly to "dejewify" the Bible. These texts had been circulated throughout Germany, accompanied by instructions to religious leaders and theologians to re-present Christ as non-Jewish.

Within these Reich Church "Bibles", the Ten Commandments had been re-presented as twelve, of which the first was "Honour your Führer and master" and the second "Keep the blood pure and your honour holy." The Lord's Prayer now began "Adolf Hitler, you are our great Führer" and ended "Führer, my Führer, my faith, my light – hail my Führer."

Even the word "Christmas" had been officially forbidden in Reich circles since 1938 and the Hitler Youth were blithely chanting a new, official song that denounced the need for "Christian virtue" as well as "Pope and Rabbi", because "our leader is our saviour" and "we want to be pagans once again".

Every senior SS and Gestapo officer knew of Himmler's obsession with the occult and his derision for Christianity; the strange goings on in Himmler's Westphalian Wewelsburg Castle had been witnessed. Many SS and Gestapo officers from Berlin had accompanied gangs of prisoners from Sachsenhausen to Wewelsburg in order to oversee the enforced rebuilding of its towers and turrets. They had heard and seen occult rites and rituals conducted at dead of night by men in SS uniforms, Himmler presiding.

Karl's father had ranted often enough about these heresies, and the "Hitler Bibles" did not long survive once in the hands of devout believers. But while Karl understood why his father was shocked and incensed, he did not care to ponder ideology or theological matters of any kind. Once he had decided it was all irrelevant nonsense – once he had embraced science and the logic of engineering as life's lawgivers – why should he care if Hitler denounced the Hebrew Bible as a "fairy story"?

But now? Now, empirical evidence was all around him that something which could not have roots in socialism or humanism, or even evolutionary theory, was at work. There could not be a doctrine, since men had begun to philosophize, that could defend or explain the deliberate abjuration of morality on the scale necessary to enforce murder as constitutional law; cruelty as government policy. The imponderable profanity of his country's leaders was, for Karl, evidence in itself of an objective, normative morality as far removed from that which governed Germany as it was possible to contemplate. As Karl knelt in prayer in the dimly lit Italianate splendour of this Catholic church, contemplating a wall-mounted representation in sculpted relief of the crucified Christ, he had absolutely no doubt that he was addressing the only possible antidote to the extravagant evil that gripped his country.

"Bless me, Father, for I have sinned," he said clearly and calmly to a priest he could not see, once in the confessional box. "It has been... about fifteen years since my last confession." And Karl got quickly to the point. He told the silent priest of the abominations he had witnessed and assisted. He was able at last to weep freely without fear of interrogation or rejection as he repented of his part in the murder of countless children and defenceless mental patients.

He spoke of his profound love for his wife and the terrible longing he had suppressed in order to survive for so long. He poured out his anguish at how violated Greta and his parents – all decent Germans – had been each time he had put on his SS uniform once he had been assigned to T4. And Karl finished by divulging to a trembling priest Heydrich's plans for the absolute destruction of Jews; plans to make Poland nothing more than a centralized operational hub for the systemized annihilation of a race, and then, once genocide and ethnic cleansing had been effected, Poland would be annexed to Germany; a breeding ground for Aryans and

Hitler's *Herrenvolk* ideology, which visualized nothing less than world domination.

When at last he had finished speaking, Karl bowed his head and waited. After a long silence, the priest spoke.

"My son, this was a heavy burden indeed. Greater than any man should have to bear. I share it with you, and with you bring it before Christ, lay it at his cross. I will do all I can as one man under the authority of this government, but as a man whose allegiance is firstly to a much higher authority, to urge my church in the pursuit of justice. But our suit must be first of all to God, for he alone knows how the innocent may be saved. Against him, evil cannot prevail. It is not possible. Take heart."

The priest paused for a long time. Karl could hear him praying quietly, murmuring fervent prayers in the darkness behind the grille that separated them. After some time, he resumed, "As for your soul, my dear son, God himself has declared, 'Though your sins be as scarlet, they shall be as white as snow; though they be red like crimson, they shall be as wool' and so you are absolved of all your sins and I pray that your turmoil will be replaced by the peace of Christ which surpasses all understanding."

There followed more whispered prayers, discernible incantations in Latin. "But my son," the priest eventually continued, "without true and lasting repentance, confession is impotent. What can you do to avoid sin in the future?"

Karl composed himself, paused long enough that he could clearly speak the sentences that had formed in his mind and heart several times since he had begun his confession.

"I know what I have to do, Father. My prayer now is that I have the courage to do it."

When finally he walked out of St Michael's Church, Karl paused and turned to contemplate the statue of the archangel Michael that stood fierce upon the cupola, wings outstretched, cross held aloft in the manner of a warrior about to do battle. Removing his SS cap, Karl saluted his new general.

CHAPTER ELEVEN

Hedda's joy on accompanying her daughter as she was wheeled on a gurney into the ambulance on the morning of Thursday the 28th March 1941 was indescribable. On the day Agnette should have died, she was going home. The official release papers were all signed and countersigned, and Hedda had been briefed by Matron on how to take care of her daughter: how often to turn and move her to avoid the formation of bedsores; how to change the catheter bag. A nurse would visit to change the catheter itself in due course and to check that Hedda was coping.

Hedda watched the matron's colourless face as she talked, listened to the emotionless enunciation of every word and loathed her anew. She said nothing when the matron had finished, though she would very much have liked to ask her how she reconciled her duty of care with her conspiracy to murder helpless infants. But Hedda's priority was to get her own daughter safely away from Brandenburg hospital and home.

As she walked past the rows of beds, the closed doors of the silent side rooms on her way out of the ward and into the white March sunlight, her knowledge was an almost intolerable burden. What could she do?

Hedda had spoken excitedly to Agnette about going home: how Anselm would be overjoyed to see her; how beautiful the new house and garden were, and now that it was spring, Agnette could soon go outside again, feel the fresh air she so loved when she was well.

When they reached the house, Ernst and Mathilde were there. Ernst had taken the morning off work to welcome home his granddaughter, and Mathilde had busied herself telling Marguerite what to do in preparation for Hedda's homecoming. Agnette's room was fresh with flowers and the bed was made up with beautiful, rose-patterned sheets. A "darling chime-mobile", which Mathilde had been unable to resist in a shop on Bellevuestrasse, was suspended from the ceiling and swung lightly in the breeze from a window opened to air the room. "But it is quite on the chilly side in here now, Marguerite," Mathilde had announced when all was complete. "Shut the window, please." Marguerite had no objection to being ordered around by Mathilde; she was too overjoyed to be welcoming Hedda and Agnette home to care.

Anselm ran from room to room pretending he was an aeroplane, and seemed unable to contain the energy and elation he felt at the imminent return of his mother and sister. Cook had made a huge brunch for everyone of potato pancakes with apples, milk and a pot of steaming coffee. There was a general air of celebration and happiness in the house, which it had not known since the Gunthers had assumed residence months before.

And then the ambulance arrived, and the orderly and the driver lifted the gurney gently from the vehicle and into the house. When they reached Agnette's room, it was Ernst who stepped forward and lifted his granddaughter from the gurney and laid her with great tenderness upon the turned-back bed. The men and the ambulance left, and there was hugging and laughter and the unqualified joy of a three-year-old boy whose world had just been restored.

"Heil Hitler, Muller." Oberführer Walter Gunther walked into Karl's office without knocking. He was carrying under his arm a large brown envelope.

Walter's appearance in his office for the second time in about a week did not surprise Karl. He knew Gunther suspected him of something. His heart, though, hammered in his chest as he rose from his chair in dutiful greeting of the Oberführer. This must not be the moment of his arrest. He still had so much to do.

"Sit down, Muller," began Walter, noting the absence of a return salute and allowing it to sweeten further the pleasure he would take in devastating this man he had come to loathe. Walter found a chair, sat down, removed his cap and placed it on top of the package upon his lap. "I shall come straight to the point. Regrettably, it has been necessary to put your wife back into the asylum from which you rather inadvisedly removed her. She will be back there within a week at the most." Walter studied Karl's face as it visibly paled. "This is most distressing for you, I can see. Take a moment to compose yourself."

Walter unbuttoned his coat and took a packet of cigarettes and a lighter from an inside pocket, tilted his head a little and squinted against the heat of the gasoline flame as he lit the cigarette. Flicking the lighter shut, Walter held the cigarette in his left hand while he dropped the lighter into his right coat pocket, then drew heavily on the cigarette, watching Karl's face as he exhaled.

"Who authorized this?"

"Hmm?"

"I said, who authorized this?" Karl was shaking with anger. This he had not anticipated. The one prayer he had asked God to answer before he was arrested and undoubtedly killed was that he would see Greta again. He needed to furnish her parents with more money, make arrangements for Greta to be cared for. He intended to tell Clara and Hans about T4, so they would act quickly to save their daughter. He just needed another few hours to get away, to catch the train. He just needed to finish some paperwork and concoct a story about having to inspect a furnace or some gas chamber somewhere near Leipzig so that he could say goodbye to his wife.

"You need to watch your tone, Officer Muller," Walter retorted menacingly. "I think you have forgotten your manners."

Karl could not speak. His fury was almost murderous. He rose slowly from his chair, and Walter watched him, a raised eyebrow the only sign that he remarked Karl's actions and demeanour. He drew again on his cigarette.

"But," continued Walter, "since you are so interested, Dr Brandt advised me of your protocol breach. Dr Kaufman was most upset that you had shown such scant regard for medical procedures. You had no right to remove your wife from his care." Walter lapped Karl's fury like nectar. If he could provoke Muller to an act of gross insubordination, he could precipitate his incarceration for treachery against the Reich and avenge what he was certain had been Muller's betrayal to Hedda that Walter had decreed Agnette's death.

"I had every right to get her out of there." Karl's eyes burned as Walter's grew colder. "She is my wife. I did not consent to her admission to that place and I am paying for her care. It has nothing to do with you – or the Reich."

Walter unleashed his temper; leapt to his feet. The brown package and his cap hit the floor. Spittle flecked his lips when he spoke. "It has everything to do with the Reich!" he shouted. "Everything you do, Obersturmführer Muller, has to do with the Reich. If you urinate, it is Reich business! And you will not – do you hear this, Muller? – you will not behave in a way which brings into disrepute the integrity of a Reich officer or... or the conduct of this office. Your wife, Muller, was assessed as seriously ill – she was and is a mental patient."

Possibly, Karl would later reflect, it was because he realized in that moment Gunther's evident insanity that he did not smash his fist into that distorted, salivating leer. In any case, a quite irrational calm spread from his chest outwards so that he was able to contemplate Gunther with a level of equanimity. He experienced a sudden peace, not unlike weariness, and sat down once more.

Before Karl's inscrutable, fearless gaze, Gunther had no choice but to retreat. He smoothed his hair, wiped his mouth. Karl still said nothing.

"So," Walter said at last, quietly but with great menace, "your precious wife is back where she belongs, in the lunatic asylum."

Still Karl stared at him. Walter's rage was inflamed anew at the man's dumb insolence. It seemed all hopes of provoking him to assault were receding. He had begun to imagine shooting Muller in self-defence. In frustration, Walter shouted, "And stay away from my wife, Muller!" But he regretted the words as soon as they issued from his mouth.

"What?" Karl's face crumpled into an incredulous grimace. "Is this what this is about? You think... Oh, my goodness. You think I am having an affair with your wife? Is that it, Oberführer Gunther?" Karl allowed himself an incredulous smirk; could not help enjoying the look of horrified embarrassment on Walter's face, the hot blush that rose from his throat to his face. "This is revenge for an affair I am not having. Is that right?"

Walter saw in an instant what a catastrophic blunder he had made. If Muller complained about this incident and cited personal revenge rather than defence of the Reich as a motive for Walter's behaviour, Walter would be a laughing stock and all credibility with Brandt and Himmler would be lost. Worst of all, perhaps, Muller might escape censure.

"Actually, Muller..." Walter tried hard to sound nonchalant and regain ground. He turned his back on Karl, walked towards the door, turned and walked back quickly to lean heavily on Karl's desk. "I couldn't give a crap about... that. But you have compromised the work of this office by acting dishonourably; by countermanding the assessment of a Reich psychiatrist and a T4 doctor, without consent or... or consultation. Dr Brandt has been made aware – by the psychiatrist. Concentrate on that, Muller." But Walter's tirade was now a lot less convincing. "Oh, and another thing, you have not been doing your job, *Officer* Muller."

"Oh?"

"No, you have not!" Walter's face was crimson. Sweat had broken out in beads on his brow and along his top lip. A noticeable tremor made his head unsteady. "Indeed, I have had to address your tardiness in reorganizing the drugs consignment to the children's wards, following a complaint that no paperwork had been received."

"I see." Karl was now perfectly calm. "No one has said anything to me. The bombing which destroyed the drugs was only last Sunday – less than a week ago. I have been busy with other things, Officer Gunther. But again, forgive me –" Karl's tone was one of feigned respect – "I am a little confused about why you have been monitoring my work quite so... personally. Do I report directly to your office now, sir?"

"You, Muller..." Walter stood upright, trembling with wrath and embarrassment, "you report to any T4 officer who is your superior. Is that clear?"

Karl nodded his understanding, all the while meeting Walter's eyes.

Walter retrieved his cap from the floor, replaced it on his head, stooped again for the package. "Your attitude is insolent, Muller. You may not be as clever as you think you are, so be careful. Be very careful."

Still Karl regarded Walter, watched him struggle to regain composure. There was a long pause while both men simply looked at each other, then, as if he had waited until he was calm enough to deliver the words, Walter spoke again.

"I have one last thing to say to you, Muller. I mentioned the crematoria at Mauthausen before." At this, Karl's confidence deserted him and he lowered his eyes. "Well, the specifications have come through to my office." Walter threw the large brown envelope from where he stood, halfway across the office, onto Karl's desk. "From Reichsführer Himmler's office on Prinz Albrecht Strasse. Reichsführer Himmler is due to visit Mauthausen on Monday. You need to have the plans ready by the time he goes. You will be going on the same day. The details are in that envelope."

"I am to have the plans finished, and go to Mauthausen, by Monday?"

"Yes, Muller, that is correct. You have the weekend to work on them. On Monday morning, you must take them to Mauthausen, where you will meet with Reichsführer Himmler. You will go no later than eight a.m. to the NW 7 office, IG Farben, and sign for a consignment of 260 kilos of prussic acid and potassium cyanide, and you will travel with the driver of the delivery lorry to Mauthausen. The driver will be waiting for you in the loading bay. Is this clear?"

"Prussic acid?" Karl was trying to keep up with these instructions, make sense of what he was being asked to do. He could not link any of this with what had just happened.

"This is called doing your job, Muller. Remember that? You are to go to Mauthausen with the consignment. You hand over your plans for the crematoria, and also you will be part of a test of this substance to be conducted on the premises. You will report on its efficacy, Muller. That is your job too, remember?"

Walter, now composed once more, regarded Karl with cold hatred.

"Not to your taste, Muller?"

"I am merely trying to remember my orders," returned Karl quietly.

"Don't bother," came the sneering retort. "They are all in the envelope. Just make sure you are at IG Farben no later than eight to pick up that load. Do not be late. Reichsführer Himmler hates lateness." And having delivered the actual order that was his legitimate reason for visiting Karl's office, Walter raised his hand slowly to his cap and uttered the words "Heil Hitler".

Karl sighed and just as slowly returned the salute but not the salutation. This treachery too Walter intended to report to Himmler before Muller arrived in Mauthausen the following Monday.

Karl hated the very idea of returning to Brandenburg hospital, and yet he always knew he would have to return if he was going to discover whether Agnette Gunther had been saved. It was hard not to suspect that somehow his revelation to Hedda of her daughter's fate was responsible for the special interest and evident hatred Gunther had developed for him. But if it were so, why had Gunther not had him arrested? Possibly, Gunther's personal antipathy was simply because he suspected Karl and Hedda of conducting an affair. Karl had to take the risk.

When he arrived at Brandenburg hospital once more, neither Agnette nor Hedda was in the side room he had visited previously. Karl checked the other rooms along the corridor, then resorted to enquiring of the staff.

Knocking on, then entering, the office door, he found Matron attending to paperwork. She looked instantly irritated that she had been disturbed and barely altered her expression when she beheld Karl. The matron recognized him immediately and also recalled her instructions from Dr Heinze to report his appearance and behaviour on the ward, and particularly any interaction with or interest in Frau Gunther.

"Yes, Officer Muller, may I help you?"

"I am looking for Agnette Gunther. Reich business," he replied.

"Indeed. Well, I'm afraid Agnette Gunther is no longer in the hospital." Then she added, looking directly at him, "I am surprised you do not know."

Karl looked momentarily perturbed. "Well, you have the advantage, Matron. I have been very busy. Please, enlighten me and then I can cease to disturb you."

Matron sighed, turning in her chair to face him. "Dr Heinze himself signed the release papers allowing the child to go home this morning – orders directly from the Reich Office." She raised an eyebrow at Karl's evident surprise. "She will be cared for at home by her mother."

Karl tried to look as if it had been foolish of him to forget such a detail. "Of course!" he exclaimed, rolling his eyes. "I had forgotten. The paperwork is on my desk. There is just so much to take care of. Thank you, Matron. Apologies for the interruption." And he pushed the door open fully, proceeded as boldly as he could into the office, and without seeking her permission, went into the records room that adjoined it and shut the door. He was hoping Agnette's file had not yet been moved. He needed Hedda's address. Karl had just managed to locate and replace the file, having noted the address, when the matron opened the door.

"Is everything all right, Officer Muller?"

"Of course everything is all right, Matron. Is there a reason why it should not be?" He regarded her irritably, walked past her and through the office to the ward.

Five minutes later he was in his car and heading towards Oranienburg, praying that Walter Gunther would not be at home. Within the same period of time, Matron had dialled the number of Oberführer Gunther's office in Berlin and asked to speak to him directly. Within moments, Emilie had put her through to Walter. "Officer Muller has been here," she said. "He asked for your daughter by name, Oberführer Gunther. He went into the records room. I don't know what he was doing in there, but he has left now."

Walter, who had been brooding on his faux pas with Muller since it happened and was becoming increasingly self-reproachful that he had lost his opportunity to compromise and arrest Muller, was effusive in his gratitude for this most interesting information. He congratulated Matron on her zeal in service of the Reich. Matron smiled to herself as she replaced the telephone on its cradle; it was not possible to attain a higher accolade.

It was late afternoon when Karl knocked on Hedda's door. He had waited for a long time, watching the house. Gunther's Daimler was not in the drive. Finally, though he could not be certain Walter was not home, Karl got out of his car and walked up to the front door. If Gunther was in, Karl would simply ask quietly to meet with Hedda in Walter's presence and ascertain that there had never been an affair. He would claim effrontery and distress that a superior officer had levelled at him such a dishonourable implication.

In the event, no such stratagem was necessary. Marguerite answered the door and then showed in Karl, leaving him waiting in the hall while she fetched Hedda. Hedda was shocked to see Karl Muller, but also could not hide her elation. Her eyes filled with tears of joyous gratitude.

"Karl! You really should not be here," she whispered loudly, "but come…" She beckoned him into a room off the hall and shut the door quietly. "Oh, Karl, do you know? Do you know Agnette is home? It is just wonderful, and it would never have happened without you. Thank you, thank you so much! I can never repay you for what you have done." Then she was suddenly earnest, came forward and took one of his hands in hers. "If you had not told me about…" she looked warmly into his eyes – "then my little girl… well, she would be…" Hedda could not finish.

Karl smiled at her, covered her hands with his remaining free one and pressed them affectionately. "I am overjoyed for you, Hedda," he said warmly, then he gently pulled away from her, "but I have to ask you something." She nodded, her eyes inviting him to proceed. "Please, how did this happen? Do you know how it came about that Agnette was released?"

"Oh, yes," Hedda started, then checked herself, for she remembered how she had sworn to keep secret the confidence Karl had entrusted to her; that he had said his life depended upon her discretion. She blushed. How could she explain? Then she instantly justified her actions by reminding herself that her daughter was upstairs and safe. That was all that mattered. And Karl, well, he was here, wasn't he? Her father had no idea who had alerted her to Agnette's fate.

"Karl, I am truly sorry," she began, "but I had to do something. I know you promised you would help, but how could I be certain you would be able to do it, and in time to save her? I had to do something."

"What did you do, Hedda? Who did you speak to?" Karl's voice was calm and non-threatening. He understood her desperation to save her daughter. He just needed to know the extent of the danger he was now in and whether he had time to do what he was planning.

"Well – please, I…" Hedda tried to think through all the implications. Would her father be in trouble now?

"Did you speak to Walter?"

"No! No, Karl, I never said a word to Walter – you have my word on that. Walter is a monster! I don't know how I am going to manage to keep my mouth shut long enough to…" She stopped, looked at Karl, her fear evident in her eyes. "He beats me," she blurted. "He will certainly kill me if he finds out I have told anyone of what he did."

Karl did not look shocked, but it was more important than ever to know if Walter knew he had been discovered in his betrayal of Agnette. "Who did you tell, Hedda? Please." Karl smiled at her. "Please. I am not angry. I don't blame you for doing whatever you could to save Agnette. I would do likewise. But I have to know who you spoke to. You see –" and he faltered, for he had no wish to add to Hedda's burden or cause her to lose her nerve and so denounce herself to Walter – "Walter paid me a visit today – this morning. He seems unusually angry."

Hedda looked instantly terrified. "I swear, Karl. I swear to you upon my life!"

He raised his hand to stop her, shook his head. "I believe you, Hedda," Karl soothed. "I believe you have said nothing to Walter. I believe you have not betrayed me." He smiled again. "But he has done something… something which makes me think he is more than… suspicious."

"What? What has he done, Karl? Why was he angry with you?" Hedda had not given much thought to how Ernst could have helped to effect Agnette's release. She knew well enough that he had colleagues in the government; on that she had been relying. But one thing of which she had been certain was that her father had no idea who had given her information about Agnette, and if Ernst had spoken with Walter, well, surely he would have said something to her? He would surely have warned her? It was odd that Walter had not come home at all this week, but... Gradually the likelihood that Walter had determined to discover how his daughter had been saved seemed entirely likely. Now, she feared for her father.

"It seems he has... taken pains to be involved in getting my wife sent to a mental asylum."

"What?" Hedda felt dizzy with the horror of it all. "Oh, no, no, no." She found the nearest chair in the room and sat down.

"My wife became very depressed before Christmas. She was not well anyway, as I told you, but I had been away for such a long time... and, well, she... Well, she..." Karl fought the emotion that threatened to stop his speech. "She tried to commit suicide, and it was too much for her parents to cope with. She was assessed and put into an asylum in Leipzig. I went down and took her out of it, soon after Christmas. You know what can happen to people who don't get well quickly enough..." He looked at Hedda and she closed her eyes, nodded. "The great pity of it all is that she – Greta – actually wrote me a letter a couple of weeks ago, saying she felt so much better..."

He had to stop. The weight in his chest was almost a physical sensation. He felt that if he allowed himself to sink under it, he might never get up. Only the thought of seeing Greta once more sustained him. "Well, it seems your husband and a certain doctor he works with took it upon themselves to have Greta readmitted. Now..." Karl was again stirred by anger. "Now I fear the worst. Walter came to my office this morning and took considerable pleasure in telling me of Greta's reincarceration."

"But Karl –" Hedda was on her feet, her voice earnest and pleading – "how could he have found out it was you? Why would he be trying to hurt you?" But even as she asked the question, it occurred to her that Walter was cruel and arrogant enough to destroy a man he only suspected of deceiving him with his wife.

"Hedda, tell me, please," asked Karl quietly once more. "Who did you tell about Agnette?" When she looked away from him, shook her head, he added, "I shall not betray your trust. You have my word. And if I did, think how you could betray mine!"

"I spoke to my father," said Hedda flatly. "I drove to Berlin the day after you told me and I told my father that my husband was planning the death of my child."

Karl frowned and tried to imagine how this had resulted in the eminent Dr Heinze, a medical director of T4, signing Agnette's release. "Who is your father, Hedda?"

"He must not get into trouble!" she declared.

"Hedda, I have given you my word. Who is he?"

"He's no one," asserted Hedda confidently, "just a chemist, but he is on the board of IG Farben and I know he works with some important people and I was desperate – you understand that – so it was worth a try. Anything was worth trying, Karl, to save my child, but I didn't want other people to get hurt."

"A chemist? On the board of IG Farben?" Karl repeated the information, struggling at once to remember Hedda's maiden name.

"Yes," she went on. "Like I said, he's on the board, so I wondered if he could, you know, exercise some discreet influence or something. And he did! The next day, Agnette was home."

"What is his name, Hedda? May I know?" Karl's voice was very calm now, his tone gentle.

Hedda looked into his kind, dark eyes, thought of how he had risked everything to help her and how he had spoken with such love of his wife, and she decided to trust him. "His name is Ernst Schroeder." Karl closed his eyes. "What is the matter, Karl?" Hedda's tone was alarmed once more. "You cannot know him?"

Karl opened his eyes. He suddenly looked very, very tired. "You are Ernst Schroeder's daughter?" How could he not have known? The irony was almost comic. He allowed himself a wry laugh.

"You know him?" Hedda was incredulous. "How can you know my father?"

255

"I know him, Hedda," he said quietly. "I work with him. And so does Walter."

Hedda's eyes widened in disbelief. She shook her head. "He is just a chemist," she protested. "He makes... he makes drugs, medicines and..." Her voice faltered as she looked into Karl's eyes; as his expression encouraged her to make the connections. The pieces of information found each other and another monstrous thing came to birth.

"I am so sorry, Hedda." Karl felt enormous compassion for her. He knew how debilitating it was to be unsure of anything – suddenly less than certain of the difference between reality and the unimaginable. "Like I have said before, it is better not to know what people do for a living these days. I really am truly sorry, Hedda."

Then he wished her well, expressed again his profound joy that Agnette was safe, and took his leave. He had to get to Greta before the net closed around him.

Walter was considering going home. He couldn't go home this Friday evening because he was now very drunk. He had been sitting in his Berlin apartment and trying to determine why he was so reluctant to face Hedda. So, she knew he had signed Agnette's death warrant. That was embarrassing. OK, it was more than embarrassing, he admitted to himself; it was a lot of stuff he had no wish to contemplate. Like the stuff about his parents. Well, it was too late to get maudlin about it now. To hell with it! He had done his duty, after all. In each case, he had put aside his personal feelings and put his country first. Wasn't that what every great warrior had to do? Country first! He had behaved honourably and he had raised the glorious Reich above the personal, petty considerations of one man's heart. Himmler himself had commended him. Well then, how dare anyone point the finger and accuse him of dishonourable behaviour or... or... whatever it was they thought.

Yes, it was all very sad. Very sad that his daughter had been bombed by the RAF – they were the enemy, not him! The British had done the damage in the first place and as good as killed his lovely daughter. The doctors had declared her to all intents and purposes dead – not him! How unfair it was to point the finger at Walter, as if he were the culprit in all this.

He pushed himself up from the floor where he had been leaning against an armchair and draining a very good bottle of whisky. It was American and had been given to him by the commandant of Sachsenhausen at a dinner party the week before last. "Hah!" Walter laughed aloud to himself at the irony of toasting the Reich with enemy liquor. The US were backing Britain to the hilt in this war; that was common knowledge. "Swines!" he muttered.

He rose unsteadily to his feet, realized his boots were still on and sat down heavily in the armchair. He tried to get one boot off, failed miserably, then sat back and laughed out loud again. "Emilie!" he shouted at the top of his voice. "Emilie! Come and get my boots off!" Then he laughed at his own hilarity in imagining his rabbit-like secretary popping up in his apartment, like something out of a fairy tale. He reached down to the floor, retrieved his bottle and knocked back the last of the whisky while considering Emilie's lack of sexual allure. He held up the empty bottle and eyed it disappointedly, becoming very serious. Emilie hated his guts. Even if he did find her attractive – which he certainly did not – she wouldn't touch him with a very long stick. That was embarrassing too. Actually, he wasn't sure if there was anybody who did like him. His wife certainly didn't. Well, he didn't like her either. But she was beautiful. And she had loved him once. He was pretty sure of that.

His heart suddenly ached for his beautiful wife as she had been when she was young and vulnerable; for his lovely daughter; for his mother, his father; for all that might have been. Even in his advanced drunkenness, Walter could not allow such sentiment to overwhelm him. He threw the empty bottle across the room.

He wished he'd picked up some tart earlier. That would have been a distraction. It was no fun being alone and drunk. He put his head in his hands and waited for words; the right words to describe why he couldn't go home and deal with Hedda or look at his daughter. He had done what Brandt suggested and ordered his child removed from the hospital. Ernst had confirmed to him that Agnette was home.

A word kept flitting past his inner sight, as if typing itself again and again, stenographed on endlessly spewing reams of paper, and he could not focus on it. But, as he finally passed out, it was as if the monosyllable were able at last to get his undivided attention and he understood what his heart could neither quell nor cease to manufacture: guilt. Guilt. Guilt. Guilt.

When Karl arrived in Leipzig it was very dark. He drove tentatively through the city streets, fearful at every moment that he would be stopped and arrested by Gestapo officers. But the ones he saw on Leipzig's streets this night were relaxed, clustering under the downward-deflected light from hooded street lamps. The officers laughed with girls or smoked cigarettes in spotlit drizzle, their rifles slung loosely over their shoulders. Others patrolled the shadows, nosing sharklike from restaurants to clubs along the city streets. All seemed peaceful enough, unless, Karl reflected grimly, you knew of the terrified Jews huddled and praying for deliverance in ghettoes, forbidden to be on the streets; unless you knew about the countless hospital and death-camp night shifts from Hamburg to Munich, Warsaw to Mauthausen, in which quotas were being met to ensure the annihilation of Jews, defective Germans and anyone opposing evil in Germany who had been unable to escape detection.

Karl parked several streets from the Erlachs' house and walked the remaining distance. It was impossible to tell if anyone was still awake when he reached the house, for the windows were blacked out. When she opened the door cautiously in response to his quiet knocking, Greta appeared to Karl as if she had been cut out from light. The most wayward wisps of her hair were defined against the electric glow of the hallway, and the contours of her angular frame were etched and haloed from his perspective of darkness.

She saw the SS uniform and was instantly afraid – made as if to close the door, for fear of being upbraided for having opened it so widely in blackout – but Karl spoke her name. Greta gasped in joy and disbelief. Within moments, he was in the hallway and holding his wife in his arms as he had dreamed of doing for so long. And Greta was repeating his name over and over in a delirium of love and relief, while kissing his face, and then they stood looking at each other, laughing through tears at the perfection of the vision each beheld. Greta was frail and thin, and her prolonged depression had taken its toll on her features, but to Karl she had never looked more beautiful; his love for her had never been more complete.

During the course of the evening, while Clara excitedly lay before him a late supper, Karl heard how, since he had brought Greta home in January, she had gradually recovered from the heavy sedation under which Dr Kaufman kept his patients manageable. And slowly, slowly she had started to get better. He heard how Hans and Clara had tended lovingly to her needs, sat vigil with her through long nights when she could not sleep and missed her husband most desperately.

As Karl had instructed, the Erlachs sought the advice and ministration of another psychiatrist, a kindly man who put more store by compassion and common sense than mind-altering medication. His name was Professor Schmidt, a professor of psychiatry at Leipzig University. He had spent time with Greta, listening to her anxieties and assessing the extent to which her depression was reactive rather than organic. He encouraged her to read again, to go to the library and take an interest once more in the law.

At first, Greta had seen no point in such an activity, for Hitler's Reich forbade her to practise law. But Professor Schmidt was gently adamant that what Greta needed was to reclaim that part of her which had been sentenced to death by the Third Reich: her intelligence. Hitler's sudden prohibition of women's right to work in the professions, combined with Greta's increasing outrage at the perverse social injustices being enshrined in German statute, had "derailed" her, according to Professor Schmidt. She had been dehumanized, he thought, by the statutory imposition of "feminization" throughout the Reich, which dictated that the highest aspiration an Aryan woman could embrace was the reproduction of Aryan stock. Add to the mix the loss of her husband, as she saw it, to this same Reich, and Greta's depression was a predictable outcome.

Greta herself knew, in any case, that she was in possession of an excellent mind which, if not exercised, had a tendency to depression. And so, at first tentative and terrified, Greta had walked, leaning on her mother's arm, to the library. To begin with, she was unable even to focus on the words of the books she took from the shelves. The concepts, the vocabulary of law, once her native language, eluded her comprehension, as though the cognitive processes necessary to give them meaning had ground to inaction through neglect. But, encouraged by her parents' loving persistence, the panic began to subside and something deep within her was reawakened. Within a few weeks, Greta was rising and getting dressed before her parents, able to walk the mile or so to the library on her own, eager to return to her books and the benevolence of a world welcoming her back.

But there was a price for her restitution: a disturbance of mind of a new order. Greta learned, by reading back copies of *The Reich Gazette* filed in the Leipzig University library, of the increasingly bizarre judgments of the "People's Courts" which were not subject to the due process of the time-honoured legislation on which her own university course had been founded. Judges whose names she had revered and whose rulings she had learned as precedents, were now summarily sentencing hundreds of people to death; people whose only crime was that they were Jewish or objectors to the increasing evidence of the abominable, inhuman cruelty of Hitler's Reich. Judges, for whose integrity and brilliance Greta had once harboured profound respect, were executing people summarily, within hours of sentencing; relying on a series of legal amendments imposed without reference to the Reichstag.

To Greta, the absurdity of this new "legal system" was overwhelming; the ceding of reason to insanity, obvious. Innumerable lawyers had already been condemned to death or imprisoned without trial by Hitler's judiciary, and Greta knew she would be one of them, were she allowed to practise. But the very clandestine nature of her research, the realization that she was part of a resistance network that was busy weaving a safety-net of sanity beneath the surreality of Nazi despotism, was itself an antidote to Greta's depression.

Soon, the only drug she needed was her books. She took to studying avidly the newspapers, making her father buy every paper he could. She gasped and exclaimed in horror and indignation as she read Goebbels' weekly propagandist journal *Das Reich*, in which he lauded Hitler's "brilliant statesmanship" and his wielding of the "weapon of truth", justifying the persecution of Jews on grounds that "every Jew is an enemy", whether "he vegetates in a Polish ghetto" or "carries out his parasitic existence in Berlin or Hamburg". Goebbels shouted from his lead articles in *Das Reich*: "The historic responsibility of world Jewry for the outbreak of this war has been proven so clearly that it does not need to be talked about any further."

Why could the people not see that this was more fictional than a Grimm fairy tale? What had happened to Germany's intellect? Her conscience? Greta emerged from the stupor of her depression into a wakefulness undefiled by Third Reich brainwashing. By the time Karl stepped into the hall on that rainy Friday evening at the end of March 1941, she was fully alive and ready to make her husband aware, if he were not already so, of the truly abominable nature of the master he served.

CHAPTER TWELVE

Walter woke up very early on Saturday morning in an armchair in his apartment living room, still wearing his boots. That his eyes were open and he was conscious, he was aware, but he felt as if his eyes were the only physical bits he could account for, blinking stupidly from the midst of an indeterminate mass that was the rest of him. Little by little he understood he was very cold. The headache that kicked in when he tried to move told him that he was still drunk. He fell back again, opening and closing his mouth in a bid to salivate. He might just stay there a little while longer. It wasn't that cold...

Around the same time in Leipzig, Karl woke suddenly and tried to make sense of the excitement and well-being he felt. For a couple of seconds, he could not place himself; could not make sense of the floral wallpaper and the absence of a window directly before his vision. And then memory illumined his thoughts and he turned joyously to behold his wife still dozing beside him. He closed his eyes in prayer and gave thanks.

Saturday passed in an irritating haze for Walter. Hours after he had finally slept off his drunkenness enough to get up from the chair, remove his boots, take off his uniform, and shower, he felt as though his brain were wrapped in gauze. He regretted the bottle of Chablis he had downed alone, over dinner, in a small restaurant on Wilhelm Strasse before he had come home and cracked into the malt whisky. He had wanted to obliterate thought, but had succeeded rather in isolating only those thoughts that could not be etherized. Even his dreams had been lurid and disturbing, though their residue was impressive rather than memorable. The impressions added significantly to the heaviness and melancholy of his mood.

Now, as Saturday late afternoon encroached and his weekend was half over, Walter was filled with a sense of waste and a gathering resentment against Hedda for the state he was in. His moroseness sharpened to fury the more focused his faculties became. That was quite enough, he resolved; he would damn well go home to his house this evening whether she liked it or not! It was his house, and if she did not like his being there, well, she could get out.

Karl and Greta rose reasonably early, for there was much they needed to do and say in the little time they had together. They had talked into the early hours of the morning, in a series of conversations that were simultaneously affirming of their love and profoundly distressing.

As gently as he could, Karl had explained to Greta that he needed no convincing of the heinousness of those who were busy perverting the country's legislature and the population's perception of justice. He held her hand and confessed his particular part in applying Reich "law", and described to her haltingly and often in tears how Hitler had used the law to redefine not only human rights but what it was to be human enough to deserve life.

Greta reminded Karl of how the Reich Citizenship Law, 1935, had deprived Jews of the right to vote or marry non-Jews, and stated in Section 4 (1): "A Jew cannot be a citizen of the Reich", and how outraged and despondent this had made her, yet she had been forbidden to discuss her feelings at work. That, she said, had been the start of what she was now calling "the illness". Her use of the phrase detached Greta from her depression and convinced Karl more than ever that his wife was better. It was with great remorse then that he prepared her for what would surely be a test of the robustness of this new state of health: that her husband would surely and very soon be subject to Reich "justice".

Amid tears and affirmations of love and contrition, Karl achieved the absolution he needed from his wife, and then he had to explain to her why he was home; that in what was certainly an act of vengeance for Karl's reneging on his duties, a senior SS officer who had authorized the euthanizing of his own daughter had also authorized Greta's return to the asylum.

"But I am better!" Greta protested, terrified. "You can see I am well!"

And Karl had kissed her hands and then her face, and smiled through his tears, nodding. "And that, my darling, is the miracle I had not counted on," he declared. "We must get to Professor Schmidt today, as soon as the hour is reasonable. We are going to need his help."

As for Greta's persistent questions about what Karl was going to do to defend himself, he could only avoid telling her he had no idea and as little hope. Instead, he insisted he would be fine and was well able to look after himself; that he was resourceful and also a senior SS officer; he would think of something. The priority was to ensure Greta was safe.

At around eight o'clock on that Saturday morning, Greta dialled the telephone number Professor Schmidt had given her for use in the event of emergencies. Within fifteen minutes, they were hurrying along the leafy street where the Erlachs lived, as indifferent to the crisp brightness of the day as were the first buds on the waking trees to their consuming anxiety.

Professor Schmidt had asked them to meet him at his office in the psychiatry department of the university hospital. He had developed a real fondness for Greta Muller. When her distraught parents had first come to him, asking him to assess their daughter, telling him of how Greta's SS officer husband had removed her from the asylum and insisted she was to be cared for at home, he had been most reluctant to get involved. He had an intuitive abhorrence of the SS that he found hard to moderate. At work, he usually managed to confine himself to ironic "hmphing" when colleagues discussed the ways in which National Socialist legislation was affecting psychiatric practice, but there were times when the insanity of Reich impositions on his work was too absurd to go unchallenged. He had been the cause of some uncomfortable coffee breaks in the faculty staffroom.

The Law for Prevention of Genetically Diseased Offspring, for example, meant that medical practitioners had a duty to register with the state diagnoses within certain categories, and then apply to the Reich Office for the mandatory sterilization of those patients. In the eight years since this law was passed, Professor Schmidt and his colleagues had had their patient records inspected regularly by the chief professor of psychiatry, as well as the dean of the university medical school. Their lectures were regularly observed to ensure they were in no way subversive of Reich philosophies and ideologies. Professor Schmidt had seen his students become blonder and less culturally diverse, until only Aryan stock that had grown up singing the Hitler Youth anthem sat in his lectures and took dutiful notes. It was so obvious to Professor Schmidt that this in itself was a symptom of the most acute national psychosis.

But in spite of his strong reservations when it came to being involved with anything to do with the SS, there were several things in the course of Frau and Herr Erlach's appeal for help that caught his attention. Greta had been a law student at the university and, it seemed, her husband was also a Leipzig alumnus who had gone on to study medicine at Berlin. This disposed him to sympathy, and then stirred a memory.

"Is this young Muller, your daughter's husband, any relation to Dr Muller, who has an office in Luxembourg Strasse?" he had asked of Hans Erlach at their first meeting.

"Well, actually," Hans had answered, "yes. He is his son. The reason we have come to you, Professor Schmidt, is that Karl's father, Dr Erich Muller, said you were a good man and that he knew you and your family. We hope this is not inappropriate – some conflict of interest or something?"

"On the contrary, Herr Erlach," Professor Schmidt had responded, smiling warmly. "It is very much to your advantage. I shall see your daughter. Bring her as soon as you can."

On discovering that Greta Muller was no less than the daughter-in-law of his family's trusted GP, Professor Schmidt had consented to see her. And Schmidt was familiar with Dr Kaufman, and knew his treatment methods precisely accorded with Reich requirements. It was therefore a bonus that his obviously bright and delightful new patient was being delivered from Kaufman's clutches.

When Greta burst into his office on this last Saturday morning in March, her complexion ruddy from the wind and excitement, Professor Schmidt was delighted by her vivacity and evident good health.

"Professor Schmidt!" she exclaimed. "Thank you so much for seeing us. Please, you must help us. This is Karl." She stopped long enough to look from the doctor to her husband, and the men nodded a greeting to each other. "Karl, my husband, has such stories of terrible things being done, Professor – of Reich officers condemning sick children to death!" She paused, looked intently into the old man's eyes, watched them narrow in an attempt to process the information and guess its import to immediate circumstances. "He works for an organization in Berlin called T4. They actually dedicate themselves to the systematic – and wholly criminal, I may add – destruction of anyone – children, psychiatric patients – anyone who is considered 'genus unworthy of life'. They actually call these people 'unworthies". Can you believe it?"

Professor Schmidt turned his attention to the young man in civilian clothes who bore a striking resemblance to his father.

"Professor Schmidt, sir," began Karl, "in the next few days – perhaps today, I don't know, but very soon – someone will come to the door of Greta's house and try to take her back to the asylum. Just after Christmas, I removed her from there. The doctor – a Dr Kaufman – was most unhappy. He complained formally to the Reich Office that I had not observed procedure and I had no right to remove Greta from his care. Now, a very senior SS officer has authorized Kaufman to take Greta back into the asylum. I have been directly informed of this decision. Please, sir, help me to save my wife from this injustice."

Finally, the professor could speak. "Why have they done this without consulting you, or me, or anybody? What they are proposing is highly irregular." He had been sitting at his desk and now he rose from his leather chair and came towards them. He was bespectacled with a neatly trimmed grey beard, and what remained of his hair was also cut very short. He sat on the edge of his desk and removed his glasses, folded them and lay them on the desk. He motioned to Greta and Karl to take seats.

"I am afraid I upset this particular senior officer, sir," explained Karl, "and this is an act of revenge." Greta looked at her husband, extended a hand across the gap between his chair and hers. He took it, looked into her eyes, saw only love. Karl explained briefly how Walter Gunther had condemned to death his own daughter and how Karl had breached Reich security in order to save the child.

"But this is barbaric!" exclaimed Professor Schmidt. Then he added, "Though such things are no longer surprising to me." He sighed, folding his arms. "Let us focus on procedure, for that is what we must rely on. Sentiment and emotional protestation will get us nowhere, as you, I am sure, Herr – Officer – Muller, are all too aware." He looked into Karl's troubled eyes, held his gaze a moment. "Now, I have Greta's notes."

"You do?" Karl was instantly cheered. "I was so worried that Kaufman would refuse to give them to you. What a relief!"

"Indeed. Well, the good Dr Kaufman was most reluctant to part with them. I had to go to the asylum personally and demand them. He would not give them to my secretary and nor would he post them. Nevertheless, they are in my possession now." He paused and looked at Greta. "I have to say that I refute his diagnosis."

"Which was?" enquired Greta.

"Which was," continued Professor Schmidt, "that you, Greta, were suffering from an acute depressive disorder of a genetic origin. The symptoms, I concur, were present: difficulty sleeping, feelings of hopelessness, loss of appetite, despondency and so on. You would agree, Greta, these were symptoms from which you suffered pretty consistently for a period of roughly two years up to your admission to hospital?" Greta nodded.

Professor Schmidt put on his glasses once more and, turning, reached behind him for a file on his desk, and scanned Greta's notes. "He says your primary depressive episode was extensive, lasting over a year, starting around the end of 1935 – when you lost your job?" She nodded again. "And, it is fair to say, at the time when you were admitted to the asylum, you had had a recurring depressive episode of roughly two years' duration, culminating, upon admission, in a serious suicide attempt." He looked at her again, she nodded her assent. "This led Kaufman to revise your diagnosis to manic depressive insanity with destructive tendencies – severe melancholic depression or 'mood disorder'. In such a case, the illness deteriorates, and persistent thoughts of self-destruction contribute to the patient's general hopelessness. The sleeplessness increases, which affects the ability to make rational decisions and so forth. In short, the patient becomes irresponsible for his or her own well-being."

Professor Schmidt paused once more, smiled at Greta, then looked at Karl before continuing. "These diagnoses are textbook, and they are the logical outcome of what I call an 'observational' psychiatric approach – one which does not involve psychotherapy of any kind. But –" and here Professor Schmidt became animated – "I fundamentally disagree with Kaufman about the root cause of these episodes and therefore their diagnosis and treatment. Kaufman has recorded that your depression, Greta, was endogenous – that is, organic, genetic, an illness originating within the body. I, however, believe –" here he looked at Greta over his glasses – "that your depression was, on the contrary, initially reactive, due mainly to being prevented from pursuing the career you loved – from being able to think and reason with specific purpose." He looked back at Karl. "Greta was suddenly, and for no good reason, disallowed from practising law, and more than this, she was recategorized as a human being. This, for a fiercely intelligent lawyer who had been a straight honours student graduating top in her class, was intolerable – as Greta has since made clear."

Here, Professor Schmidt paused again. Greta was crying quietly, tears rolling down her cheeks, and Karl raised her hand, kissed it. Professor Schmidt went on gently, addressing himself once more to Greta. "Kaufman has made no reference to your qualifications, Greta, or to the trauma you endured when you were dismissed from your position in Berlin. But that is not surprising, given that you, my dear, were a victim of the Reich he so closely supports."

Karl nodded, asking quietly, his voice evidently affected by emotion, "And how did he treat her, Professor? When I picked up Greta from that place, she was barely conscious."

Schmidt sighed, turned a few pages in the file, read for a moment before responding. "He was administering increasingly high doses of an opioid-based drug believed to relieve the symptoms of endogenous depression, mainly anxiety, and of course it sedates."

"But what is the point of that?" asked Karl. "Surely it is not a cure?"

"No. There is no medicinal cure for depression, Herr Muller. Drugs may relieve symptoms in many cases and allow a psychiatrist to communicate with a patient about possible causes of the illness. Opioids have been known to significantly reduce the risk of suicide, so allowing continuity of therapy and treatment, and increasing the chances of eventual recovery, but drugs do not cure depression."

"But is there any evidence that Kaufman tried to communicate with Greta?" Karl asked incredulously.

"Karl, darling, I can speak for myself," interjected Greta, smiling at him. "Kaufman never tried to speak with me. That I remember. We patients hardly saw him."

"Indeed," concurred Professor Schmidt. "There are no notes which indicate he attempted to engage you in any therapeutic sessions or introduce psychotherapy to his treatment regime. His next approach would have been ECT. You were due to receive that in the second week of January."

"ECT? Greta!" exclaimed Karl. "What might he have done to you?"

"Almost certainly a great deal of damage," interjected Schmidt, "but Kaufman relies upon it as a sort of 'kill or cure' therapy. He has written many papers on the clinical application of ECT in the treatment of depression. Sometimes, again, it has to be said that ECT works when all else fails, with some patients, with some kinds of depression. But Greta's depression he had misdiagnosed."

"Are you saying he experiments on his patients?" Karl asked.

"I would not make such an unsubstantiated statement, but... his trials demand large numbers of patients... and he does not seem to discriminate as carefully as I would like between depressive types when it comes to application of ECT. You understand? And I risk much in expressing it. Fewer questions are asked these days, as you know, about the ethics and the outcomes of such treatments."

Professor Schmidt looked from Karl to Greta, smiled, closed the file and removed his glasses once more before adding, "You saved your wife from vicious and unnecessary treatment, Herr Muller, which would almost certainly have destroyed her. I don't think that is too emotive a prognosis. Greta needed nothing more than intellectual stimulation, renewed purpose and someone to believe in her again. Her present health is testament to that. You enabled this to happen."

"Sir," protested Karl, close to tears, "you have done this. And I will never be able to thank you enough."

"I am starting to feel invisible again!" enjoined Greta, but she was laughing and crying in profoundest gratitude to both of them.

"And so," continued Karl after a few moments, "how do we keep Greta out of that place?"

"Simple," concluded Professor Schmidt, looking directly at Greta. "I get my report on your progress to Kaufman, personally, by first thing tomorrow morning. I shall outline the psychotherapeutic and cognitively supportive regime I have implemented in your care – without going into great detail, naturally. For example, I shall mention only that I have encouraged you to begin reading and studying again; that your intelligence is prodigious and requires stimulation. I shall not speak about your legal career. I shall pronounce you cured. I shall say that I am reporting to him directly because it is a professional courtesy, and I shall thank him for his cooperation and tell him some of his work is very interesting, etcetera, etcetera, but I shall not hand back your file."

"Why not?" asked Greta. "Out of interest."

"Because, my dear girl, one day you are going to practise law again and such a file would be prohibitive to that most therapeutic of courses."

"But what if they come to the door? What if they turn up with SS authorization to take her away?"

"Then someone, Herr Muller, must call me immediately, day or night, and I shall be at that asylum within fifteen minutes, and I shall take great pleasure in watching Greta demonstrating her mental health in the most convincing manner she can muster." He smiled widely at Greta. "And if that most impressive show of reasonableness does not impress him, then I shall challenge him to produce any diagnostic test he can manufacture to assess my patient before my very eyes. And if all else fails –" Professor Schmidt paused again, and this time looked very serious indeed – "I shall play merry hell until Kaufman begs us – Greta included – to leave!"

Greta suddenly leapt from her chair and kissed the professor on the cheek. He blushed, nodded, made a vague expansive gesture with his hands and smiled widely. "Now tell me, my boy," he began once more after a few moments, "what is all this stuff Greta was saying – about 'unworthies'? Some organization called 'T4'?"

272

CHAPTER TWELVE

And so Karl once more unburdened his soul, while his wife and her doctor listened in profoundest silence to a story far more horrible and less credible than fiction ever contrived.

When Walter finally sobered up enough to think of driving home to Oranienburg, he changed his mind. If he went home, the evening would be spent rowing with Hedda and why should he ruin what was left of his weekend? So, he put on a clean uniform and went out on the town. What he needed to cheer himself up was at least one beautiful woman and some beer. No wines or spirits tonight – just good, honest German beer. Tomorrow would be time enough to deal with his wife.

And in Leipzig, having secured Professor Schmidt's promise of assistance in delivering Greta from the asylum, Karl and his wife were free to enjoy what might well be the last Saturday evening they would ever spend together.

When he walked into the house on Sunday evening, Walter was struck by how quiet it was. It was not until he had crossed the hallway, entered his office and sifted through the post that had been left on his desk that he became aware of occasional childish laughter and the soft drone of Hedda's voice as she spoke to Anselm upstairs. They were in the bathroom, Hedda getting Anselm ready for bed. Walter was nervous and he resented it. He took a whisky bottle from his desk drawer and swigged from it; loosened his collar. Well, there was only one way to deal with this and that was head on.

He crossed his office, and once in the hall made for the stairs. Both Anselm and Hedda were startled by Walter's sudden appearance at the bathroom door, for they had not heard him come back. Hedda had been hoping that he would not come back at all that week but go to work from his Berlin apartment. She therefore had no time to prepare her reaction. She had brooded and agonized and fumed about Walter's willingness to sacrifice her daughter's life to an inhuman Reich, but she had been unable to imagine how the situation would resolve itself. Clearly, the marriage was over. It had been over in all but name for a long time, but Walter's betrayal of Agnette annulled it summarily as far as Hedda was concerned. The problem was, how did she escape with two small children, one immobile, when she had no independent income? She had to be careful. Somehow, Hedda had to get Walter to agree to divorce and a financial settlement. If he assisted her removal from his house and his life, everything would be much easier. He might even be keen to grant her freedom easily and generously in exchange for her agreeing to "forget" what he had done to Agnette.

But when she saw him leaning against the bathroom door, she was unable to disguise her revulsion. Walter also perceived the sudden fear in Anselm's face; how the smile died in his eyes as he turned from the basin where he had been brushing his teeth and saw his father.

Walter sneered. "I need to talk to you, Hedda. Right now, if you please."

"Wouldn't you like to say hello to your daughter first?" Hedda could not prevent the response, or the loaded sarcasm in her tone, as she took Anselm's hand, ready to lead him to his room.

"Agnette is home, Vati," said Anselm quietly, looking from his father to his mother.

Hedda smiled, tugged his hand reassuringly. "Come, Anselm, let's get you into bed."

"When you have done that," said Walter tersely, "come downstairs, please." And he pushed himself away from the door-frame, headed for the stairs, passing Agnette's room without pausing.

Some ten minutes later, Hedda joined him in the drawing room. Marguerite had just finished laying a fire in case the evening proved chilly, and now she smiled nervously at Walter and Hedda, leaving the room with exaggerated care as though reluctant to disturb some hallowed silence. When she had carefully drawn the door to, Walter started to speak. Hedda, perched on the arm of the chintz roll-back sofa, watched him intently, her loathing and anger two serpents circling her heart.

"I know you are aware of the situation with Agnette," he stated, standing square before her, his hands behind his back. "It is all very unfortunate and I shall make no excuses. I did my duty." Hedda could not help the horrified, inarticulate exclamation that escaped her. Walter held up one of his hands, the other still behind his back, as though stopping traffic. "I do not care for your opinion!" he almost shouted, then lowered his voice again. "What's done is done. Neither," he added, looking at her directly and fixing her with a warning glare, "do I intend to explain or excuse myself to you."

"You said that," retorted Hedda, venomous loathing darkening her eyes.

"But," he continued, "what I am most interested in is your informant."

Hedda rose to her feet and took a couple of steps towards him. "I do not intend to explain myself to you either, Walter. You should be more concerned at what you are capable of – murdering your own daughter." Her voice rose and her chest heaved suddenly as the words struck. "How could you do such an abominable, disgusting thing?" Her breathing was laboured and her face contorted with hatred. Instinctively, Hedda knew this would not work. This would end only in her being abused by a man she now knew was capable of murdering children, his own included. She had to withdraw. She could not protect her children if she was incapacitated or dead. She stepped back and tried to regulate her breathing. The physical retreat seemed to temper Walter's response, for though his fists clenched, he remained where he was.

"What do you know of difficult decisions?" he shouted. "Of putting duty to your country above all else? Hmm? What does the likes of you know about how hard life can be? You know nothing!"

There was that note of hysteria in his voice. Hedda braced herself for the inevitable.

Outside in the hall, Marguerite, who had been putting on her coat ready to go out for the evening, stopped and removed it. She tiptoed back across the hall to the kitchen and found Cook had also stopped midway in her cleaning of the kitchen. The two women exchanged frightened glances, stood in attentive silence.

Back in the drawing room, Hedda kept her mouth shut and watched Walter work himself into a frenzy. He paced up and down the room clenching and unclenching his fists, then he stopped and turned on her again. "I know it was Muller who told you," he yelled. "I have witnesses! I know he came to the house on Friday." Of course, this was a bluff, a surmise based on the Brandenburg matron's telephone call to his office to let him know Karl had asked for Agnette's whereabouts, gone into the records room and then left. Hedda simply continued to look at him. He took her silence for affirmation. "Don't play stupid with me. There's no point – I *know* you're stupid." He clenched his teeth, lowered his voice and came towards her. "There is no point denying what I can prove."

Spittle hit her cheek. Hedda turned her face from him in disgust. "Well, if you have proof, why are you shouting at me?" she asked quietly, then turned back to him. His face was inches from hers. She saw how the veins in his temple pulsed, how high his colour was. The numbness began to set in moments before he grabbed her hair and yanked her head back, spoke into her upturned face.

"I'll take that as a confession," he spat.

Hedda pulled her head forward in order to be able to speak. Even breathing was difficult, so vicious was the angle at which he held it back. "I have confessed nothing," she managed at last.

Walter was enraged. Still holding her by her hair, he raised the other hand and hit her hard across the face. Curiously, Hedda felt the sound his hand made rather than pain as he struck her jaw, but the jolting sensation in her neck told her the blow was serious enough. When he let her go, she had difficulty righting her head. She lifted her hand to her mouth and was not surprised it encountered blood.

"This is how you deal with everything, isn't it, Walter?" she said thickly, tasting the blood and realizing it was coming from inside her mouth, running down her chin.

"I know it was Muller!" he shouted again, moving away from her. He had not meant to strike her so soon or so hard. If she disappeared inside that shell of hers, he'd get nothing from her. He ran his shaking hands through his hair, tried to collect his thoughts. There was a lot more at stake here this time than allowing Hedda to be insolent and get away with it. This time, he convinced himself, it was about exposing an enemy of the Reich.

When he spoke again, it was with some measure of control. "There is little point in this... unpleasantness." He paced again, more slowly than before. "The facts are these: Muller used his position to gain access to Agnette's records. He had a... special relationship with you. That, by the way –" and he looked at her with unconcealed contempt – "is immaterial." He allowed himself an ironic guffaw. "That aspect of all this, believe me, is of no interest to me. I would find it hard to care less about you, Hedda. As long as you do not humiliate me, I don't give a damn who you screw. Let's get that clear." He continued, in a tone one might use to discipline a disappointing child. "What I am disgusted at is Muller – his betrayal of the Reich. Because that is what he did, Hedda. When he told you about Agnette, he betrayed his country. And he..." here Walter grew agitated again, came towards her, widening his eyes and grinning maniacally, raising his right index finger to drive home the point – "he is no saint!" His eyes glistened with malice and he shook his head, smiling all the while. "Are you aware your lover has gassed children? Hmm? Do you know how he was able to get information on Agnette? Because he was busy checking up on how many cripples and vegetables he had to order drugs for, to put them out of their misery!" Hedda could not disguise her horror. "Ah, he didn't tell you that bit, huh?" Walter was shouting again, his tone triumphant, eyes alight with amused fury. He got closer to her again, his face almost touched hers.

Hedda closed her eyes. Her face and neck were now very painful. Her mouth was already swelling and her left eye was starting to close. Her mouth kept filling with blood. She said nothing, bowed her head, blood and saliva dripped onto the carpet. Hedda lifted a trembling hand to wipe her mouth, and even through the pain she contemplated the bestiality, the breathtaking cruelty of these men under whose authority her country was dying. Karl had certainly alluded in veiled terms to his part in this horror and Hedda knew he worked with Walter. But he seemed so abject, so harrowed by it all, she had pitied him. Walter's brutal statement of the truth filled her with renewed revulsion and anger. All these men! Murderers, traitors; every one of them. Her own father included.

She lifted her head, and through the blood and pain she addressed her husband. "I know what he is. He told me all about it." She spoke with great difficulty. "I know what you are, Walter, that is for sure. And before you get to it, I know what my father is too." Then she added quietly, "You are all cowards. You are murderers." And suddenly she was filled with righteous rage and knew no fear, only the need to spit and scream her derision and horror and hatred into his face. She leapt at him, slapping and thumping his face before he could defend himself. "You are scum!" she screamed. "You beat women, you kill children – you agreed to let them murder your own daughter! *You* are unworthy! You call the people you murder... by... by drugs and gas and... God alone knows what else... You *monster*!" Hedda was inarticulate with fury. Walter was still too shocked at her eruption of rage to react. "You call those helpless people 'unworthy'? *You*?"

When Walter finally recovered his wits and knocked her across the room she hardly noticed. When she crumpled onto the floor he kicked her hard and repeatedly while she did her best to defend her face and body by curling into a ball and covering her face with her arms. Her thoughts were still of how foul and degenerate was the betrayal by these men of all that was vulnerable and sacred. Then at last he left the room, tearing the door open and leaving it gaping. He had what he wanted.

Ignoring Anselm's screaming, for the boy had emerged from his room at his parents' raised voices, Walter slammed into his office, removed his jacket and his Parabellum holster, and flung them both on the floor. Hardly able to prevent his hands from shaking long enough to dial the number, he got through to the exchange and demanded the operator put him through to Reichsführer Himmler's personal number – it was an emergency. The ringing tone sounded two, three, four times. "Pick up the phone!" Walter hissed into the receiver through clenched teeth, though he covered the mouthpiece.

"Hello?" At last, Himmler's voice. The greeting seemed to come at the end of laughter. There were voices in the background, the unmistakable tinkling of glass. Walter closed his eyes, tried to modify his tone. He needed to sound as if he were in control.

"Reichsführer Himmler, sir?"

"Yes? Is that you, Gunther? What is the problem?"

"I am sorry to disturb your evening, mein Reichsführer Himmler, sir, but I have some information I think will be of interest."

"Oh?"

"I have proof that Obersturmführer Muller – he works for IV Office, if you recall, sir?"

"Yes, yes, Gunther – I know him. What has he done?" And then Himmler said something to someone else, which Walter could not distinguish. "I am having a gathering, Gunther – some people. Will this take long?"

"Not long, sir. Muller is a traitor." Walter paused. There was silence on the other end of the telephone. "He..." Walter tried to think how to phrase his next words. "You recall what I told you about... my daughter, sir?"

"Yes."

"Well, it seems Muller discovered this. He told my wife."

"What?" Himmler sounded shocked. "You are sure of this?"

"Yes, sir, perfectly sure. She has said so. It has all been most… difficult. She – my wife – told her father. Luckily, he is Ernst Schroeder, the chemist at IG Farben?"

"Yes, yes."

"And now my daughter is at home. I had to tell Dr Brandt. He said to get the child out of the hospital – to avoid questions."

"I see. Brandt is here, as a matter of fact. A messy business, Gunther. Well, if you are sure, then we must arrest Muller. See to it."

"Yes, mein Reichsführer Himmler, sir. Forgive me, but that is why I am ringing. I believe there is a way we can do that quite easily. He is due to meet you at Mauthausen tomorrow?"

"Yes," confirmed Himmler, "he is."

"Sir, might I respectfully suggest that is an opportunity to not only arrest him, but to incarcerate him immediately?"

"At Mauthausen? You mean, keep him there?"

"Yes, sir. He is an enemy of the Reich. I have proof." There was a long silence. Walter began to lose confidence that he had done the right thing in contacting Himmler so impetuously. Perhaps he would think Walter impertinent, or petty. He began to justify his actions. "What if my wife's father had not been a T4 employee? Muller might have blown our security completely. As it is, I do not know how my wife will behave, who she might tell. She is, as you can imagine, sir, extremely upset."

"All right, Oberführer Gunther," Himmler responded at last. "It is a good plan. And well done. You have excelled in your duty yet again. Commiserations on the other matter, Gunther," he added. "It cannot have made for a pleasant weekend. Your wife's discretion, I am afraid, is your responsibility. Do whatever you need to do, Gunther. I am sure your wife will see reason in the end. Heil Hitler. Oh, and Gunther –" Himmler had been about to ring off when the thought occurred – "how does Muller know your wife?"

"They are... old friends, sir."

"Ah! Well, goodnight, Gunther."

"Goodnight, sir. Heil Hitler!"

Walter had Himmler's authorization to sort out the problem. Himmler, who knew what Walter had done to Agnette and understood. Himmler, who was so close to the Führer, so senior in the Reich, had agreed instantly that the situation was serious and had trusted him to contain it – however he saw fit.

When Walter left the drawing room, Hedda had picked herself up from the floor and moved into the hall, drawn by the piteous wails of her son. Marguerite sat with him on the upstairs landing, stroking his hair and soothing him. But when Anselm saw his mother, the blood-soaked blouse, her swollen face, he cried anew, tears rolling down his blotchy face, his body racked with sobs. He held his arms out to Hedda through the banister railings. Looking up at Marguerite, Hedda said softly, "Take him back to his room, Marguerite. Stay with him till he is quiet, and then go. You said you were going out this evening. Go. I will be fine."

Marguerite shook her head. "I don't think you are fine, Frau Gunther," she practically whispered, all the time stroking Anselm's hair. "I don't want to leave you and the children."

"Hedda!" Walter shouted to his wife before he reached her, emerging from his office and leaving the door open.

"What do you want, Walter?" she asked flatly. "I am tired and Anselm is upset. Let's just leave it." She spoke from the middle of the hallway, holding her face and trying to make her words clear through the spit and blood.

"I am afraid that will not be possible," he replied as he reached her. "You see, you are now a security risk."

"What?" Hedda stared into his mad eyes, made a grimace of disbelief. "What are you saying now?"

Walter sprang forward and grabbed her by her wrists, began hauling her roughly towards the drawing room. Hedda pulled against him, twisting and yanking her arms in an effort to unlock his fingers from their bruising grip on her arm. She did not, above all, want to be alone with him. She sensed that she was in very real danger. Anselm's cries began again and filled the hallway at this new disturbance and he ran from Marguerite before she could stop him, and began to descend the stairs.

"You will not hit me and get away with it," Walter snarled at Hedda, tightening his grip on her wrists, his breathing laboured with the effort of dragging her across the hall. At the drawing room door, he released a wrist in order to grab the door frame and achieve some purchase against it to pull Hedda across the threshold. With her free hand, Hedda hit and scratched him for all she was worth.

Anselm was finally in the downstairs hall and padding on his bare feet as quickly as he could to where his parents fought. "Mutti!" he screamed hysterically, over and over, reaching Hedda and grabbing her skirt. Marguerite, who had come flying down the stairs after him, grabbed him and pulled him away from his mother just as Walter succeeded finally in pulling Hedda into the drawing room and kicking closed the door.

"I hate you!" Hedda shouted at him breathlessly, her back to the door. "You are a monster! Just give me a divorce. Give me enough money to take the children and get away from you, and you'll never see us again."

"Not that simple, unfortunately," he snarled back at her, out of breath from the struggle. "Your boyfriend has done you no favours, I am afraid. In telling you so much, he has endangered your life too. Do you seriously think I am going to trust you to keep your mouth shut? Himmler himself knows that you are a security breach, you stupid, stupid, simple idiot! Even your own father knows you are a risk. Who do you think it was who came to me and told me you knew about Agnette? Yes! That's right!" Walter was luxuriating in Hedda's obvious horror as her worst fears were confirmed. "Vati! Dear old Daddy! Did Muller tell you what Daddy does for a living? Hmm?" Walter's face was screwed into an ugly grimace, spittle flecked his lips and Hedda had to turn her head to one side in order to avoid contact with his skin. Tears began to fall unchecked down her face. She was exhausted and heartbroken.

"Please." Hedda closed her eyes, raised a hand and gently pushed against his shoulder. He slapped it away. "Please, Walter, stop this. I can't take this any more."

"A pity, because I have a lot more to say." Walter grew more vicious as his wife finally wilted. "Do you know how many meetings I have sat in with your dear papa? How many of his boring presentations I have endured while he droned on and on about ratio of body weight to litres of gas needed to extinguish cripples and lunatics and Jews... Any filth, you name it, Daddy knows how to dispose of it with optimum efficiency. Oh, and do you know who built the gas chambers and enabled these most efficient ways of delivering cyanide or diesel fumes to little girls and boys? Yes, that's right! The dashing Herr Muller!"

Walter released Hedda. She sank to the floor and put her hands over her ears, sobbing desperately in a heap against the door. He bent down and shouted at her. "I am no worse than any of them – these men you so admire. They are no better than me!" And he followed the last word with a swift, sharp kick to her hip.

"Stop it! Stop it!" Anselm's voice was shrill and he was kicking the door relentlessly, beating it as hard as he could, over and over again, for Marguerite could not restrain him. After a while, he ceased to scream and cry but continued hitting the door mechanically with clockwork fury.

Cook was in the kitchen, praying, kneeling on the floor, hands together, lips moving silently, rocking.

"Ella!" Marguerite suddenly screamed to her. "Ella, call the police! Help me, Ella!" But the cook wouldn't or couldn't hear, and Anselm would not calm down, and Marguerite was worried about Agnette. She needed to check on Agnette.

"Agnette is as good as dead!" shouted Walter into Hedda's face. "It would be kinder to let her go."

"No!" Hedda was again animated. "You are worse than either of them – you are evil and mad!" She lifted her head, stared wildly at Walter through her tears. "Even Karl Muller – who is not even related to Agnette – he could not watch her die." Walter lifted his hand and slapped her hard across the face again, then grabbed the top of her arms and pulled her to her feet, but she continued, shouting at him above the constant sound of Anselm banging at the door. "And Daddy, whatever else he has done, he rescued Agnette. He got her out of that godforsaken hospital you put her in, while you didn't even have the guts to visit her, can't bear to look at her because you know you condemned your own daughter to death."

"She was as good as dead!" he shouted at her, shaking her violently. "Agnette died a long time ago!"

"No!" Hedda screamed. "She is getting better. She is going to wake up." Walter stopped shaking her, looked at her in horror. "Yes, Walter, Agnette is waking up and you would have killed her."

"I don't believe you – you are a liar," he responded, his face contorted in a grimace of hatred. But there was fear in his eyes.

"Why don't you go and see for yourself, Walter?" Hedda returned, matching his hatred, holding his glare.

"Well, I'll tell you who won't be waking up soon," hissed Walter. "Your boyfriend, Muller, because guess where he'll be tomorrow?" His eyes widened and an exaggerated, maniacal grin split his face. Hedda, beyond terrified, just looked at him. "In a concentration camp; that's where!" Walter relished her shock. "And in a few days, he should be sucking in carbon monoxide with a room full of other scum – probably in a gas chamber of his own design!"

Marguerite had finally left Anselm to go and check on Agnette. The child was still kicking and banging on the door, but less fiercely and at longer intervals. He seemed to have fallen into a sort of terror-induced stupor. He just kicked and banged and kicked and banged.

"Shut the hell up!" Walter suddenly shouted in uncontrolled rage at his son through the door, and as he turned and lowered his face to shout at what he estimated was Anselm's height, Walter's grip on Hedda's right arm loosened. In a swift, sharp movement she elbowed him full in the nose and he reeled backwards, his hands raised to his face. Hedda grabbed the door handle and opened the door, caught Anselm up in her arms and lurched with him into the hall. Seconds later, Walter was on them, and all three sprawled onto the parquet floor.

What happened next occurred in a sequence of events no one who witnessed it could recall clearly. Anselm seemed to slide across the parquet, beneath the stairwell towards Walter's office. Walter lifted Hedda from the floor by her hair and then put his hands around her throat and began to throttle her. Marguerite emerged from Agnette's room and cried out. Everyone remembered Anselm shouting, "Leave my mutti alone!"

Hedda sank to her knees as Walter tightened his grip around her throat and then, at some stage in the proceedings, moments before Hedda would certainly have lost consciousness, the deafening report of a gun. It obliterated thought and sense, and fractured memory as glass splinters. Cook was in any case still in the kitchen. Walter was preoccupied with Hedda. Only Marguerite and Anselm could have recounted what passed with any accuracy.

Suddenly, Hedda fell forward, gasping and choking in an effort to draw breath as Walter crashed down beside her on the parquet, felled by a close range gunshot wound to the back of his head. What Marguerite would always remember most clearly of all, was how the gun spun on the parquet when it was dropped and how the light from the trembling chandelier flashed on the spotlessly polished silver of its barrel. Walter was dead.

CHAPTER THIRTEEN

When the ambulance arrived it was clear at once this was a crime scene and so no one touched the body until the Gestapo also arrived. Statements were taken, the gun was fingerprinted and removed in a plastic bag. The body was finally put into the ambulance. A paramedic treated Hedda's injuries. Some sort of major domestic dispute had occurred – that much was clear. But who had pulled the trigger of the gun was less clear. The maid insisted vehemently it was an accident.

The wife said nothing throughout the questioning, but the maid insisted Hedda could not possibly have pulled the trigger because she was being assaulted by the victim at the time. Someone, though, had put a hole in the back of a senior SS officer's head and killed him. There was a cook, a badly beaten wife, a semi-comatose girl in an upstairs room, a maid and a small boy who stared and shook, and was in deep shock. Until the gun had been forensically examined, there were no legitimate conclusions to come to. The Gestapo officer decided that the present occupants of the house would remain under house guard while investigations began.

The following morning at eight o'clock, an IG Farben administrative manager was waiting with a lorry driver outside a loading depot. He had a clipboard and occasionally exchanged idle talk with the driver. He looked often at his watch. They were waiting for the senior officer to arrive, who would sign for the 260-kilogramme consignment of prussic acid and vacuum-sealed packages of potassium cyanide to be transported to Mauthausen.

By eight-twenty a.m. the man from IG Farben was evidently impatient. He had a great deal to do. The lorry driver, a burly man in his sixties, was relatively unconcerned. He moved away from the tetchy official and sat on a low wall, lit a cigarette. The first morning of April was chilly but very bright. It promised even to be warm by midday, for the sky was sweet and blue. At eight-forty a.m., the lorry driver moved from the wall to the ground and, leaning against the wall, folded his arms and closed his eyes. It was almost 300 kilometres to Linz. It would take most of the day to get there in the truck, stopping at every checkpoint. He was in no hurry. He had no plans to return until the next day and no wife waiting for him. He would be paid, whatever. He dozed off.

The IG Farben employee left the truck and walked back to his office, from where he telephoned his administrative director. The director telephoned the IV Office on Voss Strasse, asking for Karl Muller and an explanation for his failure to show up. No one had seen him. So the director telephoned the T4 headquarters on Tiergarten Strasse and asked for Oberführer Gunther, as was his signature on the order form. No one had seen him either. Eventually, in despair, the manager called an IG Farben executive director to inform him of this highly irregular situation. By ten o'clock, a substitute officer from the Hygiene Division, T4, had been allocated to accompany the consignment to Mauthausen, and the camp commandant had been notified that the delivery would be approximately two hours later than scheduled.

Emilie, Walter's secretary, was becoming quite stressed. The telephone would not stop ringing and she had no idea where her boss was. He had not left her a message or tried to telephone to explain his absence, and no one was answering his home or his apartment telephone. By the time Reichsführer Himmler called just after lunch, to express his dissatisfaction to Walter that Karl Muller had disappeared, Emilie was frantic.

"I am so very sorry, mein Reichsführer Himmler, sir," she pleaded, "but I have no idea where Oberführer Gunther is. People have been telephoning all morning. No one seems to know where he is, and he is not answering his phones."

Himmler was intrigued. Both Muller and Gunther disappeared? After what Gunther had told him the day before, it was difficult not to make connections. "Telephone the Gestapo office on Albrecht Strasse," he commanded her. "This is most suspicious. Get back to me on the following number when you have some information." And he left her the Mauthausen number and went to have lunch with the commandant before the commencement of the afternoon's extermination demonstration.

The scheduled high point of the day's events was to ascertain the relative lethality of cyanide gas when produced by a reaction of hydrogen cyanic acid with potassium cyanide. Distinguished IG Farben chemist and director Ernst Schroeder would be supervising the trials. The climax of the day, though, for Himmler, was to have been his sudden request that Karl Muller remove his SS uniform and slip into prison clothes. To his annoyance, this particular entertainment was increasingly in doubt.

Emilie could not find anyone at Gestapo headquarters who would give her information on the apparent disappearance of Officer Gunther, although they told her not to expect him at work that day. She dutifully contacted the commandant's secretary at Mauthausen and passed on the advice she had been given. Then she relaxed. A day without Gunther in the office was almost like a holiday. She would go out for lunch.

Hedda had stayed up all night after Walter's body was removed, rocking Anselm to sleep on her knee while sitting at Agnette's bedside. When at last the boy was fast asleep, Hedda lay him tenderly beside his sister and covered him over, then returned to the armchair beside the bed. Marguerite slept in Hedda's room. Her sobbing eventually subsided into silence in the small hours of the morning.

Armed Gestapo officers were posted by the front and back doors, and one patrolled the perimeter of the house. At around seven a.m., a haggard looking Marguerite appeared in Agnette's room.

"What happened, Marguerite?" Hedda whispered.

"It was an accident, Frau Gunther," replied the maid, beginning to cry again. "Anselm found the gun. I... I went to get it from him. It went off."

Hedda sighed, shrugged her shoulders. "Will you please prepare some breakfast for Agnette? And tell Cook to make breakfast for the rest of us. Ask those police officers too. They must be hungry."

In Leipzig, Karl had snapped to consciousness around five a.m. He was sweating profusely and had been restless all night, surfacing repeatedly from a maelstrom of bad dreams. It was certain now that they would come for him; in just a matter of hours. He should be in Berlin, preparing to accompany a consignment of lethal chemicals to Mauthausen. He should have been working all weekend on designs for new gas chambers. He was critically and dangerously AWOL.

He turned to watch his wife sleeping and his heart filled with tenderness but also regret for what he had been unable to do for her – and for what he was about to do. He wanted to kiss her, but dared not in case she awoke. Slipping from the bed, he grabbed his clothes, tip-toed from the room, then dressed hurriedly in the bathroom. Downstairs, there was no sound apart from the tick of the wall clock in the hallway.

Karl moved around in the gloom, the light from the rising sun blocked by blackout cloths, and found some paper and a pen. He scribbled a note to Greta telling her not to worry about him; that he loved her and would love her eternally. Leaving the note on the dining room table, he took the notepad and pen and pushed them into a pocket. A few minutes later, he was in his car and driving towards the church where he used to serve as an altar boy.

It was some surprise to Himmler that Walter Gunther was dead. Irritated by the message from Gunther's secretary that she could discover nothing of her boss's whereabouts, he had contacted Gestapo headquarters himself and spoken to a friend there: a senior Gestapo officer.

"Get Muller," he had instructed. "Even if he is not involved in Gunther's death, he is a traitor. When you find him, put him in Tegel prison straight away. I shall deal with him personally when I get back. Oh, and Fritz," Himmler had added, "someone ought to tell Gunther's secretary that he's dead – poor woman doesn't know whether she's coming or going."

It didn't take long to discover that Karl's Berlin apartment was empty and had not been used for some time. His personal files revealed that his family were in Leipzig. A phone call to the Leipzig Gestapo set in motion the search for Karl, which began at his parents' house that Monday afternoon and soon relocated to the house of his parents-in-law. There they discovered a very distressed Frau Erlach, who handed them a note apparently written to her daughter that morning and which indicated Karl did not envisage returning. No one had any idea where he might be.

When Emilie got back to the office after a leisurely lunch in a nice little café on Friedrich Strasse, she discovered an envelope on her desk, addressed to the secretary of Oberführer Walter Gunther. Terrified Gunther had returned, found her absent from her desk and sacked her, Emilie opened the envelope with trembling hands. A short note read: "Regrettably, Oberführer Walter Gunther is dead. Please inform callers and await further instructions. The Reich Office has been informed and you will be reassigned in due course. In the meantime, report for duty as usual."

"Oh!" exclaimed Emilie aloud, and then, "What a relief!" She sat down with an abandoned flop in her office chair. A grin crept like sunrise across her face.

Karl sat for more than two hours in St Mary's Church, contemplating the shortening shadows across the chancel as the sun rose higher in the sky and lit up the stained-glass windows in its north-easterly facing wall. Karl remained in the shadows, immune to the chill, coming to terms with what was undoubtedly the end of his life. Then he wrote a letter to his father and mother, designed to make peace with them, but mainly to give them peace. He admitted he had sinned in his work as an SS officer, and that he deeply regretted his part in the affliction of human suffering for which the Reich was responsible. He begged his parents' forgiveness and asked them to pray for his soul. He told them he had recently been to Confession.

At around nine a.m., the priest emerged from the sacristy. He genuflected before the altar, then turned around and proceeded arthritically down the aisle. Karl rose and waited for him to come close before calling to him gently. The old priest narrowed his eyes behind his glasses in an attempt to focus on and recognize the man who had called him. When that failed, he approached Karl, removing his glasses, finally peering into Karl's eyes. Recognition dawned. "Are you young Muller?" he asked. "Erich's boy?"

"I am, Father. Though not so young, perhaps."

"Young to me, my boy; young to me," Father Friedmann responded, smiling. "What brings you here, my son? I thought you were up in Berlin now?" He replaced his glasses, stepped back, folded his arms and contemplated his erstwhile altar boy. "You look peaky. Don't they feed you in the SS?"

"I'm a little tired; that's all." Karl extended the letter he had written. "Would you give this to my father when you next see him, please?"

"He was here yesterday, at Mass," responded Father Friedmann, accepting the letter. "Have you not seen him? I thought you might be home on leave." He nodded at Karl's chest and legs as if to indicate his civilian clothing.

"I have been with my wife. It's a little complicated."

"Ah," nodded the priest, "yes. Life is more complicated than it used to be, eh?" He looked sadly into Karl's troubled eyes, his own kindly face creasing into a warm smile. "I will give him your letter, my boy," he said quietly. His expression became serious. "It is good to see you, Karl. Very good to see you, dear boy." And the priest put out a hand to shake Karl's, briefly covering their joined hands with his free one before pulling gently away and continuing down the aisle and eventually disappearing into the street.

Karl knelt in prayer for a little longer, then rose, crossed himself, and when he reached the end of his pew he genuflected before turning his back on the altar and following in the direction taken by the priest. Soon, he was in his car and on his journey back to Berlin. He was not surprised to find two Gestapo officers outside his apartment as he approached the door some hours later. He did not slow his pace, but lifted his arms and walked until the muzzle of a rifle prevented his walking any further.

At around the time Karl was speaking with Father Friedmann, replacement Gestapo guards were relieving those who had been on duty at Hedda's house overnight. The changeover was good-humoured, the first guard having been well fed with ham, cheese and fresh bread, as well as refreshed by the excellent coffee Walter always kept in plentiful supply at home.

Hedda had finally risen from the chair she occupied beside Agnette's bed and carried the still sleeping Anselm to his own bed, tucked him in and kissed his head before going into her own room, removing her clothes, wrapping herself in a dressing gown, then going to the bathroom for a shower. Everywhere ached. Her mouth and left eye were agonizingly painful and she could barely open her mouth. She wondered if her jaw could be broken; was too tired to care much. However, she was not prepared for the sight that met her eyes when she looked into the bathroom mirror. Her face was grotesquely swollen, and her left eye had blackened overnight, as had the flesh around her mouth. Dried blood still caked the corners of her mouth and when she opened it, fresh blood trickled in a ready rivulet over her lower lip and down her chin. Her neck was impossibly stiff and she could only walk in a poker-like fashion, so that turning right or left could only be done by a full military-style swivel of her whole body. There were dark marks on her throat where Walter had tried to throttle her. She had a terrible headache. Every now and then, a sob rose involuntarily around the region of her heart like a bird making a bid for freedom, but somewhere near her throat it died and sank heavily to her chest once more.

Hedda was numb to all feeling but pain. She simply stood under the cascade of hot water from the showerhead, experiencing the soothing warmth of the water.

By mid afternoon, the April sunshine was warm. It poured itself over Berlin, flooding the Tiergarten lawns and flirting with the bronze eagles of the new Reich chancellery on Wilhelmsplatz, lavishing itself on the golden cross of Kaiser Wilhelm's memorial church spire.

"Frau Gunther?" Marguerite, still tearful, her face strained by anxiety, dark circles beneath her eyes, stood beside Hedda's bed, compulsively twisting and untwisting her apron in and out of tight spirals. Hedda, who had been dozing lightly, opened her eyes with difficulty. "It is such a beautiful day. I wondered... might I please ask the guards if I may take the children into the garden?"

Hedda seemed to consider the request, frowned, closed her eyes again. "Children?"

"Yes, Frau Gunther. I would very much like to carry Agnette into the sunshine – if you agree. I can put her on a blanket. It has been so long since she saw the sunshine. Anselm, also, would like it. I think it might do us good..."

Hedda seemed to consider for a moment, then moved her shoulders in a shrugging movement. "Sure. Go ahead. Why not?"

Within an hour of Marguerite's request, two events of import occurred. One was wholly expected, given the circumstances, and the other was entirely unexpected. First, Marguerite screamed repeatedly for Hedda to come outside, the pitch and excitement in her voice jolting Hedda to a most unwelcome state of immediate terror and alerting the Gestapo officers to stand to attention and present their rifles in readiness for action. No sooner had the intense excitement following this outburst subsided than there was new consternation of a very different nature. A very large, very official, very shiny black car turned into the driveway and came to a dignified halt before the house. A chauffeur in a peaked cap alighted and held open a rear passenger door to enable a tall man in full SS uniform to step from the car onto the gravelled driveway. It has to be said, though, that if Hitler himself had emerged from the Mercedes, Hedda would not have cared, because ten minutes previously, Agnette had begun to speak.

What a strange commotion greeted the Reich officer as he walked, hands behind his back, towards the front lawn of the Gunthers' residence. Two Gestapo officers stood to attention, rifles gripped in their right hands, their left hands appended to their foreheads in rigid salutes. Behind them, a third was unsure whether to drop his rifle from the attitude he maintained as he followed the chaotic antics before him with his bayonet, as though he were somehow causing the women to move.

On the lawn, apparently oblivious to the statesman's arrival, were two women dancing together – or trying to; they had linked arms, but one of them was having evident difficulty moving, and when she revolved to face the Reich officer, he was shocked by the swelling and bruising to her face. His eyes narrowed as he appeared to try and make sense of what he saw. Was this some grotesque scene of abuse, perverse amusement instigated by the Gestapo, forced upon these women?

On the grass were two children. One was clapping his hands and turning circles in that awkward, concentrated way young children have, lest they fall. The other, a girl, was laughing and moving her head in an attempt to keep track of the whirling, noisy women. The concern of the officer that the Gestapo officers were malefactors was soon relieved.

"Halt!" eventually cried out the one with the bayonet. "Stop it!" But when the women ignored him, he put his hand to his helmet in consternation, dropped his bayonet, lifted it again, looked anxiously towards the officer, gave up and stood to attention with his colleagues.

At last, the women stopped revolving, doubling over breathlessly, falling into each other's arms. They quietened, stood separately, and faced the official, chests heaving from exertion.

Marguerite's smile died completely, but Hedda's did not. That she had been caught laughing and dancing the day after her husband's death did not bother her. Even this harbinger of certain doom could not dampen her spirits, for at last, after almost eight months, Agnette had found the door out of the darkness. As if revived by the spring light, she had suddenly exclaimed, quite clearly, "Lovely sunshine!" and then "Mutti?" Ever since, she had been talking, asking where she was and what was wrong with her mother's face and where was Anselm and hadn't he grown! And how was Marguerite? For answer she had been kissed and kissed and hugged and cried over and kissed again. Marguerite had even linked arms with one of the policemen and swung him around, at which he could not resist laughing and had spun her a turn or two before remembering she might be a murderer.

"I am sorry for the chaos," explained Hedda as well as she could through her swollen mouth and breathlessness, "but my child has just begun to speak after almost eight months of being in a coma." She smiled and immediately brought her hand to her face in response to the pain it caused. The offical stared at her injuries, noted the tight, black slit in the swelling that was her left eye. His own eyes were brown and kind, and he smiled – warmly, it seemed to Hedda, though she knew better than to trust him.

"Am I addressing Frau Hedda Gunther?" he asked in that practised, pseudo-courteous manner the rank and file of the SS used to initiate conversations with people they intended to harm. Hedda sighed, looked at him as if to imply she was in no mood for his games; she knew what was coming. She nodded.

"Mutti?" Agnette's voice was pleading. "What is happening?"

Hedda turned from her visitor and knelt beside her daughter, kissed her face, stroked her hair. "I just need to talk to this gentleman for a moment, darling. I'll be back soon, I promise."

And Anselm, crouching down beside his sister, looked delightedly into Hedda's face, then at his sister. "Shall I talk to you, 'nette?" he asked. "I can talk to you if you like."

Hedda stood up again with some difficulty, looked at Marguerite. The maid appeared terrified, returning Hedda's glance with an agonized expression.

"Shall we go inside?" said the officer. "I haven't got much time."

Dr Brandt was bringing to a close a difficult conversation with Dr Kaufman, who had phoned from his asylum in Leipzig. "Yes, yes. All very irritating, my dear Dr Kaufman." He was soothing, while trying to carry on writing some clinical notes he needed to get shipshape before he left the office that evening. The Führer was in one of his foul tempers – so bad for his health. Brandt had warned him repeatedly that if he did not meditate more and fret less, he was setting himself up for some sort of coronary episode. And where would Germany be without the brilliant leadership and military expertise of its leader? The illustrious Führer must call him as soon as he felt any sort of agitation, and Brandt personally would come immediately and attend to him. Having received news that the Italian invasion of Greece was failing miserably, Hitler had lost his temper completely and spent a good deal of time on the telephone, screaming at Goering. Then he had turned his attention to the terrorizing of several land army generals, threatening them with court martial or worse if they did not instantly come up with fail-safe invasive strategies to take Greece by dawn on the 6th April, in Operation Marita.

Brandt needed to get to the Führer's side where he paced and ranted along the splendid gallery of the Reich chancellery, no doubt in a state of near apoplexy by now. It had been at least fifteen minutes since he had called.

"Well, is this Schmidt fellow right? Is the patient much better since you saw her last?" Brandt's secretary had come in, offered to hold the papers still and present them to him for signing while he spoke on the phone. Brandt nodded and indicated his gratitude to her, widening his eyes and smiling. "Well, Kaufman, if the patient is talking and acting reasonably, then the depression must have lifted, surely? I understand your frustra– Yes, quite. I know, bu– " Brandt rolled his eyes, changed the telephone to the other ear and lifted his left shoulder to trap it, leaving his hands free to continue his paperwork.

His secretary stepped back, taking with her the papers he pushed across the desk towards her. "I know. If I may finish? There's a couple of things you need to know. Firstly, I did not authorize Oberführer Gunther to readmit this woman to the asylum. He took that upon himself... Yes... he had told me about the circumstances... Yes, I did know Muller had taken her out in a most irregular manner..." He finished writing, put down his pen, took back the telephone in his right hand and gave the call his complete attention. He had to end it and get to the Führer. "Dr Kaufman, I'm afraid Oberführer Gunther is dead, so we cannot rely on his assistance. Yes, most unfortunate. We found out today. Yes, tragic; can't discuss the circumstances. He worked for me, you understand? You need to defer to my judgment on this, Dr Kaufman. I am also a medical practitioner, of course, and although not a psychiatrist, I have a little understanding of the nature and prognoses of a range of mental illnesses."

Kaufman was shocked at the news of Gunther's death. This, plus the assertion from Brandt that he had not authorized Greta Muller's readmission to the asylum, had significantly weakened his case. His fury was, in any case, simply blowing itself out since that smug, interfering Schmidt from Leipzig hospital had shown up again on Sunday morning and ruined Kaufman's breakfast by presenting him – in his own home – with a report that stated Greta Muller was well. He insisted Kaufman's diagnosis and treatment had been in error. Kaufman could only repeat to Dr Brandt how affronted and insulted he was by it all.

"Yes, yes, dear chap. Well, if she's better, then she is better. I think you should just let this one go, old man. After all, we have a great deal more... rewarding work for you to do. We are most impressed with your work down there... Yes, yes, absolutely..." Brandt rolled his eyes as his secretary returned to the office. He indicated to her the remaining papers on the desk. She smiled and took them away. "Well, you know what the Romans used to say, Kaufman: 'aquila non captat muscas'... Don't you? Well, let me translate for you then: 'the eagle does not catch flies'. We have bigger prey for you, Kaufman. I'll be in touch, OK?" There was another pause while Kaufman asked him what should happen about Greta's notes, as Schmidt still had them. Brandt lost patience. He had started to rise from his chair, was trying to put his jacket on while still talking. "Look, Dr Kaufman, my esteemed colleague, just let it go. What does it matter, in the end, if he has her notes? After all, I'm sorry to say it, but she is now his patient. The procurement of her case was unorthodox, but he seems to have cured her, so it would be –" he wanted to say petty – "beneath your professional dignity to pursue this. A waste of your valuable time, dear chap."

Finally, having wriggled into his jacket, closed his briefcase, which had been open on his desk, and put his pen into a top jacket pocket, Brandt ended the conversation with a sweetener. "I tell you what. I'll get my secretary to make an appointment for me to visit your place personally. How's that? We'll discuss business and have some dinner. Yes. Yes, call my secretary. Goodbye... yes, goodbye, Dr Kaufman... Yes, quite... No, no, my pleasure. Till we meet..." And he rolled his eyes again, replaced the telephone. "I never want to meet that man," he pronounced to his secretary in a tone that made it clear this was an instruction, and he rushed for the door.

"Please, Frau Gunther, sit down."

Hedda paused before complying, taking in the immaculate uniform, the polished boots, the leather gloves the Reich officer held in his right hand more as an accessory than a necessity, given the weather. He removed his cap. He seemed instantly smaller. He was balding and quite angular, but his dark eyes were remarkable, their kindness incongruous with his station. He reminded her of Karl Muller.

"I didn't kill my husband, Officer...?" she began.

"Goering," he said. "Today, I am Reichsmarschall Hermann Goering."

Hedda stood up, too quickly. Her head spun and she had to sit down again. She lifted her hand to her face. The pain was remarkable. "You are not Hermann Goering!" she stated emphatically, though the effort of expressing her indignation increased her pain. "You look nothing like him. I have met him."

"*You* may have met him," answered the man, "but I can assure you those clowns have not." He nodded in the direction of the Gestapo officers in the garden.

Hedda looked at him, incredulity and confusion fighting for dominance of her expression. She put a hand over her swollen left eye to focus better the right one. "What is this?" she asked, almost in a whisper.

"Frau Gunther, I had no idea your husband was dead, but from what I have heard – and from what I observed when I arrived – I think this may not be a bad thing?" He sat forward on his chair, undid a top button. "God alone knows how they wear these stupid things; it's strangling me!" he declared, screwing up his face as he fought with the collar of his uniform. "Actually, this is quite a good fit, don't you think?" He winked at her. "Borrowed from my big brother." Then he remembered the seriousness of her plight and that of her daughter, and realized he may have less time than he thought, under the circumstances. "I am Albert Goering, Hermann Goering's brother. The man driving my car? He's a worker at my factory in Pilsen. He's also, by the way, a member of the Czech Resistance, so we must not be caught." He winked again and tapped his nose as if to elicit her complicity and discretion.

"Why are you here?" asked Hedda, wholly unable to make sense of anything. The last twenty-four hours seemed a roller-coaster of surreal events. She wished she had some painkillers.

"I can see you are in pain. Did your husband do this to you?" She nodded. "Yes, last night."

"And how did he die? Did you kill him? I wouldn't blame you."

"No! I told you I did not. He was shot, but I... I don't know how it happened. I am pretty sure it was an accident."

"The maid?" Goering indicated the direction of the garden again. "Defending you perhaps?"

"Why are you here?"

"I got a letter from Karl Muller. You know him, yes?"

"From Karl? I don't understand." Hedda felt light-headed. The pain in her jaw from talking, her intense headache, made thinking very difficult. She desperately needed to sleep. She had not slept properly since the night before Walter had been shot.

"I will explain everything to you, but not now. In brief? He told me your daughter was in terrible danger – that your husband had agreed to have her killed."

"He told you that?" Hedda was struggling to make the connections.

"Is it true?"

"Yes. It is... it was true."

"He asked me to help you, if I could. I could, so I am here. I planned to pick you up from your house, take you to the hospital and use these papers." He produced some folded papers from his breast pocket and handed them to Hedda. She struggled to read them, so he took them back. "Here, allow me. They are release papers for one Agnette Gunther, signed by the illustrious Hermann Goering. That is a very fine forgery, let me tell you. I cannot tell the difference myself!" He smiled at her again, folded the papers and put them back in his pocket. "Anyhow, then I was going to ask you where you wanted to go. I hoped I was not too late. It has not been easy to arrange all this." He indicated his uniform, nodded towards the front garden again, meaning the car.

"I see!" Hedda was impressed, her heart softening once more towards Karl. He was, it seemed, a good man after all.

"My husband knew about Karl," she remembered suddenly, becoming alarmed. "Where is Karl?"

"I have no idea," responded Goering. "I can make enquiries later, but if you want to get away from here, and take your daughter, it seems now might be a very good time to go, don't you think?"

"You can do that? Just get us out of here?"

"If we move fast. I'll tell them I am Hermann Goering, Reichsmarshall, and I have been informed of the murder of my colleague, Officer Gunther. I shall say I am taking you personally into custody, along with your murdering maid and your brats – lay it on thick, SS-style, you know? – and I shall insist you get into the car, just as you are."

"Will we all fit?" Hedda could hardly think straight at all. "What about luggage? What about... things?"

"Sorry. Just you. I have some money. Have you?"

"Yes... Yes, I have a few thousand marks in notes and I have a chequebook which gives me access to a housekeeping account. My husband has several accounts, but they are in his name."

"I have some very close banker contacts in Berlin who can perhaps help with all that, but not for a while. The authorities will be watching your husband's accounts very closely. For now, let us go. There is no time to waste. If anybody more senior than those goons outside turns up, Frau Gunther, the game will be up. Shall we go?"

Hedda got to her feet. "I must get the money – upstairs." Albert nodded, adding that she should proceed with all haste. Hedda went as fast as she could to her bedroom, retrieved the cash, a handbag and a coat. This reminded her that the children and Marguerite might need coats. Who knew where they were going? It was only April and the weather could be very cold. She grabbed an extra jacket from her wardrobe for Marguerite, hastened to Anselm's room, then Agnette's, yanked coats from hangers. In Agnette's room, she paused briefly before Steen's portrayal of the Iphigenia sacrifice, framed and hanging on Agnette's wall. She eyed anew the little boy with his broken crossbow, fleeing from the scene in tears. He had not before struck her in such relief. Neither, for that matter, had the ghostly female figure who sat upon a balustrade in the background, clearly presiding, waiting in some way.

Albert called her from downstairs. "Frau Gunther? We really must go."

"Where are we going?" she asked as she rejoined him in the hall.

"Well," replied Albert, standing up and putting on his cap, "the hell out of Germany for starters!" And he flashed her a brilliant smile. "First, top speed to Prague, and you and the children and the maid will stay in a convent there. It is all set up. When you are all ready to travel again, I will have papers and false ID for you, and you will travel by rail to Switzerland. You may have to split up – the maid and the boy, you and your daughter – I don't know yet. Your little girl is conspicuous. We shall see later. For now? Let's get away from Berlin and the Gestapo. Agreed?" Hedda nodded in terse compliance.

Just before they emerged into the late afternoon sunlight, Goering warned her in a quiet voice: "Look the part, now; serious, OK?" She looked into his dark eyes and watched them harden, nodded again. It would not be difficult to look terrified. He grabbed her arm, led her into the garden.

"You!" He signalled to one of the guards. "Pick up that child and put her in my car, back seat." The officer ran to comply.

"May I please see your identification, sir?" The closest officer looked at the insignia on Goering's sleeve and coloured immediately, saluted. "Mein Reichsmarschall, sir!"

"I am Hermann Goering, second only to the Führer himself, my brave officer," declared Albert Goering. "And I am taking these treacherous, murderous women and their brats to the Reich chancellery, where they will pay – directly, if you understand me – for what they have done to my esteemed friend and comrade, Oberführer Gunther. Now, officer, if you please, get that woman into the car and that boy also. This one –" and he shook Hedda by the arm he held – "will sit in the front with me."

The children cried out in alarm, Marguerite wept anew and soon, all were bundled into the car. The stony-faced chauffeur looked on with an expression of disgust and slammed the door shut once Goering had climbed into the leather-covered front bench with Hedda. He tipped his cap at the Gestapo officers, who saluted in return before assuming his position in the driver's seat, and then they drove away from the house in Brandenburg, never to return. The three policemen watched until the car had disappeared. All of them looked very sad indeed.

CHAPTER FOURTEEN

Cardinal von Preysing could not get Karl Muller out of his head. Karl's letter had greatly disturbed him. His close friend Cardinal von Galen of Munster, and fearless opponent of National Socialism, had replied immediately when he received a forwarded copy of the letter in which Karl had detailed the activities of T4. Did von Preysing think this letter was genuine Cardinal von Galen had wanted to know. Could such heinous destruction of innocents be taking place under their very noses, throughout Germany?

Von Galen had investigated. Catholic parishioners throughout Munster were asked to tell their priests if they had had any exposure, direct or otherwise, to strange occurrences in hospitals. Had they had children taken away from them? Did they know people whose children had been registered as genetically defective and then "required" to reside in special paediatric units? The response was overwhelming – and convincing.

When Cardinal Orsenigo admitted to Cardinal von Preysing that Muller had come to the nunciature and tried to see him – had left him a similarly explicit letter – von Preysing conducted his own enquiries. The bishop's palace was an administrative headquarters for financial and official church business throughout the region of Brandenburg and Berlin. There were many lay staff who could discreetly liaise with records offices in Berlin, especially where Catholics were employed in administrative roles. It eventually transpired that Karl Muller was born in Leipzig to Catholic parents. Discreet connections with the parish priest, Father Friedmann at St Mary's, Leipzig, confirmed the parents still attended Mass. Von Preysing visited Father Friedmann.

Father Friedmann confided to the Bishop of Berlin that Karl Muller seemed to have got into some "official trouble". The priest very much feared that Karl had fallen foul of the law or had taken his own life. He had written a letter, which Karl's father had shown him. The letter read like a suicide note. His family in Leipzig, including his wife, were very distressed by his disappearance. Karl was not responding to any attempts to contact him, and the SS met all enquiries with vague statements about his being "unavailable".

When von Preysing pressured Orsenigo to use his official contacts to discover the fate of Karl Muller, the nuncio reluctantly complied. He was, though, he made it clear, most uncomfortable about this foray into Reich business. A few days later, over an excellent dinner, at which the nuncio's esteemed SS guests drank far too much Riesling, the cardinal remarked "casually" that some young SS chap had turned up on unstated business some weeks past – "name of... let's see –" he had paused, agreed the Riesling was excellent – "Muller? Kurt, no Karl, Muller?" The name elicited an unguarded guffaw from one of the Reichsministers present. Orsenigo added pragmatically that he had, of course been far too busy to see Muller. The cardinal sighed, lowered his eyes and unfolded his pristine napkin, spread it over his upper thighs.

The Reichsminister who had laughed was refilling his crystal wine glass, but with his left hand he simultaneously made a slit throat gesture. If it had been a certain Officer Karl Muller, SS, who had come to see the nuncio, he remarked, then he wouldn't be bothered by any more such house calls. The cardinal raised a quizzical eyebrow, cocking his head a little to the left in an attitude of polite interest. Apparently, the statesman continued, pausing mid sentence to gulp his wine, Himmler himself had decreed Muller's death by beheading following several weeks of interrogation in Tegel prison.

The nuncio said "Ah!" and nodded, as though the puzzle were solved. "Oh, Celeste," he had exclaimed, "these beans look so fresh and appetizing!" Cardinal Orsenigo smiled warmly at his housekeeper as she deposited the bowl of steaming vegetables on the table, genuinely pleased to change the subject.

And so it came to be that Cardinal von Preysing, Bishop of Berlin, discovered that Karl Muller had been executed as a traitor to the Reich, without even recourse to a People's Court. The bishop wrote a brief note to that effect to Cardinal von Galen, the Bishop of Munster, expressing his heartfelt regret at the fate of this good man.

On the day Karl Muller should have arrived at Mauthausen to meet Himmler, Ernst Schroeder was also there. It was a strange day for Ernst. He had arrived at the new extermination camp by chauffeured car, having received a request by telephone from Himmler himself to be present at the gassing trials. It had been Himmler's intention to establish Schroeder's unequivocal loyalty to T4 in the light of Gunther's revelations that his wife, Schroeder's daughter, had confided in her father her distress that a T4 doctor had ordained her child's death, with her husband's concurrence. Himmler had intended to arrest and incarcerate Muller while Schroeder watched, just to make it absolutely clear to everyone involved that treachery would be discovered and ruthlessly punished.

It had been most vexing for Himmler that his experiment was thwarted; that Gunther was dead and then Muller failed to show. Vexing and boring. Himmler had to spend hours watching a sweating and irascible Professor Schroeder train clumsy SS personnel to mix prussic acid with potassium cyanide in increasingly precise and lethal quantities. And then there was a series of tedious trials, in which seemingly endless droves of stinking and bedraggled prisoners were dispatched at intervals.

The Mauthausen experiment was eventually pronounced a success, though. By the time the third gassing had finished, and over 300 prisoners were piled in long lines of three bodies deep in a large space masquerading as a shower room, it was confirmed that this method of killing people using cyanide was more effective than the carbon monoxide methods applied previously. Modifications to the chamber, to equip it with pipes for conducting cyanide gas or, better still in Schroeder's estimation, Zyklon B canisters, would be an improvement. Karl Muller's assignment to design more chambers that allowed for both methods of mass murder would be given to another engineer at T4, with an operational date of three months from the day's trials.

And, it was fair to say, the day had not been entirely devoid of amusement. Himmler had been able to announce to Ernst, over coffee, that his son-in-law was dead. Oh yes, Himmler confirmed gravely. Dead. Shot at home – possibly by Schroeder's own daughter. It seemed she had discovered her daughter was to be euthanized.

Himmler avoided looking at Ernst straight away, put sugar cubes in his coffee and stirred it carefully. "Oh, yes!" he added, as if he had forgotten something important. "Apparently – according to Gunther, anyway – it was Karl Muller who revealed Agnette's fate to Frau Gunther. Karl Muller! Can you believe it?"

As Himmler lifted his cup to his mouth, he contemplated Ernst with an assumed neutrality of expression that the latter could not return. The professor was visibly trembling. His jaw was working furiously.

"So sorry, Schroeder," exclaimed Himmler, as though apologizing for some minor breach of manners; "this must be a shock." He sipped his coffee again, looking away as if sensitive to Ernst's battle with tears.

At last the scientist was able to speak, though his voice was barely audible. "Does Hedda know of my... involvement with T4?" There was a long pause while Himmler savoured the question, put down his cup carefully on its saucer and sat back. He folded his hands in his lap and his mouth twisted as if he were weighing the possibility. Ernst began to doubt Himmler had heard him. He sat forward in his chair and spoke again. "That I knew about Agnette? Does Hedda know?"

"Now there's a thing," said Himmler at last. "I don't know, Professor. Walter is dead. I should imagine the exchange before the trigger was pulled was pretty... heated. People say such indiscreet things under those circumstances, don't they?" For the interrogative, Himmler looked directly at Ernst. The professor was unable to respond or return the gaze. He frowned deeply and closed his eyes, as though in pain. Himmler leaned forward to retrieve his coffee cup as a tear escaped the corner of Ernst's left eye. Himmler watched it run beneath the heavy brown frame of his spectacles and disappear into his moustache.

For around three hours that day, Ernst watched prisoners die from cyanide poisoning at Mauthausen. Finally, the whole process took what he had gauged theoretically would become the standard ten minutes or so. Some of the men cried loudly before the gas was released into the chamber. Some cried quietly and some simply hung their heads. All were naked, humiliated, already half dead from labour and starvation. Ernst watched them retch and vomit, convulse, defecate and finally asphyxiate. He watched the camp guards shoot the ones who wouldn't die. His hands shook increasingly violently as he recorded the details of the experiments. By the time it was all over, he could barely sign the test papers to authenticate them.

Himmler watched Ernst and smirked. He had few doubts that the good professor of chemistry and director of IG Farben would be a very loyal Reich employee from now on.

All the way back to Berlin that night – he could not contemplate remaining in Mauthausen – Ernst sobbed quietly in the welcome darkness and solitude of the chauffeured car. That he had been unable or unwilling before to confront the reality of what he now did for a living seemed to him stupid beyond comprehension. And then he thought of Agnette; how she would have died from starvation or drug overdoses deliberately administered while she lay helplessly staring at the sky through a hospital window. And now – now Hedda knew about him and his part in all this... horror. He had no doubt of it. He knew how Walter loved to goad and provoke. His son-in-law would have taken great delight in denouncing Ernst to Hedda. It may even have been the reason she pulled the trigger. If Hedda had done that! His lovely, innocent daughter who had so recently declared her love for him, now caught up in a mire of deceit, betrayal, murder – certainly doomed to execution.

He relived again and again the moment he had so tenderly lifted Agnette from her hospital gurney to her own bed the day she had been brought home from Brandenburg hospital. How happy that day had been. How happy he had made Hedda on that day.

Ernst asked the chauffeur to drop him off at his office in Berlin. He needed to get something, he said. No, the driver needn't wait. Relieved to be dismissed, the chauffeur had driven home at once. It was two a.m.

At his desk, Ernst appeared composed once more. He leaned on the desk and joined his hands, staring ahead as if he were trying to think his way through some difficult calculation. At last, with a sigh, he bent to his left and opened a drawer in his desk. Taking from it a bunch of keys, he arose and crossed the office to a large metal cabinet, then fumbled with the keys to isolate a small silver one, with which he unlocked a drawer and pulled it open. It revealed perfectly arranged white boxes in rows. He removed a box, examined it for a moment, took it to his desk and once more sat down. Then without further hesitation, Ernst opened the box, took out a cyanide capsule, put it in his mouth and bit down hard.

A HISTORICAL EPILOGUE FOR THE READER

No consideration of the horrors that debauched Germany in the decade 1935 to 1945 is complete or accurate without deference and gratitude to those Germans who never accepted what was happening and who fought Hitler on a front where he could never hope to defeat them: the spiritual. Often, they paid with their earthly lives, but we cannot know this side of the grave what armies they joined and led in eventual, resounding victory.

Kurt Gerstein, on whose experiences and troubled life the character of Karl Muller is loosely based, was a Christian. He was beaten up and arrested repeatedly in the mid to late 1930s for speaking out against Nazism. He was expelled from the Nazi party. However, inexplicably for some, he joined the SS in 1941 and became SS Obersturmführer Kurt Gerstein. Many think his decision was prompted by the T4 euthanizing of his mentally ill sister-in-law. It seems Kurt may have wanted to influence things from the inside. Indeed, Christopher R. Browning, a historian, claims Gerstein was "a covert anti-Nazi who infiltrated the SS...", and in a letter to his wife, Gerstein wrote: "I joined the SS... acting as an agent of the Confessing Church."

But Gerstein's work inevitably required him to do things wholly in conflict with his faith and political motivation. Because he was an engineering graduate who began to study medicine (his studies were interrupted by the outbreak of war), Gerstein was appointed Head of Technical Disinfection Services for T4. He witnessed terrible atrocities in the course of his job and also, inevitably, contributed significantly to them – for example, by supplying Zyklon B to Auschwitz.

Gerstein wrote many letters and reports on the atrocities committed by Hitler's government throughout the war, and he tried to alert the Vatican and representatives of the Catholic church, as well as several foreign officials, to what was happening in the death camps and hospitals throughout Germany, Poland and Austria. But his missives and appeals had little or no effect. He died a war crimes prisoner in 1945 – an alleged suicide, but he may have been murdered by other SS prisoners. His death, as his life, remains problematic and mysterious.

Albert Goering, Hermann Goering's brother, was a fierce opponent of Nazism, using his connections and influence to save many Jews and Resistance prisoners from execution. He often persuaded his brother – and even on one occasion, it is alleged, the brutal and terrifying SS general Reinhard Heydrich – to release prisoners from concentration camps. He is known to have forged passports and release documents, and to have set up bank accounts that he used to deliver people from certain death or incarceration. Albert is credited with many heroic acts of bravery and kindness, fiercely protecting his workers in the Pilsen factory where he was Export Director from the cruelties and censure of the SS.

It is even reported by eyewitness survivors that Albert once took off his jacket and got down on his knees to assist a street-cleaning detail of Jews who had been ordered to scrub a pavement with toothbrushes for no other reason than that this would be humiliating.

Cardinal von Galen's three famous "Road of Pain" sermons, delivered in 1941, were secretly copied throughout Germany and caused outrage for good and bad reasons, but Hitler dared not touch him, for fear of the public outcry that would ensue, for von Galen was much loved by the tens of thousands of Catholics in Munster. Von Galen's fierce and fearless condemnation of Hitler's Reich's atrocities earned him the epithet "the Lion of Munster".

On Sunday the 3rd August 1941, in St Lambert's Church, Munster, the Bishop Clemens August Count von Galen delivered a sermon that included these words:

Dearly beloved Christians! The joint pastoral letter of
the German bishops, which was read in all Catholic
churches in Germany on 26 June 1941, includes the
following words. "It is true that in Catholic ethics there
are certain positive commandments which cease to be
obligatory if their observance would be attended by unduly
great difficulties; but there are also sacred obligations of
conscience from which no one can release us; which we
must carry out even if it should cost us our life. Never,
under any circumstances, may a man, save in war or in
legitimate self-defence, kill an innocent person."

I had occasion on 6th July to add the following
comments on this passage in the joint pastoral letter:

For some months we have been hearing reports that
inmates of establishments for the care of the mentally
ill who have been ill for a long period and perhaps
appear incurable have been forcibly removed from these
establishments on orders from Berlin. Regularly the relatives receive soon afterwards an intimation that the patient
is dead, that the patient's body has been cremated and that
they can collect the ashes. There is a general suspicion,
verging on certainty, that these numerous unexpected
deaths of the mentally ill do not occur naturally but
are intentionally brought about in accordance with
the doctrine that it is legitimate to destroy a so-called
"worthless life" – in other words to kill innocent men and
women, if it is thought that their lives are of no further
value to the people and the state. A terrible doctrine which
seeks to justify the murder of innocent people, which
legitimizes the violent killing of disabled persons who are
no longer capable of work, of cripples, the incurably ill and
the aged and infirm!

... Article 211 of the German Penal Code is still in
force, in these terms: "Whoever kills a man of deliberate

intent is guilty of murder and punishable with death."
No doubt in order to protect those who kill with intent
these poor men and women, members of our families,
from this punishment laid down by law, the patients who
have been selected for killing are removed from their home
area to some distant place. Some illness or other is then
given as the cause of death. Since the body is immediately
cremated, the relatives and the criminal police are unable
to establish whether the patient had in fact been ill or
what the cause of death actually was. I have been assured,
however, that in the Ministry of the Interior and the office
of the Chief Medical Officer, Dr Conti, no secret is made of
the fact that indeed a large number of mentally ill persons
in Germany have already been killed with intent and that
this will continue.

Article 139 of the Penal Code provides that "anyone
who has knowledge of an intention to commit a crime
against the life of any person. . . and fails to inform the
authorities or the person whose life is threatened in due
time. . . commits a punishable offence". When I learned of
the intention to remove patients from Marienthal I reported
the matter on 28th July to the State Prosecutor of Münster
Provincial Court and to the Münster chief of police by
registered letter, in the following terms:

"According to information I have received it is
planned in the course of this week (the date has been
mentioned as 31st July) to move a large number of
inmates of the provincial hospital at Marienthal, classified
as 'unproductive members of the national community',
to the mental hospital at Eichberg, where, as is generally
believed to have happened in the case of patients removed
from other establishments, they are to be killed with
intent. Since such action is not only contrary to the divine
and the natural moral law but under Article 211 of the

German Penal Code ranks as murder and attracts the death penalty, I hereby report the matter in accordance with my obligation under Article 139 of the Penal Code and request that steps should at once be taken to protect the patients concerned by proceedings against the authorities planning their removal and murder, and that I may be informed of the action taken."

I have received no information of any action by the State Prosecutor or the police.

I had already written on 26th July to the Westphalian provincial authorities, who are responsible for the running of the mental hospital and for the patients entrusted to them for care and for cure, protesting in the strongest terms. It had no effect. The first transport of the innocent victims under sentence of death has left Marienthal. And I am now told that 800 patients have already been removed from the hospital at Warstein.

We must expect, therefore, that the poor defenceless patients are, sooner or later, going to be killed. Why? Not because they have committed any offence justifying their death, not because, for example, they have attacked a nurse or attendant, who would be entitled in legitimate self-defence to meet violence with violence. In such a case the use of violence leading to death is permitted and may be called for, as it is in the case of killing an armed enemy. No: these unfortunate patients are to die, not for some such reason as this but because in the judgment of some official body, on the decision of some committee, they have become "unworthy to live", because they are classed as "unproductive members of the national community"... The facts I have stated are firmly established...

"Thou shalt not kill!" God wrote this commandment in the conscience of man long before any penal code laid down the penalty for murder, long before there was any prosecutor or any court to investigate and avenge a murder... And now the fifth commandment: "Thou shalt not kill", is set aside and broken under the eyes of the authorities whose function it should be to protect the rule of law and human life, when men presume to kill innocent fellow-men with intent merely because they are "unproductive", because they can no longer produce any goods... Little man, that frail creature, sets his created will against the will of God!... Foolishly and criminally, they defy the will of God! And so Jesus weeps over the heinous sin and the inevitable punishment. God will not be mocked!

This sermon by Cardinal von Galen was considered by the Nazi Office of Propaganda (in its own words) "the fiercest frontal attack unleashed on Nazism in all the years of its existence". It was circulated far and wide, reached soldiers on the frontline, was bought secretly by Jews and Christians throughout Germany. Those who heard it in their churches are reported to have leapt to their feet, crying out in agonized relief and support, many bursting into tears as it went on:

Now defenceless innocents are killed, barbarously killed; people also of a different race, of different origins are suppressed... We are faced with a homicidal folly without equal... With people like this, with these assassins who are proudly trampling our lives, I can no more share belonging to the same people!

And he threw at the Nazi authorities the words of the apostle Paul: "Their God is their belly."

In August of 1941, Hitler ordered the cessation of T4 programmes, following public outcry. The denouncement from Catholic and Protestant pulpits was largely responsible for the

316

cessation of this horror – although the euthanasia of children and psychiatric patients continued secretly to the end of the war. Simultaneously with his T4 cancellation order, Hitler issued strict instructions to the Gauleiters (regional leaders of election districts) that there were to be no further provocations of the churches for the duration of the war. Instead, he vowed, once the war was won, he would exact a cold and merciless revenge against those bishops and priests – the "Blacks", as he called them – who had dared to speak out against him.

However, on 31st July 1941, Hermann Goering wrote this memo to Reinhard Heydrich:

> To Gruppenführer Heydrich:
> Supplementing the task assigned to you by the decree of January 24, 1939, to solve the Jewish problem by means of emigration and evacuation... I hereby charge you to carry out preparations as regards organizational, financial, and material matters for a total solution of the Jewish question in all the territories of Europe under German occupation.
> ...I charge you further to submit to me as soon as possible a general plan of the administrative material and financial measures necessary for carrying out the desired final solution of the Jewish question.
>
> Göring

The White Rose German Resistance Movement (1942–3) was championed by students, in particular three young people: a brother and sister in their early twenties, Hans and Sophie Scholl, and Alexander Schmorell – all passionate Christians. They leafleted extensively, depositing their flyers in prominent places where ordinary Germans would find them and thereby some hope against Hitler's tyranny. Alexander, Hans and Sophie were beheaded in 1943. Alexander, just twenty-six when he died, was canonized in Munich in 2012. An extract from his first White Rose flyer appears at the start of this book. Here is his last:

> When he [that is, Hitler] blasphemously uses the name of the Almighty, he means the power of evil, the fallen angel, Satan. His mouth is the foul-smelling maw of Hell, and his might is at bottom accursed. True, we must conduct a struggle against the National Socialist terrorist state with rational means; but whoever today still doubts the reality, the existence of demonic powers, has failed by a wide margin to understand the metaphysical background of this war. Behind the concrete, the visible events, behind all objective, logical considerations, we find the irrational element: The struggle against the demon, against the servants of the Antichrist. Everywhere and at all times demons have been lurking in the dark, waiting for the moment when man is weak; when of his own volition he leaves his place in the order of Creation as founded for him by God in freedom; when he yields to the force of evil, separates himself from the powers of a higher order; and after voluntarily taking the first step, he is driven on to the next and the next at a furiously accelerating rate. Everywhere and at all times of greatest trial men have appeared, prophets and saints who cherished their freedom, who preached the One God and who with His help brought the people to a reversal of their downward course. Man is free, to be sure, but without the true God he is defenseless against the principle of evil. He is like a rudderless ship, at the mercy of the storm, an infant without his mother, a cloud dissolving into thin air.

The final word should, I think, go to the extraordinarily courageous White Rose activist Sophie Scholl, executed by beheading in February 1943 at the age of twenty-one:

> I will cling to the rope God has thrown me in Jesus Christ, even when my numb hands can no longer feel it.

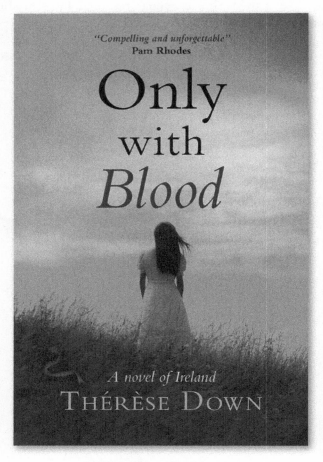

"Compelling and unforgettable"
Pam Rhodes

Only with *Blood*

A novel of Ireland
THÉRÈSE DOWN

ISBN: 978 1 78264 135 3

e-ISBN: 978 1 78264 136 0

'A multilayered, compelling page-turner. This is a must-read.'
Historical Novel Society